Shirley Smith was born in Yorkshire. For some time she worked as a headmistress in Manchester and as an inspector in South Yorkshire. She began writing four years ago after an operation and now belongs to the Fosseway Writers' Group, which this year won the national trophy from the National Association of Writers' Groups. This is her first novel.

DEAR MISS GREY

When beautiful Lucy Grey and her brother, William, become orphans, their futures are organized by hard-nosed Aunt Esther. Whilst Will is sent to Oxford University, Lucy is found a post in London as governess to Lord Hallburgh's two motherless children. However, Lucy soon senses a strange and threatening atmosphere in the household, run by Edmund Hallburgh's much older sister, the autocratic Honourable Caroline Hallburgh, who is physically disabled. She sees the growing friendship between Lucy and Edmund as a threat to her own position and is determined to break Lucy Grey . . .

SHIRLEY SMITH

DEAR
MISS GREY

Complete and Unabridged

ULVERSCROFT
Leicester

First published in Great Britain in 2002 by
Robert Hale Limited
London

First Large Print Edition
published 2003
by arrangement with
Robert Hale Limited
London

British Library CIP Data

Smith, Shirley
    Dear Miss Grey.—Large print ed.—
    Ulverscroft large print series: general fiction
    1. Orphans—Fiction
    2. Large type books
    I. Title
    823.9'2 [F]

    ISBN 0–7089–4798–0

Published by
F. A. Thorpe (Publishing)
Anstey, Leicestershire
Set by Words & Graphics Ltd.
Anstey, Leicestershire
Printed and bound in Great Britain by
T. J. International Ltd., Padstow, Cornwall

This book is printed on acid-free paper

1

'Oh do cheer up, Lucy,' urged my brother. 'Things are not as bad as they seem. You may be sure that Mama will come back with good news from our rich Aunt Esther and we'll be out of Queer Street at last. If only you will stop moping, you will find everything is going to work out for the best.'

I saw a few more blue caps at that moment and scrambled quickly through the hedge to add them to the field mushrooms in my basket, so I did not answer him. Instead, I straightened up and looked across the flat Midlands countryside towards the village of Cottenham.

The fields were neat and brown after the autumn ploughing, and the trees in the little copses were fringed with deep tinted leaves of orange and gold. The sun had already sunk down to the horizon and glowed a dull ruby red. To me, the dark evening sky expressed more than words can tell of my lowered spirits and vague feelings of dread. It seemed as if what had happened to us, far from being the end of a chapter in our lives, was really only a beginning: the beginning of something portentous and sinister that would affect us for ever.

William though, continued to chat encouragingly, as if he had no cares at all, which I supposed he hadn't really, being a boy and only eighteen years old. He was carefree and cheerful, with a man's physical strength and a boy's confident optimism about life. I wished I could share his hopefulness, but the death of my father had profoundly affected both myself and my mother and I seemed unable to shake off the terrible melancholy which beset me. I tried to banish these morbid thoughts from my mind and concentrate on the task in hand and to be cheerful for William's sake.

The trouble with mushroom gathering, I reflected, was that it was the humid damp weather which brought them to appear, almost overnight it seemed, and after an hour tramping through the fields, my feet were now soaking wet. The thin old half boots were no protection against the muddy grass and I shivered as I drew my threadbare old cloak around me.

'Let us go back now, William,' I suggested. 'Then we can surprise Mama with a dish of hot mushrooms and a little bacon for her supper, when she returns.'

William made no reply but smiled and took

the basket from me to carry it home. We set off, keeping to the familiar paths by the manor fields, and were now walking in single file past hedges which were alight with the glow of autumn berries. Their beauty served only to make me even more aware of my unaccountable feelings of sadness and despair as I wondered what the future held for us.

'I own I am quite weary and more than a little anxious about Mama's visit to Aunt Esther Grey,' I said. 'Poor as Dibden Cottage is, we might find even that has been taken from us and we will be parish paupers.'

'Oh that's nonsense,' Wills laughed over his shoulder. 'Depend upon it, dear sis, I'll wager the old trout is being generous and will get us a better house and make Mama an allowance.'

I walked on in silence. My father had only been dead for two weeks when we had to vacate the Rectory to make way for the new incumbent. Papa had been the Vicar of Cottenham for seventeen years and had served his flock well. He was a gentle, unworldly man, much given to study and the pursuit of rare butterflies and it was our mother who was the mainstay of the household. In spite of the genteel poverty in which we lived, Mama had always been so strong, overseeing the household, visiting the

3

sick and supervising the dairy and the vegetable garden. Somehow she had managed to keep poultry, make jam and preserves and even teach William and myself our letters and numbers. Later, she had earned a little extra by taking in and looking after young crammer students while Papa prepared them for Rugby or Winchester. He had been particularly successful at this and, with the excellent food and kind attention that the students received, soon had a good name among those of the gentry who wished to place their sons at the vicarage. These parlour boarders were as much as Papa could cope with but my mother's driving force ensured that he never wanted for a good supply of students.

But there's nothing so cold as charity, I thought bitterly. My father's elder brother who had inherited all Grandfather's money was married to Aunt Esther, a veritable 'old trout' just as William said. Her sloping head had the large, slack mouth and round, wet eyes of a dead fish laid out on the river-bank, waiting to have its hook removed. Her lacklustre hair was always scraped back under a lace cap and her fine clothes adorned a frame which was all but skeletal. She was very much in charge of my uncle, being a rich woman in her own right, and it was she who had grudgingly provided us with the small

4

leaky cottage where we were now to eke out our existence. She had got the carter to remove Mama's last few sticks of furniture with almost indecent haste after my father's funeral, so that we had no chance even to harvest the few vegetables and fruits growing in the walled garden at the Rectory. These had been so carefully tended by my mother all summer and even they were now denied her.

We turned the corner of the lane and William quickened his pace a little as though impatient to get back, and soon we were walking down the path to the almost derelict cottage which was now our home. The low windows were dark and unwelcoming, the door, scarred and pitted with age, was stiff and unyielding and, as we pushed it open, the rooks rose in a crowd from across the fields and flew over the low-browed, mean little house. William bustled about getting kindling from the kitchen to light the parlour fire while I removed my cloak and boots and spread the cheap deal table with a clean cloth and three plates.

'It does seem hard,' I sighed, as I hung my bedraggled bonnet near the fire, 'that we should be in such reduced circumstances. Poor Papa as the younger son, worked so hard for no reward while Aunt Esther and

Uncle James are so comfortable. I am sure they could spare us a little. It is so unjust when our cousins can go to the assembly balls and parties and we have nothing but this poverty-stricken cottage and wearisome toil.'

'Fustian!' exclaimed William cheerfully. 'We ain't in need of the old trout's charity. I still have my gun and there's good fishing at Wembeck Lake. We can manage, Lucy, and anyway I've never wanted to attend simpering misses at hunt balls and such. Though I daresay it would be diverting for you, dear sis,' he added as an afterthought. 'But you are such a good friend and companion, I forget you are only a girl. I'll oil the old door tomorrow,' he went on kindly. 'Put on the pan, Lu, I think I can hear Mama.'

He lit a candle and placed it in the window and then went to open the door to our mother.

Mama was tiny and had once been very pretty, but years of scrimping and making do to retain the position of a lady, and struggling day in day out with two children and no servants, had left her face lined and her hair hanging in grey wisps. She stood in the narrow doorway almost too weary and despondent to move and I took her pelisse and bonnet from her and led her to the fire.

'At least we have plenty of wood, Mama,' I

said, as cheerfully as I could. I knelt by her chair and gently chafed her hands with my own to try and warm them.

There was no answer. Mama stared fixedly at the fire and tears as big as peas rolled silently down her withered cheeks. William busied himself in an embarrassed way with cutting up the bacon and cleaning the mushrooms, pretending that nothing untoward was happening. I know that he is not an unfeeling sort of lad: he felt our father's death very keenly and yet was unable to grieve openly like Mama and myself. His only comfort seemed to be in doing something practical, like chopping wood or collecting the windfall apples from the orchard, never in speaking words of comfort to Mama and myself. He cleared his throat nervously and indicated that the supper was now ready. Mama was still silent and I wiped her face gently and urged her to sit at the table and eat a little.

It was obvious that her heart wasn't in it but she made a brave effort and even praised William's cooking. Finally, when she was calm, she was able to recount the happenings at our uncle's house.

'I was so shamed, Lucy, at having to go cap in hand to your aunt and uncle, but I was sure — sure they would not see their brother's children in such straitened circumstances when — when they have so much,' she faltered.

I squeezed her hand gently. 'So they granted you nothing?'

She gave a tired sigh as though she were ready for sleep. 'My brother-in-law says that we may keep this cottage,' she whispered. 'It is ours in . . . in . . . perpetuity. Although William is older than is usual for young men going up to Oxford, he had already gained the entrance requirements while your dear papa was still alive. Their lawyer has drawn up a fund for him to undertake a course of study and enable him to seek gainful employment at the end of his time there.' She stopped and gave a painful gulp, unable to continue.

'I knew it,' said William bitterly. 'They treat us like paupers instead of family. The old trout and Uncle James have always hated us. Well, I shall refuse to go up to university. I shall stay here and look after you two. You'll see.'

'Shh. Wills dear. Please. It is a chance for you. The only chance you may ever get. And your aunt and uncle will make you a modest allowance all the while you are studying. We can sell some of your father's books perhaps and you may learn a decent profession and advance yourself in the world instead of mouldering here in Cottenham. My only sorrow is my darling Lucy.' She broke down in tears once more.

'Why? Wh — what . . . about me?' I stammered, the feeling of dread once more pressing on my heart like a heavy stone.

Again she took a shuddering breath and went on, 'You know that your poor father left nothing and your aunt and uncle have refused to consider an annuity for you until such time as you may marry. I pleaded for it, Lucy, truly I did. I sank my pride and pleaded with them to provide for you, but they turned away and affected to be deaf . . .

'Then how is she supposed to live?' demanded William indignantly, while I sat in a state of frozen horror at what was coming next.

'Your Aunt Esther has arranged a . . . a . . . position for you, Lucy.'

'A position?' I echoed foolishly.

Mama wiped her eyes wearily. 'Your aunt has refused to countenance any financial support to enable you to stay here. She says that I . . . I . . . may do such sewing and needlework as is required for her household and will in return be given meals and . . . and money for candles and fuel, while you may . . . may . . . engage in genteel employment.'

I went first hot, then cold. 'What sort of employment?'

'Your Aunt Esther has arranged for you to become governess to the children of Lord Hallburgh.'

She said it in a rush as though to soften the impact. I was silent, dumbfounded. Never, in my deepest depression had I thought of the possibility of being parted from my home and my mother. I had heard of Lord Hallburgh of course, but I didn't recall ever having met him. He had a family seat in the neighbouring village of Wembeck and farmed extensively on many acres of surrounding land, but it was managed by land baillifs and His Lordship remained in London. Both she and William looked so downcast at my aunt's arrangements, I felt I must reply.

'But Mama,' I finally managed, 'I have no leanings towards being a teacher, no experience of young children whatsoever. How can my aunt countenance such a position for me?'

I jumped up in some agitation. 'I shall go and visit my aunt and uncle myself and protest with all my heart against this detestable plan which will take me away from my beloved mama and put me with strangers, in a position which will be so demeaning and humiliating.'

'No,' said William sadly. 'It's of no use, sis.

The old trout don't like you. Never has. If you weren't so young and pretty, she might not be in such a rush about getting you out of the way. Don't get into a quake about it, though. You're a clever little puss, always have been. You'll come about, just see if you don't. Why, it wouldn't surprise me if you meet a rich suitor in the big city,' he added, meaning to be kind.

His well-meaning words had quite the opposite effect on me. Gradually, as I thought more rationally about the situation, I became more and more angry and declared myself unwilling to fit in with any of Aunt Esther's plans.

My mother moaned feebly at this and William poured her a glass of wine, but she had no appetite for it and, with more tears, begged to be excused, as she was exhausted and wished to retire to bed. I helped her up the worn old stairs of the cottage and lit her bedside candle while she said her prayers. William had put some hot coals in the grate and I stirred them into a warm blaze and fetched a hot brick wrapped in a bit of old blanket to warm her feet.

'Would you like me to put out the candle, Mama?'

'Yes, please, my dear. I am unutterably weary. Today has been such a sore trial for me. Kiss me, Lucy . . . If only your dear papa were here . . . '

She closed her eyes and once more the hopeless tears squeezed from under her eyelids. I looked down at the thin, prematurely worn face and felt a surge of love and tenderness for this gentle woman who had worked so selflessly for others and was now cast into such an agony of unhappiness by her greedy relations. The lace on her night cap was old and frayed, and her life of shabby gentility had roughened her hands and faded her hair, but had not been able to eradicate her indefinable air of ladylike dignity or the classic bone structure of her beautiful face. For the first time in all my twenty years, I felt that I and not she, was the parent. Her strength and energy seemed to have fled from her with my father's death and our positions now were entirely reversed. Mama was in need of my strength and nurture and I felt I must now take responsibility for her frail condition.

'Good night, Mama,' I breathed, as I bent to kiss her, but she was already in the blessed oblivion of sleep and so I went downstairs to William.

We sat on either side of the fire sipping our wine rather gloomily and speculating about the future. My brother, with the resilience of youth seemed to have already come to terms with our new circumstances.

'At least we shall be able to meet sometimes,' he said soothingly. 'After all, I shall be in Oxford and you will have a little money of your own to enable you to travel home on the stage coach and visit Mama. Things could be worse.'

But not much worse, I thought sadly, as I studied my handsome young brother. We are very alike even though I am two years older than William. We are both tall and slim, but he is broad-shouldered, easy and boyish in his movements. We both have reddish hair but mine is red-gold while William's is red-brown like Papa's. We both have hazel eyes, but mine are flecked with green and William's are darker. Although my features are naturally finer and more girlish, there is no mistaking that we are brother and sister and I was unhappy at the idea of being parted from him. I wondered how long it would be before we were able to meet again and how much we would have changed in the meantime.

The warmth of the fire and the wine soon made me feel a little more relaxed and easy about our plight and as for William, his cheerful, open disposition would always triumph over any adversity. I was sure that his life at the university would be successful and that he would make good use of his time there. I knew that our papa's example and Christian precepts would always stand him in good stead and keep him from the temptations and follies which beset a number of young men of his age. I sighed as William stirred a log with his foot causing the sparks to fly up the dark chimney.

'Great changes in our lives, William,' I said sombrely.

'Yes indeed,' he replied, 'but opportunities also, dear Lu. Let us take them at the flood, sis. What do you say? Who knows? The position in London might be the adventure that you and I used to dream of when we were small children in the safe haven of Cottenham Rectory. And we will always have the thought of that haven to cling to when life deals its body blows,' he added soberly.

I nodded, stretching my feet out to the welcome warmth of the fire, but felt apprehensive about the mysterious Lord Hallburgh and his as yet unknown children. They were still on my mind when I finally climbed into bed next to Mama and fell into a dreamless sleep.

The next day dawned sunny and crisp and brought an unexpected visit from Aunt Esther and Uncle James. I was baking, while William was out in the back, skinning and cleaning a rabbit that he had shot for our supper. The anxieties of last night were still at the back of my mind, but I was finding kneading the bread dough while the oven heated up, very soothing. Mama, meanwhile, had kept to her bed, feeling more than a little exhausted after the events of the past few weeks. William and I had picked apples and blackberries on our long rambling walk and I had planned a fragrant fruit pie for dinner. The atmosphere was warm and pleasant, until our visitors arrived, that is.

James Grey's chaise drew up in the lane at our modest wicket gate and he handed down my Aunt Esther with the respectful deference that she always commanded of him. I was just drying my hands after putting the dough to rise when I saw them walking purposefully down the path towards our front door, which William had fortuitously oiled that very morning.

Mama was as refined and gracious as always as she rose from her bed and came down to extend a polite welcome to my aunt and uncle, but I stood silently hostile waiting for them to state their business.

They had merely visited to make sure that we all understood the kind and generous arrangements that they had made for us. After the greetings and a nervous rearranging of the chairs by Mama, William was sent for and they seated themselves comfortably before the fire.

'You do understand, do you not, William, that you are beholden to your dear Uncle James for his kind generosity in providing for your education?' Aunt Esther asked him patronizingly.

William went scarlet and ducked his head in embarrassment. 'Yes, Aunt, but I do assure you there is really no need . . . '

'No need, you foolish boy?' she interrupted him. 'How can you achieve a respectable position and a refined occupation and keep your dear mama in her old age, without the benefit of education?'

William pushed out his lips obstinately and prepared to argue with our bullying aunt, but seeing Mama's anguished glances, said nothing, and shuffled his feet uncomfortably instead.

Uncle James cleared his throat and said as kindly as he could, 'Everything is in hand now, William. The college expects you on Friday next and I have managed to procure you clean and cheap lodgings in a decent house in Irvine Street. I know you will be older than the other students, but you will do well at your studies and bring credit to your mama. She will be pinning all her hopes on you, old fellow.'

William was silent, but not so Aunt Esther. 'So, that is settled, dear boy. No need to fret about your mother and sister, for I have with my considerable influence, gained Lucy a position in an inestimably fine household in London. None other than' — she paused for dramatic effect — 'that of Lord Hallburgh! He is a gentleman of the highest *ton*. As governess to his son and daughter she will have the opportunity to mix in genteel circles, which becomes a refined spinster who is the daughter of a clergyman.'

I glared at her at being considered a 'refined spinster' at the age of twenty, but she merely gave a self-satisfied sniff and exchanged triumphant looks with Uncle James. I opened my mouth to protest at the peremptory way that my own future was being decided for me, when again I caught Mama's look of anxious terror. Last night, I had felt very protective of her as she lay in bed, so frail and sad; now, looking at the work-roughened hands and red-rimmed eyes, I realized I could not stuggle against my imperious aunt's arrangements for me: Mama did not wish it. Now that Papa was gone, she had no spirit for struggle. She wanted only peace and quiet and could even face penury and humiliation at the hands of her mean relations, because inwardly she longed only for the day when she could join him.

All these thoughts flashed wildly through my mind as I waited, quietly sullen, for my aunt to reveal her plans for me.

Seeing that I intended to remain silent, she continued somewhat smugly, 'Staples will call round for you on Friday with the gig. Your tickets will be purchased for the stage-coach which leaves the Crown at Wembeck at six o'clock. William will go with you on his way to Oxford. Hallburgh's sister writes to me that she will arrange for you to be met by a respectable member of Lord Hallburgh's household when you reach London. You will be conducted to the house in Melbury Square.'

It was useless to protest: my fate was sealed. Like it or not I was going to be the governess of two young children as yet unknown to me. Aunt Esther gathered up her reticule in a purposeful way and stood up to leave. It seemed she was satisfied that she had done right by us and was now not prepared to waste any more time on discussion.

'Come, James,' she commanded her husband, and he stumbled hastily to open the door for her, as she nodded coldly to Mama and swept out.

The carriage turned back along the lane

and was soon out of sight, the wheels rumbling faintly along the rutted track. We remained silent for a few minutes, each with conflicting emotions. Then William muttered something about the rabbit and Mama went slowly to set the table. Occupied with our own thoughts, we neither looked at nor talked to each other. I put in the loaves to bake, and an unnatural calm descended on the three of us as we reflected on this sudden change in our situation.

None of us had any appetite for the rabbit or the fruit pie and we all shed some tears at bedtime, but with the spirit of youth, William and I were at least able to look forward to the unknown and plan for our departure on Friday morning.

Mama, on the other hand, seemed frozen in her unhappiness and misery. It seemed that only sleep could give her the escape she needed and she was soon in bed and unconscious of the world. The cold stillness of the autumn night hung in every corner of the cottage as I lay awake at her side and thought of my future. I regretted now that I had not asked any questions of my Aunt Esther about the situation in Melbury Square. I had never been to London and knew nothing of the lives of fine ladies and gentlemen. All the people we had met and known in Cottenham and nearby Wembeck, were modest country folk, with only Squire Sheldon and his family standing above the others in prosperity and position. Even Uncle James and Aunt Esther, comfortably situated in the biggest house in Cottenham, lived a quiet lifestyle. As for Hallburgh Manor, it seemed to be closed for many months of the year. An old couple took care of the actual house and an army of workers under the farm manager groomed the grounds and gardens meticulously. No mercy was shown to trespassers or poachers by the stern game-keeper and his lad. I was not aware of the times when Lord Hallburgh visited his estate. I had never seen him and speculated fleetingly as to why his sister should be making the arrangements for my employment. Did he not have a wife? What ages were the children? I knew there were a boy and a girl, but that was all. Finally even these troubled thoughts failed to keep me awake and at last I slept.

In spite of my aunt's well-laid schemes, the next day, instead of packing our boxes, William rode in haste on our neighbour's hack to fetch old Doctor Browning from Wembeck. Our mother had developed a sudden chill and a fever which meant she could not be left unattended and so our journey must be postponed. I sat with her and bathed her forehead which was burning hot, although she complained constantly of the cold. I applied compresses and put more hot bricks at her feet, praying that the good doctor would hurry. Hurry! But it was of no avail. Because of her frail state and lowered spirits, the chill quickly turned to pneumonia. In spite of Dr Browning's best efforts, within twenty-four hours, Mama had her dearest wish and had joined her beloved husband, where she wanted to be.

In fairness to our stingy aunt and uncle, they met the cost of the simple funeral and even provided some sparse and mean refreshments for the few close family mourners who gathered at the grave in Cottenham churchyard. I stood numb and silent, in a borrowed black bonnet and an old black dress of Mama's which I had let down to fit me. Our pitiless aunt did not cast a single solitary flower over the cheap pine coffin, but I had gone out early and picked some rosemary and jasmine to make a little tribute tied with black ribbons, to mark my mother's passing. The mason was commissioned to alter the simple inscription on Papa's grave, to include her name, and that was that. The starkness of the arrangements cut at my heart, but there was nothing I could do. Now that they were both at rest, it seemed to me that I had been turned to stone. I could barely struggle with the household jobs much less accomplish all the cooking, and in any case, food seemed unimportant. My numbness lasted for the next few days, as William and I tried to comfort each other. We assured ourselves that she was in a better place and would somehow always be at the side of us in our struggles and efforts to be what our parents would have us be.

In its way, life is as inexorable as death. In spite of all the bitter and painful tears that we had shed, one week later our boxes were packed ready for the stage-coach. I contrived to put in my precious writing case, because I was determined to have the solace of letter writing in my banishment to the big city and I had managed to alter some cast-off gowns of my cousin's ready for my new life as a governess. William was far more confident than I and insisted that he needed only the bare necessities for Oxford, but that he must take all his favourite books for company to his lodgings in Irvine Street.

'For you must know, Lucy,' he said seriously, 'that I have enough breeches and Pa's old neckcloths to support me until I leave the college.'

I ignored this and was much occupied with

last minute darning of linen and hose, folding, sponging and pressing clothes and packing some food for our journey. At last, all was ready, and we set off at five o'clock in the morning in Aunt Esther's gig, which had duly arrived to take us to Wembeck. We gazed and gazed back at the cottage until it was only a speck in the distance and the small wicket gate had finally disappeared from view. This was the end of our old life and both my brother and I were aware that the future was precarious for each of us in our separate ways.

When we arrived at the Crown, there was already a small knot of people waiting in the silent mist of the early morning. No one spoke until I saw old Sarah Smith, getting down stiffly from the horse and cart and struggling with a huge, shabby portmanteau. She was finished with keeping poultry, she confided, and was going to live with her daughter, for she was a lone widow woman and considered she was too old to farm on her own. William dashed forward to help her and then the coach came up to the front door of the Crown. The boxes were loaded on the top and we took our seats inside. At six o'clock precisely, we set off on our journey.

All through that long day I sat silent and afraid, giving only half my attention to old

Sarah's comfortable chatter, watching the countryside unfold and gradually ebb away as we approached the city. William would stay on the coach until he reached Oxford. He seemed quite cheerful, but as for myself, I had no idea what the future might hold for me. I only knew that I longed to wake up and find that it was all a bad dream and that I was back safely once more with Mama and Papa in Cottenham Rectory.

But all too soon, the coach drew up at the London coaching inn and we kissed and promised to write soon. I was met by a taciturn but respectful groom, driving the rather splendid Hallburgh carriage. He was very smartly turned out and carefully loaded in my modest boxes and offered his hand in a gruff greeting.

'Pleased to meet you, Miss Grey,' he said. 'My name's George Baxter, Lord Hallburgh's groom.'

He carelessly tossed a few coins to the two small urchins who had laid some straw for me to stand on while he lowered the steps of the carriage. Looking down into the pinched faces of the two small boys, I felt they were not old enough to be away from their mama's leading strings, never mind working for money, late at night in the city. They gazed back at me intently from eyes that were prematurely old and wrinkled, their hands held out mutely in supplication. I fumbled clumsily in my reticule and produced a few coppers which I pressed into the thin hand of the older boy and then Baxter handed me into the carriage.

'Don't mind these lads, miss,' he said, quietly disapproving. 'They's got more money'n us and knows how to get more. Like the Good Book says, the poor is allus with us, Miss Grey.'

'But they're so young,' I faltered. 'Surely they should be home in bed, now that it is so dark.'

'Mayhap, miss,' he said in a more kindly voice. 'But perhaps they has no homes to go to, like.'

Climbing into his seat, he clicked up the horses and we set off for the Hallburgh London residence. Gradually, the dirty crowded alleys of the inner city gave way to the more gracious streets and beautifully proportioned houses of west London. Although I could see very little of it in the dark, I was aware that we had entered a much more affluent and fashionable part in the west end.

We finally drew up at the town house in Melbury Square. Baxter handed down my boxes and beat a smart tattoo with the brass knocker on the imposing front door before leading the horses round to the mews at the back of the house.

The shiny, dark-green door was opened almost immediately by a footman who led me into the drawing-room to meet a lady who was seated alone by the fire. A screen was tilted towards her to shield her face from the heat and she had a piece of dainty embroidery on her lap. My first impression was that she was very beautiful, elegant in a dress of greyish-blue, very fashionable in 1815 among young ladies of the *ton*, except that she was not young. Her jet-black hair had a white streak from the widow's peak to the back of her head, where it was modishly dressed in immaculate curls, caught up in a tortoiseshell comb. The whole effect was one of incomparable grace and beauty, very like the impressions of Greek maidens on some of the coins in my father's collections.

She caught me looking at her and greeted me with, 'Ah, Miss Grey. Come in. You must be tired after your journey and ready for your bed. I am the Honourable Caroline Hallburgh, sister to Lord Hallburgh.'

She rose with some difficulty and walked slowly towards the bell pull. She was not a tall woman and yet she had a great deal of presence. I suddenly had the feeling that in spite of her charming manner, she would be deadly if she were my enemy.

'I shall summon the maid and she can show you to your room.'

I saw that her feet were oddly twisted and encased in very small black boots, and I tried not to stare at them as she moved haltingly across the floor. Again she was aware of my gaze and gave a wry little smile.

'Yes, I am a cripple, Miss Grey. Condemned to limp and creep about the world like a snail, with only sticks to support me.'

I did not know how to answer her, and felt myself blushing scarlet to the roots of my hair at my crass manners. Fortunately the maid appeared and immediately, Miss Hallburgh turned towards her.

'Oh, there you are, Annie. Please conduct Miss Grey to her room. I shall speak with you in the morning, Miss Grey, when you are rested.'

And I was dismissed. Wearily, I followed Annie upstairs to my small bedroom on the second floor.

The maid pushed open the door and whispered, 'I've put you a bit of supper on the side table, miss, and some lemonade, in case you want a drink.'

She had also lit a fire in the small grate and put hot water and towels for me on the wash

27

stand. I sat down on the bed, suddenly overcome with exhausted loneliness and a desperate longing for Dibden Cottage and my dear mama.

'It's not so bad, miss. You'll get used to it,' she said kindly. 'And those children are lovely, a real pleasure.'

'I do not even know their names,' I said despondently.

'Why, Master Thomas, Tommy lad, he's four, rising five. Miss Sarah, we call Sal, she's seven and she's a little charmer, Miss Grey.'

'And what of their mama?' I asked curiously.

'Dead, poor lady, these three years,' Annie said stiffly and then, 'Well, I'll bid you good night now, miss. I'll wake you in the morning and bring you your washing water in good time.'

'Good night, Annie,' I responded dully. 'And thank you.'

She left quickly, closing the door behind her noiselessy and I was left alone. I washed quickly and said my prayers and got into bed. The food I left untouched, but I was grateful for a drink of the lemonade left me on the bed table. My thoughts before I went to sleep were muddled. My employer's sister, in particular, intrigued me. She was attractive but somehow dangerous. How or why I did not know, but I was soon to find out.

2

The next morning, I needed no rousing, but woke up early and was waiting nervously when the maid appeared with fresh water. Annie seemed friendly and approachable and I confessed to her that I was surprised to find Miss Hallburgh apparently in charge of her brother's household. I wondered also that she could not deal with the children herself. She seemed quite young enough.

'Oh no, miss,' Annie said calmly. 'First of all, His Lordship is away sometimes for weeks on end. He has estates in Scotland as well as his home in the country. He's also in Paris frequently and Miss Hallburgh is a semi-invalid. She is a good deal older than her brother, being, though you'd hardly credit it, forty-eight. She's remarkable, her being so active and in control of things, like.'

Just how active Miss Hallburgh, 'Aunt Caroline' was, and how much in control, was yet to be revealed to me. I had also to discover to my cost the strength of that remorseless will which made her not only remarkable but so dangerous to be near. I knew nothing of that then and protected by my naïvety, was able to smile at the maid with unaffected friendliness, for after all, she had been the first one in Lord Hallburgh's household to show me kindness and consideration.

'You said last evening that Lord Hallburgh's wife is dead, Annie.' I probed discreetly.

'Why yes, miss. Poor lady. Her life was not happy, Miss Grey. She was so young when they married and His Lordship was consumed with jealousy and all. She hadn't many friends, miss. It was such a terrible shock when she had her accident . . . '

Annie clapped her hand to her mouth and lowered her eyes as if regretting that she had said so much and though I was intrigued at what she had told me, I had no wish to pry or quiz servants, so I merely smiled and thanked her again for making me so comfortable.

Annie departed and I was soon ready, standing in the middle of the room, smoothing down my only presentable gown nervously and wondering what today would hold for me. There was a tap on the door and I opened it to find a tall stranger with a sallow face and heavy dark brows. She was extremely thin, and with her black gown and severely dressed hair was the very opposite of the chic Frenchwoman I was used to seeing in the fashion plates of the *Ladies' Magazine*.

'Good morning, Mees Grey,' she greeted me unsmilingly. 'I am Yvette Moreau, personal maid to Miss Hallburgh. She wishes to see you, mademoiselle, *immédiatement*. Be so good as to come with me.'

It was dark on the stairs and she had a peculiarly swift and silent walk, which gave her almost the appearance of a black bat swooping and gliding through the gloom. She opened the imposing double doors of the drawing-room.

'Mademoiselle Grey,' she announced.

Her voice and whole demeanour changed as soon as she spoke to Miss Hallburgh. It was as though a flame had been lit behind those dark unfathomable eyes of hers as she looked at the other woman in the room. Her voice was soft and cooing, almost caressing, and I realized at that moment that these two would make a formidable pair if we should ever cross swords. Nevertheless, I advanced into the drawing-room with what confidence I could muster as Yvette left, quietly closing the doors behind her.

Today, I had time to take in the beauty and grandeur of the room where Miss Hallburgh awaited me, in a wicker basket chair which had small silver wheels. There were cushions of embroidered oyster satin at her back and her feet rested on a little footstool but were completely hidden by a satin quilt. I looked around me with fascinated curiosity.

The drawing-room at Melbury House was huge and opulent. Several large pictures depicting handsome, glossy racehorses adorned the walls, and over the fireplace hung a massive mirror topped with gilded cherubs and a mask of Bacchus. Swags of golden grapes and vine leaves were entwined down each side of the frame which shone richly in the morning sunlight. This mirror was echoed by another, which hung between the tall, floor-length windows on one side of the room. The long, cream and gold brocade curtains reached the floor and were tied with thick silken ropes and massive gold-coloured tassels. On several of the elegant small tables there were ormolu candelabra with tall wax candles which gave an air of symmetry and dignity to the whole room. There were substantial armchairs in rose-patterned silk which were set in pairs, and at the outer edges of the room, occasional chairs of satinwood. Everything was arranged to give an air of quiet genteel luxury and good taste. I was utterly absorbed with my observations for quite a few moments, but the main focus of my attention was, of course, the mistress of the house, who sat quietly inscrutable, awaiting me and noting my every movement.

I wondered fleetingly why my Aunt Esther had not thought to inform me that Lord Edmund Hallburgh did not live alone and that his sister ruled his household. I was to learn later that Caroline Hallburgh liked to dominate everyone, especially those who were young and inexperienced like myself, who, she believed, could be more easily intimidated and thus subdued to her iron will. Perhaps she suspected that I was one of those young women who hoped to take over not only the young children, but the father as well, once I had been engaged as governess. She was certainly of a mind to quell any such notions this morning.

She sat upright in her invalid's chair, her small white hands resting on the satin quilt. She was altogether of such a pretty and dainty appearance, she could have been a piece of my Aunt Esther's Dresden china. Her dark and luxuriant hair with its strange exotic streak of white, was piled high and dressed in the Grecian manner, hanging in bell-like ringlets at the back. The style of her hair revealed the delicate shells of her ears, set with lustrous diamonds. The clasped hands were equally adorned with fine diamond rings. As she sat in her chair with her twisted feet hidden by the quilt, I felt that she looked far too young and pretty to be eight and forty.

Anyone so slight, so lovely and yet with such an infirmity, must be a generous and worthy person whom I could easily love, I thought, with a sudden surge of compassion for her. I had yet to learn how her beauty belied the real Caroline Hallburgh, how much her pampered young face owed to the ministrations of her faithful Yvette and how successfully it hid the powerful and cunning personality from everyone. In my youthful innocence, I believed that all the staff and servants at Melbury House adored her and were all at her beck and call. I discovered later that Annie, the maid, and young Thomas, were the exceptions to this. They both knew the real Caroline, of course. Annie with her memories of the past, and Tom because he had the clear-eyed perceptiveness which is the gift of some little children. As my father was wont to say in his sermons, 'except ye see with the eyes of a little child . . . '

But I am ahead of myself. Back to the present, that first morning when Miss Caroline Hallburgh smiled so graciously on me and extended her exquisite little hand with its bejewelled fingers.

She said in that deceptively soft and sweet

voice of hers, 'Welcome to Melbury House, Miss Grey.'

I took the small white hand respectfully. Although it had not been my own choice to come here as a paid governess to two unknown young children, yet I was conscious of the position of trust that was offered to me and was determined to do my best, for Mama's sake. As yet, I had no idea of the dark passions and bitter hatreds which remained seething behind Miss Hallburgh's gracious smile. Life in a small country village had not prepared me for the evil destructive jealousy which could eat away at a woman like this. I was tall and strong. Even though I was a pauper and dependent on her charity, yet I was young and pretty and whole and could walk unaided. In short, I had all that cruel fate had denied to Caroline Hallburgh, in spite of her wealth and position. Above all, I was energetic and capable of taking complete charge of the two beautiful young children, whose upbringing, now that their mama was dead, she so wished to control and rule herself.

Edmund Hallburgh, it seemed, wished to appoint a governess for them. Thomas and Sarah needed someone who was able to devote time to them and be a suitable companion while they were still young themselves. Eventually, I guessed, Thomas would go away to school and perhaps even Sarah would be enrolled in one of the newly fashionable academies for young ladies. Until then, maybe it would be better for them to live with someone like myself who could give them lessons, take them on walks, play with them and divert them in an active way, such as their aunt could never do.

I looked at her more closely.

'Please be seated, Miss Grey,' she said, her pale-grey eyes fixed on my own. 'I would like to have some discussion with you if I may.'

Her voice was as soft as ever, but now had a certain plangent quality to it, and though she was utterly charming, I felt the frequent pin pricks as though she were verbally sticking sharp needles into my vulnerable flesh.

'You are only twenty years old. Where were you brought up?'

'In the vicarage at Cottenham.'

'When is your birthday?'

'On March thirty-first, ma'am.'

'Mmm. The day before All Fools' Day,' she said with a thin smile. 'And what about your own education, Miss Grey?'

'Mama taught William and myself our letters and numbers until I was seven. Then Papa decided that as we were so near in age he might teach us both together and Wills — my brother — and I followed the same reading in the Classics and Mathematics and, of course, Logic, as Papa's paying pupils. Mama taught me my first pianoforte lessons and I was able to join my friend, Miss Pembleton, up at the Hall, and share her lessons in music and dancing. When my brother went to school, Papa let me read with him in the library and discuss anything I had read. Both my parents were of the same inclination to . . . to . . . have me develop my intellectual interests and continue my music studies.'

Miss Hallburgh gave a slight smile. 'And your parents, are they both living?'

'No. My father died in September and my mother two weeks ago.'

'So, you have only your brother in Cottenham?'

'Yes, although he is at present up at Oxford.'

'And what will he do after that?'

'He will hope to gain some suitable genteel occupation.'

She shuddered and grimaced, in a rather obvious way.

'I cannot imagine any true gentleman wanting to engage in employment.'

I smiled. The remark was so affected as to

be ridiculous and yet, I was very much aware that Caroline Hallburgh was neither ridiculous nor stupid. The elaborate shudder and the remark about a true gentleman was meant as just another little pinprick to demonstrate her power and make me feel that my family and I were of little or no worth at all. Not just unpretentious, but positive paupers, in her eyes. I refused to allow myself a reply.

'So your brother is at present studying at Oxford?'

'Yes. My aunt and uncle stood as his sponsors and are funding his studies.'

'Forgive me, Miss Grey, but am I to take it that you are not very prosperous?'

It was clear that she enjoyed applying the goad yet again.

'Not prosperous at all,' I replied evenly. 'Being a younger son, my father had only a very modest going-on and was unable to provide for us.'

'You are fortunate then to come to London and be offered a good situation.'

If my, 'Yes, ma'am,' sounded less than enthusiastic, she appeared not to notice but returned to her probing.

'You are quite a personable young female, Miss Grey. Very pretty, in fact. Did you not consider any other course of action?'

If she was alluding to marriage as a course of action, the question had never arisen. None of the local young gentry had been attracted to the idea of a poor country girl as a wife, especially such a solemn bookworm as I. The reference to my appearance made me blush. My brother Wills always loyally maintained that if I but had the right clothes, I could be quite a dasher and in any case was quite taking when I smiled.

I looked round at my magnificent surroundings. Everywhere in this room were the hallmarks of luxury. Fine furniture and sumptuous drapery provided a setting fit for a queen. It was obvious that Miss Hallburgh had no conception of the stultifying atmosphere which poverty brings. Though afflicted physically, with Yvette's help she was going to retain the beauty she had had as a girl in spite of her age and infirmity. I found this sort of bravery in adversity, wholly admirable. As I glanced around, not knowing how to respond to her remarks, I caught a glimpse of myself in the long gilt-framed mirror on the opposite wall.

I seemed to myself to look very impoverished, in my dark drab gown. Yet I knew I had a fine complexion and that sort of thick red-gold hair which has a curl and lustre to it that is entirely natural. I also knew I had a good figure — tall and slim like Papa and, as Wills has told me many a time, large and lustrous eyes and an appealing smile. I suppose I ought to smile more often, just to show off my good teeth. My hands are long and slender and I quite astounded Fanny Pembleton's piano teacher by being able to span an octave when I was only nine years old. There was, in fact, one young man who had liked me: Squire Pembleton's son, Fanny's brother, Richard.

'You have such elegant strong hands, Miss Lucy, and they reflect the whole of you,' he would tell me. 'You are altogether a strong and elegant sort of girl.'

He was sent off to the university before our friendship could develop further and that was that. His parents did not wish to encourage any liaison with a poor parson's daughter such as myself and made sure that his interest in me was nipped in the bud.

Miss Hallburgh continued her inquisition.

'And where exactly is your home, Miss Grey?'

'My aunt has given us a small house in Cottenham.'

'And you have formed no — er — attachments?'

'No, none,' I said, and smiled to myself.

Noting my smile, she said, 'Well if you take

this position with any hope of meeting some nice young man, Miss Grey, your hopes are doomed to disappointment. My brother is absent for quite a lot of the time and we have no eligible rich society blades who leave visiting cards.'

I was aware of another thinly disguised barb directed at me and I began to feel rather angry.

'I have no thoughts of marriage on my mind, Miss Hallburgh.'

'Quite so,' she murmured smoothly. Her voice was all honey and silk. 'Just one last question, Miss Grey. Earlier, you mentioned your musical ability.'

'Yes, indeed. The music teacher hired by Squire Pembleton urged me to go further — to study at the conservatoire, even. But quite apart from our very straitened circumstances, one has to be confident of being so talented to make a mark in such an exacting profession, and in spite of his urging, I relinquished the idea.'

My voice trailed off uncertainly. I was acutely aware that Miss Hallburgh valued none of my talents, musical or otherwise, she merely despised me for being poor.

'I'm afraid your musical aspirations will have to be fulfilled through teaching the little ones,' she said in a sharper voice. 'And depend upon it, Miss Grey, you will have no opportunity for any drawing-room performances here.'

I looked at her, quite at a loss as to why she seemed so triumphant at the death of my musical ambitions. She stared back at me. She really was so charming, so attractive with her dainty prettiness, if you ignored the imperfections of her feet. Yet she was not a woman to be pitied. There was so much venom beneath the sweetness of her words.

'I shall be satisfied to guide the children in their first musical steps, Miss Hallburgh. I desire no personal glory, musical or otherwise.'

'Quite so,' she said. 'As long as you remember that Lord Hallburgh and I have no occasion to require any recitals from young girls like yourself.'

I flushed. 'It would never be my wish to do so,' I replied indignantly.

'Capital,' she smiled again. 'I am so glad we understand one another. And you should also be aware that one of your duties will be to keep the children quiet and disciplined when we are entertaining. When there are guests for meals, you will, of course, have a tray in the schoolroom unless my brother particularly wants the children to be in company.'

'Very well, Miss Hallburgh.'

I knew in my heart that Miss Hallburgh wished me to take all my meals in the schoolroom, but I was soon to discover that Thomas and Sarah were the jewels in their papa's crown and he wished them to be present whenever he dined at home, which meant that I, of course, would also be part of the social scene.

Miss Hallburgh then went on to discuss my salary, which was a generous one. It was to be thirty guineas per annum, but would be reviewed after one year. I realized that I had my Aunt Esther to thank for negotiating this agreement on my behalf.

She then told me about the running of the house in Melbury Square.

Yvette Moreau was her special attendant. There was Annie who was in charge of the children's rooms, and mine of course, with a nursery-maid in attendance, but there was also the full complement of cook, house-keeper, butler, maid servants, footmen, groom and stable lads, and daily attendance by the woman who came in to do the rough work, not forgetting Saunders, Lord Hall-burgh's valet. It seemed to me like a palace in a fairy-tale. After being used to penury for so long, the wonderful food, respectful servants and well-organized household was like something I had only read about in books. I wondered how the two children were accommodated in this exclusively adult world. I was at the same time both eager and apprehensive about meeting them. Would they like me? Would I like them?

It seemed to me that in spite of agreeing to my Aunt Esther's suggestion of myself as governess, Miss Hallburgh was not very taken with me, but had merely decided that my respectability and level of education was the best that could be purchased for the salary that was being offered. She now desired to bring the interview to a close and asked sweetly if I had any doubts or questions. Somewhat foolishly, I asked how the children had managed without their mama.

Her pretty lips tightened and she said somewhat coldly, 'We do not bring up any reference to Lady Hallburgh in front of the children.'

'Why . . . why . . . is that?' I stammered. 'Cannot they remember their mama?'

'We do not mention my sister-in-law in front of the children,' she reiterated. 'They know nothing about her accident, merely that she died and has gone to a better place. Kindly summon Yvette, Miss Grey,' she ordered curtly.

The discussion was at an end. I moved to the bell pull and Yvette appeared as if by

44

magic, or as if she had been lurking outside in the hall.

'Ah, Yvette, Miss Grey and I have concluded our discussion. Kindly bring Thomas and Sarah to me at once.'

'At once, *madame*,' Yvette repeated adoringly.

I sat silently while she went to fetch the children. Miss Hallburgh spoke to her personal servant with a harshness that seemed very unkind in view of Yvette's obvious love and attention to her. Yvette was, I soon discovered, a weak and rather stupid woman, in spite of the powerful love she felt for her mistress and the tigerish way she defended her every decision. In my own quiet way, I have always been independent. Papa always exhorted us to: 'tell the truth and shame the Devil', so I have often been truthful to a fault, although without being discourteous, I hope.

I was to grow accustomed to Miss Hallburgh's autocratic ways and the way that Yvette fawned on her and responded to the oft repeated words, 'at once', so promptly. It was on that first morning that I realized that this was no empty phrase. Every single command from the little lady in charge of Melbury House, was carried out 'at once' as a matter of course.

Yvette returned almost immediately with the children and they stood watchful and rather shy just inside the doorway.

'Thomas, Sarah, come in if you please,' said their Aunt. 'This is your governess, Miss Grey.'

She watched them with impatient amusement as they approached me hesitantly. Then she expertly moved herself in the wicker chair as far as the great windows and half turned towards us, sometimes gazing out and sometimes observing us narrowly while my young charges and I made our new acquaintance.

'Why, good morning, children,' I greeted them, and held out both my hands.

They responded politely enough, but they each had a guarded expression as though distrustful of strangers.

The little girl was tall and thin for seven years, dressed in a dark-blue dress with a white pinafore and a lace collar. She was dark-haired and had the clear grey eyes of her Aunt Caroline. The little boy was fairer with blue eyes and still had some of that infant chubbiness which I found very appealing. Both of them were beautifully dressed in immaculate stockings and shiny shoes. Both seemed nervous in the presence of their aunt, although Miss Sarah ran across the room to her side as soon as the greetings were over. She leaned over and planted a kiss on her aunt's cheek in what seemed to me to be a most artful and unnatural gesture for such a young girl.

'Oh how charming, my dear,' Miss Hallburgh gushed at her. 'Was not that a very graceful young lady, Miss Grey?'

I caught Sarah observing me over her aunt's shoulder. She was watching my reaction closely and I had the feeling that she was not as charming as her aunt supposed. Perhaps she had learned to be as servile as the others at Melbury House, I thought.

Aloud I said, 'Yes, very charming, Miss Hallburgh.'

I turned my attention to her little brother. He was standing rigid with shyness in an agony of embarrassment, while Miss Hallburgh stroked Sarah's dark curls and beckoned to him imperiously.

'Come along, Thomas,' she ordered him. 'Where is your kiss for Aunt Caro?'

Thomas shuffled his feet and gazed stubbornly at the floor.

Aunt Caro was determined to have the child kiss her and said more sharply, 'At once, if you please, Thomas.'

Slowly and sadly, Thomas walked towards his aunt with bent head and dragging feet.

'You are a very disobedient, unnatural little boy, not to wish to kiss your aunt. You deserve to be sent up to your room and made to stay there.'

Thomas began to tremble and burst into tears. I stepped forward instinctively to take his hand, but Miss Hallburgh turned on me and said venomously, 'No Miss Grey. Allow Thomas to obey me if you please. He was told yesterday that he must kiss me like Sarah does, or he will be left in the schoolroom to do extra letters, and no picture books or toys.'

I thought this was unspeakable, but I realized that I was powerless to intervene and let my hands fall to my sides. Once more, I saw the girl looking at me from beneath her dark lashes, while Thomas now buried his face in his little chubby hands and sobbed loudly. I wondered fleetingly if Lord Hallburgh was aware of how his youngest little child was being bullied and coerced so unkindly by his Aunt Caroline. And why was she so lacking in even-handedness when dealing with the children? I was eventually to find explanations of all this, but for now, Miss Hallburgh merely expressed her disapproval by dismissing us from her presence.

'You may go now children and show Miss Grey the schoolroom. Ring the bell for Yvette, if you please, Miss Grey. And remember, no toys or picture books for Thomas today.'

'Oh please, Miss Hallburgh. As it is my first day, may not Thomas be excused this once? I'm sure it is merely because he is a little shy ... ' My voice trailed away at the expression of naked hatred in Miss Hallburgh's pale eyes which were now like pitiless grey flint.

'Be so good as to not question my decisions regarding Thomas and Sarah, Miss Grey. It is not becoming in one who is in a less than influential position in this household, to challenge my authority over my own brother's children.'

Once more, I was aware of the knowing glance of young Sarah as Yvette Moreau appeared to conduct us to the schoolroom, so I merely nodded my acquiescence and took hold of Tom's small hand as we left the room. I determined to make the copying out of letters a wholesome and enjoyable exercise for him and would make up for the lack of his toys by re-inventing some of the nonsense games which had so diverted Wills and myself when we were taught by Mama. The little boy clung to me desperately as we followed the bat-like Yvette out of the drawing-room. Sarah skipped confidently ahead of us, but every so often would turn to give me that knowing unchildlike look which I felt boded

no good for my future schoolroom management of this spoilt young girl. I wondered
where and how she had learned such devious
and unchildlike tactics at such a tender age,
and whether I would be able to keep the
peace between the brother and sister. I
wondered which of their parents they
favoured and before we even reached the
schoolroom, I heard the deep voice of their
papa, calling to them.

'Tommy! Sal!'

The effect was instant. Ignoring Yvette's
protests and my own attempts to restrain
them, both children turned and raced like
lightning down the stairs whence we had
come and, with squeals of 'Papa! Papa!',
hurled themselves at the tall figure in the
entrance hall. Following more sedately, I was
in time to see Lord Hallburgh fall on one
knee and clasp the children to him. He
glanced upwards at this moment and his eyes
met mine. In the dim light of the hall, his
pale-grey eyes, so like Miss Hallburgh's,
glinted like silver, although, unlike hers his
black hair showed no streaks of grey. He was
the most handsome man I had ever seen, with
the sort of profile one could see on some of
Papa's Greek coins. His age I guessed to be
about five and thirty and I recognized the
same finely moulded lips as his sister, except

that they had a curving sweetness which was far removed from her own somewhat bitter expression. He was immaculately dressed in pale-beige pantaloons and highly polished Hessians and had tossed his many caped overcoat and gloves to the footman. Then he stood up, gently putting the children from him and smiled at me.

'Ah. You must be the new governess,' he said. 'My sister wrote and told me that you had been engaged to teach Tommy and little Sal. Forgive me, your name just escapes me for the moment, Miss . . . ?'

'Lucy Grey.'

'Of course. I do beg your pardon, Miss Grey, and am delighted to make your acquaintance. These two children have been in need of some schooling these two years and more and I know my sister has had it in mind to appoint a young woman of good education to the post, so I am confident that you will effect some improvement in these two little jackanapes.

'Papa I am not a jackanapes,' squealed Tom, his tears forgotten and a smile wreathing his little chubby face. 'Papa, will you read me a story?'

Sarah scowled and said spitefully, 'Aunt Caro says Tom isn't to have a story book and he has to copy his letters instead.'

Edmund Hallburgh was now looking through the cards and letters on a silver salver on the hall table. He was obviously unaware of the tremendous importance given to Miss Hallburgh's sanctions against his motherless children. He answered rather absently.

'Well, my naughty little boy, you must obey Aunt Caro in all things.'

To me he said, 'She is the most wonderful and loving aunt in the world, Miss Grey. You have seen for yourself her terrible affliction and yet she never complains and runs Melbury House with the utmost efficiency. What would we do without her?'

He never even noticed the light in his little son's face go out like a snuffed candle or the secret little smile which appeared at the corners of Sarah's pretty mouth. As for me, it was only later that I learned how much Edmund Hallburgh owed to his elder sister who had nurtured him and virtually reared him after their parents died. Perhaps I reflected, this was the one and only time in her selfish existence that she had devoted genuine love and care to another human being. All through his schooldays at Eton and afterwards when he went up to Oxford, Caroline Hallburgh had provided the rock and anchor for a lonely young boy orphaned at such a tender age. All the comforts of a family home had been organized for him. A tutor to accompany him on the Grand Tour had been appointed with as much care as though he were a prince. It seemed that to Caroline Hallburgh, her brother *was* a prince. I wondered how she had reconciled herself to his marriage with Lady Catherine and his obvious devotion to their children.

I took hold of Tom's warm little hand and tried by means of a sympathetic squeeze, to convey some comfort and reassurance that things were not as bad as they seemed and that somehow, I would try and make everything all right again. His father turned at this moment, still with the cards and letters in his hand.

'Be so kind as to conduct the children to the schoolroom, if you please, Mademoiselle Moreau,' he said to Yvette. 'Miss Grey, I would like to have a word with you.'

He led the way to the library and opened the door politely, waiting silently to allow me to pass. I glanced curiously at the comfortable, distinctly masculine room. It was obviously the domain of a man of superior understanding and a cultivated mind. Art and architecture were very well represented and there was a sprinkling of heavy books on legal topics, indicating Lord Hallburgh's responsibilities and public duties as a land owner.

Some of the volumes reflected his country house interests, fishing and riding and there were several finely illustrated books on foreign travel and natural history, particularly birds. Lord Hallburgh's personal tastes were reflected in the choice of classical literature and his love of travel in the rolling maps attached to the bookshelves.

I caught him watching me as I gazed round avidly at the well-stocked shelves and comfortable easy furniture. There were more fine prints of famous racehorses, which I later discovered had been bred by his grandfather. There were also some botanical studies of exotic foreign flowers and brightly coloured birds. But the room was dominated by the portrait of Catherine, Lady Hallburgh which hung above the fireplace. She was posed in a blue velvet riding habit, with a little feathered hat of matching blue. In one slender hand, she grasped a riding crop, and in the background could be dimly discerned a wooded landscape with a mossy bridle-path leading into the middle distance.

I withdrew my gaze from the picture with some difficulty and concentrated on the elegant figure of Lord Hallburgh.

He had seated himself casually on the edge of a rather imposing desk and placed his pile of correspondence beside him. His expression was difficult to fathom and I stood rather uncertainly in front of him, unsure as to what was expected of me.

'Please sit down, Miss Grey,' he ordered in his distinctively deep voice.

I obeyed, and he immediately said, 'Forgive me, but you look so young, only a child yourself. Hardly old enough to be governess to my two young rascals.'

'I am twenty,' I said indignantly, 'and quite old enough for my position, I assure you.'

'Oh, you assure me, do you, Miss Grey?' he laughed. 'Well let me assure you, twenty seems positively infantile to me. I am already turned thirty-two and so am rapidly becoming an old gentleman!'

I was very taken with his humour and friendliness and compared it fleetingly with Caroline Hallburgh's bitter sarcasm. I was emboldened to ask about something which was pressing on my mind. I took a deep breath.

'Lord Hallburgh,' I started clumsily. 'I w-w- I wondered . . . '

'Yes?' he asked, his expression still kind and polite, like that of a father with a shy child.

'Well, the thing is I wondered why . . . why your sister does not wish the children to . . . to . . . '

'Yes?' he said again, still patient and gentle

with my stuttering.

'They may not mention their mama,' I finished in a rush, and felt my face flush scarlet as my eyes were once more drawn irresistibly to her portrait.

His face hardened and the finely moulded lips became a thin straight line. All vestige of kindness and humour left that handsome face and he stood up abruptly and walked towards me. For one mad moment I had the idea that he was going to strike me and I stood up defensively my colour draining away. I floundered now, hardly daring to meet his eyes as I realized the enormity of my behaviour. But it was too late to retract and I stumbled on.

'It is merely that Miss Hallburgh has said that her name is ... is ... not to be mentioned. It seems ... so ... so unnatural. Lady Hallburgh's picture hangs there on the wall. What would you wish me to do if ... if either of them should mention her?'

His eyes never left mine as he said, 'My wife was killed in a riding accident three years ago. In truth, little Thomas barely remembers her. But if either of the children speaks of their mama, then of course you must not forbid it. I ... ' He hesitated and his jaw hardened. 'I do not entirely agree with her, but my sister means to ... spare us pain,

Miss Grey, that is all.'

I wondered if that was really all. Perhaps Caroline Hallburgh hated the woman who had taken her brother's love and the children for reminding her of it. I said nothing, feeling that I had over-stepped the mark by asking such questions and he changed the subject.

He continued in a courteous voice, as though our conversation had not happened, 'I hope your work here will be very successful, Miss Grey. I would be very agreeable to your using the library if you should require it in the course of your duties. I know you to be a gentlewoman and used to a civilized and genteel home in your father's house, so please feel free to avail yourself of anything in my modest library. I have no doubt it will not be easy for you to take on the care of two young children. If any difficulties arise, you must not hesitate to let me know.'

With these few kind words I was dismissed. He rose and moved to open the door for me. It was obvious that Edmund Hallburgh did not wish to discuss his wife and that she was a closed chapter in his life. Nevertheless, I was intrigued by the beautiful woman whose portrait hung on the library wall and I was consumed with curiosity to know more about her. He again stood aside as I left the room and there, immediately in front of me was

Caroline Hallburgh. She was still in the chair on wheels and was so close to the door that I wondered if she had been listening all the while to my interview with Lord Hallburgh.

'Ah, Miss Grey, your pupils await,' she said in a falsely hearty voice. 'I hope you have not already been putting my brother about with any of your schoolroom problems. Remember, my dear, I am always ready to listen to any of your concerns. No need for you to get into a taking about anything, or bother him with trivia concerning the children.'

I knew all this was being said for Lord Hallburgh's ears, so that she could be seen to be superior to the humble governess. Her voice changed to purring, caressing sweetness as she moved the chair smoothly into the library and greeted her brother.

'Edmund, my own darling. So you have finally left Paris behind and returned to us. My dear, how wonderful to see you.'

I did not stay to hear his response, but went upstairs to look for my pupils.

Much later, when I had more time to reflect on the experiences of the previous few days, I realized what a disadvantage Miss Caroline Hallburgh had put me to and how wrong-footed I had been when daring to face my employer with such impertinent questions about his dear wife.

I must have seemed both crass and insolent, I thought, to be asking such searching questions of someone of the stature of Lord Hallburgh. In heaven's name, I told myself, what on earth did it concern a nonentity like myself? Whatever had possessed me to quiz His Lordship on the management and affairs of his private family life?

I was also acutely aware of how displeased Miss Caroline Hallburgh would be, if she ever had occasion to discuss with him the paltry views of the lowly, impoverished governess, regarding his children's memories of their dead mama.

I blushed to myself many a time, as I remembered with the utmost chagrin, his obvious disapproval and disdain at my ill-thought-out questions during our first interview.

Finally, wearily, I came to the conclusion that what is done is done. If Lord Hallburgh could not forgive me, then God must.

This was small comfort and the ensuing days would prove the uphill nature of the struggle that I would have, to preserve my integrity as a Christian and my principles of loving goodwill to my fellow creatures in the face of Caroline Hallburgh's bitter enmity.

The young children were easy to love and

nurture, being as yet mostly untried and unspoilt in the race of life. Lord Hallburgh was an unknown quantity and his sister, Caroline, a force to be reckoned with.

'Say not the struggle naught availeth,' as Papa would say, but yet my spirit quailed somewhat at what lay before me in this household with so many unresolved problems and tensions from the past.

3

Miss Hallburgh had prepared special accommodation for me so that I might be alone with the children. A spacious airy bedroom on the second floor had been changed into a schoolroom with two tables, bookcases and an easy comfortable chair for my use. The window seats were fitted with soft cushion squabs and there was a bedroom for the children leading off from it. My own modest but comfortable bed chamber was but a few steps down the corridor.

Yvette had already set the two children on task according to their aunt's instructions and was supervising their progress with hawklike intensity. There was an air of tension in the atmosphere and all three looked up as I entered the room. Sarah was on a piece of coloured mat, playing with some small brightly painted wooden dolls in rather a desultory fashion, while poor little Tom sat in solitary splendour at the schoolroom table, laboriously trying to copy letters onto his slate. His eyes were still red and his plump little cheeks still stained with his recent tears, as he worked with silent sad absorption on his task.

Yvette herself sat in the chair by the window. Her expression was one of grim satisfaction at having successfully carried out Miss Hallburgh's instructions to the letter. I felt as though I understood all three of them, as I walked over to the window and gave Yvette a friendly smile.

'Thank you Mademoiselle Moreau,' I said to her politely. 'I have finished my interview with His Lordship and am now ready to take over my duties in the schoolroom.'

She did not reply, but merely nodded, twisting her thin lips into a disapproving embittered grimace and left the room as silently as always.

'Good morning, once again, children,' I said smiling at them. 'How pleasant for you that your papa has returned home for a while.'

'Yes, and I may go out riding in Papa's curricle if I finish all my school tasks,' Sarah said proudly. 'But baby bunting Tom must stay and do his letters, Aunt Caro says so.'

I was to become used to the impatient movements of her slender hands and the arrogant flash of her bright grey eyes when she felt that she was addressing a servant or an inferior. She was a young girl who already showed great promise of a fine intelligence and boundless energy, but I knew her quick brain would resort to cunning and laziness if left to her own devices. I felt that she already knew how to wheedle and flatter her Aunt Caroline, who would never see any flaws in Sarah's character, but would continue to indulge and spoil her. She would have to be handled with extreme care, as one would handle a spirited horse.

Tom pushed away his slate and sank his face onto his hands whispering, 'I hate Aunt Caro. I wish Papa could live here all the time.'

'Baby, baby bunting,' Sarah jeered again. 'I shall tell Aunt Caro what you said and you'll have no supper.'

She was absolutely radiant at the thought that Tom would be punished further. He cried louder than ever, much to his sister's amusement, and I felt constrained to intervene between them.

'Thomas,' I said, taking one of his clenched little hands in mine. 'Please do not cry. Sarah did not mean what she said and there is no need to take on about it so. She is merely funning you.'

By the scowl on her face, I could see that young Sarah certainly did mean what she said, but I determined to persuade her of the wrongness of her threats.

'Sarah,' I said to her gently, and I took one

of her hands in mine also, 'I find it very difficult to believe that you are a girl who is proud to tell tales. Do you really enjoy getting little Tom into trouble?'

For a moment, she lowered her gaze and had the grace to look somewhat discomfited, but almost immediately, threw back her head and gave me an arrogant stare.

'My Aunt Caro says that I must always tell her what Tom says and does. It isn't tale-bearing, Aunt Caro says so.'

She gazed at me defiantly and attempted to pull her hand away from mine.

'But does not your inner judgement tell you that it is monstrously unfair to repeat such things to an adult, and that your own love and concern for your little brother must make you want to shield and protect him?'

She shuffled her feet and stuck out her lower lip with a rebellious expression on her pretty face. 'Yes, but Tom did say that he hates Aunt Caro. It is the truth,' she muttered, sullenly.

'Just because it is the truth does not mean you have to be disloyal to your brother by repeating it, Sarah. To speak the truth and shame the Devil over your sincerely held beliefs is a strong and Christian thing to do,' I persisted. 'To tell tales of your young brother is weak and cowardly. Do not you see that?

Surely you will not enjoy playing on your own while poor Tom is copying out his letters over and over again. Will you?'

Sarah now ceased trying to pull away from me. She once more shuffled her feet about in an agony of indecision and inner struggle.

Blushingly, she finally acknowledged, 'No. I have no wish to play on my own, Miss Grey. I am sorry, Tommy.'

'Good,' I said. 'That is quite the most bang-up thing to do, Sarah.'

I gave her a beaming smile and patted her hand in a friendly manner before releasing it. I realized it was only a small and temporary victory of Sarah's good nature over the poisonous nurture of her Aunt Caroline, nevertheless, I was content. I knew there would be other struggles of a similar kind with this wayward young girl, but for now, peace reigned in the schoolroom and the three of us were content with each other.

I showed Tom how to draw every letter as a humorous character. Letter 'S' was Mr Sam the snake. Letter 'K' was Mr Kit the kicker with one leg kicking up and one down. The 'B' was Mr Baker who always carried his baskets of bread before him and so on. After a while, Tom had forgotten his troubles and was laughing with pleasure at our letters game. In spite of herself, Sal, too, was attracted and left her dolls to join us at the table. It was a joy to see the genuine pleasure that the two of them had in this simple activity, which had been invented by my own dear mama for my brother and myself, when young. Sarah was a quick and able pupil. Her alert mind grasped every concept in reading and mathematics almost at once, her only fault being to flit butterfly-like to another topic as soon as her concentration waned. Even so, I was very satisfied with the progress of both children and when we had cleared away the books and eaten the lunch that Annie had brought up for us, I promised the children a walk in the park opposite Melbury Square. I helped them with their outdoor clothes and put on my pelisse and bonnet and we walked down the stairs towards the front door.

'Ah, I thought I heard your voice, Sal. Has Miss Grey released you from your school-room prison for the day? What about our drive, my darling?'

I immediately recognized that distinctive deep voice, and to my surprise, Lord Hallburgh's study door opened and he stood before us smiling at me and the children.

Noticing Tom's sad expression, he added quickly, 'And my dear old Tom, of course. What about a turn round the park? See and be seen with Papa's new matched greys?'

Tom looked even more forlorn, and Sarah muttered, 'Aunt Caro says that Tom must not go. He has to practise his letters.'

'Fudge, Sarah. We shall all go,' Lord Hallburgh said. He gave his son a pat on the shoulder and included Sal and me in his open smile.

'Perhaps I could stay with Tom,' I ventured tentatively. 'Miss Hallburgh did say that he . . .'

'Mmm yes,' he said, stroking his chin. 'But I am sure to make it evens with Caro later. She cannot deny Tom his little treat on my first day home. Give me a minute and Baxter will have the curricle brought round for us, Miss Grey.'

I remained silent, pleased at the prospect of an outing but full of foreboding at this airy flouting of Miss Hallburgh's wishes. Sure enough, when we were outside the front door, being helped up into the curricle by Baxter, Caroline Hallburgh came round the corner of the terrace in her special chair and stopped in front of me like an avenging angel.

'I thought I had ordered Thomas to spend today at his letters,' she said, with an angry glare. 'He is not to have a treat riding in his papa's curricle after his rudeness to me.'

I thought it best not to reply to this when

the papa in question was present himself, already in the driving seat and with Baxter preparing to swing himself up at the back. I merely pressed both of the children more safely into their seats and my gentle pressure also served as a warning to them to remain silent.

Lord Hallburgh answered for us, very politely and evenly. 'Why, it is all of a piece, Caro. The little scamp has been hard at it all morning learning his letters and Miss Grey has pronounced herself well satisfied with his progress. May we not put it behind us now, please? It is such a fine afternoon for giving the greys an airing.'

He gave his sister that particular and unexpectedly sweet smile that I was to recognize over the coming months. I realized with a flash of perception where Sarah had acquired her great charm. It was not effective in mollifying Miss Hallburgh though. Her delicate pretty face grew pink and she replied somewhat tartly, 'I will not have employees countermanding my orders, Edmund. Surely you realize how unsuitable it is for a mere governess to interfere in my discipline of the children. Thomas has been told repeatedly that he must greet me properly, and it is not likely that he ever will if Miss Grey rewards him for refusing to do so.'

Tom shrank back into the buttoned upholstery of the curricle and his hand sought mine. I could sense his terror and wished fervently to give Miss Hallburgh a set down. I held my tongue however, hoping that Lord Hallburgh would stand up to the tyrant in his household and I was not disappointed.

He looked down at his sister and gave a laugh. 'Why, Caro, my dear, it is not like you to get into such a miff over the little ones. Come now, what do you say? Shall we not let his crimes pass unrecorded this time? It is my first day at home after all. I'll wager Baxter will not be too pleased if the greys miss their exercise. If Tom is a little beyond the pale as far as manners are concerned, it must be because he favours his uncouth papa.'

Again, he gave his particularly pleasant smile.

'Miss Grey has promised to teach him all the refinements required of a young gentleman of quality, but alas,' and he shrugged his broad shoulders which were elegantly encased in a coat of superfine blue cloth, 'Rome was not built in a day. Please excuse him this time, dear Caro. Please, my dear.'

No one could resist this appeal delivered in such a handsome and fetching way. Miss Hallburgh had to concede to her brother and did so with feigned good grace. 'Oh very well,

Edmund, but you spoil the children dreadfully.' However, I knew from the clenching of her pretty white hands and the tightness of her shapely lips that it went against the grain with her.

Her brother laughed again. 'Yes, I spoil them,' he conceded. 'But now we have a fierce dragon in the schoolroom who will not allow me to break the rules in the future. Miss Grey is such a force to be reckoned with that we must all obey her.'

I felt dear little Tom visibly relax and he gave a wriggle of pleasure at the thought of myself being a fierce dragon. Miss Hallburgh, however, was not so amused. She did not appreciate his little joke in my praise. She turned her cold eyes on me. They were full of contempt.

'But there is no need for you to accompany the children on their drive, Miss Grey, if their papa is in attendance.'

Lord Hallburgh spoke again before I had time to answer. 'Does the fierce schoolroom dragon wish to do something else? Have you other plans for this afternoon, Miss Grey?'

'Why no,' I stammered, blushing inanely. 'We were to go a walk, you see . . . I . . . No . . . I would be delighted to go for a drive.'

'Capital, my dear Miss Grey. We shall go then. Goodbye for the present, Caroline. We will have a couple of turns around the park and return in about an hour.'

Miss Hallburgh directed a look of pure venom at me, but fortunately this was observed only by little Thomas who once again put his hand in mine as we set off on our jaunt to the park.

Lord Hallburgh was content at first to allow the perfectly matched greys to trot sedately while Baxter sat with arms folded high on a box seat at the back. The autumn sun was warm as we drove through the gracious streets and on towards Hyde Park. I began to relax and enjoy the sights, as people watched our progress round the square, with the two children remarking excitedly on everything that they could see. As we drove, I was acutely aware of the proud set of Lord Hallburgh's handsome dark head, his smart clothes and immaculate Hessians. He looked every inch the true Corinthian, the nonpareil that he truly was. I felt immeasurably proud to be with him. He was a member of the highest *ton*, one of the richest in London and, yet I quickly felt, one of the most charming men alive. He seemed completely without arrogance or conceit, one who could command respect and liking not only from an insignificant governess like myself, but from the powerful and wealthy. I felt privileged to

71

be out with him that day. I saw how natural and youthful he seemed in his relations with his children. He appeared to cast all cares aside as he chaffed and joked with Thomas, who clearly worshipped his father, and then changed his approach to one of gentle teasing with Sal. I observed a change even in Sarah when she was in her father's presence. She seemed so much more open and less calculating with him than when she was in the stilted company of her aunt. I resolved to try and help her to cultivate this aspect of natural childhood and to gain some openness of character, regardless of her aunt's wishes.

Lord Hallburgh showed the same consideration and kindness to me, in the way that he went all round the various rides in the park, pointing out different areas where I might walk with the children and the botanical gardens which he said were worth a visit.

Then he stopped the curricle and Baxter walked the horses while we explored the maze. Of course, the two children ran off eagerly to try and reach the centre first and I laughingly followed them running to keep them in view. Sarah reached the middle first and Tom and I ran hand-in-hand to join her.

I had not realized that we had left my employer behind until I heard his distinctive deep voice calling, 'Hello! Miss Grey, Sal,

Tom. Where are you?'

At once we turned and ran back the way we had come, but with one or two false turnings and dead ends, we were all three of us breathless and glowing as we reached Lord Hallburgh again. I pushed the thick hair back from my face, aware that I had lost the combs which kept my unruly locks in place. He was standing in the sunlight, tall and slender but with the light reflecting the fabric of his coat, on his wide, strong shoulders.

His eyes looked as bright as glass as he said laughingly, 'Dear Miss Grey, I thought I must have to send the Watch out for you if you had not returned from the centre of this maze. And my dear children, lost forever,' he said with mock melodrama to Sal, who giggled and took his hand.

'But you seem to be a swift runner, Miss Grey. A positive Diana in flight.'

'I am so sorry,' I said. 'It was such a pleasure . . . The fresh air . . . Running with the children,' I finished breathlessly, raising my hands to try and tidy my hair.

I saw the handsome pale eyes, so like his sister's, looking at me with frank and admiring appraisal and I lowered them again, rather self-consciously.

'You look like one of the children yourself,' he said quietly. 'What a young slip of a girl you are, to be sure.'

'She is not a dragon, Papa,' said Thomas gleefully. 'She is just a slip, is she not?'

'Do not be rude, Thomas,' his father corrected him. 'I am so sorry, Miss Grey, I should not have made that observation. *Pas devant les enfants*, you know. Forgive me.'

Embarrassed, I took Sarah's hand and walked towards the curricle where Baxter helped her up into her seat. I waited for Thomas and once he was inside with his sister, I took my place beside them. Lord Hallburgh climbed into the driving seat and took up the reins and we set off for Melbury Square.

Tom was silent, surreptitiously sucking his thumb when he saw that his sister's attention was diverted by the passing scene. I glanced down at him. He looked enchanting with his shining curls made untidy by the wind. I knew that the outing had done him good and that he had forgotten, for a few hours, his aunt's subtle persecution and bullying. I hoped that in time, he would gain some resistance to his tormentor.

A tide of warmth and affection welled up inside me, as he whispered, 'I love you, Miss Grey. It was so lovely and airy in the park and I love to be with Papa.'

'And I enjoyed it also, Thomas, being out

with you and your Papa,' I answered, giving him a little squeeze.

I little realized what results my rash admission would have when it was repeated to Miss Hallburgh. Tom lay back against the cushions and sighed with contentment. I too was content. I had enjoyed immensely that glorious hour of escape in the company of Lord Hallburgh and his children. He had not been the lordly aristocrat, overweening or arrogant, but an ordinary affectionate papa, out for an hour with his children, driving his own carriage, whip in hand, conversing with me as well as the young ones. As we clip-clopped along at a very steady pace through the quiet streets around Melbury Square, he now turned his attention on me more fully.

'I own that I still find it absurd to think that you are nearly one and twenty, Miss Grey.'

I detected no patronizing or pomposity in his tone, only the merest friendly interest of an employer towards a younger person in his employ.

'Oh, but I do assure you it is so, sir. I often wish I had a few more mature aspects to my nature and appearance that would make me more credible as the 'fierce schoolroom dragon', as you described me.'

I wondered fleetingly if my banter would be considered out of place, but he merely laughed and said, 'Now you're bamming me, Miss Grey. I assure you that we are all of us delighted that you are not in any way a dragon. But I trust my sister's judgement entirely in her choice of a governess for Sarah and Thomas. And you have such a youthful and pretty name.'

I was emboldened to say, 'It is an old name, from the Greeks, I think. It means 'Light'.'

'It suits you perfectly,' he said, briefly.

It was an indifferent seeming compliment, tossed lightly over his shoulder as he steered the horses expertly towards home, and yet I felt my cheeks grow hot and I busied myself with tucking a rug round Tom's knees, as he had now fallen asleep.

'This must be a very different life for you from the one you were leading in the country, Miss Grey,' he continued. 'My sister tells me you were used to live in Cottenham Rectory. Tell me a little about it: I have estates quite near there, at Wembeck.'

'Indeed, sir, and I know the whereabouts of Hallburgh Manor. Well, my father had a living at Cottenham, but he is recently dead and so my aunt arranged for me to come to London as a governess.'

There was so much I wanted to say, so much sadness and, yes, anger that for a few moments, I did not trust myself to speak. At the same time, I experienced a surge of tenderness towards my two motherless little charges, especially Thomas.

There was a pause as though he was aware of my strong emotions and then he asked politely, 'And do you have theories, Miss Grey, as do some of those in charge of the new educational seminaries for young ladies? Ideals of a curriculum designed for intellectual as well as social life? Mm?'

'Now it is you who is ribbing me, sir. No, I have no such pretensions,' I answered him. 'But with the wonderful example set by both my parents, I do have some ideas of developing a child's heart as well as intellect. In particular, as regards feelings towards our fellow creatures. It is of great importance to me.'

Suddenly, boldly, as Baxter was handing me down from the carriage, I turned to Lord Hallburgh and said, 'Perhaps Your Lordship may wish to know at first hand my practice in the schoolroom.'

'I would so,' he responded, courteously. 'You might not be a dragon, Miss Grey, but I can see by the set of your chin that you are determined to make something of my two young rapscallions.'

He gave me a warm smile which encouraged and delighted me, and went on, 'It is quite an undertaking, to have the care and guidance of two young children. Thomas, of course, is still an infant.'

'But he is eager to learn,' I countered.

He smiled fondly. 'And my only daughter is somewhat wayward and I think you will find, rather lacking in application.'

'But she has a lively intelligence and great charm. I'm sure she could be guided to use her gifts in a way that would help her to do well in life.'

'My dear Miss Grey,' he said. 'You are the most loyal female dominie that I have ever met. I hope your pupils deserve you,' he said, more sombrely. 'My own schooldays were not so happy. Both my parents died when I was young and my dear sister, Caroline, was mother and father and governess to me, who was but a young and lonely lad until I went away to school. My life would have been intolerable were it not for the home she made for me. Being so much older, she had the wisdom to help and nurture me in the holidays. I owe her a debt of gratitude that I can never repay.'

I listened intently to him, feeling that these confidences from such a grand person as

Lord Hallburgh must be very significant indeed. Whatever Caroline Hallburgh was or was not, it was obvious that she had exerted the most profound influence on her brother's life.

We were both diverted from our conversation at this moment by Tom, who, still rather shaky from sleep, was lifted down from the carriage by Baxter and attempted to run after Sarah to the front door. He fell painfully in the gravel and, though he tried to be brave, his chubby face crumpled with tears. As I ran forward to help him, Sarah was unable to resist a smirk and a jeer at her little brother's expense.

'What a little cry baby, to be sure,' she mocked. 'Cry and stick your finger to your eye, little baby Tommy!'

In spite of my concern for Tom, I turned immediately and bent in front of her so that my eyes were on a level with hers.

'Sarah,' I said calmly, 'what did we say, this morning? Did we not agree that it was in no way loving or commendable for a girl to mock and tease a younger child, especially her own small brother?'

She looked up at me with her father's handsome pale-grey eyes and then lowered her gaze. I waited for a moment and then whispered, 'Come and take Tom's hand with me, and we can go upstairs and make his knees better. Please, Sarah.'

She tossed her head, embarrassed, but then looked towards her father. Lord Hallburgh gave no acknowledgement to his daughter's charming smile, merely saying, 'Get along, young Sal. Help Miss Grey with Tom and I shall see you at dinner.'

I scooped Thomas up into my arms and carried him through the front door and upstairs to the schoolroom.

4

Dinner was not a formal meal that evening. How could it be when we had to accommodate two such young children? I accompanied my charges, who had now been dressed in fresh clothes, by the nursery maid. Sarah was in a pretty muslin dress with a wide ribbon sash and little white satin slippers and Thomas in the usual little boy's outfit of skeleton suit in dark-blue velvet and a little frilled white shirt. The outfit was decorated with gold braid and gilt buttons and Thomas was very proud of it because he thought it made him look like a soldier. If only I had a more handsome gown, I thought. My drab grey dress was heavy and unfashionable; the neckline had been adjusted very inexpertly by the village dressmaker and I was aware that it was not a good fit. I am not one to repine and am not a vain woman, but I reflected that at my age, even an inexpensive gown which was new, would suit me. Annie had done her very best with my hair and I was not displeased with the result, as I examined my reflection in the mahogany-framed looking-glass. Steady, green-flecked eyes gazed back at me and I put up a hand to smooth the short curls framing my rather wide brow. It was an unnecessary gesture. She had gathered my hair into satin ribbons at the back and this was a style which I knew revealed the small dainty ears set close to my head. My face as yet needed no artifice. I still had my country girl's complexion and the full red lips which I had inherited from my dear Mama. I thought of William's remarks about my perfect teeth and resolved to remember to smile as often as I could.

The magnificent dining-room was panelled in oak and had a fireplace at each end of the room. The beautifully carved chairs were each drawn up towards the antique silver chargers on which reposed exquisite china plates marked with the Hallburgh coat of arms. I had never experienced anything so grand and noble as the table laid for the Hallburgh family dinner, with the sparkling candelabra and shining silver cutlery. In the centre of the table was a crystal bowl of exquisite hot-house flowers, their heady scent dominating the room.

Lord Hallburgh sat at the head of the table. He looked as always, both fashionable and elegant, the dark evening clothes suiting his tall figure. His hair had been styled in a fashion made popular by Lord Byron and he seemed in a relaxed and gracious mood.

There was no one sitting at the foot of the table, which I supposed would have been his wife's place in days gone by. Miss Hallburgh was on His Lordship's right hand side and the children and I sat opposite to her. I had a feeling of slight panic and queasiness at the idea of sitting so closely and intimately with these two handsome and wealthy people. I tried to calm my nervousness by attending on the children.

I did my best to be inconspicuous, tactfully cutting up Tom's meat for him and giving warning frowns towards Sarah when I felt she was gulping her food too quickly. I deliberately avoided Caroline Hallburgh's cold gaze and concentrated on getting through the meal without being noticed. Nevertheless, Lord Hallburgh addressed the occasional kindly remark to me to which I responded with as much composure as I could muster. Caroline Hallburgh pointedly ignored me throughout the meal and her icy disdain was in sharp contrast to his easy friendliness. I was conscious merely of her baleful stare every time I looked in her direction, which, I hasten to say, was not often.

I contented myself with the thought that when the children were in bed, I would write to William and give him my impressions of life in Melbury Square. I took particular note of her exquisite gown and beautiful hand-painted fan, which she languidly wafted across her face between courses. But it was the exciting Lord Hallburgh I most wanted to convey in my word picture for William.

In spite of my pretty hairstyle and newly pressed dress, I still felt like a poor country cousin. Caroline Hallburgh, by contrast, was splendidly attired in a gown of dove-grey watered silk, which showed off her delicate complexion and unusual pale eyes to perfection. Though she laughingly claimed to Edmund that it was 'but a cobbled-together supper and but a poor push after what he had been used to abroad', the fact was, it was far grander than anything I have ever been used to at home. There was such a delicious assortment of courses, expertly served by the butler and two young footmen, it was difficult for me to choose what to eat and what to leave alone. My senses were overwhelmed by the heady game stew and the fragrance of the fresh fruit. Although I was distracted by my two young charges, I was still able to enjoy the sweetness of the wine jelly allied with the crispness of the tiny butter biscuits. The whole range of exquisite tastes was accompanied by a smooth Bordeaux wine, served in sparkling crystal glasses.

At last it was over, and Miss Hallburgh

signalled to me to take the children upstairs to prepare for bed. Lord Hallburgh was to be left to enjoy his port and tobacco while she took some tea in the drawing-room. The children bade a polite good evening to their papa and I escorted them to the door.

Thomas clutched my hand and pressed himself against my skirts as though anxious to be gone upstairs, but we were stopped abruptly by Miss Hallburgh.

'Thomas, are you not forgetting something?' she demanded coldly.

She had left her place at the table and walked slowly towards us using two sticks to help her. Outside the dining-room, Thomas pressed even closer to me and began to nervously chew at his fingernails.

'Take your fingers from your mouth, child, you are no longer an infant. Come and kiss me before you retire for the night.'

Thomas stood stock still, but did not offer to comply. He looked up at me as though appealing for help. I could do nothing.

I gently removed his hand and said coaxingly, 'Kiss your aunt, my dear,' but he mulishly put his fingers back into his mouth and lowered his eyes. I was in an agony of concern for him and yet was powerless to prevent his aunt's demands.

It was obvious that Miss Hallburgh had

very rigid ideas on the nurture and upbringing of young children.

She tightened her lips and said, 'Take your fingers from your mouth at once. Do as I say. This defiance must not be allowed to continue.'

Desperately, I bent over Thomas and whispered, 'Be a good boy, Thomas and kiss your aunt.'

Miss Hallburgh now turned her wrath on me. 'Kindly do not intervene when I am dealing with Tom's bad behaviour, Miss Grey.'

I recoiled from the cold hatred of her grey eyes. 'I . . . I beg your pardon, ma'am, I understood that I was engaged to be governess to the children.'

'Just so,' she hissed. 'But this is a matter of my discipline and the upbringing of my brother's child.'

Thomas now abruptly pulled his fingers from his mouth and threw both arms round my knees, sobbing, 'Please take me to bed, Miss Grey. I hate Aunt Caroline. Please may we go to bed?'

Sarah sniggered at this and was immediately quelled by an ugly glare from her aunt. 'Take him up, Miss Grey, and get him ready for bed. I shall come and deal with him presently, when he has had time to reflect on his bad behaviour.'

I was distressed by this, but was obliged to comply. I made one last attempt to persuade her to a more reasonable attitude towards the little boy.

'Please, Miss Hallburgh,' I began.

'No more,' she said imperiously. 'I will not have my orders countermanded, Miss Grey. Let go of her at once, Thomas.'

Thomas did so, but set up a loud weeping and distraught sobbing which was painful to hear.

I cast around me, indignant at the way she had treated a young defenceless child and was so angry that I was emboldened to say, 'Forgive me, ma'am, but I cannot countenance one of my pupils being treated in this unfair way. Either I am in charge of these children, or you are. With respect, we cannot both be responsible for their education and discipline.'

Although I spoke quietly, I was aware that Sarah had now become very watchful indeed and was looking at me with a mixture of respect and surprise. As for Miss Hallburgh, her voice rose shrilly above the cries of poor little Thomas, as she rounded on me with the utmost venom. Perhaps she had not imagined that a humble governess would dare to address her in this way, but although I have been brought up with the concept of Christian meekness and forgiveness, I am by no means timid, especially in defence of the young and helpless. Her chin quivered, and her beautiful face turned stiff with the force of her barely repressed hatred. Her eyes flashed like frozen ice chips and she opened her mouth to speak, but no words came. It was as though she was literally speechless with rage.

It was into this highly charged atmosphere that Lord Hallburgh emerged from the dining-room. He advanced languidly and spoke with studied calm. 'Upon my word, Caro, a fellow cannot enjoy a quiet cigar with this din going on. What on earth can be the reason for such hullabaloo? Poor Tom is howling as though the hounds of Hell are after him,' he added, as though to soften the severity of his words.

Tom's howls subsided into a few sobs and once more I was aware of Sarah looking very calculatingly at her father and aunt.

In the brief silence that followed Tom's tearful hiccups, she said, by way of explanation, 'Aunt Caroline said that Tom must take his fingers from his mouth and give her a kiss. Miss Grey says that she is our governess and is in charge of us, so we must do as she says.'

Her bright grey eyes, so like her father's, flicked from one to the other of us. What a perceptive intelligence the girl had, I thought, for one so young. What strength of character for either good or evil, she displayed. There was now complete silence. The atmosphere in the large gracious hall was tense with suppressed emotions. Even Thomas seemed to be holding his breath. His father ordered Sarah to take him up to the schoolroom and wait for me there. She obeyed instantly and led the little boy up the stairs without a backward glance.

He spoke first to his sister. 'You seem to have got yourself into quite a taking over something, Caro,' he said gently, giving her an affectionate but quizzical look.

I watched helplessly as Miss Hallburgh's face changed from delicate English rose to an almost crimson red. Her pale eyes bulged as though she were about to be affected by an apoplectic fit, and her bosom heaved with the desire to be my accuser in the unfortunate scene which she herself had just caused. I awaited the onslaught of her reproaches and blame towards myself with my head held high. None was forthcoming. Instead, to my amazement, she pulled out a scrap of lace handkerchief from the sleeve of her gown and proceeded to weep most affectingly.

'Oh Edmund,' she sobbed. 'You know how I've always worshipped those two dear children, especially since their poor mama is no more. I have endeavoured to be friend and counsellor to them as well as a loving aunt, but meet with only base ingratitude from Thomas, who rejects all my attempts at natural affection and nurture. Miss Grey does not, as yet, understand his wayward nature, and I fear she seeks to allow a quite unbecoming familiarity from the child. I . . . I . . . have tried my very utmost to do what is proper for the children; I can do no more,' she sobbed, and broke off to dab her eyes in a most dainty and affecting way. Then she darted a glance at me from under her lashes in a replica of Sarah's earlier expression.

'My dear Caro, please do not upset yourself,' he urged her. 'Everyone realizes we owe you a debt of gratitude for your kindness and the sacrifices you have made.'

He spoke directly to me for the first time. 'My sister has been an absolute nonpareil in her care of us since . . . Catherine . . . since . . . my wife — ' He broke off.

'Yes. I realize that,' I replied quickly, trying to ease the situation for all our sakes. Caroline Hallburgh obviously knew how to play on this admirable man's emotions and was prepared to do so without any conscience.

Mademoiselle Moreau glided into the hall at this point with an embroidered shawl which she proceeded to drape tenderly around Caroline Hallburgh's shoulders, while darting dark looks of hatred in my direction. I continued to stand there while Miss Hallburgh basked in the attention of the two people who meant most to her. Over the lace handkerchief, her silvery eyes met mine momentarily and I recognized the triumph in her glance. I realized that Edmund, like most men, saw only what he wanted to see and did not wish to look beyond the surface in his dealings with women. I felt passionately that I would like to urge him to trust to my management of his little son and daughter, but I realized this was not the most opportune time.

Again, he laughingly cajoled her into forgiving Thomas and letting his bad behaviour pass. At this, Miss Hallburgh became the womanly saint so beloved by Yvette. She smiled forgivingly and agreed that it didn't signify and that she had already forgotten Tom's transgressions. I felt very uneasy at the little scene which was being played out for her brother's benefit. I knew in my heart that if Edmund had not been present, Tom would have been treated in a much harsher fashion and I could not rely on His Lordship's presence in all future disagreements.

Gradually, with calculated stages, she allowed herself to be comforted and coddled into smiling equilibrium, as both he and Yvette held her hands and coaxed her into taking some tea.

Finally, he turned his attention to me. 'And what was the problem about Tom's nail biting?' he asked, in a more relaxed manner.

'Oh, nothing of any import,' I stammered, noticing Caroline Hallburgh's beady look. 'Perhaps he was a little overtired. I shall go upstairs and calm him before bedtime.'

He turned smilingly once more to his sister. 'You see my dear Caro. You are all that is good in your care and feelings for the children. But you must concern yourself with your own health and comfort, now that we have Miss Grey. She is everything that is commendable in a governess. Her discipline is absolutely dragon-like and you must leave the children entirely to her competent ministrations.'

I knew this speech and his small attempt at a joke, would not endear me to Caroline Hallburgh, or her faithful Yvette, but having regained his affectionate regard, she dared not say more. He further antagonized her against me by continuing urbanely, 'Our inestimable Miss Grey's first name is Lucy, Caro. She informs me that it means 'light' and who knows? She might be able to bring some light to those two little jackanapes of mine.'

There was no reply from his sister and I mounted the stairs to the schoolroom very conscious of his lazy relaxed laugh and the frigid disapproval of the maid, Yvette and her mistress.

A few days later, I learned that Lord Hallburgh had left for Scotland and I had to face the prospect of life at Melbury House with none of his support against Caroline Hallburgh's strange tensions and hatreds.

5

My Dear William

I have taken particular pains to be alone in Lord Hallburgh's library this evening, so that I might write to you about my new life in the big city. In return, I hope you will find some time to reply and describe all your doings at Oxford. I can reassure you about my continned health and wellbeing, although sometimes, I think my progress with the children at Melbury House is rather slow. It is all so new and different after Cottenham, and teaching young children is tiring as well as rewarding. At the moment, dearest brother, Lord Hallburgh is in the country, hunting in Scotland, as I understand it. This evening, Miss Hallburgh is giving a small select dinner party and my little charges are happily settled in bed with the nursery maid in attendance. I have long since finished my supper in the schoolroom and have indulged myself in writing to dear Fanny Pembleton, from whom I have as yet, received no word. No doubt, she is enjoying the assembly balls at Bath and will write in due course. I hope you are able to decipher my crossways writing and will reply soon. I would be so delighted to receive your news and gossip about your fellow students and to know that you continue in good health and spirits. It is not so long now to Christmas and then we shall meet and talk to our hearts' content. Please bring back with you any clothes which need darning or repairs. I shall be delighted to accomplish anything which is helpful to you. I remain, my dear brother,

Your loving sister,
Lucy.

I had settled myself in a soft, high-backed chair by the fire in Lord Hallburgh's library to write my letter and no sooner had I finished and sanded it, than I was aware of the door opening and of the unmistakable smell of a gentleman's cigar pervading the warm and cosy atmosphere. I gathered my writing things together and stood up somewhat reluctantly to confront a complete stranger who seemed just as astonished as I was to find another person in His Lordship's library.

He was very smart in his evening dress, his hair dressed in the continental manner, and had about him an almost indefinable air of foreignness which was not unattractive.

'Oh, your pardon, *mademoiselle*,' he said, and gave me a polite bow.

Although he was young and handsome, yet he had an appearance of almost snake-like cunning. He was so polished and suave that I knew at once this must be a Frenchman.

'My apologies, *mademoiselle*. You must be the young lady who is governess to the Hallburgh children. I am Doctor Marcel Trabut, I was not aware that the library was occupied.'

'Yes, I am Miss Grey,' I replied, picking up my writing case and preparing to return to my room.

'I am so sorry to disturb you, Mademoiselle Grey,' he said again.

'It's of no consequence, sir,' I replied. 'I must in any case go and check on my pupils.'

'But you are so charming, *mademoiselle*, and you look so young yourself to be in charge of those children.'

He walked gracefully to the fireplace and threw his cigar butt into the glowing embers.

'I'm here as medical adviser to Lord Hallburgh's sister. Please . . . I have no wish to disturb you. I merely hoped for a quiet smoke before joining Miss Hallburgh and the ladies. She is, as you know, in constant need of attention for her various ailments.'

His dark eyes, so languid and sensual, raked me up and down, lingering somewhat embarrassingly on my shabby gown and worn house shoes.

'You were not at the dinner this evening?'

'No I had supper upstairs with the children.'

'A pity,' he said, rolling his eyes and pressing his hand to his heart with mock sadness. 'A lovely young girl like yourself could have done much to lighten the tedium of a rather boring dinner party.'

I did not care for his manner and made determinedly for the door.

'You must excuse me, Dr Trabut, I have to go and make sure that the children . . . '

'Please, do not leave me so soon,' he urged. 'I get so few opportunities to converse with young fresh people. All my clients seem to be elderly or dull, or both.'

Again I caught him observing me with his bold, calculating stare. I wondered what Lord Hallburgh thought of him. I was to find out that His Lordship had little patience with this charlatan and only tolerated him for his sister's sake. At the same time, I felt I must be polite to him. After all, he seemed to be the family physician and it would not do to show any lack of civility. Seeing my hesitation, he made an effort to engage my attention further by changing the subject.

'Have you had chance to look at these studies of the racehorses by Clifton Tomson?

His Lordship's father was a very keen breeder of horses and won many trophies in all the classic races.'

Unconsciously, I found myself drawn towards a gilt-framed picture of a stunningly glossy black horse, which, Marcel Trabut informed me, had won purses of over £30,000 for Lord Hallburgh's father.

'The famous Bounty Hunter, and a great favourite of Catherine, Lady Hallburgh,' he said admiringly.

He never stopped talking in that smooth continental way of his and I was trapped like the proverbial fly in the spider's web while he confided he had just returned from Paris.

'A symposium of the foremost physicians from continental Europe,' he explained. 'Discussing the latest methods of preventing the spread of infectious diseases which beset our various populations. It was fortunate that Miss Hallburgh was not afflicted too severely by her ill health, while I was away,' he said with a cynical smile.

'She makes a fetish of being frail, mademoiselle,' he said softly. 'But she is by no means as delicate as she would like others to believe.'

I was stung by his disloyalty.

'So why, then, cannot you be honest with

98

her and encourage a more robust approach to life?' I asked, more indignantly than I intended.

'My dear Miss Grey,' Dr Trabut said even more softly and viciously, 'Miss Hallburgh has built a whole house of cards on her invalidism. Take away that and she will collapse into nothing. Nothing,' he repeated. 'All the sympathy and concern that she attracts by reason of her infirmity would disappear, and yet, I tell you, she is far more physically able than you think.'

His lips curled thinly. 'Her brother sees nothing of what is going on, of course.'

'What do you mean?' I asked, intrigued in spite of my better judgement. I was reluctant to gossip behind Lord Hallburgh's back and yet, I must confess, I wanted to know more.

He now turned towards the picture of Lady Hallburgh and pretended to be studying it.

'Well, the beautiful Lady Hallburgh, for example,' he murmured dreamily. 'What a wonderful woman! What an angel in human form. His Lordship worshipped her of course. Everyone did. And then . . . her tragic end. Has Caro not told you about her?'

'No, indeed,' I said stiffly.

I did not wish to know about Lord Hallburgh's beautiful wife, but even so, I was now incapable of leaving the room. I was both reluctant to listen to him and yet consumed with curiosity at the fate of the lovely young woman who had been mother to Sarah and Thomas.

Marcel Trabut drew another long fragrant cigar from his leather cigar case and turned it between his fingers, almost like one who is about to perform a parlour trick or some sleight of hand. He turned back to the picture of Bounty Hunter, an almost sleepy expression on his sallow face.

'And this was the creature which caused Her Ladyship's death, *mademoiselle*. She was in Leicestershire where His Lordship is partial to the hunting. Lady Hallburgh took out Bounty in preference to her more usual, tractable mount. It was thought that she must have lost control of such a difficult horse and either caught her head on a low branch, or been thrown by the spirited stallion. When they found her she was lying with a broken neck, but the horse was grazing peacefully, not three hundred yards away.'

I gazed at the picture of the magnificent horse and thought of the beautiful young woman in the portrait and my two motherless pupils. For the first time, the woman of my imagination seemed to be a living, breathing entity, no longer a beautiful cipher doomed never to change or grow older.

'I suppose you have been instructed never to mention her name.' He turned suddenly to look at me directly.

'I . . . I . . . don't know,' I stammered. 'Miss Hallburgh certainly seems of the opinion that it is best not to mention her to the children.'

'Quite so, Mademoiselle Grey,' he murmured slyly. 'In truth, the little one cannot remember his Mama and I will take my oath that *la jeune fille* never alludes to her at all.'

'But why is this?' I burst out, against my better judgement. 'After all, her portrait is . . . for all to see and must be a constant reminder of the unhappy circumstances of Her Ladyship's death.'

'Miss Hallburgh is very influential, *ma petite*, but even she was unable to persuade His Lordship to remove the offending picture and expunge the memory of Catherine forever.'

'But why should she wish to?' I interrupted him again, far more passionately than I intended. 'Surely the picture is a precious reminder of a dear wife and mother?'

Again, the slyness of his expression showed through his pretence at politeness. He smiled cynically at me. 'In a marriage, my dear, things are never quite what they seem. Catherine Hallburgh often suffered from nervous debility and her husband was frequently preoccupied with estate matters.'

What was he implying? I wondered indignantly. That the kind and dignified Edmund Hallburgh was a neglectful and unloving husband? A cold and absent father? A jealous monster guarding his wife as a miser guards his gold? I found this difficult to believe. From the little I had seen of him, he seemed almost a saint. Yet what did I know? A young unmarried girl who had never even known a man and had lived in a country parsonage all her life; I was hardly qualified to judge such a complex situation as marriage.

Aloud, I said, 'But I believe he held his wife in great affection and esteem and has never recovered from Her Ladyship's death.'

'But he also had deeper passions, Mademoiselle Grey. Her great beauty and spirited behaviour sometimes drove him to the depths of despairing jealousy. Who knows what unspeakable actions his mad rage might have caused?'

I now looked at the loathsome doctor with the utmost disbelief.

'I am quite sure that your insinuations against Lord Hallburgh are wicked, sir,' I exclaimed recklessly. 'To suggest otherwise is a vile calumny.'

'But you are young,' he murmured softly, almost caressing me with his sensual dark eyes. 'Remember, I have been an observer of this family for some years, and the onlooker sees most of the game, *n'est ce pas?*'

I now felt exceedingly uncomfortable and, though I longed to leave the room, yet I wanted to know more about Edmund and the beautiful Catherine. Was Dt Trabut seriously implying that Her Ladyship's death was not an accident, but murder, caused by her husband's jealous rage?

Somewhat feebly, I said, 'I know nothing of the circumstance of Lady Hallburgh's death, but surely, it was an accident?'

'Perhaps,' he said in a silky voice. 'But she was in a mad, reckless mood when she went out riding that day. It may be that her own unhappiness made her careless to the point of suicide.'

I was so shocked at this, I hugged my writing materials closer to me and made to leave the room. He must have seen my disgust and horror at his revelations, because he put a white manicured hand on my shoulder as though to warn me.

'No word of our little tête à tête, *mademoiselle,*' he said in a sibilant whisper.

'Especially to Miss Hallburgh, you understand. She was no friend to Lady Hallburgh, when that unfortunate young woman was alive, and would take it ill if you were to rake up the unhappy past. She passionately resented her brother's love for his wife and was jealous of the place Catherine had in his affections.'

I bade him a formal good evening and sped up to my room, my cheeks still burning at this last revelation.

It was a long time before I was able to compose myself for slumber; my thoughts were whirling uncontrollably and my emotions so highly charged, I had to get up and sit by the window for a few minutes. I looked out onto the moonlit terrace. The November weather had turned cold and there was a halo around the moon. The formal urns with their evergreens were stiff and lightly tinged with frost. The whole scene was of stark coldness. I shivered in spite of the warmth of the room. Broodingly, I sorted out my feelings about the situation at Melbury House. I felt that Edmund Hallburgh was a good and loving father, and a kind and courteous employer. How then could I imagine a situation where he had driven his unhappy young wife to bring about her own death?

Nevertheless, Marcel Trabut had introduced an idea into my mind which I found extremely disturbing and which, in time, would prove to be a disruptive element in all our lives.

6

Next day, I had resolved to speak discreetly to Annie, but she had fallen ill and in her place was a sour old body who kept herself to herself and resolutely had nothing to do with me. I missed Annie and was determined to visit her at her sister's lodgings in East London, but this caused another crisis between myself and Miss Hallburgh.

'My dear,' she said sneeringly, 'how can you take this illness seriously? Persons of that order manage to be ill when it suits them. It is just so much flummery. Ten to one, her sister has a more lucrative job for her that will last but a few days and then we will see Annie returned to full health. Believe me, this sort of thing is common among that class of people.'

But I obstinately refused to believe this of Annie. She was the only one who had shown any consideration or respect for me and I wanted to return her friendship.

'Nevertheless, Miss Hallburgh,' I persisted, 'I have some time off on Friday and am persuaded that I have a right to spend my few hours as I wish.'

It was obvious that Miss Hallburgh despised and disliked me for my decision, but even she was unable to physically restrain me from my resolve to visit Annie and take her some small comforts. The staff were surprisingly generous when they knew where I was going. A slice of fragrant game pie, a little claret left over from Miss Hallburgh's dinner party, an embroidered handkerchief with some hartshorn from the nursery maid, all appeared as if by magic as soon as my decision was made known. Miss Hallburgh's disapproval did not weigh at all. I was able to take a hackney cab and see for myself that Annie was indeed poorly and in need of support and kindness, until such time as she was recovered sufficiently to be back at work.

This was not the only time during those weeks when Lord Hallburgh was absent from Melbury House, that Caroline Hallburgh and I were set against each other. I consistently tried to be polite and tolerant towards her, but Lord Hallburgh had given me the task of caring for his children and giving them the training and discipline that they needed and so I was firm in my resolve to run the schoolroom in my own way. It was indeed salutary to recognize how well disposed the staff really were towards me after I had stood up to her and insisted on visiting Annie. I was heartened and encouraged by these little acts of friendliness from the other servants, except for Yvette Moreau, of course.

I realized that this rather sly and cunning woman was, in fact, reporting back to Caroline Hallburgh everything which happened between myself and the children. She was frequently able to visit me in the schoolroom with a trite or unimportant message from her mistress and always appeared with a look of sour triumph when she delivered these salvos. They seemed planned to interrupt my teaching and this was very trying. Once the children had been unsettled it was sometimes difficult to calm them again.

When Annie returned to work, she was as loyal to me as ever and now quite devoted and wishing to serve me. Thomas also, was now completely won over. He was utterly compliant and easy to handle and once, when he was tired and about to lie down in bed as I wished him goodnight, he said sleepily, 'Good night then, Mama.'

I must confess that this brought tears to my eyes, and I left the nursery bedroom without comment. Fortunately, Sarah was still saying her prayers to the young nursery maid and did not hear. But even she was much improved and her behaviour was only awkward when she had been in her aunt's company for some time.

The tensions between Caroline Hallburgh and myself occurred mostly over my training of the children's behaviour, rather than the content of my lessons. She had the knack of undermining and sneering at the principles of honesty and consideration for others which I was trying to inculcate into the children. She did this on an almost daily basis, first, by enticing Sarah to her, then offering a bribe or privilege before contradicting my instructions or discipline. This was in sharp contrast to the actions of their father, who, before he had gone to Scotland, had used to come into the schoolroom occasionally and sit quietly, examining their notebooks and paintings. He would always praise what he saw and encourage the children positively to mind what I told them, always upholding my order and organization. Once, he even laughingly pretended to be a pupil himself.

'And do you think my mathematics so abysmal that I should wear the dunce's cap, Miss Grey?' he had said with mock despair, much to the delight of the two children who laughed with pleasure while they awaited my response.

Naturally, I had entered into the spirit of this fun and sternly decided that he must practise number bonds to one hundred until he was more proficient in addition and he had shown suitable humility and declared himself ready to work hard for improvement.

He was so kind to me, so considerate and civilized, with no trace of pomposity or patronage, the sort of man to impress a young inexperienced country girl like myself. I had grown to enjoy the deep manly voice, the graceful, beautifully dressed figure of the gentleman who sometimes brought us a few sweetmeats into the nursery or took us out for an airing in Hyde Park. These trips were very rare, but memorable. He was always so kindly and, what is even more attractive, he was utterly charming and I looked forward to his visits to the schoolroom.

By contrast, while he was in Scotland, my life was somewhat lonely and bereft and I was excluded from the social circle enjoyed by Miss Hallburgh. I had no idea when he would return. Even in my most sombre moments, I could never associate him with the sort of hateful, unloving husband who could drive his poor wife to suicide, whatever Dr Trabut might say.

Now that Dr Trabut had discovered my existence, he seemed to be forever in the library or passing through the hall at the same time as myself and I was conscious that these were not altogether accidental encounters. I took my own measures to avoid him, but one evening, he persuaded Miss Hallburgh to allow the children into the drawing-room after supper. Annie and I made sure that they were both dressed suitably for company and I duly presented them before their aunt and her guests at seven o'clock.

Thomas, as always, was reluctant to be with his aunt but I coaxed him and in the end, he submitted with a good grace. After the children had been petted and fed with sweetmeats for a while by the matronly ladies present, they were then asked to recite. Thomas of course, stuck his fingers in his mouth and held his head down in his shyness. I was finally able to get him to lisp a little rhyme from the *Mother Goose Treasury* and he was then fussed and made much of by all the ladies, much to Miss Hallburgh's disapproval.

'But what about dear little Sarah?' she asked dotingly. 'I'm sure she knows far more advanced pieces than those. What can you recite for us, my darling?'

Sarah was now over-excited at all the attention her little brother was receiving and said impulsively that she could recite a poem by Mr William Wordsworth. This suitably impressed everyone, but only I knew that Sarah had never learned this poem by heart. She had merely heard me repeat the words of 'The Rainbow,' when we were on one of our outings and the rain had cleared to disclose a perfect shimmering arc across the London sky.

'Sarah,' I whispered to her desperately, 'you do not really know this poem. Why not recite the verse about the 'Naughty Little Doll', which I taught you last week?'

She squirmed away from me, her face flushed with the attention she was receiving and struck a pose in the middle of the drawing-room.

'My heart leaps up when I behold
A rainbow in the sky,' she declaimed confidently.

'So . . . so . . . was . . . so was it — '
She broke off in confusion, not knowing how the poem continued. I took her hand, not daring to look at Miss Hallburgh, who sat stony-faced and angry, while her guests murmured indulgently and gave some encouraging applause at little Sarah's lapse.

'Try again, *petite* Sarah,' urged Dr Trabut, giving me a sympathetic glance, but there was no such understanding from Caroline Hall-burgh.

'You may take the children upstairs, now, Miss Grey,' she said coldly. 'It is obvious that more effort needs to be made with Sarah's education.'

It was clearly of no use to protest at the number of little poems and pieces that I had already taught the children. They were not to be given a second chance and neither was I. It was a pleasure to their aunt to put me on the wrong foot and I had to swallow my chagrin and merely wish her a polite good evening and take the children to bed. I felt the animosity and spitefulness of her attitude very keenly. It made me feel even more isolated and on edge, but I knew that I was unable to effect any change in her and I had to shrug it off.

The next day, I tried to reason with Sarah and point out to her that if she had performed what was suitable and within her capabilities, she would not have been so humiliated in front of the company.

'It would have been better to recite one of the poems you know well, rather than make a cake of yourself in front of your aunt's guests,' I said to her softly and kindly.

Sarah's sensitive little mouth, so like her beautiful mama's, trembled uncontrollably at my gentle censure and her large eyes filled with tears. I realized at that moment what an unhappy little thing she really was underneath all the bravado and the showing off with her Aunt Caroline. I sensed that this was a turning point in our relationship for both of us, as I put my arms around her and whispered words of reassurance and comfort.

'There, there, Sal. Do not fret yourself, my little darling. We will say no more, my dear. Everyone makes mistakes, that is how we learn. Come now, dry your eyes and let us see if Tom remembers any of his letters from yesterday. He loves it when you test him and play with new words.'

Tom did indeed remember them and Sarah's tears were soon forgotten in the new game that I showed them of making words with little letter cards. We were soon all laughing at the humorous pictures I had drawn on the back of the cards, so that Tom could turn them over before he guessed what they said.

The children had become so affectionate towards me and I had become so fond of them in return, that there was nothing I would not do for them. We had so many enjoyable activities and walks in London that I soon knew the area around Hyde Park as well as I knew my home village of Cottenham.

The only problem was the continued unpleasant efforts of Miss Hallburgh to make my life difficult and unhappy. It seemed she resented a young and pretty woman gaining the respect and trust of her nephew and niece, and actually enjoying them, having fun, uncomplicated by any prejudice or jealousy on my part. Whatever the reason, she made it her daily activity to try and make my life miserable by undermining everything I tried to do with them. She was particularly vindictive to poor little Thomas, who was totally unable to understand the petty spitefulness of his aunt and unable to cope with the absence of his papa and the confusion wrought by Miss Hallburgh's interference.

This was difficult enough, but my other problem now was the continued and unwelcome presence of Marcel Trabut. His incursion into my schoolroom territory was very trying. The doctor seemed to find a chance to visit his wealthy patient three or four times a week and was often invited to stay for supper. He made every opportunity to come up to the schoolroom, ready to indulge in one of his sly conversations about the Hallburghs. He was always full of innuendo and half-finished sentences. I tried to freeze him out, tried to be dignified and distant, tried always to be busy and preoccupied with the children when he entered the schoolroom uninvited, but he was impervious to my set downs. He always insisted on kissing my hand when he departed, invariably holding it for a moment longer than necessary, his dark, liquid brown eyes gazing soulfully into mine.

Miss Hallburgh took me to task over my reluctance to welcome the doctor into my domain.

'It has come to my attention, Miss Grey,' she admonished me, 'that you are less than civil to Dr Trabut when he has occasion to visit Melbury House. I quite fail to understand how someone in your position can have the effrontery to be so ill-mannered to a gentleman like Marcel Trabut, while at the same time, of course, throwing your handkerchief in another direction.'

'I . . . I . . . do not take your meaning, Miss Hallburgh,' I said at last. 'When could I possibly have been disrespectful or discourteous to Dr Trabut?'

'Why, when he visited you in the schoolroom yesterday,' she snapped petulantly.

'But I was in the middle of teaching the

children their numbers,' I explained, as calmly as I could.

'Numbers. Letters. Sums,' she snapped. 'There is no need to give yourself such airs, Miss Grey. Anyone would think you were head of a seminary instead of being merely a spinster governess, dependent on my brother's charity.'

These hateful words issued from her sweetly curving red lips as though she had just remarked on the weather, or the latest book at the subscription library. I remained in frozen silence as I looked at her cold, slate-grey eyes and pretty pink cheeks. She was as beautiful as ever this morning with her pale-lilac dress and with amethysts and diamonds at her ears and throat. The glossy black hair with its distinctive white streak had been dressed with Parisian elegance by her faithful Yvette and her little boots were of purple satin. I must have stared at her for full twenty seconds before the import of her words fully entered my consciousness.

'Forgive me, Miss Hallburgh,' I said, feeling my face flush with indignation. 'Your pardon, ma'am. Did I hear you aright? What do you mean by your remarks on my 'throwing my handkerchief?' I would be obliged, ma'am, if you would explain that to me.'

She was obviously chagrined at having revealed herself to me in this way, but she was determined to outface me and try to retain the high moral ground.

'Why, only that you do not treat my brother in this unwelcoming fashion, Miss Grey. If he is in the schoolroom, he is treated as an honoured guest and you have time aplenty to let him pretend to be one of your pupils and to play nursery games with you and the children.'

I realized she was referring to Lord Hallburgh doing the numbers to a hundred when he had pretended to be a dunce. I knew, of course, that this information had been extracted from Sarah after Yvette had reported back to her mistress.

'It would be totally inappropriate for me to deny Lord Hallburgh entry to the schoolroom, Miss Hallburgh, when I am accountable to him for the education and training of his children,' I said, with what dignity I could muster.

I knew how she could not bear to have her brother like me or approve of what I was doing, nevertheless, I was not prepared for the spiteful remark that I had 'thrown my handkerchief in his direction'.

'I still do not understand what you mean by your remarks about my personal conduct,

Miss Hallburgh. Pray explain exactly how I have 'thrown my handkerchief towards His Lordship',' I persisted, now feeling only cold anger at her patronizing attitude.

The floodgates of her hatred and malevolence towards me were unleashed at this and her face was suffused with the passion she felt against me.

'You little hussy,' she hissed. 'Do you not know that I am aware of how you trail after my brother when he is at home, using the children as your excuse to entice him into the schoolroom and making yourself available to go in his carriage for jaunts around the park? You make it so obvious that you have a *tendre* for him. Such behaviour is entirely unsuitable for a person in your position. You would do well to know your place, my girl, instead of setting your cap at a man of his rank.'

I was too mortified to answer her. How dare she speak to me like this? What had I ever done to deserve such malice? Even if I did have a *tendre* for him, it was entirely unsuitable for her to voice this. My mind was in turmoil. Was what Miss Hallburgh said true? Did I really have such obviously tender sentiments towards my employer? I hadn't thought along these lines and yet, I had to admit to myself that I did indeed like and respect him exceedingly. More than this, I positively admired and revered him, very much as I had revered my father. In fact, I would willingly lay down my life for him or the children. There was absolutely no comparison between my hero, Edmund Hallburgh, and that toad, Trabut. I wondered what her reaction would be if I repeated some of the doctor's more colourful gossip about Lord and Lady Hallburgh and their private life together. Equally, I could have revealed to her the base intentions of her physician, how he came to make himself a nuisance to me, not to make much of the children, or indeed take any interest in them whatsoever, but merely to enjoy some dalliance with a woman he felt could not protest at his attentions. I could also have mentioned how he had revealed to me her own lack of frailty and her imaginary illnesses in his usual indiscreet fashion. All this I kept quiet about, however and merely removed myself from her presence.

'Your pardon, Miss Hallburgh,' I muttered, 'I am needed upstairs,' and I fled away from her, before I was tempted to say too much.

In the privacy of my modest room, I thought long and hard about my recent encounter with Caroline Hallburgh. I was glad that I had been able to exercise some restraint and had not repeated any of Dr

Trabut's indiscretions to justify myself to her. After all, she was not my employer and Lord Hallburgh had expressed himself well satisfied with my work. I decided that I could maintain a dignified silence and not succumb to her bullying.

The next day brought a scrawled note from my tormentor, as though in some way she wished to mitigate the horrid accusations she had laid at me.

'*Miss Grey*

We will say no more of our little discussion. Perhaps I mistook your motives, so let us not be in any huff about our disagreement. Doctor Trabut has asked if he may take us out with the children to Vauxhall Gardens. I have agreed and have ordered the carriage to be brought round at two o'clock, tomorrow. I hope you will have the children ready to accompany us.

C.H.

How dare she refer to her insulting accusations as a 'little discussion'? I was still very mortified and had a mind to cry off from the visit to Vauxhall. It was obvious that Miss Hallburgh felt that she had been hasty in her speculations about me and that this was her way of building bridges to try and mend the rift. She was not a fool, and after all was aware of how well Lord Hallburgh thought of me and of the influence I was exerting on Sarah and Thomas. He would not forgive her if she succeeded in driving me away, that much is certain. After a brief inner struggle, I decided that I must try and be amicable if not for her sake, then for the children, who are much affected by tensions between the adults in families. So far, I had not ventured to look too closely or honestly into my heart about her insinuations of my feelings for Lord Hallburgh. It was something I did not wish to address at that particular time, so I put these feelings from me and replied civilly that I would have the children ready promptly and that we would accompany Dr Trabut and herself on the outing. The pity was, I thought, that she had managed to take the edge off what should have been an exciting and interesting experience for me, before it had even begun.

Nevertheless, the trip went ahead and Miss Hallburgh managed to be very pleasant, perhaps because of Marcel Trabut's presence, I was not sure. She was even forbearing with poor little Thomas who did not bite his nails once. The children were ecstatic at the sights and sounds of the Gardens. They revelled in the acrobats, jugglers and fire-eaters, and loved the small stage where the story of Columbine and Pierrot was so colourfully played out, with music and dancing. We had supper in a little private booth, arranged by Dr Trabut and they were able to choose what food they wanted to eat. Both were tired but happy as we came home to Melbury House. It was long past their bedtime, but Annie and the nursery maid were waiting to whisk them off to be washed and put into their beds, as soon as we arrived.

Caroline Hallburgh had been unusually pleasant to me that evening and before I retired for the night, the bat-like Yvette glided up to my door with a message that there had been a letter from Lord Hallburgh to the effect that he was returning from Scotland and we were all to spend Christmas at his family home, Hallburgh Manor in Wembeck.

7

The next few days passed in a flurry of activity as we all of us put our minds and efforts to the move into the country. I must confess that I felt excited at the idea of being near my own home village of Cottenham and of being able to see my dear brother and some of my friends again this Christmas. I had received a reply to my letter from William which was both despondent at his present financial situation and, at the same time, youthfully hopeful for the future. He was also looking forward to Christmas when we could see each other again. Even Fanny Pembleton had taken the time, amid her giddy round of social engagements, to write to me and enquire how I did.

For my own part, I was unaccountably elated at the thought of seeing Edmund Hallburgh over the festive season and having the opportunity to be in his company once again. I even managed to distance myself from the hateful attentions of Dr Trabut, so high were my spirits with anticipation of the pleasures to come. At the same time, I strove to keep the two young children from becoming too excited, both at the change of scenery and at the advent of Christmas itself.

Annie and the nursery maid were soon busy preparing and pressing clothes for the holiday at Wembeck and it seemed they talked of nothing else as they ironed and packed the children's things. Our visit was to last until after Twelfth Night and they would need clothes suitable for the church services and for riding their ponies, as well as for the Christmas party in the Great Hall at Hallburgh Manor. As for myself, I had to clean my old country boots and darn my stockings. I would have to make do with what I had, for there was no possibility of a new gown or slippers.

For some reason though, Miss Hallburgh continued to be charming to me and, although I could not guess why this was so, I resolved to make the best of it and basked in this new atmosphere of unexpected cordiality. One morning when the excited preparations were at their height, Yvette appeared as silently as always, but carrying a dress of black watered silk, with little puffed sleeves and a frilled hem. Her sallow face never slipped from its expression of twisted disapproval as she delivered her message.

'My mistress sends her compliments, Mademoiselle Grey, and begs you will accept this dress as a gift. It is one that Mees Hallburgh has grown too stout for and it may be of some use to you, while you are still in mourning.'

I coloured up with mortification at this patronizing message. No doubt Caroline Hallburgh thought I would disgrace the family party and proclaim my abject poverty in front of His Lordship's tenants in my one and only plain but decent dress. I was about to refuse the gift in a very spirited manner, but I never had the chance.

Annie looked up from her goffering iron and said quietly, 'Why, what a lovely dress that is, Yvette, and how becoming for Miss Lucy's colouring.'

She turned to me in her usual friendly manner. 'I could so easily put some pin tucks in the bodice, miss, and let down the hem a little to fit you properly.'

Her ingenuous eyes met mine with such admiration and affection, that I felt ashamed of my ungracious reaction to the gift.

'Why yes,' I mumbled. 'Pray thank Miss Hallburgh, Yvette and say that I am very conscious of her generosity in such a pretty gift.'

Yvette nodded sourly and withdrew, while Annie left off her ironing to exclaim over the fine dress.

'Hardly worn more than twice I dare say, and the style is much more suitable for a beautiful young lady like yourself than for an older person, such as Miss Hallburgh,' she smiled.

Once the children were in bed, she came to my room and cut and sewed and tucked and hemmed, until the dress was done. We stood before the small plain mirror, I craning my head to see the effect of the gossamer light fabric on my naked creamy shoulders, Annie hanging back a little, rapturous in her admiration of my changed appearance. Even I was taken aback at the way this fine gown revealed sudden unexpected aspects of my youth and beauty. I had never had anything so grand before. The feel of the silk against my body was so voluptuous and sensual, it made me blush with pleasure. The dark fabric was not only a foil for the colour of my hair, but revealed the whiteness and fine texture of my skin. As I stared into the mirror, the image which stared back at me was no longer that of a girl, but of a lovely young woman. The effect was almost unnerving but yes, exciting too. I resolved to use half of my precious shillings on a lacy embroidered shawl, such as I had seen in the mantua makers in Bond Street. I turned to kiss Annie and to thank her for her hard work and found she had tears in her eyes.

'Oh how beautiful you look, Miss Lucy,' she whispered. 'As beautiful as . . . as . . . my poor dead lady,' she exclaimed impulsively and putting her apron to her eyes, she hurried from the room.

I continued to stare at myself in the looking-glass. I was glad that at least I would not disgrace Lord Hallburgh this Christmas. But did that mean I was casting my handkerchief in his direction? I thought not, but admitted to myself that I would not be averse to his admiration and approval. I removed my new dress slowly and thoughtfully and packed it carefully in my trunk. Tomorrow I had some hours away from my duties and I would go out and buy a shawl to match the dress.

Preparations were now well under way and it was decided that Annie and I would take the children and the nursery maid and would go down to Wembeck ahead of Miss Hallburgh and Yvette. Annie would help the housekeeper at the Manor to open up and air the rooms before his sister came to supervise His Lordship's preparations for the festive season. The butler would organize a full complement of staff so that everything would be in readiness for Lord Hallburgh's arrival on Christmas Eve.

Neither Caroline Hallburgh nor Yvette Moreau bothered to wave farewell to us as we set off in the largest of the Hallburgh family coaches with all the luggage, luncheon baskets and children's toys which we could ever need for a stay in the country. Baxter drove us expertly through the city and onto the turnpike road to Oxford where private rooms had been arranged for us. He unloaded the luggage and led the horses away to be fed and watered while the nursery maid and I made the children comfortable and gave them supper and a little wine and water. They had been at a pitch of high excitement and anticipation during the journey, hardly eating anything from the basket of victuals provided by the cook. Now they were absolutely unprotesting as they were led away to their beds with the promise that we should make a very early start in the morning. After I had heard them say their prayers, I, too, made my way to bed in the pleasant anticipation of being able to spend my day off with my brother, William, while we were at Wembeck.

The next day was the sort of dreary, dark mid-December day that always heralds the approach of the winter solstice and we were glad of the fire bricks under our travelling rugs as we set off on the second part of our journey. The children were quieter now and I was able to lean back against the leather squabs in the back of the carriage and let my thoughts roam at will. I wondered how my dear William was and whether he was already down from Oxford for the Christmas vacation. I thought of all that had happened to me in the last few weeks and most of all, I must confess, of when I would see Edmund Hallburgh again.

This was to be sooner than I anticipated, for he arrived even before his sister. On 20 December with four days to go, his curricle drew up at the door and the stable lads were roused to see to the horses as Lord Hallburgh swept in, bringing a whiff of the dank country cold with him. He tossed his gloves and hat onto the hall table and rubbed his hands together as though to ward off the cold. There was no sign of the butler who had long since retired to bed, but as I put my head round the door of the library, I was in time to see Lord Hallburgh shrugging himself out of his many-caped greatcoat. He glanced up and, seeing me, strode towards me. I instinctively reached for the bell pull to summon a servant to attend him, but he stopped me immediately.

'No, do not disturb anyone, Miss Grey,' he smiled, chafing his hands. 'I shall merely warm myself at the library fire.'

He turned from me as he spoke and bent to hold his hands out to the flames. The light caught his glossy, elegant head and his dark hair was alight with deep chestnut glints. As for me, I hovered in the doorway, uncertain as to what I should do, fascinated as always by his handsome appearance. He seemed to me to be even more attractive and personable than I remembered him. I wondered if I should leave him and go to my room, but perhaps he would think me uncivil to absent myself so abruptly. I looked towards my sewing and the book which I had left on the seat beside the fire and resolved that I must scoop them up, think of a graceful remark and make my exit.

He seemed to read my thoughts without even turning round. 'I beg you not to let me interrupt your activities please, Miss Grey,' he murmured in his deep amused voice. 'But I have had a long journey and am uncommonly hungry.'

Now he turned to look directly at me, his slate-coloured eyes sparkling with fun. I at once became conscious of how I must look, my face flushed with the warmth of the fire and my hair undressed and hanging down in its soft natural curls. Thankfully, I was at least wearing a decent dress, with a fresh lace jabot and white cuffs.

'Are you hungry, Miss Grey?' he asked, continuing to regard me, so steadily that self-consciously I put up a hand to smooth my hair.

'No. Leave your hair alone, Miss Grey. It looks utterly charming *au naturel*. You have not answered my question. It must be some time since you had dinner and you are young and healthy. Are you now hungry?'

'A little, sir,' I replied somewhat shyly.

'Then we must find some food,' he said decisively. 'Come, ma'am, take my arm, allow me to escort you in to supper and we shall see what the kitchen yields up.'

He took a candle from the sconce beside the fire and offered me his arm. My heartbeat seemed unaccountably to increase as I took it solemnly and accompanied this tall, elegant figure as he led me across the hall with mock ceremony. The kitchen was in darkness, of course, cook and the maids having long since gone to bed. The copper pans glowed brightly in the candlelight and a fire still burned in the huge cooking range. There was cold chicken and pheasant on the pantry slab and some soft yellow butter to put on our bread. I cut up the meat as neatly as I could while Lord Hallburgh opened a bottle of red wine and poured it into two of the plain kitchen glasses. He reached up to the dresser and lifted down a huge brass charger, which he used as a serving tray.

'So, Miss Grey, ma'am,' he joked, piling the bread and meat onto the tray and adding the wine bottle and glasses. 'Will you do me the honour of supping with me this evening?'

My heart fluttered with excitement and nervousness. 'Why yes, sir,' I answered gravely, entering into the spirit of his play-acting.

What fun! I realized for the first time in weeks, that fun and merriment were noticeably lacking from my life, since William and I were no longer together. Of course, the two children were lively company, but they were not adults and I felt suddenly that this was going to be a night to remember.

He bore the supper in triumph to the library fireside and we seated ourselves on either side with a small supper table in between. He cast off his smart superfine jacket and turned back the sleeves of his immaculate shirt, then loosened the elaborate cravat, unwinding it and tossing it on to the floor. I watched fascinated as the dignified Lord Hallburgh turned himself into a tired and weary traveller, just an ordinary father who had journeyed home and was ready for his supper. He caught me looking at him and stared at me over his glass.

'You are looking very pretty tonight, dear Miss Grey. And the lace at your throat is very becoming.'

I swallowed painfully, unable to meet his gaze and did not reply.

'Are you happy with my two little brats?' he went on.

'Why, yes, of course, sir, they are both very charming,' I managed to say and then took an unladylike gulp of my wine.

'I hope you manage to get some free time away from your responsibilities,' he continued soberly. 'You are so young to be out of the real world and just with little children all the time. You should be having some pleasure in your own life, I think.'

'But I am . . . I do . . . ' I stammered. 'I have many pleasures. Like tonight. It is so unexpected and enjoyable to be having supper with you like this.'

He looked into the fire thoughtfully, his eyes now very dark and brooding. 'Yes, at this late hour when all the world is asleep and two people are on their own, things do seem more simple,' he agreed. 'My life is the very opposite of unexpected and pleasurable. It is always one of responsibility to others, to public duties and formality, managing country estates and observing the rules, of obligations to my tenants and those who depend on me. And yet, Lucy, when I was younger and Catherine and I were first married, we were often able to have firelight suppers like this and we could laugh together and forget the stupid social conventions. How wonderfully carefree youth was then . . . '

He took another drink from his glass while I sat inadequately silent, not knowing how to reply, not daring to interrupt his train of thought. First of all, I was amazed that he had called me Lucy. Then, that he had mentioned the children's mother by name. Perhaps I thought wildly, he is going to tell me more about Catherine and the mystery of her untimely death. But, as I sat motionless, not wishing to break the spell, he gave an impatient shake of his head as though angry with himself for revealing his private thoughts. He rose and put down his glass and the spell was broken.

'You must be tired and ready to retire to your room, Miss Grey,' he said, not using my name this time.

'No, really, sir, I am not at all tired,' I protested with all the energy of youth.

'Well, you ought to be, after your efforts at lion-taming in the schoolroom and your long journey up here,' he smiled. 'And I must own, I shall not be sorry to seek my own bed. Come, my dear, we will extinguish the

135

candles and leave the tray for the servants to deal with in the morning.'

Quite unexpectedly, he stood before me and taking both my hands in his, raised me gently to my feet. He did not immediately release me, but said, 'What a light and graceful creature you are, to be sure, and what a dear sweet girl. I hope life never changes you, dear Miss Grey.'

Then he bent his head and gently pressed his lips to the palm of each of my hands in turn. The pressure of his mouth was firm but not demanding, the warm lips touching me for only a few seconds and yet as I gazed down onto his handsome bent head, I felt over-whelmed and intoxicated by his touch. I gazed up at him wanting more of his caress, but he stepped back from me and bowed with mock formality.

'Goodnight, dear Miss Grey,' was all he said, and then he held the door for me to leave.

I had wished the evening would never end, but it seemed over before it had begun. I was deeply disappointed as I went up to my room, even though I was telling myself not to be such a fool. Edmund Hallburgh had meant nothing by his playful gestures. He had merely been kind to one of his servants. His confidences were just those of a busy man, relaxing by the fire after a long journey. I told myself all this, but in my heart was the wild improbable dream that I might be more to him than this.

I never knew how Caroline Hallburgh found out about our impromptu evening meal, but find out she did. When she arrived on the day before Christmas Eve, Lord Hallburgh was out with the Wembeck Hunt and I was summoned to her room immediately after lunch, by the taciturn Yvette who gave me the look of triumphal bitterness which signified that I was in trouble.

As in London, Miss Hallburgh had her own suite of rooms in her brother's house, furnished to her own taste and with her own maid and personal physician in attendance. She was awaiting me with a great deal of the pomp and circumstance that surrounded her when she was on her own territory.

I approached her door with unaccountable trepidation and knocked politely.

'Enter,' she ordered in that familiar imperious voice.

Today, she was still in her house dress, with frills up to her throat, lounging on a very deeply upholstered day bed. I wished her good day as politely as I could and gave her my most cheerful smile. This did nothing to appease her evident annoyance and, in fact, served only to increase the dissatisfied expression on her handsome face. She gave me a look of undisguised dislike and began to berate me even before I had closed the door behind me.

'It has come to my attention, Miss Grey,' she blazed, 'that when Lord Hallburgh arrived from Scotland the other night, you were brazen enough to accompany him to the servants' quarters and help yourself from the kitchen in order to indulge in a late supper party in the library. How dare you exceed your duties in this way? I demand to know what you think you are about to show such disrespectful familiarity to your betters. Well, girl?' she continued angrily, when I did not at first reply.

I pressed my lips together so as not to voice the angry retort that was in my mind to deliver. Instead, I looked at her as calmly and evenly as I could and only answered quietly, 'I was invited to sup with my employer, Miss Hallburgh. You surely would not have had me refuse? The children were safe in their beds. The servants had retired. It is not my place to control your brother's supper arrangements. Nor, with respect, is it yours, Miss Hall-burgh.'

'Be silent, girl. How dare you address me so disrespectfully?' she hissed.

'I am very sorry, Miss Hallburgh,' I said as placatingly as I could, 'but I am unable to understand your disquiet at my actions. I merely accepted Lord Hallburgh's invitation to eat with him when he returned from his journey.'

My quiet answers, far from calming the situation, seemed to almost drive her into a frenzy. 'You cunning little jade!' she exclaimed. 'Just because His Lordship is partial to a little late night supper when everyone is asleep does not give you *carte blanche* to join him. I have already had occasion to speak to you about setting your cap in that direction. It is conduct completely unbecoming in a person of your social class.'

My face now flamed with anger and hurt pride, but my reply was icy as I said, 'My class, ma'am, may not be of the aristocracy, but, nevertheless, I have been brought up a lady by my parents and know the value of good manners. Surely you cannot think that my reputation would be compromised by having supper with one so honourable as Lord Hallburgh?'

She was now quite beside herself and could hardly gasp out any words. Her usually smooth face was suffused with fury as she tried to reply. The delicately white, beringed fingers clutched convulsively at the gossamer shawl which was draped around her shoulders. She struggled desperately to control herself, but was now almost apoplectic, and no words came.

Curiously, as Miss Hallburgh's ire reached boiling point, it had the effect of making me cold and calm in contrast, and I continued steadily, 'I confess to being appalled and disgusted that one of the servants has found you willing to listen to below-stairs gossip about someone as admirable as your own brother.'

She now found her voice. 'Miss Grey, you will leave this house at once. Needless to say, I shall not give you a character for a new situation.'

For the first time, I felt a pang of disquiet at my recklessness in standing up to her. I was appalled at the thought of leaving Tom and Sarah and my friend Annie, particularly at Christmas. I had so enjoyed gaining the confidence of the little ones and I liked the comfort of life in London. How would I obtain another position without a character? How could I tell Aunt Esther? The ignominy of rejection was terrible enough, but how could I bear being dismissed from his service, never to see *him* again?

At this thought, the iron really entered my soul and I said proudly, 'Forgive me, Miss

Hallburgh, but I do not consider that you are my employer. You have no right to terminate my employment as governess to Lord Hallburgh's children. That, with respect, ma'am, is his alone. I am completely innocent of any wrong-doing. You have not only compromised my own good character by implying unsuitable behaviour in the matter of Lord Hallburgh's invitation to me to have supper with him, but you have cast a slur against your own brother by these unfounded suspicions. My actions were innocent. I am therefore determined to await his return from hunting before I leave his house, so that he may assure you that this is so.'

I observed the effect of my words on her and saw that she was making an effort to rein in her temper now that she realized that she had gone too far. The struggle was palpable. She was silent for some moments, so I followed up my remarks by pressing her further.

'I recognize that His Lordship is well satisfied with the standard of education that the children are achieving. I am therefore convinced that he will be as mystified as I am myself at your reasons for getting rid of me. However, if he is of like mind as yourself and holds me in such low regard, I will go and pack my things.'

Still she was silent as she picked petulantly at the lace at her throat. I waited with held breath. I had played my best card in the battle of wills with this woman. Would she call my bluff and report everything in her distorted way to Lord Hallburgh and insist on my dismissal? What a strange disordered personality she had. It seemed as if the oily Dr Trabut was right. It was as though her mind was as disabled as her body and that this had affected her intense love for her brother. Perhaps having nobody else in her life, she had lavished such jealous love and worship on Lord Hallburgh that it had turned her brain. She had certainly brought him up and nurtured him with an intensity and single-mindedness that was worthy of the most devoted mother. But she seemed to inhabit an unreal world where her cloistered life contained so few people that she had to be the central character with everyone else as pawns in her game of love and power. I wondered fleetingly what had been her game with poor dead Catherine. Had her insane jealousy helped towards the early death of the tragic young wife? And why was she jealous of me? A nothing of a governess. A penniless nobody. Why try and destroy a person of no consequence like myself? What would happen to poor little Tom, I thought with a shudder, if I left him to his Aunt Caroline? But such agonies of conscience were not going to help the present situation. I took a deep breath.

'Miss Hallburgh,' I said firmly, 'perhaps you have thought better of your instruction for me to leave the house. I have no wish to leave Thomas and Sarah. I think it would go ill with them to have another change of governess while they are still so young. May we not forget our differences and work towards the happiness and stability of your young niece and nephew?'

She still made no reply and I wondered what it was that passed through that tortured mind.

Finally, she said, with sullen reluctance, 'It is true that I have no wish to worry Lord Hallburgh with this, so I will forgive your unsuitable behaviour this once. As long as you do not let it happen again.'

The sneering patronizing tone of her words put me on my mettle yet again and I answered spiritedly, 'I have not behaved badly, Miss Hallburgh, and refuse to acknowledge any rebuke from you. If you still feel you have cause to regret anything that I have done, I would rather resign my position now.'

'No,' she muttered. 'Lord Hallburgh would be very put about to be without a governess at Christmas.'

'But I cannot stay if you think my behaviour unsuitable,' I persisted. 'Perhaps I should wait until Lord Hallburgh returns from hunting and ask him to give an opinion.'

This was the final straw. She dared not lose face by involving her beloved brother in such a petty dispute. He would cut through her petulance and resentment and recognize that I had done nothing wrong; she had merely given way to her jealous temper. Suddenly, her whole demeanour changed and she began to act the part of the helpless invalid. The pale-grey eyes brimmed over with tears and she allowed her pretty lips to quiver pathetically.

'I am so sorry, Miss Grey,' she whispered sadly. 'I know you meant nothing by your actions, but you must understand, my brother means everything to me. He has had such a tragic life and . . . and . . . so many young ladies have made a set for him . . . I am sure that you would not wish to be counted as one of those creatures.'

'No. Certainly not, Miss Hallburgh,' I said firmly.

'No, of course not. Let us try to be friends then, my dear,' she said pathetically. 'I have had such a dreadful night after the journey from London. Even Dr Trabut's special tincture was not able to relieve my pain. I know you are young and strong and do not wish to be burdened with an older woman's problems, but it is sometimes very difficult for me. You must understand.'

She put out a soft, white hand to try and grasp my own, but I understood her only too well. I stared stonily ahead and refused to succumb to this sudden wheedling. I knew instinctively that Miss Hallburgh was acting out a part and was not sincere in anything. Nevertheless, she seemed to have got over her angry temper and, feeling relieved, I made my escape back to the schoolroom.

8

Later that afternoon, even while I was reading a story book to the children, I was inwardly in some turmoil as I thought over Miss Hallburgh's treatment of me. I supposed it to be true that Lord Hallburgh had been admired by many young ladies and I guessed there must have been one or two who tried to encourage him into the marriage stakes since the death of his wife. The joy and happiness that I had been feeling at the memory of our informal supper party had now ebbed away and I was feeling cast down by the wicked and malicious things that Caroline Hallburgh had said to me. I had the most uncomfortable feeling that in spite of her declared wish for greater understanding, she would be watching me closely to try and wrong foot me in front of her brother at the first opportunity. Even the thought of seeing William on Christmas Day failed to raise my spirits, and it was all I could do to retain an equable temper when dealing with my children.

'My' children. In truth, they are not my children, but affection and desire for a mother's love seemed to be reflected in the warmth of their attachment to me, and in the care and concern which I felt towards them. I tried my utmost to be cheerful and bright in the face of their excited hopes for Christmas and to assure them that all good boys and girls would be rewarded with presents and sweets when Christ's birthday arrived.

In the days before Christmas Eve I was intent on trying to curb their natural excitement and to calm them down a little. Even in the middle of a story, little Tom would start to talk of toy soldiers and a wooden fort that he hoped Papa would buy for him and, of course, Sarah wondered if Aunt Caro would remember the doll she wanted. As for me, I endeavoured to stress the spiritual message of Christmas, as my own dear Papa had tried to do when William and I were small. I felt at last that they were beginning to understand some of what I had told them and suggested that in the afternoon we should go for a walk in the grounds of Hallburgh Manor and blow away our schoolroom cobwebs. Annie and the nursery maid helped me to wrap the children in warm and comfortable clothes and I donned my old cloak and country boots.

It was very invigorating weather and we walked briskly keeping close to the path near the boundary wall of the Manor and did not venture into the fields. Soon the children were running and skipping ahead of me and I managed to forget my own troubles in the glow of their enjoyment and high spirits.

As we returned, it came on to snow which excited them even more and they whooped with delight. The sky was leaden and the snowflakes large and slow and fluffy. The children were entranced. They literally tumbled in at the front door, laughing and glowing with their exertions, and we were suddenly met by Lord Hallburgh himself, the footman removing his outdoor boots and the maid hanging up his greatcoat. He was seated on a brocade stool, his long legs stretched out for James to pull off the boots. He looked up and smiled, the gesture lighting up his handsome face as the young footman helped him into a pair of soft indoor shoes. I smiled back at him, taking in the glossy dark hair, made slightly untidy by the weather and physical exertion. He looked remarkably like Lord Byron today with his romantic dark looks and snowy cravat, except that his mouth was more firmly shaped and more manly in its firm contours. It had none of Byron's soft pouting sensuality. I was not to be allowed to contemplate his lips for very long, however.

'Papa!' shrieked Sarah, casting herself upon

him and ignoring Annie, who was hovering about, waiting to help her out of her outdoor things.

We brought a draught of cold air with us into the hall and Thomas hung back a little, not wishing to take off his coat and, meanwhile, chewing at his nails. I was trying to persuade him from this habit and I gently removed his fingers from his mouth before giving Annie my bonnet and pelisse. Lord Hallburgh greeted me very affably and, as soon as the children had taken off their outdoor clothes, we moved into the drawing-room. He sat down on a chair by the fire and the two children clambered onto his knee. I was struck again at his kindness and affection towards these two. So different, I thought, from the general, rather distant conduct on the part of most society fathers.

'It is snowing, Papa,' Sarah exclaimed excitedly. 'The old woman in the sky is shaking her bed and the feathers are falling down on us.'

'Has Miss Grey told you this fairy-tale?' he said, laughing at her.

'No, it was Annie, Papa.'

I saw a rather constrained look on his face and realized that he was still disapproving of Annie's influence with his children.

I said quickly, 'There are so many quaint

149

reasons given for snow and storms, Annie was no doubt telling a story that was told to her.'

'Oh, quite,' was all he said, but I felt his dissatisfaction and unease with what he felt to be a servant's superstition.

'And, Papa, why does Annie not look after us any more?' demanded Sarah, throwing her arms about her father's neck.

I saw again that strange closed expression on his face before he replied evenly, 'Why, you silly goose, you have Miss Grey now and she is in sole charge of you. You must both try your hardest to learn your lessons and do as your teacher bids you.'

He leaned his head back rather wearily, the lines around his mouth suddenly etched more deeply and he looked very melancholy. I beckoned the children to the table where I had put out some of the games they liked to play.

He said in a low voice, so as not to be heard by Sarah, 'Annie is an admirable servant, but I find that she talks too much and too unwisely about things that have happened in the past and that are best left unspoken.'

'She has been with you a long time, sir,' I said, at last. 'And she seems a most willing and loyal worker.'

'That is true. I know that when Catherine,

my wife . . . was alive . . . Annie was her trusted maidservant. Looked after everything for her, supervised the children, saw to her clothes, in fact, was someone who was in Catherine's confidence. To be honest, I always felt that this trust was somewhat misplaced and later events proved me right.'

I had no idea what all this meant.

I continued to look at him expectantly and, as our eyes met, he gave a deprecating smile as though to reassure me. I had the feeling that he now regretted ever broaching the subject in the first place.

'Well, that is a chapter closed now, I suppose. I shall say no more.' And he moved his hands rather restlessly on the arms of the chair.

I wondered why he felt first so compelled to talk about his wife's maidservant, and then, why he felt equally driven to close the subject without saying more. It seemed very puzzling, the way people started to talk about Catherine and then so suddenly called a halt.

While I was distracted with these thoughts, Sarah suddenly darted over to a little side table and picked up a pretty musical box. 'Papa! Papa! May we play with Mama's musical box? Oh please, Papa. I shall be so careful and Miss Grey has never heard the little bird singing.'

It was the first time since I had known Sarah that I had ever heard her mention her mother. Even in their prayers at night the children only ever said a little verse to express the end of the day's joys and a supplication to God to keep them safe through the night, never any more personal prayers such as 'God bless Mama and Papa'.

I glanced involuntarily at the clockwork linnet perched on a little shelf in its cage of gold wire and waited with bated breath to see what Lord Hallburgh's reaction would be.

I saw his face assume a hard expression. There was a deepening crease between his brows and his mouth became a tight, thin line.

He said with an attempt to be calm, 'I think not, Sarah. Miss Grey and I do not wish it at this moment. Pray, put it down and return to your game with Thomas.'

But Sarah was wilful as usual and not to be gainsaid, even by her father.

'Oh please, Miss Grey,' she begged. 'Please say you would like to hear Mama's little bird singing. She always let us listen to it if we were good.'

In my head, I was begging Sarah to desist from all this and not to create an unhappy atmosphere of tension, like her Aunt Caroline.

Lord Hallburgh stood up. 'I said 'No',' he repeated sternly, and there was no mistaking the finality of his tone this time.

I gave Sarah a warning look, but she was now set on a misguidedly determined course and pestered him further. 'Oh please, Papa. Tom and I have been very good today. Mama always let us . . . '

'Yes, yes, Mama always let us,' echoed little Tom, although it was obvious that he could hardly remember his mama at all, much less what she did or did not allow them to do. He ran up to his father and clasped his arms around Lord Hallburgh's knees.

There was a moment of shocked silence. 'Now please, children,' I remonstrated with them. 'Your papa has said you may not play with the musical box and I think it time we went up to the schoolroom . . . '

Then the unthinkable happened. Thomas released his father's knees and ran to try and snatch the pretty toy from his sister. The two children each began to tug at the little musical box and then suddenly, Thomas let go and, as Sarah staggered back, she dropped the linnet's cage onto the ground. There was a quite sickening sound as the clockwork mechanism sprang apart and unwound and the pretty toy lay destroyed on the floor.

I gazed in horrified silence and then

Thomas burst into tears. Sarah was profoundly shocked at what she had done and her face became as white as her dress. I dared not stop to think about it but hurried across the room and picked up the broken musical box carefully and laid it back on the table, not venturing to look at Lord Hallburgh.

Sarah who was now completely out of temper snapped angrily, 'It was not my fault. We should be allowed to play with it. Mama always let us. You cannot always bury the past with the dead, Annie says so!'

Then she, too, burst into tears and looked towards me as though for comfort.

My heart missed a beat at the child-like repetition of Annie's words, which I knew she did not understand. I stole a look at her father's face. He stood as though turned to stone, his face ashen. I realized that no one could rescue the situation now and repeated rather too late that it was time to go upstairs.

'Come, children,' I said, holding out a hand to each of them. 'It is time to go up to the schoolroom.'

'No,' he said. 'You children go up on your own. Miss Grey will join you presently.'

His eyes were angry and I could see a small pulse beating in his tight jaw.

Both children were now crying loudly, both obviously overwrought, but I had to watch the poor little lambs shuffle out disconsolately, while their father stood taut as a bowstring by the fireplace.

'I am so sorry,' I faltered. 'I blame myself for allowing this to happen. Perhaps it would be possible for the clock repairer to mend it, do you think?'

'It is of no moment, Miss Grey,' he said curtly. 'It was a bauble, a mere trifle. I bought it for my wife in Venice. It is true that she did allow the children to play with it before dinner, on many a happy afternoon in days gone by.'

He looked so angry and melancholy as he uttered these words that my heart went out to him and to the two motherless children who had left the room in disgrace.

'I must apologize, Miss Grey. It must seem beyond sense for a father to argue with two small children like that and over such a silly trifle. But you see, the emotions and memories that were revived by their desire to play with the thing were . . . quite . . . quite . . . unbearable.'

'Yes, of course,' I said with some unease. 'But it is I who should beg pardon. I was in charge of the children and I let things get out of hand. Poor Sarah is quite overwrought.'

'Yes. I was very stern with them, was I not?' The ghost of a smile appeared on his lips.

'Words cannot express the comfort it gives me to have one such as yourself to guide my children and lead them along the right lines. You are so young and your presence so unobtrusive and yet you bring great strength to them. For this, I thank you, Miss Grey.'

I was utterly overwhelmed at this speech. That I, a nonentity, just a country miss, could bring comfort to one as eminent as Lord Hallburgh was almost unbelievable to me and yet it filled me with a deep and utter joy. In spite of the unhappy scene I had just witnessed, my heart was singing with delight.

'Perhaps I should go to the children, sir,' was all I could manage to say.

'Yes, yes, of course,' he replied. 'Poor Sarah. I was too hard on her. But you do see how much I needed to get a proper teacher for them. My wife . . . when she was alive . . . entrusted them too much to Annie's care and, of course, a lot of servants say unsuitable things in front of the young. Just silly and idle gossip of course, but it can do lasting harm.'

Yes, like Doctor Trabut and Miss Caroline Hallburgh, I thought.

I waited and he went on, 'My wife had not your musical gifts at singing and the pianoforte you see, Miss Grey. The little musical box was very dear to her heart. But it is not true that I have tried to bury the past,' he burst out suddenly. 'I adored my wife but no one may live with the dead, however close we were in life.'

I nodded mutely, not wanting to look at the handsome face which was now so distorted with emotion.

'You must try not to listen to gossip from the servants Miss Grey. You have become almost one of the family and it is difficult, I know, not to take notice of Annie's chatter. Now you understand why I do not care to have my . . . my . . . Lady Hallburgh's name mentioned.'

No, I did not understand. I was completely puzzled by all that I had heard and seen, but Lord Hallburgh then continued in a calmer voice as though nothing had happened, giving me leave to go up to the children.

'And Miss Grey,' he said courteously, 'there is a jeweller's in Bond Street where I have an account and you may purchase, if you will, another little musical box for Sarah. It will no doubt help to ease her childish sorrow somewhat.'

He saw me looking at the broken toy on the table. 'I shall get the footman to dispose of that,' he said without emotion.

He walked before me to the door and held it open. 'Thank you for all your kindness to the children,' he said gravely. 'I recognize that today was merely a small reversal of all the improvements you have wrought over the last few months, so do not reproach yourself. God bless you, dear Miss Grey.'

'Thank you,' I said.

As he stood before me, handsome and courteous as ever, I felt a surge of protective affection, such as I feel for the children when they are asleep. I was almost pleased that I had never met his wife. Glad that I had not ever witnessed the deep passion of his love for her, or his devastation at her death.

I managed a rather uncertain curtsy and he nodded politely. 'Rest assured that I have noticed your honesty and the integrity with which you manage so many difficult situations,' he said, just before I left.

I knew then that he was aware of Miss Caroline Hallburgh's many vindictive acts towards myself and realized with a flash of insight that he had been astounded at some of her more spiteful remarks. Her behaviour had obviously not enhanced any affection and respect that he had for her. As I left him alone in the room, I walked with my head held high. The country church mouse was needed. Needed by one such as he. I was passionate in my resolve to serve him all my days and not ever allow Caroline Hallburgh or any one else to persuade me to desert him.

9

Christmas Eve dawned frosty and clear as the light dusting of snow from the previous day froze on paths and fields, sparkling on every twig and blade of grass. For most of the day, the children and I busied ourselves with a Christmas manger scene. I had had a good talk with Sarah, who was tearfully contrite about the breaking of her mama's musical box and promised me that she would apologize to her father and beg his forgiveness as soon as she saw him. She kissed me most sweetly and begged my pardon and so the unpleasantness of the previous day was now forgotten as we immersed ourselves in preparation for this most holy time of the year.

Several of the little animals from Tom's Noah's Ark were arranged on some straw which we had obtained from the stables. Sarah had clothed one of her tiny dolls in a swathe of blue cloth to represent the Blessed Virgin and for the whole day, the schoolroom table was covered with card and scissors and glue while we completed our little nativity scene. I helped the children to wrap up their modest presents to the people who meant most to them. Two fine lawn handkerchiefs for their papa which we had purchased from Mercers before leaving London. For their Aunt Caroline, a shimmering gauze shawl, embroidered with the lightest and most translucent silks to create almost the effect of gossamer wings. It was obvious that someone, probably Annie, had colluded in the choice of a present for myself. Sarah was at pains to hush Thomas as he attempted to blow the secret open while we wrapped and glued and painted the small parcels for our loved ones. For, of course, I was wrapping my own little gifts. For the children, a little story book each; a pretty lace jabot for Annie, to transform her workaday dress into a more elegant creation for her day off. I had purchased an accounting book for my dear William but I hesitated over a small token for Lord Hallburgh and decided that I could not demean myself and His Lordship by buying the sort of inexpensive trinket which was within my slender means. Instead, I took out of my trunk Papa's glass paperweight, which he had always kept on his desk. I cleaned and polished it until it shone. Although it was old, it was beautifully designed in the shape of a little boat. Papa had brought it back from abroad when he was young and did the

Grand Tour. I wrapped it in thin red paper and wrote my tiny greeting on a visiting card to go with it.

I thought long and hard over a present for Miss Hallburgh and finally decided to get up early and pick a sweet bouquet of winter jasmine and Christmas roses entwined with ivy and evergreens, which I arranged in a glass vase ready to put on her place at the table.

The two children were to be allowed to stay up and have dinner downstairs and I was pleased to think that this would help to pass the time for them and take away some of the unbearable waiting and anticipation that children feel at Christmas time. Doctor Trabut did not help matters by arriving unannounced in the schoolroom and distracting them, just as they were concentrating on their drawings. I had given them some sheets of paper from my sketch book and they were using my pencils to draw scenes of Christmas. I found Marcel Trabut's presence difficult to bear as I knew he had no real interest in the children, but merely came to goad and torment me. He was only intent on making mischief and I was aware that if I chafed at this and made complaints, he would just report it to Miss Hallburgh and make my life even more difficult. I therefore tried my utmost to be polite, if not welcoming, and tried to ignore him.

Thomas had drawn an enormous round plum pudding and was busily engaged in putting dots all over it to represent the fruit. Dear little Sarah pored over her paper with much crossing out and fresh starts and finally managed a picture of a lady in a grey dress. Under the picture she had written, 'I hop I can hav a china doll with silk cloths and I wud like a new mama who is kind and pritti like Miss Grey.'

Although I made no comment about it, I knew immediately that Dr Trabut had read these words and would take this knowledge back to Caroline Hallburgh, so that she would know all about the little girl's Christmas wish. I exercised the utmost restraint while he inflicted his hateful presence on me and finally, he left us. Thankfully, I summoned the nursery maid to help the children to change their clothes before I went to my own room to prepare myself for dinner.

The dress that I had chosen was yet another of Caroline Hallburgh's gifts and had a low neckline decorated with tiny bows of very fine black ribbon. The skirt which fell gracefully from under the bosom was finished with three rows of frills, each embroidered with matching silk. Fortunately, due to her infirmity, Miss Hallburgh wore her gowns rather long, but even so Annie and I had translated one of the frilled layers into a false hem to lengthen it further to fit me. I have no necklaces or jewels of any kind except mama's pearl ear-rings which she had had as a betrothal gift from my father. Not being used to an evening gown, the neckline of my dress seemed disconcertingly low and the lack of any adornment seemed to draw attention to my bosom which looked so white and smooth against the shimmering silk. I took the ear-rings out of their box and put them on and then I stood back to study the effect. A serious young face stared back at me from the small dressing mirror. My cheeks were rather flushed with the effort of dressing, and the slight pinkness of my ears lent a sparkle to my green eyes. The dress was short sleeved and revealed the white naked-ness of my arms. I took out Mama's long evening gloves from their box and drew them on. For the first time since I had arrived at Hallburgh Manor, I was conscious of a desire to look pretty and was excited at the prospect of the evening to come. I walked about the room, slowly and self-consciously, feeling the unaccustomed pleasure of the luxurious fabric against my skin, practising the art of being a woman, not a governess, hoping that I would not be too conscious of my naked shoulders in the evening dress. Annie came in at that point and brought curling irons and ribbons to do my hair.

'I allus did My Lady's when she entertained at home,' Annie confided in me. 'She hadn't a good head of hair, if you know what I mean, miss. A bit sparse, her locks were, especially after the children. But I allus did it nice. And it's a pleasure to do yours, Miss Grey. You got lovely hair. I'll do a Grecian if you wants it.'

She combed and curled and arranged some dark ribbons in my hair to very good effect, for when I next dared to peek into the mirror, I gasped with pleasure. A very smart young society lady was reflected there now with an extremely modish hairstyle and I thanked Annie warmly for her efforts.

The covers were to be laid in the dining-room at seven o'clock and I presented the children and myself in the drawing-room promptly at a quarter to seven. I was astounded to see quite a sizeable company of people assembled and Miss Hallburgh seated smugly by the fireside in her little chair on wheels, holding court quite regally as usual. I recognized one couple — Squire and Mrs Sheldon who had in the past attended Papa's church on Sundays. They smiled and nodded affably when I greeted them. There was, of course, Dr Trabut and the very handsome young Patrick Rudkin, brother to Harriet Marland. A rather elderly lady who played nervously with her fan and was obviously a distant aunt, was also part of the group, and a very dignified grey-haired dowager, Lady Dalton. Lord Hallburgh had not yet put in an appearance but as the children entered the room, they were made much of by the guests, especially the squire and his lady who had not seen them for a whole year and were much taken up with exclaiming over the way that they had grown. Miss Hallburgh meanwhile, affected to introduce me to Patrick Rudkin and the dowager.

'Lord Hallburgh and the rest of us will be attending a ball in Warborough tomorrow evening,' she said smugly. 'The Honourable Mr Patrick Rudkin and his sister, Mrs Harriet Marland, will be in attendance,' she added triumphantly. 'They are not near neighbours of ours, being from Norfolk, but they are staying at Warborough Manor and are well acquainted with my brother through Lady Dalton.'

She was very pointed in her hurried introduction of the aged aunt, treating the older woman off-handedly, almost rudely.

Since our last little contretemps, Miss Hallburgh had been at unfailing pains to be sweet and gracious to me, but I was conscious all the time of a hidden dislike and an angry impatience which was entirely because of her jealous antipathy towards me. Nonetheless, I greeted the other guests and they bowed politely and proceeded to make conversation among themselves, while the elderly aunt continued to fidget. Miss Hallburgh lowered her voice to a confidential whisper.

'For your ears alone, Miss Grey,' she said archly. 'I am so delighted and Dr Trabut is absolutely thrilled that the Honourable Mr Patrick Rudkin and his so charming sister are able to grace the Warborough ball with their presence this Christmas. My brother managed to see quite a lot of them last season when he was shooting in Norfolk and naturally, when Mrs Marland came out of mourning for her husband, he was so taken with her, he attended many of the events and soirées where she was one of the honoured guests.'

Doctor Trabut came up to us at this moment and immediately, it seemed to me, joined in the so called 'confidential' conversation with Miss Hallburgh.

'She is such a beautiful young lady, Miss Grey,' he purred caressingly. 'And as rich as she is beautiful. She has one charming little son who will inherit a legacy left by his French *grand-mére*. She has everything!'

'Yes. Everything that could appeal to a lone widower like my brother. Time has healed many of the wounds of the tragic past and he must now be looking forward to married happiness once again and the comfort of a second mother for those two dear children.'

'Are you seeing yourself as the match-maker, *madame*?' he laughed in his most unctuously honeyed voice.

'I would be so devastated if my dear Edmund were to throw himself away on a nonentity or an unsuitable bride with no breeding or *ton*,' she smiled. 'It would have to be someone *sympathetique*, like dear Harriet Marland. She is so sweet, so compliant, so able to fit in perfectly with our situation.'

I noticed the rather marked emphasis on the words 'our situation' and felt rather put down, as I realized her words had been carefully chosen for my benefit. With her unshakeable delusion that I must be out to entrap her brother, Miss Hallburgh was warning me off. I murmured an excuse and went to join the Sheldons and gave a hand each to Sarah and Thomas because now Lord Hallburgh had entered the room and having greeted his guests, he gave his arm to Lady

Dalton. The others formed themselves into pairs and we entered the dining-room for dinner.

The room was decked with evergreens in true country fashion, and the candles blazed with light down the long formal diningtable. Lord Hallburgh sat at the head of the table, of course, and his sister sat on his right-hand side. In spite of Miss Hallburgh's sly hints, there was an air of festive jollity about the meal and everything seemed to go well. The seating plan was that I had Sarah on one side of me and Thomas on the other. Opposite, was seated Mr Patrick Rudkin, who was a very polished gentleman indeed and who chatted easily of this and that, putting me completely at my ease.

Underneath all the social niceties and the formality of the dinner party, I was uncomfortably aware of Miss Hallburgh's low, confidential talk with Mrs Sheldon.

'Of course, one must not leap to judgements in such delicate matters, but I fancy I have a woman's intuition in this sort of situation and naturally, I would not for the world mention any breath of this outside these four walls, but I own I think he has a definite *tendre* for her. Oh, if only something may come of it, my dear Mrs Sheldon. Dear Harriet always looks so adorable, does she not? I am sure my brother could hardly help falling in love with her.'

I tried deliberately to close my ears to her chatter and concentrated instead on helping Sarah and Thomas to get through the meal with their best social manners to the fore. And they did not fail me. Their behaviour was impeccable and I rejoiced in the murmured compliments from the other guests at the poise and gentility of the two children.

But it was of no avail. The praise directed at Mrs Harriet Marland by Caroline Hallburgh rankled sorely with me and I was acutely aware of her darting needling looks in my direction as I strove not to listen. For his part, Lord Hallburgh was all affability and paid equal attention to Lady Dalton and myself. I stole covert glances at him throughout the meal and discovered a most amusing and droll side to his character. It was obvious that everyone was enjoying his humorous reminiscences of the shooting parties in Norfolk and I was aware that Patrick Rudkin was much diverted too, although he was not seated close enough to hear everything.

The soup dishes were removed and plates were brought in for the game and roast beef courses which were to follow. I thought enviously of Mrs Harriet Marland, a beautiful young widow who obviously had everything a man could want in a wife. Beauty, position, wealth and breeding were all hers. Jealous though I was, I had to concede that she did indeed seem to be in a special position to engage a man's attention. A sweet compliant nature, beauty and good humour enough for the most critical of suitors. Lord Hallburgh's anecdotes were evidence of that.

Momentarily, my emotions got the better of me and I thought, in a fever of hot rebellion, how I wished I were Mrs Marland, to be dressed as a fine lady as she was instead of in another's cast offs; to be attending balls and parties and conversing confidently on equal terms with someone such as Lord Hallburgh; to be seen as a prospective second mother to his children. If only I were Harriet Marland. For it had come to me then in a blinding flash of insight, that I was in love with him. The respect and admiration that I had at first felt for my employer had given way to feelings of an abiding hot passion. The strength of my emotions was so frightening to me that I hardly dared think about it. The idea of so deep and absolute a love for a man such as Edmund Hallburgh was almost too overwhelming to contemplate.

As I tried to come to terms with these totally new and unaccustomed feelings, answering mechanically to Patrick Rudkin's conversational gambits, and at the same time distractedly supervising my excited young charges, I noticed the world-weary eyes of Dr Trabut observing me speculatively. Privately, Patrick Rudkin must have felt that conversation with the Hallburghs' governess was rather uphill, but if he did, he gave no sign and for this I was thankful. Truth to tell, I knew that I had no right to think of Edmund Hallburgh in any other way than that of master and servant. I must cast out any love that I felt for him before it could consume me, for I knew in my heart that my love was strong enough to destroy me utterly. Above all, I was determined not to let Caroline Hallburgh's insidious accusations be proved true. I was not going to reveal my love by word or deed to another living soul. With this proud resolve, I endured the rest of the meal and then at a signal from Miss Hallburgh, the ladies were required to withdraw leaving the gentlemen to their port and cigars.

My way was made easier because I had to supervize the two children until the nursery maid prepared them for bed and then, when they had said their prayers and were settled for the night, I was able to return to the drawing-room.

It was Marcel Trabut who started the

tensions on that Christmas Eve. A group of wassailers had arrived from the village, swinging their lanterns and charcoal hand-warmers and, as they sang in the hall for the entertainment of the company, the children naturally demanded to be allowed downstairs again to enjoy the singing. One of the footmen was told to give the singers warmed ale and a purse of money by Lord Hallburgh and, as the guests trooped back into the drawing-room, I ushered the children back to bed.

Unobtrusively, Dr Trabut followed me. As I returned from the nursery bedroom onto the dim landing, he seemed suddenly to appear from nowhere and negligently put an arm across my shoulders, with quite unacceptable familiarity.

'Ah, sweet Miss Grey,' he murmured. 'How pretty you are looking this evening.'

I tried coolly to avoid any contact with him and extricated myself ready to return downstairs.

'But how is it, Miss Grey, that you are so cold?' he persisted, with his odious smile.

I decided not to answer this, but merely said, 'If you will excuse me, Dr Trabut, I should like to return to the drawing-room.'

'You are so quiet and retiring, dear Miss Grey,' he whispered. 'And yet I seem to think you have hidden fires beneath your cool surface. You are also a brave young woman to deal with those two unruly spoiled brats and to stand up to the oh, so formidable Caroline Hallburgh. I feel you could be such a passionate creature if you were awakened by the right man.'

'Please excuse me, Dr Trabut,' I said impatiently. 'You talk the most utter tattle and I would like to pass if you please.'

He continued as if I hadn't spoken. 'It is obvious that the great milord admires you, *mademoiselle*, but I must whisper a little word of warning. Be very careful how you deal with Caroline Hallburgh, *ma petite*. She is a force to be reckoned with as my dear Lady Hallburgh discovered to her cost.'

In spite of myself, I paused with one foot on the stair. Any mention of Edmund's lovely young wife seemed to fascinate me. The idea of that beautiful creature in the portrait being prey to the cruel Miss Hallburgh as well as to a jealous husband, held a horrid fascination for me and, in spite of myself, I was consumed with morbid curiosity.

Marcel Trabut was not an open or engaging personality. On the contrary, his conversation and demeanour were all about underhand remarks and insinuations. It was possible from his hints and sly innuendoes to build up a very unattractive picture of the sort of existence that Edmund's young wife had endured during her pitifully brief married life. I looked down the brightly illumined grand staircase decorated on every baluster with evergreens and holly in the traditional country style. I thought of the two innocent little children lying upstairs and wondered what was the guiding motive for Marcel Trabut's detestable tittle-tattle. He had made it his business to become more than friendly ever since I had taken up my post as governess to the Hallburgh children. Looking back, I realized also that Caroline Hallburgh had encouraged, nay, gone out of her way even, to throw us together. She was always suggesting some outing or excursion for myself and the children which would include the doctor and I wondered briefly if she were deliberately trying to forge some liaison between us. Perhaps her object was to displace any interest she believed I had in her brother and so create some sort of attachment between myself and the detestable Frenchman. This seemed ludicrous and yet, the fact remained that however repugnant I found him, some remark he made, some view of his about the life or death of Catherine Hallburgh would be guaranteed to hold my attention and command my interest. I found the idea of her so absorbingly fascinating that I was a slave to any morsel of information about her. I guessed that he knew this and was deliberately playing on my intense desire for further revelations about this tragic lady. Nevertheless, I requested once more, with extreme politeness, that he should let me pass so that I could rejoin the company in the drawing-room.

This he did with an ill grace, almost snarling, and standing aside abruptly so that I could pass him. I was to realize later that he went back to Caroline Hallburgh with the childish little picture and Sarah's Christmas wish for a new mama. He had craftily taken it from the schoolroom table and hidden it in his pocket.

When I finally re-entered the drawing-room with a rather heightened colour, the atmosphere was somewhat quiet. Miss Hallburgh had not yet organized any card tables and most of the company seemed to have finished their tea and were talking among themselves in a rather desultory way. Patrick Rudkin was chatting with Caroline Hallburgh and Squire Sheldon, with the aged lady hovering nervously on the fringe of the group. Mrs Sheldon and Lady Dalton were seated near the window and as Dr Trabut, followed me into the room, he went languidly to join them. My eyes instinctively sought out Lord Hallburgh and I was somewhat surprised to see that he was seated by the fire, quite near to his sister, but not really taking part in any conversation.

I was conscious that he glanced up towards the door as I entered and greeted me with a smile. 'Ah, Miss Grey,' he said. 'Please have some tea. I trust all is well with the little ones?'

He stood up and moved towards the tea cups, but his sister, travelling with surprising speed in her little chair, intervened. Summoning the footman who was clearing some of the used cups, she said quickly, 'Serve Miss Grey with some tea, and then you may set up the tables for cards.'

Lord Hallburgh smiled winningly at this point. 'But not before we have had some music, Caro,' he demurred. 'We have had the wassailers, but it would be a pity not to have something more refined on Christmas Eve. Patrick is an accomplished baritone and I'm persuaded that Miss Grey would be willing to play for us and possibly sing also,' he suggested.

While he was looking directly at her, Caroline Hallburgh preserved her expression of pleasant good manners, but only I saw the look of utter hatred and malevolence that masked her features as soon as her brother's eyes were turned to the rest of the guests. He said, 'What do you say, sir? Are you also inclined to give us a song if you have a musician of Miss Grey's quality to accompany you?'

Mr Patrick Rudkin aquiesced immediately, with absolutely no false modesty or shyness and although I had not sought this singling out of myself for attention, I felt that I must do as everyone wished. As for Miss Hallburgh, she decided not to let anyone see her furious looks and she turned on her most gracious smile as they all murmured approval at the idea of some musical entertainment. I therefore sat at the pianoforte and played and sang two very old airs by Thomas Arne while Mr Rudkin went to fetch his music. As the sound of my singing and playing died away, I was very gratified by the murmured approval of the guests and especially by the attention and warmth of Lord Hallburgh who came up to me and was most particular in his praise of my simple songs.

Young Mr Rudkin had chosen a piece by Handel: 'Where'er you walk, cool gales shall fan the glade'. It had been one of Mama's favourites and, as I played the familiar chords of the accompaniment, I felt sad tears of regret and longing welling up in my eyes, so much so that I fumbled to turn the page. Immediately, a strong firm hand was on mine and Lord Hallburgh was at my side to turn the music for me. I dared not look at him, but continued to play almost automatically, while I struggled to regain my composure.

Then the song was ended and the young man acknowledged the applause very modestly, smiling round the room and going to sit beside his sister quietly, while everyone murmured that they would like another song. This he refused very firmly and pleasantly, as it was obvious that the tables were now being set up. Lord Hallburgh declared that hot punch and sweetmeats would presently be served and that those who wished could play cards. I was conscious of Miss Hallburgh's cold eyes looking in my direction, but then her attention was turned to supervising the two footmen and making sure that the guests were served with refreshments. Under cover of the ensuing movement and chatter, Edmund Hallburgh touched my arm briefly.

'Are you quite all right, Miss Grey? You looked a little upset during Mr Rudkin's song.'

'Yes, I am all right. I was just a little sentimental at his choice of song, which brought back memories of my mother, that is all.'

His face softened immediately. 'They say no one is truly grown up until they have lost their mother. It must have seemed a veritable blow when she died at the very moment when you most needed her,' he said quietly.

'I suppose that is true,' I said sadly. 'I would give anything to have her back again. She was the best kind of mother, loving and strong and always there with her sound advice and practical help.'

His eyes met and held my own, brilliant, handsome, and kindly, with a warm friendliness of expression which I found utterly disarming. Suddenly he said, 'You sang and played charmingly this evening, and you are looking very beautiful, Miss Grey.'

'Beautiful?' I echoed foolishly.

'Yes, your hair is done differently. You look so delightful in your dark dress: it suits your colouring perfectly.'

I was so astounded that he had noticed anything at all about my appearance that I was unable to think of a reply. Then he went on to talk about the children and how proud he had been of their conduct at dinner. He was extremely diverted at some of the little tales I told him about their activities in the schoolroom.

I had no desire to mention Dr Trabut's unwelcome visits, but as he glanced round the room and noticed Trabut's eyes on us, he frowned for a moment and then said in a low voice, 'I wonder if that doctor is any good for Caro. I sometimes think that he encourages her to positively enjoy her ill health. She should get out more and shake off the vapours which seem to be affecting her. When I was a youth and in her care, I am sure she was far more capable of walking, in spite of the problems with her feet.'

I was unable to answer this. I knew from what Annie had told me that Caroline Hallburgh had been very good to her orphaned brother. There was much that I could have told him regarding her unkindness to Thomas and her spiteful attitude to myself, but I thought it best to keep silent. Then the moment was past. Smilingly, Lord Hallburgh rose and half turned to join his other guests.

'I hope you will tell me if there is anything that troubles you.'

'No. There is nothing, sir, I thank you.'

'But I expect you would not admit to it if anything *did* trouble you,' he said. 'You are so strong and contained, unless moved by the music of Handel, of course.'

At this, we both laughed and once again I

180

was aware of Caroline Hallburgh's sharp eyes on us.

'I am so pleased that you will be able to see your brother tomorrow,' he said. 'You will have some respite from your duties and be able to relax and enjoy your holiday.'

'Yes. I am looking forward to seeing William. As soon as breakfast is over and the children have unwrapped their gifts, I shall go and meet my brother at church and afterwards we will have lunch at the Bull in Cottenham. And yourself, sir, how will you spend the day?' I asked.

We both laughed again as he replied, 'Well, I shall, of course, be with my family and there is the Warborough Ball in the evening. If only I can get through the day without seeing too much of that accursed Trabut. I shall survive your absence, but you must hurry back to us, Miss Grey, when you have seen your brother. The children will miss you sorely and so will I.'

Then he was required to circulate among his guests and I chatted to Mrs Sheldon and the elderly aunt until nearly midnight, when I was able to retire to my room. My thoughts were in a turmoil as I lay in bed waiting for sleep. I went over every detail of our conversation in my mind, every nuance of expression on his handsome face, every smile, every compliment that he had given me. I pressed my restless head into the pillow and kept my eyes tight closed, but sleep eluded me until it was almost Christmas morning.

10

Neither Dr Trabut nor Lord Hallburgh were at breakfast the next morning. The Sheldons and Patrick Rudkin were present and the aged aunt and, of course, the children. They had unwrapped their presents at the first light of dawn and were pleased with them. Touchingly, they had placed a little parcel at the side of my plate. It contained some embroidered hair ribbons, which I knew Annie must have helped them to buy. If Miss Hallburgh noticed my bouquet, she gave no sign and no comment was made about my present for Edmund Hallburgh, which languished on the sideboard throughout breakfast. No one either touched it or spoke of it and I was assailed by horrid doubts as to the suitability of my actions in giving him a gift in the first place. Patrick Rudkin was all that was civil, however, and kept up a steady conversation throughout the meal with many compliments as to my singing and playing. Gradually, I began to lose my shyness with him and in spite of Miss Hallburgh's glares, I responded to his youthful jokes and his obvious admiration and soon started to enjoy his company. He gave many invitations to me to visit the home of his parents and the Sheldons also made many warm offers of hospitality. This was very gratifying and I promised to accept their kind invitations as soon as was practicable. In my heart, I knew that I would never be in a prosperous enough situation to visit either party on socially equal terms and so my promise was a polite sham.

Finally, I was free to leave the house and make my way to Divine Service. Having taken leave of the children who were to go up to the schoolroom and be supervized by Yvette until luncheon, I donned my bonnet and cloak and was driven by Baxter into Cottenham to attend the morning service and to meet my dear brother. It was the first time in two months that I had been away from Lord Hallburgh's household and I had much to tell dear Wills, who, I fancied, was a little thinner since he had become an Oxford student. His boyish high spirits, however, were undiminished. As soon as we had left the church, he strode beside me with all his well-remembered vigour and soon we were breathless with laughter as we walked briskly to the Bull.

'But you, dear sis, are in bloom!' he exclaimed laughingly. 'I have never seen your eyes so bright, or such a chestnut sheen on

184

your hair. Is it the food and drink you are enjoying at Melbury House?' he teased.

I blushed and disclaimed and went on to talk at length about Sarah and Thomas and the splendour of life in the Hallburgh household. Of course, I made no mention of the love I felt for the children's father or the petty persecutions that I endured at the hands of their aunt. Instead, I affirmed the positive affection and pleasure that the children offered me and the security and comfort of my situation.

'And what of you, Wills,' I said at last when we had finally reached the inn, 'how are your studies progressing? How do you fare with your lodgings? Are you comfortable? Do you eat well?'

Here I glanced at his thin legs which were stretched in front of him towards the cosy fire in the Bull's best parlour.

'Hold hard, Lucy,' he exclaimed laughingly. 'One question at a time, please. Yes my studies are progressing well. I have a personal tutor assigned to me who was a contemporary of Pa's when he was also at Oxford. We get on famously, Lu, and I do admire him as a scholar with a quite exceptional mind.'

He paused for a moment and then said, somewhat diffidently, 'I know my uncle and the old trout would like me to take to the law or some area of commerce, Lu, but I am more and more drawn to the church, as was Papa. Josiah Tranter, my tutor and Pa's old friend, is of the same mind. He feels I may have a real vocation.'

I said nothing at this. I knew that my Aunt Esther and Uncle James would be horrified and dismayed if my brother should choose a vocation with so little financial remuneration. Having no independent income, he would be reliant, first of all, on a curate's meagre salary and if he eventually procured a living, would be obliged to support himself on a modest stipend, unless he was able to make an advantageous marriage, of course. I looked at his lively honest face, so open and youthful in his enthusiasm and felt so sad for his innocent dreams.

Carefully, I said, 'Well, William, I know that if dear Papa were here, he would be delighted at the idea of your joining the clergy. But it is early days yet, and who knows? You may change your mind before your time at Oxford is over.'

'Yes. But I have enjoyed one or two hours a week coaching some of the Reverend Tranter's younger pupils, who are cramming for Eton, Lu. He has expressed himself pleased with my work and I have been rewarded quite handsomely by the grateful parents.'

He blushed with pride as he showed me a handful of gold coins from his pockets. We talked of old times as well, my brother and I, while we ate a wonderful luncheon with trout and duckling and a heavy pudding of honey and apples done up in an English custard. William insisted in the most manly fashion that he must settle the bill, of course. We sat for an hour or two drinking some red wine and then I had to take my leave. William was to stay the night at the Bull and then he would visit my aunt and uncle before returning to Oxford.

'I suppose they will want an account of me,' he laughed ruefully. 'As they are my patrons, I must show myself to be a serious scholar.'

'Yes, indeed,' I laughed. 'But honestly, William,' I said, as I kissed him goodbye, 'I know you are serious and I know you will do well whatever your chosen profession.'

With that we parted and Baxter drove me back to the house. He left me and took the horses round to the mews at the back and I arrived at the front door at exactly the same time as Lord Hallburgh who was walking briskly towards the house, pulling off his riding gloves. In my agitation at seeing him, I clumsily dropped my reticule and we both knelt at the same time to retrieve it. Inelegantly I banged my leg on the stone mounting block and almost stumbled over.

'Miss Grey,' he exclaimed, helping me to my feet. 'Oh my dear girl, I am so sorry. That must have hurt you. Are you quite all right?'

He had clasped his arms around me protectively and those few comforting moments, seemed to last forever. We were standing together on the steps of his elegant house. The trembling early evening stars appeared to grow even larger and more luminous as I enjoyed the marvellous safe haven of his arms. We were so close to each other that I felt the warmth of his breath against my cold face; my only thoughts were of how much I adored him. I was deeply, passionately, in love with him. He was the most wonderful and handsome man I had ever met. I had no idea what his own feelings were, but perhaps he felt impatient with my clumsiness and was merely being courteous in raising me to my feet. I was thoroughly unnerved when, unexpectedly, he broke the spell of this timeless moment. He suddenly clasped me even closer and kissed me lightly on both cheeks.

'Darling Miss Grey,' he said. 'Merry Christmas. How lovely that you are back with us. We have all felt your absence so much today. I trust that you are not hurt. Shall I summon Annie to help you off with you cloak? I am so sorry if you are shaken by your fall. Please let me help you.'

It was all I could do not to throw myself more closely into his arms. I know his words were mere politeness, but he had called me 'darling Miss Grey'. The sensation of his lips on my cheeks was absolutely thrilling to me, even though I knew he meant only to be kind. I said nothing, feeling only the pressure of such strong emotions, after first bidding farewell to my brother and now of being so constrained in the presence of the man I loved.

He opened the front door for me, and then said gently, 'I hope you are not angry at my kiss, Miss Grey. If you are, I must crave your forgiveness.'

'No,' I managed to say. 'No, not at all.'

'So our beloved governess has a very affectionate heart then? You are not just the calm and collected teacher, or the fierce dragon of the schoolroom?'

'No, of course not,' I smiled. 'Merry Christmas, sir. And I have missed you all today, also.'

I sensed that he felt relieved at my reply and we entered the hall together.

'And how does your brother? William, is it?'

'Well, sir, I thank you, and we had a most excellent lunch. William is at present staying with my aunt and uncle in Cottenham.'

'Capital,' he said gravely, and we smiled into each other's eyes, as we parted very amiably.

My spirits soared as I hurried upstairs and took off my bonnet and cloak, refusing his offer to summon the maid. I was just warming my hands at the fire that Annie had made in my room, when the silent Yvette glided up to my door to tell me that Miss Hallburgh wanted a word with me. I was reluctant to leave my fond reverie by the fire, but I was quite used to these interviews by now and knew I just had to give way to her. I sighed inwardly but descended the stairs quite cheerfully.

She was in the drawing-room, in her little chair as usual, looking absolutely beside herself with suppressed rage. She was dressed in a very modish gown of turquoise silk shot through with deep blue and with a matching turban. In her ears, and pinned to the turban, were exquisite amethysts, set round with diamonds and matched to an amethyst pendant at her throat. She looked so immaculately beautiful as always that I was surprised and nonplussed when she handed me Sarah's little drawing and the naïve little Christmas wish which accompanied it. As long as I live, I shall never cease to be amazed at Caroline Hallburgh's ability to be at once so extremely beautiful and charming and at the same time, so evil and vindictive.

'I have spoken to Sarah about this, Miss Grey, and she assures me that it was entirely her own work, but I would like to suggest that it is a most unusual sentiment for such a young child. What was your object, Miss Grey, in encouraging that sort of expression?'

'What do you mean? I do not understand. What sort of expression?'

Her eyes glared and she twisted her lips in disdainful and bitter disbelief.

'Please do not go through the pretence of not knowing what I mean. I am referring to the words, 'And I wud like a new mama who is kind and pritti like Miss Grey', which I feel are entirely inappropriate for a child of her age. Who put this notion to her?'

I stared at the bit of paper and felt myself going scarlet with embarrassment at the child's innocent words. Then indignation set in. 'Oh come, Miss Hallburgh. This is absolutely ridiculous. Surely, even you cannot think that I directed such thoughts to a little girl in my care, or was so disrespectful of

Lord Hallburgh as to dictate such stuff?'

She tore the drawing into pieces and, leaning forward, flung them into the fire. 'I must tell you, Miss Grey,' she said nastily, 'that I disapprove entirely of your encouraging young children to write such things. What was the idea, in such a useless vain exercise? You must have known that the presents for the children had already been purchased and wrapped long before we left London.'

It was useless for me to go into detailed explanations about Dr Trabut's unwelcome visits to the schoolroom and the way that he insidiously undermined my discipline. I was furiously indignant though at his underhanded action in presenting Miss Hallburgh with the child's ingenuous writing. Not for the first time, I felt besieged by these two cunning people and their sinister accomplice, Yvette. For a moment, as I looked at her evil, twisted expression, I was filled with a sort of angry panic. If my brother seriously intended to become a clergyman, and I were to lose my position here, it would be the end of any support I could hope for from my aunt and uncle. Not only that, but I would be cut off for ever from the man I loved.

I drew a deep breath to try and calm myself and said with what dignity I could muster, 'Really, Miss Hallburgh, the children's drawings are nothing whatever to do with Dr Trabut. Sarah wrote from the heart. I did not suggest or dictate to her or Thomas, how they must express themselves.'

'A likely story. Sarah would never presume to write such a thing, unaided.'

I began to tremble. Whether it was my trifling accident or the highly charged emotions brought on by my meeting with Edmund Hallburgh, I cannot say. All I know is that at that moment, my control failed me and I snapped, 'I find it despicable that a man of Dr Trabut's years should trouble to steal a child's little picture in this sly fashion and that you should stoop to not only read what she has written, but should interpret it in this nonsensical way. Does time hang so heavy on your hands, ma'am, that you both should seek to persecute and torment someone who is only trying to do her job?'

The effect of my words was immediate. Her hard slate-coloured eyes were now like slits as she glared at me. I regretted my hasty words immediately. The fact that I would not let her bully me seemed to goad her even further. She returned yet again to her vile insinuations, like a cat who continues to toss about its prey, long after the bird is dead.

'How dare you speak of Dr Trabut in that disrespectful way?' she hissed. 'He is my doctor and my dear friend, as well as a friend of Lord Hallburgh's and a frequent visitor to this household.'

Privately, I thought of His Lordship's remarks about the doctor's treatment of her and felt that he was no friend to either of them, but I bit my lip and said nothing, determined to regain my calm.

'I insist on knowing who put such an unsuitable idea into Sarah's head. 'A new mama' indeed,' she scoffed. 'As if my brother would look at a mere servant.'

'Miss Hallburgh,' I rejoined wearily, 'it was a little drawing done by Sarah with no assistance from anyone. You are making too much of it.'

This reply fired her anger again and she burst out in a fury, 'I shall send for Sarah and get to the bottom of this.'

This was calculated to make me react. She knew only too well my protectiveness towards the children and how anxious I was to spare them pain.

'Miss Hallburgh, please do not distress Sarah in this way. It is Christmas Day. I beg of you not to disturb such a time of peace and goodwill by all this unpleasantness. It has taken weeks of effort to stabilize the children and to calm their behaviour. It will all have been for nothing if you start upsetting them

194

with adult quarrels.'

'Oh be quiet, you hateful little schoolma'am,' she screamed, now completely beside herself, and she drummed her elegant little fists on the arms of her chair. I began to feel unnerved and not a little uneasy at her utter lack of control.

The silent Yvette ran into the room at this point and at once Miss Hallburgh burst into a full fit of the vapours, weeping and clutching at the amethyst pendant at her throat and panting as though breathless. She gabbled incoherently, while pointing at me. Her eyes rolled alarmingly.

'Hush, *madame*, please,' Yvette murmured. 'Calm yourself, dear Miss Hallburgh. Shh, shh,' she soothed. Meanwhile she darted spiteful, angry looks at me and said disapprovingly, 'What can have happened to upset *madame* like this. Is it something you have done or said, Miss Grey? It is bad for *madame*'s heart to have this sort of agitation. *Doucement*, dear Miss Hallburgh,' she crooned at her employer, and wafted some sal volatile under Miss Hallburgh's nose.

I did not reply to this and Yvette rang the bell and sent for Dr Trabut. He affected all tender concern for his patient, but I could tell from the cynical look and knowing little smile that this was just a grotesque pretence. While Yvette stroked Caroline Hallburgh's forehead, he opened his doctor's bag and gave her a few drops of laudanum.

'I have given her a tincture, Miss Grey. She is a very delicate lady and her health is so fragile. These sort of upsets could prove fatal to her,' he said, looking at me reproachfully, as though I had been the cause of her outburst. 'And now, Yvette will help her upstairs to bed. Let us hope that this episode will not have any serious effects.'

Miss Hallburgh was now feigning a swoon and I stood seething in silent protest as they helped her out of the room and up the stairs. My instinct was to pack my trunk and leave the Hallburgh family forever. If it were not for the children, I thought, I would go and throw myself on the mercy of my hateful Aunt Esther. But honesty compelled me to admit to myself that I could not bear to leave Edmund Hallburgh, even if his sister made my life an unbearable hell. I could not part from him ever, even if she continued to do her worst.

Summoning up as much calm as I could, I went upstairs to the schoolroom and found my two charges rather subdued. In spite of the excitement of Christmas and the presents they had received, between Yvette's supervision of them and Miss Hallburgh's interrogation of Sarah, they had not had an entirely joyous day. I endeavoured to make up for my absence by nursing both children on my knee and speaking to them gently and cheerfully about the doll and the fort with soldiers, and how pleased I was to be back with them again. Gradually, I was rewarded by a visible lifting of their youthful spirits as they slowly recovered from the tensions of the day. Soon they were playing together quite naturally as usual and, as we were not required to attend a formal dinner that evening, we had a cosy supper with stories and nursery songs before an early bed.

Miss Hallburgh, however, after sleeping off the effects of her laudanum, was recovered sufficiently to be crimped and curled by the faithful Yvette. She was helped into her ball dress of palest gold and was handed her reticule and fan and then Yvette attended her very tenderly, as she descended the staircase ready for the evening festivities.

All the guests were assembled in the hall waiting for the carriages and although I very pointedly stayed in the schoolroom, reading a book, Annie was unable to contain her excitement at the scene. She ran backwards and forwards untiringly to peep through the banisters and report on the appearance and actions of the gentry.

'Oh Miss Grey,' she breathed. 'The old dowager has on all her diamonds this evening. It is so strange how fine good diamonds look against old skin, is it not? And Miss Hallburgh is dressed up like a girl of eighteen. His Lordship is not downstairs yet, but the other gentlemen look very handsome, miss. How elegant they look in evening clothes.'

She went on in this vein, until Lord Hallburgh made his appearance and the coaches were assembled at the front steps.

'What a good figure Lord Hallburgh has in his formal clothes, Miss Grey. And what shapely legs. He needs no padding to improve them, that is sure.'

I heard the footman clang the heavy door closed and although I felt like weeping, I forced myself to be pleasant to Annie, as she busied herself tidying up the toys and straightening my room, while all the time she spoke of how well His Lordship was looking and how she expected that Mrs Harriet Marland would be dancing all night.

'She is a very beautiful lady by all accounts

and young enough to be seeking another husband.'

But finally, Annie finished her task and took her leave of me with many good wishes for a Happy Christmas and I was at last, blessedly left in peace.

11

I never heard the carriages return, because I was long since asleep in my bed, but Miss Hallburgh was up betimes and entered the schoolroom with the help of her two sticks, straight after breakfast the following morning. There were no formal lessons, I being determined to allow the children some relaxation and an opportunity to play with their Christmas toys. There was a pleasant peaceful atmosphere in the room and it came as an unpleasant shock, therefore, when the calm was interrupted by such an unwelcome visitor. I rose and greeted her politely, determined not to give her an opportunity to criticize me, but she brushed aside my greeting and stood leaning on her sticks as the children wished her good morning and went back to their toys.

She was at first very fulsome in her praise of the hospitality which they had received at the ball. She went on then to declare what a beautiful picture Mrs Marland had presented and how few times the lady had sat out a dance. This was difficult enough for me to bear, but what followed was even worse. Very softly and insinuatingly, she started on poor Sarah, who was playing with her new doll, which she had dressed in a set of specially made doll's clothes.

'And how is my little darling girl today?' She crooned with a fond smile.

Sarah started nervously, but answered politely enough. 'Very well, I thank you, Aunt Caro.'

'And who gave you the thought to write about a new mama for Christmas, my dear Sarah? Was it Dr Trabut? Thomas? Miss Grey? What made you think of it, my dear?'

Sarah's face immediately closed and became sullen. She continued to busy herself with the doll's clothes and kept her eyes lowered, refusing to answer. I felt myself seething with anger and resentment again, but I could do nothing. Thomas looked up from his task of arranging the soldiers on the schoolroom table, but it was an indifferent uncurious look. In his innocence, he had no idea of the passions and unresolved tensions which were driving his aunt and was only too pleased that she was leaving him alone. For my own part, I felt like running away and never coming back again, but I determined to stand firm.

'Miss Hallburgh,' I said sternly. 'Please believe me, no one directed Sarah to write those words. You are making much of nothing. Doctor Trabut's visits to the schoolroom are entirely unwelcome to me and I would appreciate it if he left me to my task of teaching the children without any interference. I can well do without the upset and disruption these visits cause.'

At my slightly raised tone, Tom suspended his game with the soldiers and automatically put his fingers to his mouth and began his nervous nail biting. Sarah began to pleat and unpleat the doll's silk dress while still keeping her eyes sulkily downcast.

'Children,' I said gently, 'take your toys and go and play in the bedroom for a few moments. Tell the maid I shall be there presently.'

I could see that Miss Hallburgh was going to continue with her tirade against me for allowing the child to express herself as she did. I let her continue for a few moments while I listened as calmly as I could. She accused me of all sorts of misdemeanours — flirting with Dr Trabut, creating an unpleasant atmosphere in the house, using the children to try and ensnare her brother into marriage, all the old familiar ground which she had covered so many times before. I let her carry on. I knew that with Edmund Hallburgh approving of my work, I need not fear anything that this unhappy woman could do. What did rankle with me was the ungracious way that she never mentioned one positive thing that I had done for her little niece and nephew. She had not the decency to show the slightest gratitude for the way I had worked with them and improved their behaviour, or the time and effort that I had put into their education.

It was not until she returned yet again to the subject of Sarah's little drawing and her insinuations that I had dictated the words to the child for my own devious reasons, that I finally lost my calm and was goaded once more into making a spirited reply.

'You have no right to infer such base motives on my part, Miss Hallburgh. I have only ever considered Edmund as my employer, nothing else.'

Pleased to have a reaction at last, she pounced like a cat at my use of his Christian name. 'Oh. It is 'Edmund' now, is it?'

I bit my lip at my thoughtlessness, but I was angry, nonetheless. 'You are evil and wicked to make such accusations against me,' I panted. 'I have done nothing wrong and your remarks are completely uncalled for.'

'How dare you speak to me in this disrespectful way?' she shouted, her voice shrill with rage.

But I dared anything now. My pent up passion lent me the courage to say, 'I shall leave this house at once. My work is not valued and you find only fault with all my efforts. I will not stay to be treated like this.'

I ran from the room in tears and rushed blindly along the landing to my bedroom. But as I went Dr Trabut appeared silently from the stairs and caught hold of me.

'What can be the matter, Miss Grey? Why are you crying, *ma petite*?'

I tried ineffectually to push him away but the tears were coursing down my cheeks and I could not see properly. The more I struggled against him, the tighter he held me. There seemed to be no one about and I fought even more frantically against the odious doctor and his hateful embrace, but it was useless. Although he was only slightly taller than myself, his strength was superior.

'Doctor Trabut, let me go please,' I exclaimed, angrily.

'But not before you have told me what is wrong,' he whispered. 'It is the hateful Caro, is it not? She is having one of her tempers. Try not to upset yourself, Miss Grey. I will deal with her directly. I can easily give her one of my little tinctures to smooth her down. How pretty you look when you are angry. Your lovely young lips are trembling so.'

Then, in the most insolent and insulting way, he kissed me hard on the mouth and though I struggled even more furiously, would not let me go. No man had ever kissed me like that before and I found it so distasteful, that I could not imagine being able to ever wash off the horrible sensation of his lips on mine. He was in no hurry to let me go and it was very unfortunate that at that moment, Annie should come bustling across the landing with a pile of sewing. She was horrified to see me in such a position, with my hair untidy and my face red with weeping. The arrogant Trabut gave a contemptuous laugh as he released me and gave a broad wink to Annie, as though to imply that I had found his attentions welcome. She passed on discreetly, saying nothing and affected not to notice the very compromising situation that I was in. Immediately she had turned the corner of the staircase, Marcel Trabut attempted to take me in his arms once more.

'You are wonderful. Delectable. Just ripe for wedding and bedding. Come, what do you say, my dear Lucy? Marry me and we will go back to Paris. You can be Madame Trabut any time you give your consent.'

'Never,' I said. 'You disgust me, sir.' I eluded his clutching hands and ran to my bedroom. I was shaking with fear and loathing of these people who, it seemed, were trying their best to destroy me. Much as I loved the two children and wanted to stay with them, I felt I must leave this place, or it would drive me mad. In spite of my deep love and adoration for Edmund Hallburgh I knew I must go. I washed my tear-stained face and wiped the shame of Marcel Trabut's hateful kiss from my mouth. As I was tidying my hair, there was a tap at my door and the odious doctor himself was outside, wishing to deliver a message from Caroline Hallburgh.

'Please come out,' he wheedled. 'Miss Hallburgh wishes to see you.'

I made no reply, but was thankful that I had locked my door.

'Please, Miss Grey,' he began again. 'Miss Hallburgh is unwell and is sorry for quarrelling with you. She wishes to see you. To apologize.'

'Please go away,' was all I said.

'Miss Grey,' he said softly, tapping on the door again. 'I, too, am sorry. I had no business to kiss you like that. But I absolutely adore you, my sweet one. Please forgive me, Lucy dear. We could be married if only you will say yes. I could make you a happy and wealthy woman. Miss Hallburgh has told me that she would give us her blessing. You would be the respected wife of a well-known doctor instead of a mere governess and I would take you away from all this and make you so happy. Please say yes, my sweet Lucy.'

I tried to ignore his whispered blandishments while I was deciding what to do. My instinct told me that there was collusion between Caroline Hallburgh and Dr Trabut to compromise me and I knew that the scene on the landing would be reported back to Lord Hallburgh. At the same time, she realized that she had gone too far in her vicious attack on me. Perhaps she was a little afraid that Lord Hallburgh would hear of that as well and condemn her for being the cause of my abrupt departure. As I continued to make no response to Marcel Trabut's insincere overtures, he gradually fell silent and went away.

Now it was the turn of Caroline Hallburgh herself to lay siege to my bedroom. I heard her little wheeled chair swish along the landing and then she started to whisper placatingly to me through the door. 'Please open the door, Miss Grey, and let us talk calmly.'

'No thank you,' I said. 'I do not wish to say anything to you nor to listen to your apology. I merely wish to leave here as soon as I can. Baxter can drive me to my Aunt's house, if you please, when I have packed my trunk.'

A note of barely controlled desperation entered her voice now and she began to cajole and wheedle, like Marcel Trabut. 'Please Miss Grey. Let us sort out our misunderstanding. I am sure you would not wish to be the cause of any trouble between Lord Hallburgh and myself. And your aunt would be very taken aback if you left here with no character. You would need to seek other employment, would you not? You would need a reference, surely?'

But at that moment, I cared nothing for a reference, or my aunt's reaction to my unwelcome arrival on her doorstep. My only thought was to leave forthwith, and so I made no reply. There was silence for a while and then, ever so softly, she started again.

'Marcel has told me that he wishes to marry you, Miss Grey. I hope you will accept my best wishes. I am delighted at the idea of you finding happiness with the dear doctor. I give you my blessing, my dear.'

This was too much. 'I do not wish for your blessing,' I cried out. 'Please go away. I have no wish to marry anyone, but I would not have Marcel Trabut if he were the last man on earth.'

Then everything went quiet as though she had given up and gone away. Tremblingly, I collected my meagre possessions together and began to pack my trunk. As I picked up the ribbons from the two children, the little card they had sent me fluttered to the floor, and I bent to pick it up. 'To dear Miss Grey,' Sarah had written. 'With best love from Tom and Sal.'

My fragile self-control deserted me at this. All my love and affection for the children came flooding back to me. They needed me so much; how could I abandon them to their aunt's vile moods and humours? They would never grow up whole and sane if they were left to her tender mercies. I broke down and cried bitterly.

Suddenly there was a further soft knocking on my door and this time the voice urging me to open it was that of Edmund Hallburgh.

'Miss Grey, please may I speak with you for a few moments?'

This dear, familiar deep voice caused my heart to thump loudly and made me feel first hot and then cold as my face burned and then went pale.

'Miss Grey, Lucy, are you there? May I speak with you?' he asked again.

Hastily I dried my eyes and desperately considered what to do. In all fairness, I could not refuse to speak to my employer, and yet I knew that I was going to appear at a disadvantage, my hair awry and my face stained with tears.

'Yes. One moment, if you please,' I stammered, and hurried to unlock my door. I stood like some imbecile, in front of him. The room behind me was in turmoil with my clothes and writing things piled on the bed ready to be packed. I knew I must look a fright with my red eyes and white face.

'So it is true what they tell me: you are going to leave us,' he said gravely.

'Yes ... I ... No ... I was going to ... that is ... ' I stammered inanely. It was obvious that he had taken in all the details of my intended departure, the meagre possessions on my bed and the books piled on the bedside chair. He did not rant and plead like Miss Hallburgh.

'Miss Grey, you are not yourself. These upsets in the family are absolutely damnable. When will they ever end?'

He asked this as though to himself, his voice very low and quiet. I remained silent, not trusting myself to speak, just standing there helplessly.

'Please may I see you for a few minutes?' he asked again. 'I would like to speak to you in private.'

Taking in my distraught appearance made him add seriously, 'Shall we say in the library in half an hour, when you have had time to compose yourself a little? Then we may discuss your intended departure further?'

I nodded miserably and he turned and went downstairs. I tidied my hair and washed my face, amid a turmoil of emotions. I thought back to the initial interview that I had had with Lord Hallburgh when I was first appointed. Now, I thought, he is going to terminate my employment. I am to be told to go. I shall be sent home to Aunt Esther Grey in disgrace and will have to face her cold disapproval and reproaches. I could hear the children playing in the schoolroom and bitterly regretted my hasty action in saying that I would leave them. At last I could delay no longer. I went to Lord Hallburgh's library and tapped on the door.

'Please do come in and be seated, Miss Grey,' he said very quietly. Then he leaned forward in his chair and frowned at me. 'I have had some very disquieting news, today. My sister says that you have given notice of your intention to relinquish your position with us.'

'Well,' I whispered, trying to fight back the treacherous tears that threatened to well up again, 'you see I . . .'

'And also,' he continued, as though I hadn't spoken, 'that you are about to become affianced to Dr Trabut.'

At this, I forgot my tears and found my

voice. 'Certainly not,' I said indignantly. 'That is an absolute falsehood.'

But his eyes were now turned thoughtfully to the fire. 'I must confess, Miss Grey, that I had no idea of any such interest on your part. In fact, I felt you had some antipathy towards him.'

'That is so. I dislike him entirely,' I protested.

'And yet Miss Hallburgh tells me you have been seen locked in his arms,' he said, suddenly severe. He looked at me searchingly. 'Strange conduct indeed for a respectable young woman who feels antipathy towards the man in question.'

I sprang to my feet with indignation, 'I assure you that I dislike him utterly,' I cried.

At this he looked at me again, the small pulse beating in his cheek. His eyes were more cold and hostile than I had ever seen them before.

'Then I fail to understand. Were you kissing Dr Trabut, or were you not?'

'No, I was not, at least not willingly, Lord Hallburgh. Doctor Trabut was pressing his attentions on me before I was able to prevent him. That is all. It was unfortunate that someone should have witnessed his actions and reported it to Miss Hallburgh.'

'Ah, I see.' Once more, he looked

searchingly into my face. 'That explains it.'

He almost smiled, although I failed to understand why it was important to him whether I was kissing Dr Trabut or not, or what concern it was of his anyway.

'She was certain that you were returning his ardour and that a romance had bloomed.'

This time he did smile, but I was unable to see the humour of it.

'I do assure you, sir, that it is not the case. I have no understanding with the doctor, nor do I wish to have.'

'Then why have you given notice? My sister is convinced that it is because you intend to marry Dr Trabut.'

'But that is untrue,' I protested, becoming agitated again.

'What takes place between you and the doctor is not my affair, but I own I was somewhat surprised at Marcel's declaration. He has something of a reputation of a lightweight where the ladies are concerned. A philanderer even. But you are such a beautiful young woman, it is no wonder that he has succumbed . . . '

'Please!' I almost shouted. 'No more, sir. Once and for all. I do not have a *tendre* for the vile Dr Trabut.'

Seeing my agitation, he stood up also and we faced one another in front of the fireplace.

He continued inexorably, 'In the absence of your parent or guardian, I feel I must warn you against this man. He is not to be trusted with someone as young and . . . inexperienced in the ways of the world as yourself. I would not wish to lose our dear Miss Grey unless it was to the happy haven of marriage and I would not be sure that the doctor's intentions were honourable.'

'Lord Hallburgh, pray believe me,' I said, trying to match his calm tone. 'I have no wish to marry anyone, least of all Dr Trabut. Cannot you see that the whole of this sorry situation has been engineered to ensure my discomfiture?'

'By whom?' he asked sharply.

But I was not prepared to answer this and implicate his spiteful sister. Looking round, wildly, my eye encountered the tranquil painted gaze of Catherine, immortalized in the gilt-framed portrait.

'Oh, no one. It is of no moment,' I said miserably. 'Perhaps it would be better if I returned home after all.'

'You mean to your aunt and uncle?'

'Yes. Perhaps it would be for the best.'

'I am so sorry. What will we do without you?'

He looked genuinely cast down and passed a hand across his brow as though suddenly weary and I felt a surge of compassion and sympathy for him. I thought of Sarah's little drawing and the love and affection which she had expressed. I thought next of the horror of being in receipt of Aunt Esther's cold charity and I shivered.

Finally, despairing, I cried, 'I will not go. I will stay. I beg your pardon for what I have said. I will stay with the children.'

'I would not want you to stay if you do not wish it, Lucy, but I own, we cannot get along without you. My children . . . They . . . You are their life . . . I cannot tell you how much they need you and your influence . . . They have no mother . . . now that . . . Catherine . . . My poor Catherine . . . '

He broke off as though overcome with emotion and gazed up at his wife's portrait.

'Catherine worshipped them . . . ' He stopped as if he were too distressed to continue.

'Lord Hallburgh,' I said quickly, 'please forgive me. I will not desert the children, but I know that your sister dislikes me and would be more comfortable if I left. This is why there has been a conspiracy to marry me off to Marcel Trabut. It is not my wish to leave, believe me.'

'Then stay,' he said, and smiled again, this time into my eyes.

He held out his hands to me and, greatly daring, I placed my own in his.

I was trembling with the turbulence of my emotions. I felt as though I would swoon and without realizing it, I clung tightly to those cool, strong hands.

Later, when I was able to think more coherently about what followed next, I was hardly able to believe it.

As I looked into his expressive grey eyes, I felt as though I were being pulled inexorably towards him, our eyes on a single thread.

'I am so pleased you do not wish Marcel Trabut to be your husband,' he said softly, almost in a whisper.

'No, I could never love such as he,' I said, equally softly, utterly enchanted by the silver eyes gazing so seductively into mine.

His face inexplicably drew even closer to my own.

'But you are capable of love, Lucy. You have so much love to give. You were made for love.'

Then I was in his arms and his lips found my own in a long lingering kiss. Not an insulting invasion of my person, as Marcel Trabut had done, but a tender, exciting, wonderful kiss, such as I had never experienced before.

I melted into this kiss and gave myself up

to the sweetness of his caress as though we were the only two people in the world. And for me, at that particular moment, no one else existed. I returned his kiss with all the love I had, trying, as my lips moved under his, to convey to Edmund Hallburgh, that I loved him with all my heart and soul and strength. Just for those few seconds, I felt that we truly belonged to each other and that I would willingly do anything for him.

All this happened in an instant and then just as suddenly crashed apart. Even as I ecstatically prepared to renew the pressure of my lips against his own, he suddenly sprang back and almost pushed me from him, saying, 'I do beg your pardon. I should not have done that. I am so sorry, Miss Grey. Please forgive me. That was absolutely unpardonable.'

He looked so unlike the normally dignified and self-possessed Edmund Hallburgh, that I almost had to laugh with the hysteria I felt. Instead, I struggled to contain my feelings, as he once more clasped my hands and said, 'Only tell my sister, please that you will not leave us. As for Trabut. I will make sure that he does not bother you further.'

'I think I can learn to put up with him and I do not want trouble.'

I realized that he regretted that kiss and

although I did not at the time know what was in his mind, I decided to try and make light of it. He had probably just meant to be kind, I thought, and persuade me to stay with the children.

'Please do not apologize,' I said. 'It is I who am sorry for giving way like that.'

He gave me a strange, deep look, as though he were trying to make sense of what I was saying.

'I shall now become the schoolroom dragon again.' I went on. I tried to smile as I made this stupid little joke, but his face remained serious.

'Please will you inform Miss Hallburgh on my behalf, that I will stay. I would never leave while you and the children need me, but I confess I am not able to withstand an interview with your sister at this moment.'

He nodded politely and once more, I noticed the faint beat of a pulse in his cheek, as he turned away from me and I made my way back to my room.

12

I was still unsettled in the evening, my emotions in turmoil, and the children reflected this sense of unease in the Hallburgh household. They spoke only quietly and seemed to be trying not to be noticed by their beloved Miss Grey. Every time I looked at Sarah, she withdrew like a snail into its shell. There were none of the usual protests when it was their bedtime and both gave me a quick hug when they had said their prayers.

I sighed with relief as I settled in front of my bedroom fire and drank a warm posset of milk and a little brandy brought to me by the ever kind and considerate Annie. Neither of us mentioned the episode she had witnessed with Dr Trabut, but I know she had noticed my red eyes and all the servants seemed to know of my interview with Edmund.

Tactful as always, Annie had merely said, 'Everyone is glad you are not going to leave, Miss Grey. Them children cannot do without you now, miss. Cook has sent you this and hopes it will help you to sleep.'

She put down the little tray on a footstool and departed.

But it did not help me to sleep. I sat for some three hours in front of the fire, thinking of all that had happened before I eventually felt relaxed enough to seek my bed. I had finally acknowledged to myself that there could never be anything between Edmund and myself except the respect and kindness offered by a good employer to a loyal servant. I told myself that I must never, by word or deed, reveal my feelings for him. It would be too humiliating to allow anyone to guess how much that casual kiss had meant to the sensible governess, Miss Grey.

That night, I lay with a bright December moon shining on me through the open curtains of my window. I went over again and again the events of the day and what had been done and said by everyone: myself, Dr Trabut, Caroline Hallburgh and finally Edmund. Every phrase of our conversation; every expression on his face; the cool touch of his strong hands and, most of all, the sweetness of his lips on mine, I recalled not once but hundreds of times. I lay thinking for most of the night, gazing dry-eyed at the ceiling, unable to cry any more and absolutely desolate in my lonely misery.

The morning as always brought the

comforting routine of the schoolroom and the children. I did not see Edmund, but received a pretty note, thanking me for the paper-weight and adding that it would be given pride of place on his desk. No mention was made of his sister or any of the upsetting events of the previous day.

In any case, we were now all preparing for Twelfth Night, and a return to Melbury House in London. The visitors had departed the day after Boxing Day but I was able to see William once more before he went back to Oxford. The cook, who had seemed to take me under her fiercely protective wing since my fall out with Miss Hallburgh, had sent a discreet message via Annie that I would be most welcome to use her private parlour if I wished to entertain my brother to luncheon. I accepted with alacrity. I sent round a note to my aunt and uncle, wishing them the compliments of the season and earnestly requesting that William should be allowed to have luncheon with me.

The cook sent in to us a meal fit for a king. A rich soup of collar of salmon, followed by stewed pheasant and a rabbit roasted with fragrant herbs, appeared as if by magic and, when I felt I must burst at all this food, a noble piece of cheese and some fine red apples were placed on the table.

I was both amused and disquieted at the eager, almost avid way that William tackled his luncheon and washed it down with good claret wine. I wondered anxiously how adequate his food was at Oxford and I asked him if he was getting enough to eat.

'Oh yes, Lu,' he replied. 'And I sup with Mr Tranter and his family twice a week, you know. Mrs Tranter is a splendid cook,' he confided. 'And Maria, Miss Tranter that is, often makes a very decent syllabub to round off the meal. She is such a capital girl, Lu. I know you two would get on famously if you were to meet her.'

He stopped suddenly, as though he had said too much. I said nothing, but poured him some more wine from the jug. Perhaps he was getting more involved with his tutor's family than was wise for a young student, I thought, but who was I to dare advise someone on affairs of the heart? My own situation was far from satisfactory and would certainly not bear discussion between a brother and sister. I held my tongue and was grateful that Cook's largesse did not end with this splendid feast. Not content with filling him to bursting point, she packed up a supper for him to eat on the coach. Cold beef and a meat tart with some of the cake from Christmas and a further bottle of wine were beamingly handed to him when he went to the kitchen to thank her.

'He is a young man as needs his victuals,' she said, by way of explanation, and I was inclined to agree.

Soon Aunt Esther's carriage arrived to take him to the stage-coach and we made our fond farewells, promising to write to each other and meet again at the Easter vacation.

We soon settled down to our London life again, and during the cold, dark days of January I saw little of Edmund, who seemed to be away frequently on estate business. Miss Hallburgh was never tired of telling me that he was at some house party in Leicestershire, with the beautiful Mrs Marland, of course, or attending a New Year Ball in Scotland at which the exquisite widow would be present. I spent much time burning with jealousy, imagining the joy she must be having in his company, and thinking with fond regret of his bright silver eyes and attractive smile.

In the schoolroom, things were going tolerably well. Thomas was keen to count and learn his numbers and Sarah was far more amenable and easy to handle than she had been before. I still had anxieties about her, particularly when she gave way to outbursts of temper and disobedience. So like her Aunt Caroline, I mused. She occasionally lapsed into telling tales or even untruths about her little brother, but in the main, I was satisfied with her progress. It was that rather dull and quiet time of the year when all the festivities were over and spring was still far off. Without any contact with my beloved Edmund, my life seemed vapid and boring.

Caroline Hallburgh had not changed one whit and still gained her lonely pleasure from encouraging Sarah's bad behaviour, or wreaking spiteful acts of vengeance against the vulnerable Thomas. I was still unbelieving of the time and effort that she put into her petty tyrannies against us, but I had come to realize that Edmund had only brief insights into his sister's venom. He was so preoccupied with other matters, these instances of her malicious doings soon slipped his mind. Late January was bitterly cold, even in London, and the children had to remain indoors for much of the time. Caroline Hallburgh was also confined to the house, but she occupied herself with nagging the servants and bullying the faithful Yvette.

This lady, to her credit, bore it with equanimity and with no lessening of the dog-like devotion that she gave to her mistress. Since we came back from Wembeck, I had seen little of Dr Trabut. Perhaps he had decided that I was far too prim for amorous dalliance. Perhaps Edmund had reprimanded him. Who can tell? Whatever the reason, I was profoundly grateful for being left in peace. As it was, the doctor visited several times a week, and if we came face to face, made sheep's eyes and gave me the usual soulful glances. I was easily able to deal with such schoolboy tactics.

Caroline Hallburgh pointedly tried to include me in theatre visits, if he was to be a member of the party, and even suggested once that I should accompany him to an assembly ball, but, needless to say, I declined. There was always a tension between Miss Hallburgh and myself and she showed an unspoken contempt for me which she had displayed ever since my ad hoc supper with Edmund. I had ceased to care for her opinion, however, and determined that I would live as positively as my circumstances allowed.

William and I continued to correspond regularly, and I was much struck at the apparent intensity of his developing relationship with the Tranters and in particular, Miss Maria, of course. This young lady was apparently but seventeen years of age and the only child of elderly parents. She was naturally very carefully brought up, but I guessed that if she had really given her heart to William, her doting parents would not deny her anything that she wanted, and I confessed to some anxiety at this situation. Still, I mused, what will be, will be. Any worries I had on that score would have nothing to do with the case and William, like most young men of his age, would do as he wished.

At this time, I heard again from Fanny with a promise of a meeting in the summer months when Squire and Mrs Pembleton would be having a garden party as part of Fanny's coming out year. This was something to look forward to, and in truth, in spite of the long, cold winter of Edmund's absence, the year soon rolled round to Easter and my twenty-first birthday.

Easter was early this year, and my birthday fell on Easter Saturday. To my great surprise, Annie delivered a large oblong parcel to me, done up with sealing wax with the distinctive monogrammed seal of Lord Hallburgh. It had been sent by a special courier on the mail coach and was a book of prints depicting various foreign cities. There were pictures of the Roman antiquities and the Venice Lagoon in Italy, as well as other famous landmarks in Spain, France, Greece and Turkey. There were also delightful studies of the flowers of each region, delicately coloured and tinted by hand. It was beautifully bound in Moroccan leather and was inscribed by himself in a large flowing hand: *To Dear Miss Grey, celebrating the survival of Europe, from thirty-first March, 1795, to thirty-first March, 1816, with best wishes from Edmund Hallburgh.*

Annie was obviously agog at his largesse and the extravagance of its delivery. She watched me closely as I unwrapped it with trembling hands, blushing with pleasure and gratification at his generosity. She seemed about to make some observation herself, but having opened her mouth to speak, closed it again. As for me, I was in a veritable seventh heaven as I hugged the volume to me. I actually kept the wrapping paper. It, too, was precious, having come from him, and was not to be merely discarded. Even Caroline Hallburgh was pleasant to me and had graciously indicated that I might invite William to dinner, so that she might be introduced to him.

On this occasion, she went out of her way to be graciously charming and seemed to completely win him over. Nothing was too much trouble for her. The food and wine were of the first quality and I could see that William was suitably impressed. As for myself, I thought sadly that I had become so worldly-wise under her malign influence, that

I thought cynically only of her ulterior motives. Later, as we sat alone in the drawing-room while she went to discuss something with Yvette, William stretched out his legs to the fire and said admiringly, 'What a gallant woman she is, Lu. And how admirably she seems able to manage the difficulties of her affliction.'

I considered this for a moment in silence. 'Yes, she can be very charming,' I said grudgingly at last.

'That is damning with faint praise, indeed,' he grinned at me. 'What can have occasioned your dislike of the mistress of the house, I wonder?'

'Did you not guess from my letters that I had no joy in her company, Wills?'

'Well, I did not realize that you disliked her so extremely.'

'I have to be careful,' I said. 'Letters can be read by the wrong person.'

William looked startled at this. His own straight and honest dealings with the world were based on the most moral of Christian precepts. He was ill-prepared to understand someone of Miss Hallburgh's twisted outlook.

'But you *are* happy, sis?' he asked with a worried frown.

'Oh yes,' I assured him. 'And I love the

children of course.'

'I find you altered, though,' he said, still looking at me with concern.

'Oh? In what way?'

'Well, you seem to be thinner. But very beautiful,' he added hastily.

I laughed and said that this was strange in view of the meals we had at Melbury House.

'No . . . I mean you are different Lu. There is a radiance about you . . . have you fallen in love?'

I blushed red and he laughed and said, 'So, the cap fits does it, Lu?'

With a mental prayer towards my dear papa in Heaven, I decided to perjure my immortal soul and tell a lie. 'Certainly not. But what about you?'

He lightheartedly confessed to what I had guessed already, that he was deeply in love with the daughter of his tutor, Mr Josiah Tranter.

'I have been in her company so much lately, and Maria — Miss Tranter — is such a taking little thing, Lu. She is so full of fun and humour and . . . ' Seeing my amused expression, he floundered somewhat and ended rather lamely, 'Well, it is early days yet, Lucy, and I must secure a living before I can take a wife, but I confess, Miss Maria Tranter is the one for me.'

Miss Hallburgh came back into the room at this point and we sat drinking tea while she chatted very archly to my brother about my influence on the children and how much I was admired in certain quarters, meaning Dr Trabut of course. William seemed to find her utterly amusing and charming and very intrigued by the constant mention of Marcel Trabut. As for myself, I was relieved that she seemed so calm and pleasant and not in the mood for her usual pin pricks. The evening had been enjoyable in spite of her flirtatious conversations with my brother. I was to realize later that her charming chatter to William was her way of laying the foundations of her future plans for myself.

And so, I was one year older. I had now become of age and although I felt no differently, I wished that my parents were still here to celebrate with me. Signs of spring were at last appearing in Melbury Square. The children and I were able to take up our walks again, but Edmund Hallburgh, whom I loved so passionately and whose close embrace had so thrilled me, seemed entirely lost to me. He was at Melbury House very infrequently and even then I saw him only at meal times when I was required to present the children, neatly dressed and on their best behaviour. On the now rare occasions when he invited us out for a drive in the park, Miss Hallburgh saw to it that either I was not required or that the nursery maid should accompany us.

Then, on a beautiful day in May, I was in the library, arranging some flowers from the hot houses at Wembeck, when the door opened suddenly and he was before me.

He was as charming and civil as always, but I thought he looked rather strained and tired. He glanced down at me with those unusual silvery eyes of his and gave his well remembered smile as he greeted me with, 'Miss Grey, what a pretty picture you make to be sure. If the Wembeck bailiff tries to persuade me that I must foreclose on the hot houses, the sight of your graceful flower arrangements and the obvious pleasure that they give you will be enough to make me resist with all my strength.'

I merely smiled at this and did my utmost to remain calm as we talked about the progress of Sarah and Thomas.

Then he said suddenly, 'And Trabut? Is he acting in a more gentlemanlike fashion?'

'Yes . . . yes . . . I think so.'

I directed my gaze onto the flowers, clipping and snipping the foliage and trying to effect a reasonable arrangement with hands which I noticed were trembling slightly.

'I think you have become somewhat thinner, Miss Grey,' he said suddenly. 'I hope all is well?'

I looked at him directly then and met his rather mocking grey eyes unflinchingly. 'I thought the same of you, sir,' I replied softly.

'Oh,' he laughed deprecatingly. 'Hunting with the Quorn, you know, and busying myself with country matters . . . '

He gave me his brilliant sweet smile. Then he mentioned, almost casually, that Mrs Harriet Marland with her little son Benjamin would be visiting next weekend and that the house party would include her brother and several other guests who were well up in London circles.

I added another stem of green foliage to the classic urn which was to grace the dining-table. I did not trust myself to speak, but finally managed, 'How delightful, My Lord.'

Long after he had taken leave of me, I continued to stand, gazing unseeingly at the lovely flowers, before summoning the footman to carry them into the dining-room.

Of course, Miss Hallburgh had a field day with the preparations that ensued for the weekend party. Annie was to make ready the various guest rooms and was to pay particular attention to Mrs Marland's bed-chamber. Exquisitely embroidered sheets, freshly ironed and perfumed with lavender were to be taken out of the housekeeper's linen store, and the furniture washed and polished with beeswax and turpentine. Annie was required to arrange the most expensive French toiletries and perfumes on the dainty dressing-table and, of course, I was to fill a magnificent Chinese bowl with yet more exotic blooms to grace the exquisite jardinière in her bedroom.

'Yes, Miss Grey is indeed a treasure,' Caroline Hallburgh said rather sarcastically at dinner. Edmund had just commented in a very complimentary way on my earlier efforts at flower arranging. 'I have instructed her to supervise the flowers in dear Harriet's room. Little Benjamin will, of course, share with Tom. See to it if you please, Miss Grey,' she commanded tartly.

I know that she felt I had no right to have any feelings at all, and her triumphant looks and unspoken satisfaction at the idea of Edmund's intended and his future step-son visiting us for the weekend, was more than I could bear. I was pierced to the quick by her autocratic arrangements.

'And you will be responsible for the care of

Benjamin,' she ordered. 'My brother has organized a visit to Almack's for the Saturday evening. Cook will provide nursery meals for you and the children this weekend,' she added very spitefully. 'Lord Hallburgh will be taken up with entertaining his guests and will not wish to be bothered with young fry.'

So I was to be banished from the dining-room and the salon while he entertained his beloved, but I was quite happy to be alone in the schoolroom with the children and felt sure that Benjamin would be a very sweet little boy. Perhaps as lovable as my dear little Thomas, I thought. I was obviously not to be allowed to attend formal meals with the guests, and I supposed that Edmund would not send for the children as he often did when he was at home.

On the Friday afternoon, we all assembled at the front of Melbury House in the bright sunlight and soon the coaches arrived with the weekend visitors. First, Mrs Marland and her brother, Mr Patrick Rudkin, holding between them a small boy who had none of Tom's cherubic looks, but who was almost wizened in his small-faced, weasel appearance. He was beautifully dressed, of course, and skipped forward confidently on his thin legs, his pinched, yellowish face looking strained with the excitement of his new surroundings. I stepped forward to greet him and clasped his narrow little hands in mine.

'Benjamin, welcome,' I said as warmly as I could.

I turned to motion Sarah and Thomas forward to meet our young guest. They both hung back, somewhat reluctant to join the company and I was aware of Miss Hallburgh's beady eyes watching the scene avidly as though she guessed at the pain in my heart. She was standing in the gracious imposing doorway, supported by her two sticks. Her dress was long and elegant, made of butter-coloured double muslin and hiding completely the small ugly boots which she habitually wore.

Edmund greeted his guests courteously as always; the footmen carried up the trunks and valises to the various bedrooms, and the visitors were ushered into the drawing-room by Miss Hallburgh herself. She motioned to me to remove the children forthwith. I took them up to the schoolroom where I had set out various favourite toys and books to entertain all three of them.

Tom started to misbehave almost immediately. He thrust his pugnacious little face into that of Benjamin, and said provocatively, 'Miss Grey is my teacher, not yours. She loves me, not you.'

I realized with some sympathy the hopeless misery of acute jealousy, and smiled. I kissed him and murmured that we were all going to be friends and that the three of them could share the toys and books together. But I understood exactly how he felt, because these were my own sentiments entirely.

We were required to attend in the drawing-room before dinner that evening, and looking at Mrs Harriet Marland, my heart was like lead. I could understand that Edmund must be enamoured of her. She was not only incredibly fair and beautiful, with flawless skin and full carmine lips, but was exquisitely dressed and elegant in a silk gown of palest peach that must, surely, have come from Paris. Her fashionable long white gloves accentuated her graceful slender arms and her dainty feet peeped from under her dress like little satin mice. Very fair, golden hair usually darkens as a girl grows up, but this lady had silky locks the colour of ripe corn and the bluest eyes I had ever seen. Her hair was dressed so modishly and her jewellery was so impeccable, that she looked almost too perfect to be real. Edmund himself looked utterly happy, almost like a bridegroom, I thought, jealously. He chatted animatedly with all his guests, for the Sheldons had also arrived and, of course, Mr Patrick Rudkin was in attendance.

The three children and I stood rather self-consciously, observing the company but not really being part of it. Edmund came forward to greet us with his usual kindliness.

'Miss Grey, I would like to present you to Mrs Marland. You remember her brother, Mr Patrick Rudkin?'

The brother and sister stood together, both handsome and beautifully turned out, but although Patrick Rudkin was attractive and personable enough, it was Harriet Marland who shone in her beauty like a star in the firmament.

Polite greetings were murmured. Mr Patrick Rudkin bowed politely to me. Little Benjamin hurried forward and grasped one of his mama's hands in a possessive fashion. I heard a seductive low voice as Mrs Marland murmured my name and extended her slim elegant fingers in greeting. I saw her pale, beautiful face with its curving red mouth and, as I gazed into those cornflower eyes of hers, I wished that I were a thousand miles from here and that I did not have to witness her triumph over the man I loved.

'You remember Miss Grey, Patrick? She is our mainstay and support in the education of the children,' Edmund said with a smile. 'We positively could not do without her. Is that not right, Caro?'

Caroline Hallburgh gave a rather falsely agreeable reply. 'Yes, certainly, Edmund,' she said with an icy smile.

He turned to Mrs Marland again. 'You have met Mr and Mrs Sheldon,' he said.

'And I am delighted to renew their acquaintance,' she replied, once more extending her hand graciously.

They moved away, leaving me to Caroline Hallburgh. Speaking in low contemptuous tones, she indicated that I should now remove the children from the drawing-room.

'Oh but Papa, may we not stay a little?' Sarah begged. She loved company and the Sheldons had made such a fuss of her at Christmas.

I could see that Edmund was torn between wanting the presence of his children but also his duty to the guests.

It was Caroline Hallburgh who answered quickly, 'No, Sarah. You must help Miss Grey entertain our little visitor.'

And she stared frostily at me, so I hastily collected the three children together and ushered them up to the schoolroom.

For the rest of the evening, I tortured myself by imagining Edmund and Harriet dining together with his guests. She was so exceptionally beautiful, a veritable orchid in a field of daisies, I thought. He must surely be deeply in love with her. I pictured the scene in the drawing-room after dinner, as they sat in a discreet tête-à-tête, listening to her brother singing for them, or retiring to a sofa by the window so that they might be alone, while Miss Hallburgh organized the rest of the company to play cards. Perhaps he would find an opportunity to kiss her, as he once kissed me, I thought dolefully. I was sure that an announcement of their betrothal must be imminent. I must try not to be so foolish, I told myself sternly, and took down a story book with which to entertain the children.

The next day, I had trouble all the morning with Benjamin. For such a privileged little boy, he was remarkably mean and aggressive. He did his best to upset both Sarah and Thomas in turn and, when all else failed, he deliberately began to try and destroy the little carved animals in Tom's Noah's Ark, stamping on them and finally throwing one into the fire. I must have been absolutely shocked because, for a moment, I did not react. Then I held out my hand calmly for the other one that he was intending to throw also and said, 'Give that to me if you please, Benjamin.'

'No! Shan't,' he shouted and as I tried to

gently take it from him, he sank his teeth into my hand and bit me hard. As I started back, surprised and pained by this, Sarah darted forward suddenly and fetched young Master Marland a sharp box round his ears which caused him to set up a most piercing scream. He fell to the floor dramatically and writhed and yelled, quite unnecessarily, I thought. He was watched with interest by Tom who quietly rescued his remaining toys and put them away safely.

I do not think that Benjamin Marland in the whole of his precious young life, had ever had his ears boxed. He not only screamed and sobbed most theatrically, but actually managed to lose his breath with temper and went quite blue in the face.

Hearing the screams, Annie bustled in and, picking the boy up in her arms, took him to the washstand and threw cold water in his face to bring him to his senses. He drew a shuddering breath at this and struggled out of her grasp, raced to the door and pelted down stairs shouting for his mama.

'You naughty girl,' I exclaimed angrily to Sarah. 'Why did you do that?'

I felt suddenly overwrought with the whole situation.

'He bit you, Miss Grey,' she said indignantly, and indeed I suddenly became aware that the little monster had drawn blood. 'But that was no excuse for you to hit a visitor, like that, Sarah.'

Annie scurried about, getting drinks of milk for the children, who both remained sullen and unwilling to be friends with the visitor. Benjamin's screams had, meanwhile, brought his mother and Miss Hallburgh from the dining-room. By the time I arrived on the scene, I was able to witness the very elegant Mrs Marland, scooping up her sobbing little child and glaring at me reproachfully.

'What on earth can have occasioned this upset with dear Benjamin?' she asked me very coldly. 'He is absolutely beside himself and says that you have been very unkind to him. His poor face is red as though you have struck him.'

I floundered as to what to say. It would not be acceptable to his mama if I told the truth about Benjamin's nasty little tricks. Equally, to tell the tale of Sarah boxing the spoilt boy's little ears, would not be politic at this moment, I thought.

'Well, ma'am,' I began. I became aware that the other two children had joined us and that Sarah was looking extremely uneasy at the thought of her actions being made known to her papa. I tried desperately to think of some explanation that would smooth the situation.

Miss Hallburgh now joined the Greek chorus in the hall.

'My dear Mrs Marland, what a dreadful thing to happen to your sweet little boy. How has it come about that he is so upset and while in the care of our own staff? I am unable to understand it.'

Mrs Marland's brother and Edmund had also come out of the dining-room and were gazing with some incomprehension on the scene in front of them. I saw Sarah's eyes grow round with nervousness at the thought of anyone finding out that she had hit the nasty little Benjamin and I resolved that I must, at least, protect her while the visitors were present. Miss Hallburgh was in her element now.

'To have struck a defenceless little child, merely because he wanted to share Tom's toys. This is unpardonable, Miss Grey. What a terrible example to set before the children.'

Once more I opened my mouth to try and say something, but Mrs Marland was before me. With the dignity and beauty of a tragic heroine, she turned her tearful magnificent eyes towards Edmund and exclaimed, 'Perhaps I should remove my dear Benjamin from the malign influences of the schoolroom and keep him with me at all times. He is a delicate child. We have been advised by our physician that Benjamin must not be allowed to upset himself. It causes him to lose his breath you see, and he becomes quite an invalid for days.'

Edmund looked quite bemused by it all and Miss Hallburgh, fearing that Mrs Marland would depart from Melbury House forthwith, ushered the weeping mother and child into the dining-room, leaving the rest of the Hallburgh family with me. It was obvious that the two women considered that I was the villain of the piece and that I had struck the odious little Benjamin. I looked helplessly at Edmund's stern face. He looked extremely disapproving and severe. He was gazing at me with cold distaste at the idea that I could so attack the small child of one of his guests. Sarah had gone very white and I knew that whatever happened, I could not destroy her trust in me by betraying her to her beloved father. In all our moral stories and talks, I had tried so hard to urge her to be honest, to be fair, to tell the truth and shame the Devil, but this was a monumental task for a little girl of her age. To expect her to confess that she was the one who had hit the horrid child who was tormenting her brother was unrealistic, so I remained silent. Edmund was very cold with me and totally disdainful.

'He is a very difficult child, and one who

has ungovernable passions. I expect you lost patience with him and struck him in your temper.'

I said haltingly, 'It was not quite like that. You see he was being very destructive and throwing Tom's toys into the fire. He had to be stopped . . . somehow.'

I paused and he turned his frowning gaze towards me.

'And he bit Miss Grey,' little Tom volunteered, trying to help.

'A most unhappy occurrence, indeed,' Edmund said, with a grim face and tight lips and he turned on his heel and walked back into the dining-room.

The rest of the evening was thoroughly wretched. The children were subdued and so was I. To think that the man I loved believed me to be capable of striking a little child in my care was abominable to me, and yet I could not in all conscience tell the tale on Sarah. Tom had gathered up his toy soldiers and put them safely in the fort. At bedtime, he begged me not to let Benjamin play with the Noah's Ark again. Sarah, meanwhile, remained silent and pale. The struggle taking place inside her was almost palpable. It was obvious that the conflicting emotions of admitting to hitting Benjamin and of saying nothing and letting her father believe that I had done so, were having an unsettling effect on her. We both shed a silent tear at bedtime as I tucked her in.

While I sat alone, having my solitary supper, Yvette came to get Benjamin's things. It was obvious that I was now beyond the pale and not considered fit to have the care of the precious little Benjamin. I wondered if I would be dismissed from my post when the house party was over. I could hardly bear the memory of Edmund's cold expression and disapproving looks. I knew that the evening at Almack's with the beautiful Mrs Marland, would be a glittering occasion. I was consumed with jealousy at the thought and went to bed miserably lonely and sad.

Towards dawn, I fell into a restless slumber, but awoke unnaturally early and lay for a while, still thinking of the events of the day before and the impossibility of my position. Finally, I stumbled from my bed and washed in last night's cold water. I dressed hurriedly and drew a shawl around me. It was barely daylight, but I reached for my book, *Mediterranean Cities*, my birthday present from Edmund, and as I turned the pages, amazingly, I began to feel calmer.

At breakfast-time, I was surprised that Edmund and Sarah were alone in the dining-room. Both looked a little constrained and it was obvious that Sarah had been shedding some tears, but she was smiling a little tremulously. Her papa was as tall and handsome as ever, but the cold disapproval had entirely gone from his look.

'Miss Grey,' he said softly, as soon as breakfast was over and the footman had left the room. 'Sarah and I wish to crave your pardon.'

'What can you mean?' I asked, totally bemused.

'I mean that Sarah has confessed to me this morning that unfortunately she boxed the ears of young Benjamin and was unable to admit to it when his mama thought to blame you, Miss Grey.'

'Oh, Sarah,' I said. 'Oh, my little darling girl. What a brave thing to do. I am so proud of you, my dear.'

I got up and went round the table to where Sarah was sitting and gave her a kiss.

'I told Papa that you said we must always tell the truth and shame the Devil, Miss Grey, and he agreed and said that it was the most bang-up thing to do.'

'Well done, little Sarah,' I whispered to her.

'You see how powerful the schoolroom dragon is?' Edmund smiled. 'You have instilled a very strong and honest precept into my little Sarah, for which I am truly grateful.

She was unable to bear the blame that she had on her conscience. This lesson is worth a thousand sermons, Miss Grey. I will never forget it.'

I kissed Sarah once more and whispered to her to go back to her room. I would see her presently.

Edmund held out his hand to me and, as his strong, warm fingers closed round mine, I felt full of pride for my pupil and immense joy that Edmund Hallburgh and I were friends once more.

He smiled down at me. 'Thank you, again, dear Miss Grey. What an influence you have on my dear little girl. She will grow up to be a strong and principled woman on the basis of your training.'

'I am so pleased that she was able to tell you everything herself,' I said, shyly.

'Yes, and I will make sure that Benjamin's mama knows the truth,' he said grimly. 'What a little beast he was,' and he lifted up my injured hand and pressed his lips to it very gently. Blushingly, I tried to disengage my hand from his, but he grasped it all the more firmly and looked deep into my eyes. 'Dear Lucy, I thank you once again my dear,' he said, and then was gone.

I was buoyed up all day with the happy memories of that early morning encounter. I was swollen with pride at Sarah's honest behaviour and then had the gratifying experience of Miss Hallburgh's grudging admiration at the way I had conducted myself. Mrs Marland was more handsome in her apologies and begged that I should give little Benjamin another chance. This I did willingly, and was rewarded by a much more serene atmosphere in the schoolroom as well as the obvious approval of Edmund. I still experienced some envy and resentment against Mrs Harriet Marland, however, who was thus freed to enjoy his company at the various social occasions that weekend, while I was tied to the schoolroom and minding the children. But everything must come to an end eventually, and the weekend guests finally took their leave with Edmund now visiting once more in Leicestershire. I was myself in drab and low spirits in spite of the lovely weather. Miss Hallburgh never tired of telling me how beautiful Mrs Marland looked in a riding habit and how superbly she sat her horse.

'Although, she does not hunt, my dear, she is a wonderful rider and naturally Lord Hallburgh will be invited to her estate in Norfolk later in the year. She is a marvellous hostess. My brother is so happy in dear Harriet's company. My fondest wish would be . . . but you know what I would wish, do you not, Miss Grey?'

'Yes, ma'am,' I said as agreeably as I could, for in truth the thought of the engagement of Edmund Hallburgh and Harriet Marland depressed me utterly.

13

I thought a lot about Edmund when I was alone in my room and I had great joy in his birthday gift. In my spare moments, when the children were in bed, I would take it out of its wrapping paper and sit and look at it with absolute delight, thinking of him and wishing that he could gain some joy and happiness in his own life. I even forced myself to think of him achieving marital contentment with Harriet Marland. This idea was as a death and made me weep but, oh my dear Edmund, I thought sadly. If only she could make you happy, I would be delighted to think that you were hers, even if it meant that I would never see you and the children again.

But these were fruitless thoughts. Somewhere deep inside myself, I knew that there were problems in the deep, dark past that remained unexplained and that were perhaps, inexplicable. Every time I looked on the portrait of Catherine with her calm beauty and proud expression, I wondered at the enigma of what had happened to her. What could have destroyed this beautiful woman who was assured of the love of a man such as

Edmund Hallburgh? How could she have been his beloved wife and yet not have been a happy and satisfied woman? These questions I pondered over frequently. They seemed unanswerable and yet eventually, I was to discover some strands of the tale of Lady Hallburgh, which were darker and more secret than I expected.

While Edmund was away, Dr Trabut was a frequent visitor to the house and waiting on Miss Hallburgh as though she were once more the classic invalid. I did my best to avoid him, but on the very evening that Edmund was expected home, I left the children to be prepared for bed by the nursery maid and went down to the library.

I had decided to withdraw from the shelves, a volume of the *Fables of Aesop*. I was going to use this to encourage the children to think about the hare and the tortoise and to see their own progress in the context of this famous story. I would take it up to the schoolroom and next day would build all our reading and writing activities around the well-known tale.

As I lingered among the volumes of poetry and literature, which were freely available to me if I cared to browse among them, I glanced up to see Marcel Trabut suddenly appear before me. I stepped down from the library steps. I was surprised, but even more of a shock was to follow.

'Ah, Miss Grey,' he murmured. 'I am so sorry I missed your birthday, but I would like to give you this little gift.' He handed me a bright red bag which had the name of a Bond Street shop emblazoned on it in gilt lettering.

I could see that it contained a little musical box, almost identical to the one that had been broken by the two children.

'I have searched for weeks for this pretty thing,' he murmured. 'I so much want you to have it, Miss Grey. It will amuse you as it once amused her.' And he turned his dark, soulful eyes to the portrait of Catherine Hallburgh.

I stood in somewhat of a quandary, not wanting to accept his gift but not being able to reasonably refuse it without appearing churlish. He saw me look up involuntarily at her picture and continued in his softly insinuating voice, 'Ah yes, Miss Grey. We had many hours of amusement with this little toy. Small wonder that the great *milord* was so jealous. My Lady would entertain me sometimes for a whole afternoon. She was so charming, *mademoiselle*. You also have that sort of attractiveness that draws men.'

He moved nearer to me and I instinctively moved away. He moved closer still and grasped my wrist. 'You can fire a man's desire with one single glance, my dear, as could she.' He gestured again towards the portrait. 'Come, Miss Grey, I beg for one kiss in return for my little gift.'

He tried to pull me towards him but I resisted, protesting, 'Doctor Trabut, this is intolerable. Kindly let me go. I have no wish for your gift and I do not want your kisses. They are unwelcome, sir. Pray let me be.'

'But cannot you see that this aloofness is what makes you so damnably attractive? Come, my dear Miss Grey. One leetle kiss is all I ask.'

I pushed him firmly away at this point. Perhaps more firmly than I intended, for he staggered a little and clung to the wall. 'She was so much like you, my dear Lucy. She had that quality which drives men to distraction. Cannot you see, my dear, that I am besotted with you, as I was with her?'

I was appalled by this revelation and must have shown it in the shocked expression on my face, but then common sense prevailed and I answered somewhat tartly, 'But I am not besotted with you, Dr Trabut. Kindly let me pass.'

He continued as if I had not spoken, with a dreamy, almost voluptuous, expression on his sallow face. 'Yes, she returned my kisses, with the utmost warmth, *mademoiselle*. And much, much more besides. We had, how can I say it? An understanding. And I could be the same with you, dear Lucy. I would make you so happy, *n'est ce pas?*'

As I stood frozen with horror and distaste at this hateful revelation from the incorrigible Trabut, we were interrupted suddenly by a swift movement of the door which burst open to reveal Edmund, eyes narrowed in a ferocious scowl, teeth bared in a terrible grimace of hatred. As he advanced towards Marcel Trabut, I shrank to the wall, in an attempt to become small, invisible, non existent, in the face of his fury. Marcel Trabut, however, had no such opportunity to move or defend himself.

'You lying cur,' Edmund snarled at him, and his fist shot out towards the Frenchman's chin with the force of a cannon ball.

'Milor', please!' he gasped, as he clasped his hand to his bloody nose.

He had turned a rather sickly pale colour and started to protest and gabble as though to stave off with words the savage attack that he dreaded.

'Please,' he said again. 'You misunderstand, Milor' Hallburgh. Please listen to me . . . I can explain. It is not what you think . . . '

'So many things fall into place now,' hissed

Edmund. 'I was suspicious of you, but never had proof. You loathsome swine. I could kill you and gladly swing on the nearest gibbet, to rid the world of an evil being such as you.'

Marcel Trabut was now seriously alarmed and tried ineffectually to thrust away his attacker, but it seemed that Edmund was absolutely unable to contain his passionate anger and he laid into the other man with a ferocity such as I had never seen before.

He is still insanely jealous, I thought, just as Annie had said when I first arrived at Melbury House. Doctor Trabut had hinted slyly more than once that he had been Catherine's lover and that she had encouraged and enjoyed their regular afternoon dalliance and now he was reaping the consequences of this. Edmund was hitting the doctor again and again and I grew very perturbed by what was happening.

'Oh please do not go on,' I begged him, but he continued to punch Trabut almost automatically, with a set, white face and paying no heed to the other man's screams of protest. I tried to intervene physically to stop Edmund's attack on him, but it was useless.

Now, Miss Hallburgh swished into the library in her little wheeled chair. She was as always, elegantly dressed in a pale lilac gown and with fine jewels at her neck and was closely followed by the faithful Yvette. Both women gazed in horror at the scene before them.

Marcel Trabut was at present crouching on the ground, cowering ignominiously and begging for mercy in an absolutely craven manner. There was no lessening of the violence from Edmund and he continued to snarl at the cowardly doctor to stand up and fight like a man.

Caroline Hallburgh's own face had now assumed a very ashen colour and she seemed entirely at a loss as to how to act.

'He is run amok, your brother!' shouted Trabut, pressing his handkerchief to his swollen lip. 'What have I ever done to deserve this? Miss Hallburgh. *Aidez moi!*'

Yvette took Caroline Hallburgh's hand and whispered, 'It is true, Miss Hallburgh. He must be insane. Stop him, I beg you, please, *madame.*'

Caroline Hallburgh stared at Edmund, as though for once she was completely helpless and unable to react. My poor Edmund seemed not to notice that anyone else had entered the room. He was standing with his bloody fists still clenched, but now was glaring up at the portrait of his late wife. It was obvious that all kinds of hateful thoughts were invading his mind concerning the cowardly Marcel Trabut and his liaison with the beautiful Catherine. At this point, Miss Hallburgh let out a small theatrical scream. It was done entirely for effect and to gain Edmund's attention.

'Edmund! Please control yourself. Whatever has happened? Oh my poor Marcel. Edmund, allow him to get up, please. In the name of God.'

She now burst into tears and once more Yvette offered soft words of comfort while all the while glaring resentfully at Edmund. As for myself, I continued to cower against the wall in an agony of nervous discomfort and unease at the scene which was being played out in front of me.

Yvette whimpered, 'Cannot you see that you are agitating Miss Hallburgh, sir? Please allow the doctor to get up and have his wounds attended to. I beg of you.'

Edmund seemed at last to rouse himself from his angry trance. 'Yes. Get up,' he grated angrily. 'And then get out. Leave us and do not ever return. I do not wish you to attend my sister in this house ever again.'

We all stood in a tense and angry silence while Trabut dragged himself painfully to his feet and scuttled sideways from the room, still holding his handkerchief to his bloodied nose. Even the sobbing Miss

Hallburgh was quiet until Edmund turned on his heel and also left us. At least the children had not witnessed this appalling scene, I thought. I thanked heaven that they were safely asleep in their beds. I prepared to slip away to my own room myself, sickened and appalled at the way that Edmund's love and trust in his wife had been so wantonly destroyed by the evil Trabut, but I was not to escape so easily. Caroline Hallburgh held up a forbidding hand. It seemed that now the unpleasant scene was over, she had suddenly recovered from her hysterics and had achieved a deadly calm.

'One moment, Miss Grey. I would like to speak with you, if you please. Kindly leave us, Yvette. I will ring for you when I wish to retire to bed.'

'Very well, Miss Hallburgh.' Yvette went silently as always and we were left alone.

I drew a deep breath as I waited for the inevitable interrogation. It was obvious that she had now begun to enjoy the drama of the situation. I almost pitied her. She moved her little chair towards me and I could see that her lips were quivering. She wiped them with her handkerchief.

Her hand shook, but she said quietly, 'Be seated, if you please, Miss Grey. Tell me how this trouble started. Who struck the first blow?'

'Lord Hallburgh,' I stammered. 'Doctor Trabut was no match for him. He made no retaliation. There was no contest.'

'But there must have been a reason for such a savage attack. What could possibly have happened to cause such violence? I wish to know. Poor Marcel is my friend as well as my physician. What had he done? Tell me.'

But I was unable to form the words to describe what I had witnessed. 'Please, Miss Hallburgh. I beg you, do not involve me in this. I do not wish to offer an explanation.'

'You wicked girl. You will tell me!' she shrilled, and the beringed hands began to tap ominously on the arms of her chair as she prepared to work herself up into one of her notorious scenes.

'I demand to know how this came about. I am the mistress of my brother's house. What were you doing in the library? Why were you not attending to your duties in the school-room? Tell me at once.'

But I could not. I kept my head bent and thought in an agony of love and longing of the pain that my beloved Edmund was undergoing, alone with his thoughts of the wife he believed to be faithless.

In a quieter tone, she went on, 'Miss Grey,

I absolutely insist that you tell me what happened in the library this evening. What were you doing there in the first place?'

In a low voice I replied, 'I had taken the children upstairs and the nursery maid was preparing them for bed. I came down to look at a copy of *Aesop's Fables* for the schoolroom tomorrow.'

'Go on, girl, go on,' she exclaimed impatiently.

'Very well. As I came down the library steps with the volume in my hands, Dr Trabut suddenly appeared and offered me . . . offered me a pretty little musical box for my birthday . . . I tried to politely refuse it, but . . . '

'Yes? But what?'

'He urged me to accept it as it was an exact replica of the one that . . . she . . . that the children unfortunately broke . . . I tried to refuse it . . . '

I halted in some confusion.

'So he urged you to accept a music box like the one that Lady Hallburgh had. I am sure it was kindly meant.'

'Yes . . . No . . . It is just that . . . just . . . that he . . . '

'Yes? Yes?'

'He tried to embrace me. To kiss me against my will.'

'Most young women know how to deal with gentlemen who are a little too familiar. Surely even a parson's daughter could gently deflect unwelcome attentions,' she said sneeringly. 'Or, perhaps, Miss Grey, you had led him to believe that they were not so unwelcome?'

I blushed to the roots of my hair and answered indignantly, 'Miss Hallburgh, that is quite unforgivable. I absolutely refuse to conduct any conversation with you unless you retract that remark forthwith.'

'Very well, very well, you stupid girl. What next?' she urged impatiently.

'Well,' I continued reluctantly. 'I told him that I positively did not want his kisses and he . . . intimated . . . that . . . Lady Hallburgh was always used to want them and that he had other liberties besides.'

I stumbled to a complete stop, feeling sick, my heart racing and with a terrible feeling of dread pervading my whole being. The effect of my words on Miss Hallburgh was quite dramatic. Her blustering, bullying conceit seemed suddenly broken and the small exquisite face became shrivelled like that of a painted doll. She whispered more to herself than to me, 'Oh, Marcel, you utter fool.'

'It was at that moment that he . . . that Lord Edmund entered the library and called

261

him out as a lying cur and then he hit him.'

'Oh what a terrible thing to happen,' she declared. 'My own brother to indulge in such vile, ungentlemanly conduct and to so forget his manners as to attack Marcel. He will never wish to speak to us again.'

'And should you wish him to?' I asked curiously. 'After he has maligned your poor dead sister-in-law in that way?'

'Miss Grey, you are just a country vicarage mouse and know nothing of the world,' she exclaimed rather hysterically. 'Marcel is so polished, so suave, so attractive to women. And Catherine was so spoilt, so flirtatious. I hated her. Of course, Edmund absolutely adored her, she could do no wrong. I expect Marcel was under her spell also, as were most men. And now she has even spread out her evil fingers from beyond the grave and bewitched my dear Marcel away from me.'

I watched in fascinated horror as the little china features dissolved and gradually disintegrated in one of her famous attacks of the vapours. At that moment, I experienced only compassion and pity for this lonely unhappy woman and a certain detached curiosity at her ability to turn on either charm or hysteria at will.

For Marcel Trabut there was only hatred and contempt. Whether he had or had not made love to Catherine did not at that moment concern me. I felt only sadness and concern for my dear Edmund and would willingly have killed Trabut myself if it were possible. Edmund had loved his wife with a deep and abiding love and I could not bear to think that she might have betrayed him with someone as unworthy as Trabut.

'But you!' cried Miss Hallburgh, working herself up into a frenzy. 'If only you had never come here, with your mealy school-ma'am tales against dear Marcel. Hurling your bonnet at my brother . . . Hoping to win him as your own.'

Her voice had now risen to a scream and I hastily pulled the bell to summon Yvette. As soon as she entered the room she began to calm her beloved mistress and cluck over her solicitously in a mixture of French and English, so I hastily made my escape, shaken and distressed by what I had witnessed, and hurried to my own room.

As I turned the corner on the first landing of the gracious Melbury House staircase, I almost ran into the object of my concern. He was dressed as for a journey with a many-caped driving coat and was carrying a valise with him. Two footmen scurried past us with trunks and other luggage, but Edmund paused and stood to speak to me very courteously. He looked extremely stern and his face was pale.

'Oh, Miss Grey,' he said quietly. 'I was just coming to seek you out to apologize for the bestial scene that you were forced to witness earlier and to beg your pardon for the discomfiture you must have endured.'

I was unable to reply, being too full of emotion and the recent upheaval of feelings to make any adequate response.

'I am going away for some time, Lucy, and will be in Leicestershire for a few weeks. I felt I must inform you of this as you were so unfortunate as to experience an unpardonable act of violence on my part, this evening.'

I gazed up at him, trying to will the feelings of love and concern for him which overwhelmed me, to encompass his beloved person.

'And when will you return, sir?' I asked somewhat tremulously.

'By choice — never,' he replied grimly. 'But as you know, I have much business and concerns both in London and the country, so I must return eventually.'

'But the children,' I protested. 'What of them? They have done nothing . . . '

'No,' he said, with a hardening of his jaw. 'They have done nothing and all I ask for them is that you should continue to be their guide and mentor in such a harsh world. Will you do this for me, dear Lucy? I know how difficult it must be for you. Caroline is not the easiest woman to get along with. Please. I know that I may go with a quiet mind if you are with them. Please, my dear.'

I was utterly overwhelmed at the emotion and despair of his appeal. I felt my own tears rising unbidden as he repeated the words, 'Please, my dear.'

'Of course,' I managed, consenting eagerly to his wishes. He looked so grey and bitterly unhappy that I could hardly bear to see it.

'Oh come now. Lucy. No tears, my dear. What is done is done. I know you will take good care of the little ones and rest assured, my sister is fully aware that in my absence, Dr Trabut is not allowed in this house, so you will not be importuned by him ever again.'

I fought back my emotions and tried not to let my tears spill over onto my cheeks. He was obviously as put about as I was myself. His face was drawn and terribly unsettled. It was as though he would never be calm again. I longed to hold him to me and comfort him as I would have done dear little Sarah, or my darling Tom. All I could do was to look at him with helpless, impotent compassion, my tears now running freely and I unable to stop them.

Then he put down the valise and cupped

my face in both his hands. 'Do not disturb yourself on my account, dear Lucy,' he begged. 'It will resolve itself, never fear.'

Now I gave way entirely and sobbed in his arms quite unashamedly. I felt his hand stroking my hair and then his soft kiss on my forehead. I strained towards him, raising my lips to his and he returned my kisses, more than once.

Finally, he put me from him very gently and said, 'Goodbye, my darling girl. I am eternally grateful to you. God be with you, my dear Lucy.'

Then he left me. He walked down the staircase and I heard the front door slam as he stepped out into the cool night air. Baxter clucked up the horses and then came the sound of the chaise being driven away.

I continued towards my room absolutely bereft of all that might make me happy or content. What would tomorrow bring, I wondered, without the only one who was worth living and dying for? I felt my own existence would be worthless. As I prepared for bed, I once again took down the copy of *Mediterranean Cities*, which he had given me, turning the pages and looking at the pictures with unseeing eyes while I tried to compose myself for slumber.

I understood only too well how shattered

Edmund's perceptions of his beautiful wife must be, in the light of the hateful revelations from Marcel Trabut. But life had to go on and, in spite of my deeply sad thoughts, I had to put on a face of normality in front of Tom and Sarah. I had a feeling that with Edmund's departure, Miss Hallburgh would send me yet another of her imperious summonses, but this did not come about. Instead, Yvette appeared suddenly in the schoolroom one day and reported in a subdued and rather mortified voice, 'Mademoiselle Grey, Miss Hallburgh is not well . . . but . . . Doctor Trabut has been . . . has had to go urgently to Paris . . . Miss Hallburgh has been obliged . . . obliged to engage another physician . . . Doctor . . . Doctor George Abbott from Harley Street, will now attend her. She requests that you keep the children occupied and quiet during the time of her recuperation. *Merci, mademoiselle,*' she finished in a low voice.

I merely nodded in response to this. It must have cost Yvette a tremendous effort to make this climb down on behalf of her mistress. I knew that after her unhappy experience with Dr Trabut, Caroline Hallburgh was feeling the unusual and unlooked for emotion of humiliation. I felt no ounce of human pity for her whatsoever.

14

The next few weeks were lonely and somewhat sad without Edmund. The children seemed resigned to his absence, however, and there were no further scenes from Caroline Hallburgh. The early summer continued fine and we had a message to say that Edmund planned to travel in Italy with companions from Norfolk. I wondered briefly if the group included Harriet Marland, although no mention had been made of her name. Occasionally, I caught a glimpse of Dr Abbott, but only fleetingly. He was a solid and very English medical man, always striding purposefully when he entered the house, brusque but unfailingly polite at all times. On one occasion, when I encountered him in the hall, I asked after Miss Hallburgh's health and how she did. He answered very openly and not in the usual guarded way of physicians, that she did very well and could do even better were she not so bound up with the narrow concerns of her life at Melbury House.

'For you must know, miss, that she is constantly agitated in her mental state. If this

268

problem could be overcome, her indisposition would disappear like snow in summer.'

He was reassuring also when Sarah took a feverish chill which turned into a serious cough, making her ill for at least two weeks. I felt the responsibility lie heavily on me in the absence of her papa, but George Abbott could not have been more tenderly attentive and reassuring if she had been his own dear child. He visited her every day and then for the second week, continued to call in to see how she did. Thankfully, she had all the resilience of a normal young child and once on the mend, recovered rapidly, day by day.

June was enlivened by a visit from William who was to have a few days at the home of our Aunt Esther Grey before starting work as an assistant clerk to an attorney. He had achieved this position by the good offices of the Reverend Tranter, who continued to be his guide and mentor. William's affection for young Maria continued unabated and he was now quite open with me about his love for her.

'But marriage will not be for some time yet, Lu,' he sighed. 'I have to make my way in the world and show myself capable of supporting a wife. Maria's parents are all that is kind, Lu. I shall do my utmost not to let them down.'

I wondered briefly what would be the reaction of our Aunt Esther to the news of William getting engaged, but decided to say nothing. We were able to have some happy hours together before William went on the stage coach to Wembeck and both of us looked forward to meeting once more in London after his duty call to our relatives.

These small diversions in my life in no way took away my feelings of pain at Edmund's absence, but coupled with the fine warm weather, they did much to lighten my spirits. One significant development at this time was the order from Caroline Hallburgh that the beautiful portrait of Edmund's late wife should be removed from the library and a rather insipid country scene put there in its stead. I was unaware at first of what became of the portrait. Annie reported that the order for its removal had, in fact, come from Edmund himself and that his sister had merely followed out his wishes. Much later, I saw the picture wrapped in a dust sheet and stowed in a little-used room on the top floor. With some curiosity, I lifted one corner of the cover and gazed sadly at the beautiful face. In my mind, I tried to imagine the woman who might conceivably prefer Marcel Trabut over Edmund Hallburgh. I remember I stood for many minutes, thinking of this without coming to any conclusions except that she must have been a very troubled lady indeed.

Then one morning in July, Yvette appeared unexpectedly in the schoolroom. 'Miss Hallburgh would like to see Sarah and Thomas, if you please, *mademoiselle*.'

She deliberately avoided my gaze, her sallow face rather flushed and with a very discomfited expression. I acquiesced without any enthusiasm and began to brush Sarah's hair and put in fresh ribbons while Annie took Tom to wash and put on a clean collar. Then I took them down to their aunt's boudoir wondering all the while what could be behind this request.

'Please do not let the children stay too long,' Yvette whispered urgently, as we reached the door. '*Madame* gets very tired you know.'

I merely nodded without speaking, but Caroline Hallburgh had heard Yvette's plea and exclaimed waspishly, 'I will be the best judge of how long the children should stay, Yvette. Kindly go and find something useful to do, if you please.' And Yvette left the room, her face now quite angry.

She was sitting on a sofa by the window, wearing a black gauze house gown and with little black velvet boots just visible below her dress. As always, she had on some very impressive jewels, but her face was paler than I had ever seen it. In spite of Yvette's artifice with her pomades and powders, Miss Caroline Hallburgh looked distinctly unwell. Even the children seemed to notice this and stood regarding her silently. She was at first, just as silent, and wore a very unfriendly expression, which was rather off-putting for all of us. I had instructed both children that they must be polite and considerate and ask how their aunt did and if she was now recovered from her indisposition.

Needless to say, Tom stood tongue-tied and awkward, but at least he was not putting his fingers to his mouth, merely gazing solemnly at his aunt without speaking. Sarah was more forthcoming and stepped forward very prettily, bobbing a curtsy and impulsively kissing her aunt on the carefully rouged cheek.

'Are you now well again, Aunt Caro?' she asked artlessly. 'And is your headache completely gone?'

'Oh yes, I thank you, my dear,' she responded, taking Sarah's little hand in her own plump one. 'But Aunt Caro has been very unwell, my little poppet. Doctor Abbott has almost despaired of your poor aunt's recovery.'

I thought privately that the good doctor

would be quite astounded at this diagnosis in view of his conversation with me.

'Pass that little dish of bon-bons, and you may choose one, my darling,' she cooed at Sarah, and stroked the little girl's curls with a languid white hand.

'Oh please, Aunt Caro, may I have a bonbon?' Tom asked eagerly, noticing his sister's favour with his aunt.

'Certainly not. You are a greedy, ill-mannered little boy,' she answered spitefully.

When Tom's little face puckered up and he began to cry, she relented and said irritably, 'Oh very well, stupid child. But choose a small one.'

I was aware that however much recovered she was, Caroline Hallburgh did not feel inclined to suffer infant tears and tantrums from Tom. She pointedly neglected to offer me one of the sweet-meats, but her own white fingers hovered voluptuously over the little dish and she chose one and put it carefully into her small mouth with all the sensuality of an Eastern potentate. Once more, it was brought home to me how driven by her passions was this unhappy creature and how pitiable she really was.

I was moved to say, 'We were all sorry to hear of your illness, Miss Hallburgh. I trust you will soon be completely well again.'

She deliberately turned away from me and said with a suffering expression, 'I shall never be well. My health has been destroyed by the cares and concerns I have endured on behalf of others.'

She closed her eyes and held a hand up to her smooth, white forehead. 'I feel one of my swooning attacks coming on,' she said. 'Please leave me, children. You may come and see me again another day.'

We were dismissed. I left the boudoir feeling humiliated and insulted by her lack of civility. As I took the children up to the schoolroom, Yvette was waiting in the corridor and hurried in to her mistress without speaking to me. I felt in disgrace, but without knowing what misdemeanour had made me guilty. As I set out the books and pictures for my lesson, I reflected that Caroline Hallburgh's anger was as a result of the unfortunate scene in the library and that she was no more likely to forgive my real or imaginary sins than she would those of her dead sister-in-law.

The next day brought a very welcome letter for the children, from their father. It had obviously been opened by their aunt, or perhaps more likely, had been enclosed in a letter to herself. In it, Edmund explained that a trusted fellow traveller was returning to London and had offered to act as a courier. Both children were naturally excited, jumping up and down and exclaiming, 'It is from Papa. It is from Papa!'

Although Sarah was able to pick out some of the words unaided, they both begged me to read their Papa's letter from Italy:

My dear children

I write to tell you that as the sun is going down in this lovely corner of Tuscany, my thoughts are with you and of your doings at Melbury House. I hope you are being mindful of your Aunt Caro and that you are being good and clever for our dear Miss Grey. The countryside is beautiful here, more especially the tall geen Cypressus, in such graceful contrast to the blue of the Mediterranean sky. We have travelled to Rome to see the great Coliseum and the other antiquities and are returning from our time abroad in two weeks. I need hardly add that, now the plans are laid, I am impatient to be back home with you again. Travel broadens the mind, but it can be wearisome also.

I remain, your ever loving, Papa.

I read hungrily the words, 'our dear Miss Grey' several times and wondered if Caroline Hallburgh had noted them too. Then Sarah had to have the letter and try to decipher it unaided. Soon it was the turn of little Thomas and I had to go and get the big leather-bound atlas from the library to satisfy their questions of Edmund's where-abouts and describe to them the wonderful sights which their father was enjoying in Italy.

There was also a letter from my brother, ebullient and confident as always, to the effect that Mr and Mrs Tranter had given their guarded permission for his and Maria's betrothal.

'Of course, it won't be until the end of this year when my dear Maria is eighteen. And what do you think, Lu? Messrs Willis, Hardy and Jakes have offered me a permanency as a clerk in the firm. I am now set fair to becoming a city gent as well as a married man. I have been allowed to leave Oxford early.

I was delighted for William's happiness of course, but it contrasted sadly with my own rather downcast spirits. I tried to shake off my feelings of gloom however and to offer him my sincere congratulations. In the afternoon,

I was able to take some hours away from my duties and one of the grooms drove me to my brother's lodging. William and I had a lively time, chatting and discussing his work with Mr Hardy in Lincoln's Inn Fields. It was plain he was experiencing great joy at his good news. Words tumbled out of him in his enthusiasm to describe to me what a decent fellow and all round nonesuch was Mr Hardy, and how hard he was going to work to provide for dear Maria and justify her parents' trust in him.

'For you must know, Lu,' he rattled on, 'Mr Hardy has come from just such humble beginnings as we have ourselves, but once started in law, he has never looked back. In no time at all it seems, he was making a very tolerable living at Willis and Jakes and six years on he is now a partner. Albeit a junior one,' he added hastily, seeing my quizzical look.

'And only think, Lucy, now that he has already been able to persuade Mr Willis and Mr Jakes to engage me as an articled clerk, who knows what advancement will now open up to me? Willis, Jakes, Hardy and Grey,' he murmured dreamily to himself. 'It has a pleasant ring to it.'

'And what of your idea of a position in the Church, Wills?'

'Why, Mr Tranter has suggested I might work at the law until such time as a living could be found for me. He thinks it would test my feelings towards a true vocation, Lu. What a fine fellow he is to be sure, and he is so tolerant of my marriage to Maria. I know I can trust him to advise me wisely. I must be the luckiest fellow alive, sis.'

It was a joy to me to see his enthusiasm and it took my mind from my own unhappiness, so that for a few hours I forgot even Edmund in the pleasure of my brother's company. It was obvious that with the flexibility of youth, Wills was seeing the advantages of a training in law rather than the Church, but it was early days, I thought. His financial responsibilities as a married man might be the deciding factor in these decisions.

All too soon, my few precious hours of leisure were over and Wills obtained for me a hackney cab to take me back to Melbury House. As he handed me up, we cheerfully arranged to see each other again in one more month, when he would have settled into his new position.

William had insisted on paying the cab man for me and, as I alighted near the imposing gates in Melbury Place, I had no need to pause for the fare and so turned immediately, deciding to walk round to the servants' entrance. I was sure that one of the young footmen would still be up and would let me in. I reached for the finely wrought circular handle on the huge gate and was startled as a cloaked figure suddenly rose up before me in the gloom. I gave a start as I recognised Marcel Trabut and I turned away in an effort to avoid him. I determined not to speak, but he barred my way.

'Have you no word for me, Lucy?' he asked bitterly.

'No, Dr Trabut, I have not,' I said in a low voice. 'Kindly let me pass, *monsieur.*'

'Not before you tell me how Caroline is and whether she has recovered her health,' he insisted.

His voice was no longer soft and seductive, but hoarse and almost desperate. He had lost his air of sophisticated Gallic charm and appeared now to be what he was — a rather ordinary man of less than average height.

'Yes, she is quite recovered, thank you, and is now being attended by Dr Abbott,' I said coldly.

'That foolish quack,' he exclaimed contemptuously, and I felt my anger stir.

I knew that his pretended concern for Caroline Hallburgh stemmed from his exploitation of the wealth and position she was able to bestow on him. He would probably seek out another rich patron, I thought, in order to replace the goose that laid the golden egg. I could not help it: my face mirrored the contempt I felt for him and my lip curled.

'Pardon me, *monsieur*. Foolish quack or not, Miss Hallburgh is calmer and the household quieter since Dr Abbott became her physician.'

He made no reply to this beyond a disparaging 'Humph' and an insulting observation about Edmund which I found very offensive. Once more I attempted to reach up to the handle of the gate and enter the drive of Melbury House.

'But one moment, Lucy. Do you not think I was shabbily used by Lord Hallburgh, eh? To be treated to a bout of fisticuffs and be dismissed from my position like that?'

'No, I do not,' I answered indignantly. 'If I were a man, sir, I would do the same.'

I ought to have known that he would find my spirited retort piquant, rather than a put down.

'What a pretty little shrew you are, *ma petite*,' he said caressingly with a return to his old flirtatious manner. 'Is it such a crime, *mademoiselle*, to offer a beautiful young lady my hand in marriage?' And he made his well-remembered sheep's eyes at me.

'I do not wish for your proposal, I thank you, sir. I find your attentions unwelcome, as unwelcome as your observations about poor dead Lady Hallburgh. I would bid you goodnight.'

My contempt had now obviously got under even Trabut's thick skin and his normally sallow face turned an ugly colour as we stood in the darkening shades of the dusk.

'You evil little witch,' he snarled, all pretence at continental charm now leaving him. 'I was totally besotted with you. I never even heard Milor' Hallburgh enter the room. I was enslaved. Enslaved! I never intended my remarks for his ears.'

I made no reply and he continued, 'But everything happens for the best. Why should he not hear the truth about his wife's dissatisfaction? He has his enjoyments and the work of his estates, the shooting and the sporting life. Why should he think that someone of her great charm and beauty must be content with *les enfants* and the household cares?'

I was now seriously concerned that one of the staff would come out and find me with Trabut. Baxter always took a lantern round to the stables to check on the horses after dark. If his master was not expected home, he would secure the gates. Darkness was falling apace and I felt alarmed.

'Good night, Dr Trabut,' I repeated, and to my great relief, he let me pass. I opened the gate with trembling hands and crept thankfully inside.

In spite of everything, he must still have the last word. 'Do not think, Lucy, that the Milor' Hallburgh will escape lightly from his assault on my person. The matter is in the hands of my lawyer and he will present my complaint to the courts. Lord Hallburgh will be shown up for the ruffian that he is.'

But I had already sped up to the back door and tapped softly for admittance and so heard no more.

Yet I could not help remembering what he had said and wondering if it were really true. If so, could a man like Trabut possibly succeed in a law suit against the powerful Lord Hallburgh? I doubted it and yet I was sure he would not wish for a scandal involving his dead wife. Perhaps I should broach the subject with Edmund — warn him of Trabut's threat. And yet, when he eventually came back from Italy, still looking tired and strained, I could not bring myself to mention it.

After the first lyrical welcome from the children was over, things settled down into a quiet routine. Edmund had changed though.

His face remained hard and impassive. There were no more little jaunts round the park, merely an occasional visit to the schoolroom and a very brief word to the children, his face an impenetrable mask. One thing was different, now: Edmund called me by my first name all of the time, even in front of the children. Caroline Hallburgh made no comment about this, but I caught the cold disapproval in her eyes every time she noticed this unlooked for familiarity. She was much calmer since Dr Abbott had been in attendance. Perhaps too calm as it turned out. As the glorious summer rolled on, she seemed to be much better in health and began to wear lighter, more suitable dresses, very pretty and fashionable, although always with the little boots of course. She neither smiled at me nor spoke unless she had to. If ever a woman was my enemy, it was she, and yet I still had no knowledge as to how I had offended her. Occasionally, she offered the usual carping criticisms of my work and my handling of the children, and I still had to be on guard to protect poor Tom, who was, as always, the butt of her spiteful tongue. All this was not a novel experience. I knew she would not dare go against her brother's express wishes and dismiss me from his household, and so I remained as polite and civil as my position warranted.

As for Edmund, I only saw him at meal-times, never alone. He was, as always, unfailingly pleasant and courteous, but he never once gave me his well-remembered smile and I felt that all the rapport and little jokes that we once shared were gone forever. This was far more painful to me than a hundred poisoned barbs from Miss Hallburgh and I could barely conceal my pain and suffering over the loss of his friendship. I lay in my lonely bed on those warm summer nights thinking about him and feeling despondent about my life in general and what the future would hold for me. I loved him madly, passionately, with all my heart and soul, even though I had to acknowledge that I could never be any more to him than trusted reliable, 'Dear Miss Grey'. My only happiness was to be in his presence, to be able to sit at his table, take comfort in his impeccable manners and the kind pleasantries he exchanged with the children. This happiness brought its antithesis though, the pain of my longing and the dreadful unhappiness of wanting a man who was unattainable.

Mrs Marland visited again at the end of the month, without little Benjamin this time. She was as beautiful and elegant as ever and the knife was turned even more painfully in my heart by the sight of her graceful figure entering his carriage, on the way to some opera or soirée. Miss Hallburgh took great delight in banishing me to the schoolroom again, 'For we keep London hours when dear Harriet is with us,' she gloated. 'And it would not do to expect the children to dine in company every evening.'

I was shaken by a violent paroxysm of jealousy, such as I had never experienced before and that night, alone in my room, I raged inwardly at the cruel inequalities of life. I wondered bitterly if Edmund would make Mrs Marland the second Lady Hallburgh, now that he had caused Lady Catherine's likeness to be pushed out of his sight and out of his life. But no announcement was made of an engagement during her visit and shortly after the children had gathered at the front drive to wish her farewell, I learned from Edmund that Dr Trabut was to pursue his satisfaction in the courts.

'I am to meet with my lawyer today, Lucy,' he told me, as we walked back to the house, leaving Sarah and Tom waving madly to Mrs Marland's departing carriage. 'I shall be unable to take the children for a drive.'

I merely nodded, not revealing to him that I was aware of Trabut's intentions.

For a moment there was a return to his old

manner. 'Nothing to concern yourself about, Lucy,' he reassured me. 'No need to look so downcast. Doctor Trabut is determined to seek the law over the claret I drew from his handsome Gallic nose.' He smiled sardonically as we entered the hall.

'I am very sorry, sir,' I murmured.

'No, Lucy. No sympathy. I have no intentions of allowing that rogue Trabut to drag our names and those of my . . . of . . . Lady Hallburgh through the mire of the courts. I would not wish to see any of us pilloried by the vulgar broadsheets, particularly our dear Miss Grey.'

'No sir,' I rejoined inadequately, feeling at a loss as to what to say next. 'But I would do anything I could,' I continued passionately.

For a moment, the ghost of his old sweet smile appeared in the handsome grey eyes. 'Thank you child, there is no need,' he said softly. 'No, indeed,' he went on, warming to his theme. 'I have it on good authority from some of my acquaintances, that Trabut's pockets are decidedly to let. He has lost many of his adoring female patients lately and, of course, Caro has given him the about turn, so he would want to settle out of court.'

We passed into the library, waiting for the children to return to the house. Then he said almost casually, 'And I have lately, been thinking of buying a property in Italy. To live, I mean. Young Tom will be ready for school in a few years and both children could spend their summers with me in Tuscany.'

I was stunned and could think of nothing to say, but my dismay must have shown on my face, for he went on, 'In days gone by, I loved town life and the season you know, but since . . . she . . . since my wife died, it has no delight for me any more.'

He gazed down at the floor. 'These last years have been so worthless and lacking in any joy for me, Lucy.'

For one mad passionate moment, I forgot we were master and servant. I even forgot myself sufficiently to call him Edmund. He seemed to neither notice nor care at my familiar form of address. As for me, the respectable governess, Miss Grey, I poured out a torrent of entreaty at the thought of losing my beloved forever.

'Oh Edmund,' I cried. 'I implore you to turn from the unhappy past and start to regain some composure. That villain, Trabut, may have just been mischief-making with his vile hints and sly innuendoes about Lady Hallburgh. However painful, you must pluck these thoughts from your mind, or they will fester and destroy you. You do not even know whether he spoke the truth!'

Now he clenched his hands at his side and turned to look at me, his jaw like granite. It was as though his iron self-control had finally snapped. 'Oh yes, I do know,' he ground out. 'I was . . . was . . . close enough to Catherine to know that things were not right between us. I suspected there was someone. But not that man. Dear God. Not Trabut.' He spat the name with loathing.

But still the foolish young governess persisted. 'But you cannot know for certain,' I urged.

'And what does our little vicarage mouse know of the ways of the wicked world?' he sneered. It was the first time he had ever used Caroline Hallburgh's sarcastic epithet and tears started to my eyes at this cruelty. Nevertheless, I persisted, my voice choking with emotion.

'I . . . I know nothing,' I stammered. 'But it may not be what you think. No wife who loved her husband and children would want to be on intimate terms with such a one as Marcel Trabut. Perhaps she was lonely and found long days with small children tedious and boring. She was young and beautiful. Maybe she craved excitement . . . admiration. Perhaps she found Trabut a diverting companion . . . nothing more . . . '

I faltered to a halt. I dared to look into his

face. It was white with suppressed rage and a kind of hopeless sadness which could not find expression. Then he gave a contemptuous laugh.

'Thank you for the philosophical discourse, little Miss Governess. Forgive me, but you cannot know anything. You did not meet the main player and she is now out of the race. Only her personal maid, and possibly Caro, know something of the truth. Explanations, accusations, are all equally and utterly futile.'

He finished on a note of absolute despair, shaking his clenched fists in front of him and trembling violently with emotion. Impulsively, I caught his wrists and implored him to be calm.

'Please, Edmund. Do not destroy the love and trust that you felt for Catherine, merely on the whim of an evil charlatan such as Trabut.'

I do not know what possessed me to defend the poor dead woman in this way, unless it was my natural inclination, instilled into me by my dear papa, that everyone must be innocent until proven guilty. He used to say, 'To the pure in heart, all things are pure, Lucy.'

And I repeated it to Edmund now.

For a long moment he was silent, looking down. I released my grasp on his wrists and put my hands behind my back, fearing that I had exceeded my duties in speaking to my employer like this and addressing him by his first name. Finally he spoke.

'Yes. You are right. You speak the truth as always, my dear, honourable Lucy. Do you know, since you have been at Melbury House, my darling little Sarah has not told a single lie? What a powerful influence you have, my own vicarage mouse, to be sure.'

This time the mocking name did not hurt me. We continued to gaze at each other steadily and then he went on, 'You are always so honest, are you not? Well now, I will also confess the truth and shame the Devil. I have discovered that I no longer love my dead wife. Whatever she did or did not do in life, in death it is of no moment. The passion I once felt for the mother of my children is now burnt out. Finished. It is all over. In truth, it was over long ago, but I was loath to admit to it. It was not love for her that impelled me to trounce the dastardly Trabut, but pride. It was my personal honour that was being impugned by his insinuations. There. I hope I do not shock your maidenly sensibilities too deeply by my confession. But you were right to say what you did. I shall go and see my lawyer in a more rational frame of mind. It is certain he will be able to fix on a suitable sum to settle with Trabut, and after that, I shall probably go abroad again for a while.'

He carefully removed my hands from behind my back and kissed me gently on the forehead. 'Please never leave us, my dear,' he murmured softly, and then released me and strode purposefully out of the room.

I felt so weak with emotion, that I took several minutes to recover. The children, however, knew nothing of this and bounded in with their usual high spirits. Mrs Marland's coach had taken ten whole minutes to disappear from view. Mrs Marland, herself, when she left, had promised that they might go and spend a few days in Norfolk and play with little Benjamin Marland. I looked at them doubtfully when they imparted this information and Sarah began to giggle. Tom, who had been serious so far, joined in, but I knew that the idea of a few days in the Marland household was a daunting prospect for him.

I did not see Edmund again that week. I did not know the outcome of his negotiations with Marcel Trabut, but I supposed that it had been successful as we heard no more about the law suit.

It was about this time that Annie announced her intention of retiring completely from domestic service and going to live with her sister in Cheapside. I applauded her common sense in this and recognised the benefit of moving in with someone who could be mutually supportive, and yet I was sad at the ending of my friendship with such a genuine and sincere person. She was a humble maidservant, but then, so was I a humble governess. We both had cause to be grateful to the mutual warmth of our friendship and I would be sorry to part from her.

15

My emotions at this time were very intense and I seemed to find no relief in my usual activities of reading poetry or writing to my friend. I felt that the most deep and meaningful feelings of my life were ones which I could share with no one, especially my brother or Fanny Pembleton. So I was obliged to live on the surface of life, never daring to look too deeply into my own troubled heart or contemplate the future.

One day, while the children were out for a visit to one of Miss Hallburgh's married friends, I was able to get ahead with my letter writing, even catching the opportunity to pen a few lines to my dear friend, who had now returned from Bath and was languishing in Wembeck until such time as she was ready for her coming out. Her letters were all of the dressmakers and milliners who were attending her and her mama and of the advance invitations she had already received for the coming season. Her parents were giving a ball themselves for Fanny, sometime in November, to which I was invited and William, of course. This seemed a long way off and though I accepted politely, I knew in my heart that I would not have either the clothes or the social ease to carry it off. Still, it was a kind thought on Fanny's part and reflected our long-standing friendship.

I sanded my letter to her and then was momentarily idle and lost in thoughts of days gone by, when we were girlish best friends and bosom confidantes, sharing our music lessons and being taught to dance by the Italian dancing master engaged by Fanny's mama. I wondered what would be her reaction if I were able to talk to her now on the deepest level about my emotions concerning Edmund Hallburgh and the problems I experienced with his difficult sister, Caroline. One thing was certain: I would be unable to write it down in a letter, and even verbally recounting Miss Hallburgh's malevolent actions would be difficult.

My thoughts were interrupted at this moment by a soft and gentle knock at the door, and Annie appeared somewhat apologetically with a tea tray. Her face was very tense and strained and, in spite of my welcoming smile, she still appeared very ill at ease.

'Begging pardon, Miss Grey,' she said in a low tone. 'I've prevailed on Cook to allow us a drink of tea and a few little cakes.'

She put down the tray on a side table and put up her hands to smooth back some wisps of hair that had escaped the confines of her small lace cap — a circumstance that Annie would not normally tolerate, she being such a neat little body.

I stood up from behind my writing desk and stepped forward to greet her.

'Annie,' I said, 'this is very thoughtful and kind of you. You do not usually seek me out in my free moments, especially now, when you must be busy with your own concerns. Your removal to Cheapside must be taking up a large part of your time.'

I own, I felt surprised and wondered what had occasioned this visit to my room.

We settled down and she poured out the tea, saying, 'I must apologize for intruding, Miss Grey, but I have been in Lord Hallburgh's service a good few years, first in the kitchens, then as personal maid to Her Ladyship.'

She stood twisting her fingers nervously, and I set aside my writing things and motioned to her to be seated.

'I was chosen above the others, because I had a bit of book learning, you see, Miss. My first position had been with a maiden lady who was keen on teaching me to read and write, so when she died, I was given a good character and had no difficulty in getting a job at Melbury House.'

She raised her tea cup with hands which trembled somewhat and took a sip of her tea.

'I was so shocked by Lady Hallburgh's untimely death,' she said, 'particularly as Miss Hallburgh was so unpleasant in the aftermath of the tragedy. I was staying with my sister who was ill with the croup for over a month and couldn't be left. I nursed her through it and when I returned to my work, Lady Hallburgh was dead and Miss Hallburgh seemed determined that I was to be put back to the position of a domestic and not a personal maid. It may seem trivial to you, Miss Grey, but I know that she wanted to deny me the position I had enjoyed with Her Ladyship. She was going to make sure that I would never again have any place at all in the household, or any influence with the children.'

Her speech now became an absolute torrent. It seemed that once started, she could not stop talking. I sat helpless, listening and observing, as Annie poured out her story.

'You should have seen how upset those two poor little children were at their Mama's sad accident.'

Finally, she paused and sipped her tea again, breathing rather heavily and fanning herself with a napkin. Truth to tell, I would rather not have had my precious free time disturbed in this way, and yet I sensed that Annie's decision to seek me out like this must have some serious import.

'One thing you may not know, Miss Grey,' she said hesitantly, 'is that I enjoyed Her Ladyship's trust since before Sarah was born. Lady Hallburgh was already in the family way when I became her personal maid.'

Her accent now became less refined and traces of her Yorkshire ancestry broke through as she continued her tale.

'I had been more of a companion like to the previous lady and so had a lot of experience with the gentry, but even so, it seemed such a privilege to work in a grand house like this, for a beautiful young family.'

There was another pause which I allowed to continue while she caught her breath.

Then she said in a low voice, 'It was a shame, Miss Hallburgh coming like that, supposedly to look after Lady Hallburgh before Miss Sarah were born, for she never liked me, although I am sure I gave every satisfaction to Her Ladyship. I fetched and carried for her up until the time she were brought to bed with that little girl and afterwards, I looked after her again until Master Tom was born.'

She began to twist her apron with restless fingers and gazed towards the window.

'It was after the second bairn that things started to go wrong, Miss Grey. Caroline Hallburgh considered that me and Her Ladyship were too close and wanted her to have Yvette who is a proper French lady's-maid. But Lady Hallburgh felt comfortable with me, whereas I think that Yvette gave her the shudders.'

Now that she was embarked on her tale, it seemed that nothing could halt Annie's tongue.

'In that month while I was nursing my sister, she wrote me many letters, sometimes twice a day, Miss Grey. Even the night before her accident,' she rushed on, dramatically. 'I've saved all of them. I could not bear to part with the last link to Her Ladyship and besides, I felt there was something terribly wrong with the circumstances of her death.'

I felt vaguely uncomfortable now as I viewed the package which she thrust towards me. It was a pile of letters, tied round with some narrow tape of the kind used by milliners. They were nothing exceptional to look at and were loosely wrapped in waxed paper.

'It just about broke my heart when

298

. . . when she was killed . . . Miss Grey. And in the upset that followed, Lord Hallburgh allowed his sister to stay on and let me have the care of the two infants, them being used to me you see, and the little lad already weaned. I suppose I should have given these to His Lordship then, but somehow, there never seemed a proper moment. Then, what with Miss Hallburgh's eagle eye on me and Yvette spying at every end and turn, in the end, I daresn't, miss, and the moment passed.'

Annie was now speaking very rapidly and excitedly, I felt extremely disquieted, wondering what was coming next.

'You see, Lady Hallburgh was such a good, sweet lady, so kind and generous. For her to die as she did, why it was a real shame and so unnecessary. I shall never believe it was just an accident . . . ' She broke off, her cheeks red, her bosom heaving. I was now completely unnerved and unable to deal with her obvious emotion.

'Be calm, Annie,' I urged. 'I shall ring for some more tea and you may compose yourself.'

But Annie had no intentions of composing herself. Just as soon as the footman had brought a fresh tray of tea into the room, she waited only until the door had closed behind him before resuming her eulogy over the late Lady Hallburgh.

'She was wonderful to me and such a fond mama to those two children. I was more than a maid, Miss Grey. She took me to her heart, she did. I cared for all her clothes you know, and brushed her hair for her every night. And things were well between her and His Lordship, until Miss Hallburgh started to interfere, that is.'

I sipped my tea and tried to stay quiet in spite of the turmoil within me at these confidences.

'You should not be disclosing all these things to me,' I said trying to sound repressive, but I knew in my heart that she had aroused my curiosity and I wished her to continue her tale.

'But it is the truth, Miss Grey, and who else can I disclose them to? It has been on my mind for months. I am not in the world enough to approach His Lordship and, as you know, I am leaving his service to go and live with my sister. But he ought to see these, Miss Grey.'

I gazed fixedly at the badly wrapped parcel. 'I think you should give them to him yourself.'

'No. You are the only one I can trust.'

I continued to gaze fascinated, wondering

what the letters contained.

'I would like to entrust them into your safe-keeping,' she said in a rush. 'My Lady suffered so much before she died. It's all in these letters. I know His Lordship was tormented afterwards, but she had such a pitifully short time and I know she loved him, I know she did.'

Once more, I was uneasy and said uncomfortably, 'Very well, Annie. You have said your say. I will make sure that Lord Hallburgh has them as soon as he returns.'

She clutched my hand painfully and urged, 'Lock them away, miss. Make sure as they are safe from the likes of Miss Hallburgh and that Yvette.'

I was shocked and surprised at her vehemence and hurriedly cast about in my mind as to the most suitable place to keep the letters safe until I was able to deliver them to Edmund. Annie, now thoroughly heated and quite beside herself, seemed to be unable to stem the flow of her tirade against Edmund's sister and her personal maid, Yvette. Whatever my private thoughts, I felt it better not to encourage this and instead, tried to soothe her and calm her fears. I persuaded her to finish her tea and return to her own room.

'I shall put these in my drawer, Annie, and rest assured, I shall visit you at your sister's house in Cheapside. You have worked hard and conscientiously for this family and deserve all that retirement has to offer.'

But, as she stood up to go, Annie delivered herself of one last salvo.

'My Lady was all that was sweet and good. She did not deserve to die as she did. It was all the fault of that wicked woman, Caroline Hallburgh. I know.'

On this note, I finally managed to coax her out of my room and rang the bell to have the tea things removed before going to the schoolroom to attend my pupils, who had returned from their outing.

When finally I got back to my room, leaving Sal and Tom to their supper and bed, supervised by the nursery maid, I was horrified to find that the letters had completely disappeared.

I had merely opened the drawer to take out a fresh collar for the morning and, at first, unthinking of anything untoward, I gazed at the space left by the missing papers. I felt for all the world as though they would suddenly re-appear before me. Then I searched every other drawer in the dressing chest, my writing things, under my pillow and even the bed, in a useless expenditure of anxious energy.

I was forced to acknowledge to myself the futility of the search. Lady Catherine's letters were gone; stolen, probably while I was busy with the children. I sat on my bed, sick at heart and with an apprehension which was almost a feeling of doom. Who could possibly have known about them and entered my room with the intention of stealing them? Whoever it was must be at present in this house. My thoughts naturally turned to the sly Yvette and, as I continued to sit lost in thought, my feelings of apprehension gave way to a cold anger.

I felt determined to fathom out this thing. Yvette was always listening at doors, prying into the personal secrets of the staff, constantly reporting back to Caroline Hallburgh. She was capable of entering a room silently and unannounced. She was my first suspect in this. My anger gradually gave way to resolute determination and I hastened to Caroline Hallburgh's boudoir with the intention of confronting her with my suspicions.

Yvette was lurking on the landing and made as if to accost me, but I brushed past her and made haste to her mistress. I ignored her thin-lipped, malevolent stare and continued on my way. After the most perfunctory knock on Caroline Hallburgh's door, I entered her bedroom, uninvited. It was as I thought. Yvette had obviously overheard

Annie's conversation with me and had conveyed the waxed package to her mistress.

Miss Hallburgh was seated under the window in her little wicker chair on wheels, reading Lady Catherine's private letters. Her plump pretty face was almost vulnerable in its naked prurience and she merely glanced up without curiosity as I entered the room. Then taking more note, she glared at me with obvious anger.

'How dare you enter my private room like this?' she demanded icily. 'What can you possibly want which leads you to take such ill-mannered action?'

I felt cold and sick but not at all afraid of her, so I answered boldly, 'Miss Hallburgh, I think you are holding something in your hands which rightly belongs to your brother. I demand to know who removed those letters from my keeping. I can only suppose that Yvette obtained them for you by stealing them from my room.'

Her eyes now assumed a basilisk stare of utter hatred as she glared at me and her porcelain cheek flushed a violent, angry red.

'Kindly leave me, Miss Grey,' she snapped. 'I have no notion of what you mean and shall report this intrusion to my brother when he returns. I hope he will terminate your employment in consequence.'

'Miss Hallburgh,' I demanded again, ignoring the implied threat of her words. 'I wish to know how you obtained that package, which was entrusted to me and which was in a private drawer in my bedroom.'

'Why should I not obtain it?' she demanded. 'Catherine was my sister-in-law. These letters do not belong in your possession.'

She actually screwed one of them up contemptuously and threw it on to the floor.

'But I was the guardian of those letters,' I protested again, 'and I promised to deliver them to Lord Hallburgh.'

I had absolutely no nervous fears of Miss Hallburgh at this moment and stood my ground with my head held high.

'You have somehow got hold of them from my room, I do not know how, but I consider what you have done has violated my own privacy as well that of your late sister-in-law.'

I was now in full spate and in unbridled school ma'am mode as I lectured her as severely as though she were an errant pupil. Her pretty pink face turned from scarlet to puce and she made as if to rise from her chair. But both her hands were clasping the letters, so she was unable to propel herself upwards by the arms and her legs were not strong enough for her to stand unaided.

Her lips were trembling with anger as she said viciously, 'Well, like it or not, Miss Grey. I own them, now. And very pretty reading they make. It is all lies about dear Marcel and myself.'

I felt a pang of relief that the letters contained some sort of apologia for Lady Hallburgh's behaviour.

Aloud, I said, 'I sincerely hope that they will help to explain things in a satisfactory manner to Lord Hallburgh and will help to put right the unhappy doubts that he has had about his wife. I am sure that these doubts were encouraged by your own base insinuations, Miss Hallburgh.'

'You evil doxy!' she screamed, now utterly beside herself. 'You are low and wicked to ingratiate yourself into my brother's household and then to torment a helpless invalid . . .'

'You are not helpless and you are an invalid entirely from your own choice,' I answered calmly. 'I know full well the vindictiveness which drove you to try and destroy the love that Edmund felt for his young wife. May God forgive you for that. But the letters to Annie make things plain to him at least. It will in some measure expiate the unhappy past and lead him to some more contented frame of mind.'

'Contented?' she countered shrilly. 'He will never read her trashy notes. I shall make sure of that.'

I stared in horror as she clutched them to her bosom with those white, beringed hands and made to tear them across.

'You cannot. You must not,' I protested vehemently, but she picked up her slender walking cane and, as I rushed over to her to try and wrest the papers from her, she fetched me a surprisingly powerful blow on the shoulder, which felled me to my knees and made me gasp with pain. But by now, I had a firm grasp of the bundle of letters and I hung on with all the tenacity of a terrier. Already, some of them were beginning to crumple and tear under her grasp. Loose pages began to flutter to the floor while we continued the unseemly struggle in silence. Now Miss Hallburgh attacked my hands with her cane, leaving raised purple weals across my knuckles as she attempted ineffectually, to loosen my grip. She was in the throes of some madness and was not only raining blows on me, but was attempting to rise from her wheelchair.

I staggered weakly to my feet and gave a last desperate tug at the bundle of letters. This, unfortunately, had the effect of catapulting the hapless Miss Hallburgh onto the floor and myself also in a most unladylike heap. To my horror, as Caroline Hallburgh fell forward in this undignified way, I heard an ominous crack as her head hit the floor.

She lay still, now unnaturally pale and, of course, the devoted Yvette chose that exact moment to knock softly at the door and enquire, 'Are you content *madame*? May I get you something?'

She entered the room with her usual gliding walk and screamed loudly at the sight of Caroline Hallburgh lying pale and still, blood oozing from the wound in her head and myself leaning over her.

'*Mon Dieu!*' she exclaimed dramatically. '*Ma pauvre madame. Le docteur, vite!*' and she ran out of the room to try and find the doctor.

I, meanwhile, feeling dazed and shocked, knelt by Caroline Hallburgh, chafing her wrists and forehead. I was trembling uncontrollably. I had never meant such a terrible accident to befall her and was fearful that she might even die. Soon Dr Trabut appeared with Yvette, two footmen and most of the maidservants.

All of them stared at me in silent condemnation, mutely accusing me with wide eyes of an unforgivable assault on a helpless invalid. I knew that there was no use explaining or excusing what had taken place. I stood, guilty in their eyes as almost a murderess. After the first excited hubbub there was complete silence and taking command of my disordered senses, I commanded everyone to leave except the doctor and Yvette, who helped me to get Miss Hallburgh into bed, meanwhile explaining with tight lips that Dr. Abbott was out of town and she had taken the liberty to summon Dr Trabut. I did not demur at this. He knew the patient and was used to attending her in the past. At that moment, I was just grateful for his presence.

Yvette turned on me with the utmost venom and spat out, 'You have killed her, you wicked beast.'

She burst into loud rasping sobs and Dr Trabut motioned to me to take her from the room.

When I returned, Miss Hallburgh's eyes were open and she was no longer unconscious. Doctor Trabut calmly dressed the wound in her head and prepared a draught which he patiently helped her to swallow. She lay back, white and still against the pillows, and in spite of my dislike of him, I thanked him gratefully for his swift response to Yvette's summons.

'No need to fret yourself, Miss Grey,' he

said with his usual knowing smile. 'I am used to Miss Hallburgh and know that she will soon recover from this. But you, my dear . . . you seem very agitated by tonight's episode. Try and get some rest. Summon Miss Hallburgh's personal maid and advise her that the tincture I have left must be administered every two hours. Meanwhile, take yourself to your own bed chamber and have a good night's sleep.'

He handed me a glass of colourless liquid. 'Take this with a small glass of brandy before retiring, Miss Grey,' he said. 'And we shall see what tomorrow may bring.'

In spite of feeling somewhat uncomfortable at going against Edmund's wishes in allowing Marcel Trabut to attend his sister, I had to acknowledge that the effect of his visit had been positive. I saw no one else for the rest of the night and locked the letters in my trunk. I felt absolutely refreshed and rested in the morning and, to my relief, Edmund's own physician, Dr Abbott, visited. It was obvious that he viewed Trabut's visit slightly askance and in his own very gentle and oblique way, he tried to find out how Miss Hallburgh came to fall from her chair.

'You must have pulled her with some force, Miss Grey,' he prompted me.

'No,' I faltered. 'Miss Hallburgh propelled

herself from the chair in her effort to cling on to Lady Hallburgh's private letters, which she was seeking to destroy.'

He also expressed disappointment that Trabut's services had been called upon, but I defended this on the grounds of medical necessity.

'It seems that something more than an argument took place yesterday,' he said, not looking at me.

'Yes, and I am sorry that Yvette had to call on someone who is not approved of by Lord Hallburgh, but she felt that his sister's life was in danger and I was bound to agree with her.'

I told him briefly of the events leading up to Miss Hallburgh's fall and immediately, he became more reassuring.

'You were completely justified, Miss Grey,' he said. 'I was not immediately available and this prompt action probably saved her life, although I know you will have to make your explanations to your employer when he returns. Meanwhile, she is making good progress. I would advise you that she is best left to her personal maid. I will return in the morning. I'll leave this witch hazel for your hands.'

With a kindly smile, he was gone and I was left alone. The children were unusually quiet as though sensing that something was amiss and, for my own part, I dreaded the moment when I would have to face Edmund and offer my explanations.

This came soon enough. That very evening, at seven o' clock when the children were already in bed and I was engaged in bathing the painful bruises on my hands, he arrived at the front door. As usual, he had a mountain of bags and boxes and strode in throwing off his travelling cloak and looking round with his familiar charming smile, to greet whoever was near. Unfortunately, it was the sour Yvette who intercepted him and relayed all the unfortunate events of the previous few days with her usual spiteful relish.

The summons did not come straight away. I had stayed in my room waiting for the interview that I knew was inevitable, reading and trying to stay calm, but finally, despair set in. I lay down fully clothed on my bed, my throbbing hands folded on my breast to try and ease the pain of them and I gave way to feelings of cold apprehension at what lay before me. Hopeless tears of despair started to my eyes and squeezed themselves from beneath my closed eyelids as I thought of the cruel injustices of the world and the misery of my situation at the hands of Caroline Hallburgh.

Then there came the familiar tap on the

door. It was, of course, Yvette, looking pale and strained with the effort of nursing her unpleasant mistress, but triumphant all the same when she saw my tears.

'Lord Hallburgh would like to see you in the library at once,' she said curtly.

I nodded mutely. He had sent for me. I must go to him whom I loved best in the world and face the cold accusations of his sister and her toady. Yvette turned abruptly and went back to her duties, while I took out the dog-eared packet of letters from my trunk and, in some trepidation, went to my interview with Edmund.

16

He was standing by the window but turned and greeted me as I knocked and then entered the room. His glance was polite but cold and I knew I must look a dire fright with my pale face and red eyes.

'My sister is resting at the moment,' he said coldly. 'I have been able to consult Dr Abbott and he will, of course, be attending her on a daily basis.'

I never took my eyes off him as he was speaking. He was as always dressed with the utmost elegance, but his handsome face was as hard as stone and his eyes like chips of flint. Two deep channels had appeared between his brow and at the sides of his mouth. His shapely hands gripped the edge of the polished mahogany desk and he gave me a long sombre stare. His expression was absolutely unforgiving in its cold disdain.

'I wish to know exactly what transpired between my sister and yourself, leading to this unfortunate accident,' he demanded curtly. 'And what was your object in allowing Trabut to attend her? If I had been present he would not have dared presume to enter this house.'

'I must explain . . . ' I faltered. 'You see Dr Abbott was out of town and it was desperately important . . . to . . . get help for Miss Hallburgh.'

'Desperate indeed,' he said with a look of the utmost contempt, and my explanations withered on my dry, nervous lips. I felt quite overcome at the enormity of my present situation and my legs trembled beneath me. I felt I must now collapse under the emotional strain of it all. Edmund seemed to sense this and gave me a longer, closer, scrutiny.

'Sit down, Miss Grey,' he said in a more moderate tone of voice. 'You look all done up. I want you to tell me everything, but you must appreciate that I have come back to an absolute bear garden, which seems to be entirely of your making. I can hardly credit the dreadful injury that my sister has sustained at your hands.'

I stared at the floor hopelessly, still clutching the letters and gulping painfully in an effort to control the tears which threatened once more to engulf me.

He now left his place behind the desk and advanced towards me, saying in a somewhat gentler tone, 'What in the name of Heaven possessed you to attack Caro like that?'

I answered with some spirit. 'You must have been told by now that I dragged your poor crippled sister from her wheeled chair and tried to murder her.'

'Come. Be serious,' he said sternly. 'I expect you lost control and the accident happened in an instant as these things do,' he added with some bitterness.

'And can you believe that of me?' I asked wonderingly.

'Well, hardly. It beggars belief to suspect such an action of my kind friend, Lucy Grey, so you must tell me all and put me straight.'

He seemed marginally less hostile and motioned to me to be seated. For this much, I was thankful, but at that moment, his quicksilver eyes became fixed on my hands.

'But what have you done here?' he asked, momentarily diverted from his sister's concerns. 'What has happened? You have injured yourself.'

'Yes,' I said. 'I sustained my injuries while trying to wrest these letters from Miss Hallburgh.'

I saw his face become even more grim and craggy and the well-remembered pulse began to beat in his cheek.

'And what might this be?' he demanded.

I handed him the packet of letters.

'Lady Hallburgh wrote these to Annie in

316

the month leading up to her death.'

'Yes, I recognize her writing,' he said slowly. 'I was not aware that she wrote to the maid. How came you by them?'

'Annie brought them to me because she is leaving. She begged me to give them to you as she did not want any other person to read them. She has kept them all this time and felt it only right that you should have them.'

'But how came they to be so torn and battered?'

'Your sister ... Miss Hallburgh that is ... she tried to take possession of them. She pulled me to the ground and then ... struck my hands ... with her walking cane, but ... I would not release them ... And in the struggle ... she ... she fell from her chair and struck her head. On my word of honour, Edmund, it was an accident! I swear, I never intended to harm her.'

He stared at me as though seeing me for the first time. His face registered both horror and astonishment.

Then gradually, a more compassionate expression entered those silver-grey eyes and he said softly, 'Upon my word. My darling girl, of course I believe you. I know that Caro can take on at times But your poor injured hands! How could she do this to you? How did you bear it?'

I now weakly surrendered myself to the tears which had been threatening to engulf me all day. I covered my face with the injured hands and wept.

'It was a nightmare. A bad dream,' I sobbed. 'And all the disapproval and blame lies with me! You must know that I . . . I would never deliberately harm . . . a fellow creature. It is not in my nature so to do . . . ' I concluded wildly.

'I know. I know,' he said gently. 'But Dr Abbott was not to know what really happened and, of course, I knew nothing of these letters.'

'No,' I said in a muffled voice. 'Only Annie knew about them.'

'But how did my sister get hold of the wretched things?'

With many hesitations, I recounted how Yvette had overheard Annie talking to me all about it and had been ordered to take the package from my room.

'My God, Lucy,' he said at last in a hushed voice. 'Caro has really shot her bolt this time. I cannot apologize enough for her dishonourable actions. I am at a loss to know why she should do such a thing. I am unable to even hazard a guess as to what it was she did not wish me to read.'

He stood over me now and put a gentle

hand on my shoulder. 'Poor Lucy. How devastating for you. I see that the incident was not of your making. But why did you feel that a lady's trivial correspondence with her maidservant could be of such import?'

'It . . . it . . . implicates Dr Trabut and Miss Hallburgh in the problems that . . . that . . . your wife was having,' I replied, haltingly. 'I have not read them, but Annie told me the letters would reveal the truth of what really happened.'

I covered my face again, unable to contain my sobs and suddenly, he sat by me and drew me into his arms, patting my shoulder gently and whispering as though to a distraught child.

'Hush, my poor Lucy. Try to compose yourself. You have been so brave and so terribly hurt for your efforts to save Catherine's wretched letters.'

At this, I gave way totally and pressed myself against him, sobbing unrestrainedly against his shoulder. To his credit, he allowed this assault on his fashionable jacket to last for some seconds until I gradually managed to pull myself together. Then he put me from him very gently and took up the tattered bundle of letters which he proceeded to glance through, at first casually and then with increasing concentration, his brows a black line and his eyes as cold as ice. He began to read aloud:

Mar. 15th: My dear Annie
I trust your sister is somewhat better. We are missing you here. Colonel and Mrs Ealing came for dinner last evening and afterwards we went to the theatre. The enjoyment was ruined by Caro, who as you know, insists on showing her petty hatred of me when we are alone, but is careful to be all honey when Edmund is near. I am so afraid that she is out to harm me. I know that she is jealous of my love for Edmund and feels that he rightly belongs to her. She has done so much for him in the past, but Edmund loves me. I am sure of it, so why do I feel so frightened?

He stopped reading. 'What a lonely voice comes from these pages,' he said quietly. 'Caro was obviously persecuting Catherine with her jealousy, as she had you. I understand it now. But at the time, Lucy, it was so difficult for me to believe any base motives on Caroline's part. She had always been so good, so loving to me, you see. She was my mother and father rolled into one. A wonderful sister who understood and loved me unconditionally when I was left an orphan with no one to turn to. I felt and still do, that I owed her a debt of gratitude for her love and care, that I can never repay.'

'But she has no need to be jealous of me,' I cried. 'What possible reason could she have?'

He said nothing but gave me a deeply penetrating look and turned over two or three more pages. I stood up with an effort.

'If you will forgive me, I will go to my room,' I said. 'It is not proper that I should listen to the reading of your wife's private letters. Pray excuse me.'

'No,' he said firmly, and with such ferocity that I immediately sat down again and remained where I was.

'You shall listen, because, Lucy, it is obvious that my sister and the evil Trabut have attempted to ensnare you, just as they did poor Catherine. Now, with hindsight, I realize what terrible pressures Catherine had to bear, and she so young and only recently delivered of her second child.'

I continued to sit mute while he read on. The love of his young wife and her obvious devotion to her children, shone out of those pages like a beacon, as did her innocence and naïve charm. He read a paragraph from the next letter, which was dated 26th March, a.m.

Dear Annie

*Marcel told me today how pretty I am
and that I can turn any man's head.
There seem to be so many men in
London who are content to have their
heads turned and to declare themselves
in love. I own, I am glad to be happy
married and settled down . . . '*

'Yes, he was right,' he said slowly. 'She had
the power to attract men like the proverbial
bees round a honey pot. But there was no
harm in her. I should have spent less time on
the damned estate business and more time
with my young family. What a fool I was.' He
sighed and began again.

March 26th, noon:
Dear Annie

*I am missing you. Caro has been with
us for weeks now and shows no sign of
leaving. I find it such a burden that she
is still here, so long after the birth of
Thomas. I was foolish enough to ask her
intentions in this direction yesterday, but
she insists that she is too weak to move
away from the medical care that she can
get in London. I expect she means Dr
Trabut, who as you know, constantly
dances attendance on her and encourages*

322

her pose of chronic ill-health. She is so clever at getting her talons into my darling husband and I know he will always see her as the pretty, helpless invalid, who was kind to him after the death of his mama. She has warned me not to come between her and Edmund, or I shall live to regret it. I know I can never confide these things to my husband. He would never believe me. May God forgive me, but I have to acknowledge that she is an evil witch, with the beautiful appearance of an angel, while Marcel Trabut is an out and out devil. Between them, they will be the death of me.'

Even Edmund seemed startled at these words. His face expressed the pain and shock of this last revelation and he looked up from his reading in obvious discomfiture.

'My God,' he said. 'The scales are certainly falling from my eyes at these revelations. My poor Catherine. How she must have suffered. And yet, Catherine never voiced her fears to me. She seemed always to be quite sanguine at my sister's presence in the house and my frequent absences from home. She must have gone through hell.'

'But what courage and loyalty she showed,' I answered him.

'How true,' he said in a soft voice. 'And how obtuse I must have been to suspect nothing of this.'

'How could you suspect?' I responded indignantly. 'You were not to know what was happening. Perhaps I should withdraw,' I suggested again. 'I cannot be of any assistance here.'

'No,' he said decisively. 'You must stay, Lucy. I want you to know everything. After all, you have also suffered at Caro's hands. Please stay and hear the truth of it.'

Listening to his voice as he read on was almost unbearable, as the words of the tragic young woman were poignantly revealed.

March 30th:

My dear Annie

I am so lonely while you are at your sister's and Edmund is now away on estate concerns. Only the children are warm to me. Caro and I are polite enemies and I am much perturbed at the way she is attending Sarah — always petting her and spoiling her. She gives me triumphant glances as she gains moral influence over my little Sal, while making demeaning remarks about baby

Thomas. I cannot find this suitable behaviour in a fond aunt and yet, I know that Edmund will never understand if I try and explain my fears. He will merely dismiss it as 'women's concerns'. At least I have you, dear kind Annie, to confide in . . . '

'It is true,' he groaned despairingly. 'But I always thought that having my beloved sister in attendance, after the birth of Thomas, would be a comfort and a support to my dear Catherine. I mistakenly imagined that these sort of nervous fears were a natural aftermath of childbirth and could best be coped with by the companionship of another woman. Caroline seemed so good, so loving, I always thought that she was a warm friend for my young wife. I never guessed at Catherine's desperate unhappiness.'

April 2nd:
My dear Annie
Edmund is still away, My tormentor continues to turn the screw. It is unbearable. If only my dear mama were still alive. I would fly to her and take my babes with me.

Edmund continued impassively.

April 2nd p.m.:
Dear Annie

Dr Trabut is very smooth and polished. He seems to know exactly how to handle Caro. His charm is lost on me, but he can be very amusing and flattering. Caro has invited us to attend an assembly ball this evening and he is most gallant in his attentions.

April 6th:
Dear Annie

Caro's mood seems set fair at the moment. She has said that she wants to be more understanding and that she recognizes the solitariness of my situation, alone here with the children and my husband preoccupied and busy. It is true that I am often alone and somewhat sad without you, Annie, but I question her motives in criticizing Edmund's frequent absences.

'It is obvious that she even tried to set my own wife against me,' he said bitterly. 'She, who I thought was utterly above reproach and who, in the past, had loved and cared for me like a second mama. She, who was so kind and attentive to me all through my long, lonely childhood. I can hardly credit her cruelty.'

I made no reply and he went on:

April 7th:
Dear Annie
Edmund is still in Leicestershire, but I am quite lively. Marcel invited the children and myself to Vauxhall Gardens and we took the nursery maid with us. We had a most wonderful day. Last evening, Caro invited him for dinner and afterwards, he made an opportunity to be alone with me in the drawing-room. He tried to kiss me and openly declared his love for me. I was terribly shocked, and told him it must never happen again. When I told Caro what had happened, she laughed and said that many sophisticated ladies of the ton seek comfort and distraction in mild flirtation.

'Absent husbands, my dear Catherine, can make lonely wives. Why should you not seek a little pleasure? After all, it harms no one and can be very enjoyable.'

She is certainly putting herself out to arrange many little visits and pleasures for Marcel and me. My head tells me I should not allow his friendship and yet, Caro seems to think it is harmless and I confess he is all that is amiable and cheers me with his company.

I did not venture to look at Edmund's face. It must be unbearably painful to go on reading and yet he seemed determined to accept all the blame for the unhappy past.

Oh my dear love, I thought. If only I could love you and comfort you and make this pain go away.

'An absent husband is always a source of trouble,' he mused as though to himself. 'And yet I thought she seemed so content and children always fulfil a woman, do they not? Why was I so crass as not to know that she needed more? And why did I not recognize that Caroline's love and devotion to me had over the years, turned into a bitter and twisted obsession?'

Oh, my darling Edmund, I thought sadly. You are not crass but perhaps were blind and yet, if I were your true wife, I would have been fulfilled no matter how neglectful you were.

Thursday:
Dear Annie
How are things at Cheapside? Please send good news of your sister's health, so I

may look forward to your return. Edmund will be back on Monday and we are engaged to dine with Mr and Mrs Neill the following week. Marcel has not visited for some days and Caro insists that it is all my doing. 'You are so cold and distant,' she says. 'Poor Marcel feels your lack of friendship keenly and is too hurt to visit us'.

She hints that he is wildly in love with me and that I must pen him a little note to make all well again.

Saturday:
Dear Annie

What a cruel schemer Caro is. What a weak and foolish idiot I am. I wrote Marcel a note at her instigation, expressing disappointment and regret at his continued absence, just as she wished and the effect was instant. He responded immediately and again, she made sure we were alone. He at once clasped me in his arms and pressed his lips to mine in a fever of passion and desire. For a few moments only, I wavered on the brink of being untrue to my marriage vows and to the dear husband who loves me, as my weak flesh responded to Marcel's ardent embrace and I pressed myself against *him. I felt my craven body welcoming the hardness of his own in a surge of sensual longing. For a wild moment, it was in me to throw caution to the winds and become the mistress of this charming man, who is such an ardent and skilful wooer. Only a still small voice of calm held me back. My self-respect. My love for my dear husband. My fear of losing forever my darling children and lastly, the cool, clear realization that my evil sister-in-law had planned and executed the means of my ruin in the most callous way. I drew back from the abyss to which she had led me and thanked God that I had seen my foolishness and her wicked intent in time.*

Edmund's face was now etched in stone, his eyes dull and grey, the hands holding this letter shaking uncontrollably. I bent over him and put out my hand in a vain attempt to stem his agitation.

'Please,' I begged him. 'Do not read more. This is too much.'

'No,' he snarled, like an animal in pain. 'No. It was my own blindness which prevented me from seeing what was happening. My own stupidity in not taking care to stop Caro hurting her.'

April 14th
Dear Annie

I must confess to you that my life is no longer of any value to me. I am a thing of no import and I realize now that Caroline Hallburgh has ruined me. She was waiting for me in her little wicker chair, outside in the hall, when Marcel attempted his seduction of me. They both laughed as she informed me that Edmund would hear of everything when he returns. In vain, I pleaded the fact that I had resisted temptation and remained true to my marriage. I even tried to enlist him in my defence, to assure Edmund that nothing had taken place except for a few indiscreet kisses. Marcel merely laughed and said it would be worth a few thousand pounds from Milord to keep His Lordship's humiliation quiet. He suggested that he needed the money to settle his debts at the gaming tables. Caroline also laughed, 'And, of course, you will lose your children after Edmund has banished you. But rest assured, my poor Catherine, I will bring up Sarah and Thomas as though they were my own.' My shame and humiliation are complete. Even if you were now here with me, I would wish only to die before Edmund returns home.

He stood up abruptly and moved back to the desk. The skin on my face was taut with the tears I had shed during the course of his reading. My heart was pounding with a wildly irregular beat and I was finding it difficult to keep my hands still. I forced myself to hold them on my lap as the silence continued. I did not trust myself to look at him until at last he spoke, in a defeated and leaden voice, completely uncharacteristic of his usual tone.

'Catherine insisted on taking out Bounty Hunter against Baxter's advice. It was as though she no longer cared what happened to her. She was found two hours later and Bounty, riderless, was cropping the grass nearby. She had obviously ridden like a mad thing in the two acre wood and been thrown off the horse. Her neck was broken. They as good as murdered her, my sister and Trabut. Hounded her to her death.'

He clenched his fist and punched the palm of his other hand in a futile gesture of frustration and anger.

'My own sister,' he ground out.

He looked so utterly despairing that I jumped up and moved towards him to try and offer some comfort.

'You cannot know that,' I cried. 'It could have been an accident. Baxter said that the horse was too high spirited to be a suitable mount for a lady.'

At the sight of his grey, hollow expression, I faltered to a halt. 'Oh Edmund,' I pleaded. 'What is past is done. Please do not let these people hurt you any more. Let your poor Catherine rest in peace. Those two little children are the future now.'

But he was implacable. 'Caroline caused her death as surely as if she had murdered her with her bare hands,' he persisted, and his mouth was mulishly determined. 'And that evil charlatan, Trabut, colluded in her final destruction. He should be wiped off the face of the earth.'

'Oh Edmund, please,' I begged him, unable to bear the expression on his face. 'Let it rest. Illness does strange things to people and Miss Hallburgh has been an invalid for a very long time. Can you not forgive her?'

'No,' he said harshly. 'I cannot. It may be that her illness has affected Caro's mind. She was not always like this. In days gone by she was a good and lively companion, a loving sister, a beautiful young woman, in spite of her physical impairment. God knows how she came to be so malevolent to my poor young wife. No, I cannot forgive and forget. Catherine was a naïve and vulnerable young girl. She was no match for two cunning players such as Caroline and Trabut. She may have been weak and easily led, but she did not deserve to be destroyed at the age of twenty-six by the neglect of her husband and the wickedness of her sister-in-law. I tell you, Lucy, I shall not be responsible for my actions if I should meet up with Trabut. As for Caro, I do not trust myself to interview her. After Catherine's . . . accident, she had the . . . the . . . wicked effrontery to insinuate that Catherine had galloped off to some clandestine meeting. At the time . . . I . . . thought . . . I thought it was an attempt to console me for the loss of a young and pretty wife. What a fool I was. I owe Catherine a deep debt of apology for my suspicions of her. I was even gullible enough to have her portrait removed. Well, now I have made a decision to have Caroline removed — from my house and from my life, forever. From tomorrow, she will be gone. I shall send the children to the country and go abroad for a while. The London house can be closed. It holds too many unhappy memories.'

For the first time he looked into my eyes. 'As for you, Lucy,' he said, 'I would like to thank you for your steady faith in my poor dead wife. You are, as always, as steadfast as a rock, my own dear Miss Grey.'

And to my astonishment, he squared his

handsome shoulders, took me very firmly in his arms and kissed me on the lips. I had a fleeting understanding of the plight of the poor young Catherine Hallburgh when she was afraid to respond to the passion engendered by the unspeakable Trabut. For I was constrained at returning his kiss by the tremendous warmth I felt for him and remained passively in his arms, longing to express the strength of my love for him and at the same time, afraid to display a hunger for more kisses that he might not wish to give.

He released me eventually and we stood for a few breathless moments looking at each other, before he said finally, with an attempt at calmness, 'It is very late. Tomorrow is another day and we shall have a lot to do, so be off to bed with you now. You are tired and weary. I shall speak to you in the morning.'

I went reluctantly to my room, sick at heart with all the undischarged emotions which I felt for him. If Edmund Hallburgh was determined to hide his anger and humiliation by leaving the country, there was little I could do about it. I had had no opportunity to release any of my pent-up hunger for love and passion with the man I adored. Once he had gone to live abroad, my love was doomed to failure and without any future; I decided it could lead only to my own humiliation and rejection. Even my love for his children came second to the wild despair that I now felt at the thought of his apparent cowardice in running away from the unhappy past. Before I prepared for bed, I resolved to leave London forever. I, too, would run away from a situation that I could not control. Tomorrow, I would rise early and be away before anyone was awake.

17

My departure from the unhappy splendours of life in Melbury House was accomplished with the discreet help of the dignified coachman, Baxter. As I lay in bed that night, I determined to seek out the groom and beg a lift to the Angel Inn, where I might take the stage coach back to Wembeck. Then I agonized over those two dear children and wondered how they would react when they knew I had left them. Unable to rest, I rose from my bed once more, this time to write several notes, before I was at last satisfied that I had explained gently, my reasons for leaving. Except of course, that I could not tell them the real reason for my departure. My hopeless unrequited love for their father and the misery inflicted on me by their aunt and her loathsome accomplices were secrets which would forever be locked in my heart. I packed my box and prepared to leave Melbury House forever. Then I lay down and tried to sleep, only succeeding in drifting into a restless uneasy slumber when the light of day was already beginning to filter in through the window.

I tiptoed downstairs as soon as I heard the longcase clock strike six. I knew that Baxter would be in the main stable block, getting the horses ready for the lads and I hurried across the yard to seek him out. He looked up in some surprise as I entered the tack-room in my travelling cloak and bonnet.

'Why, Miss Grey,' he said pleasantly. 'You are up and about early, miss, and look like you are dressed for a journey.'

He was obviously questioning my intentions in a very polite and respectful way. Immediately, I answered without any attempt at subterfuge. I confided in him my intention of returning home urgently and without the knowledge or consent of my employer.

'For you must know, George,' I went on, 'I wish to go at once and do not seek to put His Lordship or Miss Hallburgh to any trouble on my account. I have some money and wish you to escort me to the Angel, where I may get the stage-coach.'

He looked at me doubtfully, saying nothing, but when I attempted to press some coins into his hand, he refused them, saying gently, 'Nay, keep your money, miss. You will happen as like, need it and it is a pleasure to be of service to such a kind gentlewoman as yourself. I can take you where you want to go, but are you quite sure as you are doing right,

Miss Grey? Will you be met at your journey's end, ma'am?'

I answered quickly, 'I shall be perfectly comfortable, and as for my destination, I am sure there will be others who are travelling my way.'

I was so eager to reassure him of the soundness of my decision, that I hurriedly skirted over my own doubts about travelling back to Wembeck alone. I said nothing either of the dread fear I felt at facing my Aunt Esther, or how I was going to manage to live in Dibden Cottage, alone and with no visible means of support. As for Baxter, he said no more but harnessed up the horses and lowered the steps of the coach. He helped me in with his usual grave courtesy and handed up my small pieces of luggage. Then we were off.

I had little time to reflect on the enormity of my actions. Baxter whipped up the horses and we drove swiftly to the Angel. We were both silent as we bowled along the almost deserted streets to the staging post and for this I was grateful. When we reached the inn, the coach was already drawn up in the yard and a sprinkling of passengers stood about while others were already aloft with the baggage. I ascended from the carriage in the early morning air and bade farewell to George Baxter.

'Good fortune, miss,' he said, as he handed me my box. 'You are a right good 'un, Miss Grey, and them little childer will miss you sorely.'

It was all I could do to prevent the tears from springing to my eyes, but I managed to shake his hand and then turned to see if I could procure a seat inside. Once this was accomplished, the groom waved his whip in a gesture of farewell and set off back to Melbury House, while I clambered aboard the coach and settled down for my long homeward journey. I had made no provision as to any refreshments or breakfast and was forced to stay in the coach when it stopped at the first stage, the ground being too filthy and muddy with dung for us to alight.

But at the next coaching inn I had a little meat with bread and took a small cup of coffee to last me until such time as I should get back to Dibden Cottage, so the next stage of my journey was fairly comfortable. The moon was riding high in a cloudless sky when the stage finally arrived at the Crown in Wembeck. The exhausted passengers picked up their belongings and stumbled from the coach. Two were met by a rustic cart, but the rest, like myself, wended their weary way across the fields, or along the lanes by the light of the moon, to their own home village or hamlet.

I set off alone across country towards home, keeping to the well-worn path by Squire Pembleton's two acre field and at three in the morning, footsore and exhausted, I finally arrived at Dibden Cottage. The night clouds had now banked up and the moon was momentarily obscured as I clicked open the wicket gate and crept wearily along the narrow path. I was quite exhausted with the emotional turmoil of the last few days, and the long and taxing journey on the public stage-coach had worn my already ragged nerves to shreds. I stumbled haltingly up to the door.

The familiar, miserable squat cottage, with its straggling growth of ivy and air of brooding neglect was as cold and unwelcoming as ever, but I put down my meagre baggage and sought under the stones for the big iron key and pushed it into the scarred and bleached old door.

But never mind the lack of welcome, or the cold, abject poverty of the untenanted dwelling; it was home and for a few moments I searched near the hearth for the tinder-box and a stub end of wax candle. In a few seconds, the moon reappeared and cast her cold light through the small grimy window and I was able to discount the bleak misery of the pathetic hovel, feeling only relief from the anguish of the last few days. My fingers were still stiff and painful where Caroline Hallburgh's walking cane had punished them, but I managed to light my candle and sank gratefully into a chair and removed my bonnet. I paused there for some minutes while I tried to collect myself and achieve a calmer frame of mind. Only gradually did my breathing became more even and my body more relaxed, as I continued to sit in the cold and dismal room. It was far too late to think of getting kindling and lighting a fire, so I merely kicked off my muddy boots and went upstairs. Wrapping my travelling cloak tightly around me, I lay on the damp, musty-smelling bed to wait for the morning.

Miraculously, I slept until the burning sun streamed through the stained and misted window and the birds had begun their early morning songs. I felt somewhat renewed by my deep sleep and was much cheered by such lovely sights and sounds as these. Even though the memories of the last few miserable days of my existence crowded in on me, they were not sufficient to dampen my spirits entirely. I told myself sternly that I

must make the best of whatever circumstances fate decreed. Taking the old iron
bucket from the corner of the scullery
determinedly in my hand, I went to draw
water from the well and looked around in the
lane for some twigs to use as kindling. The
last of William's late potatoes were still stored
in sand in a hessian sack, just as he had left
them, so I resolved to buy some milk and
butter from one of my neighbours and eat as
best I could. I washed my face and tidied my
hair before setting off on the twenty-minute
walk along the rutted cart track to the Widow
Chantry's cottage. She had a cow and a pig
and I was sure of being able to buy a jug of
milk and a pat of her churned butter. The sun
was now out in full splendour and, as I
approached her cottage, I was met by four
ragged children who all pressed around me in
various states of dirty cheerfulness. As I
strode towards her house they surged towards
me as one, as soon as they saw me. They all
looked nourished, with fine straight limbs,
and all smiled shyly and charmingly as I
handed over my jug and asked how they did.

'Oh, middling, thank you, Miss Grey,' said
their mother, wiping her hands on her
voluminous white apron. 'But what of you?
What are you doing back at Dibden Cottage?
We all thought as how you had obtained a

position in London.'

I hesitated and then said, 'It has ended earlier than expected and I returned home last night.'

She said no more, but it was brought home to me at that moment that I must brace myself for the dreaded interview with my aunt, or she would be bound to hear of my disgrace at second hand from one of the village gossips. Just for now though, I took my milk and butter and prepared to hurry back to the cottage. The good wife had even put two new-laid eggs into my basket, while waving away my attempts to pay for them. I gratefully took my leave of her and carried everything back home.

Once there, I swept out all the cobwebs and mouse droppings from the floor and washed the tiny windows, thinking all the while of Sarah and Thomas and wondering how they did, while I made everything as clean and habitable as I could. Once the fire was lit, I looked in the flour crock and picked out the weevils before making some herb scones in my oven and preparing a warming pan to air the bed. If only William were here, I thought longingly. He might have been able to snare a rabbit or a pigeon to go with the potatoes. I sighed, and resolved to write to him that very evening and to my Aunt Esther also. Delay could only add to the unpleasant scene that I was sure would follow when she learned of my return. My meagre savings would not last long and my aunt and uncle would no doubt wash their hands of me when they knew that I had left Melbury House of my own free will. I knew I would have to seek another position or starve. This time, though, it would have to be through my own efforts. Perhaps I would be able to obtain something through an agency; possibly I would have to set my sights lower and take on the position of abigail or companion to some wealthy, aged dame, who would not be nearly as gracious as my darling Edmund. I squared my shoulders. Now that I had gained the confidence to travel alone on the stage-coach, I thought, I could go anywhere and do anything, almost. Whatever I did, it would not stop me from thinking constantly of Edmund and why he had kissed me and seemed to want closeness, only to reject me and put me from him.

As I proceeded with my household tasks, Sarah and Tom were also very much in my thoughts and tears pricked the back of my eyelids as I wondered what they were doing. Had they managed to read my brief note? Had someone else read it for them? Miss Hallburgh? Their father? I wondered if he would ever understand how desperate I had felt when I left Melbury House for the last time. Perhaps the beautiful Harriet Marland would be the kind and pretty new mama, so longed for by little Sarah.

Then I tried to shake off these melancholy thoughts and I sat down to write to William. After all, I had chosen to leave. I had not been dismissed and had done nothing wrong. If there was a God in Heaven, surely justice would prevail and I would be able to find other employment where I could be content, if not happy?

The letter to my aunt and uncle was somewhat harder to write than I had imagined and I drafted it two or three times before I was satisfied that it explained my actions, even though it was very brief and to the point. When I went for more milk tomorrow, I would give it to one of the Chantry children to deliver to my aunt by hand.

My supper was of buttered potatoes and herb scones washed down with the last drop of milk, and I was in very low spirits as I extinguished my candle and went to my cold and lonely bed. I felt my situation was absolutely dire. I had parted irrevocably from the only man I could ever love. The two children would still be unsettled and upset at my absence and I knew that even my dear Wills would find my actions hard to understand. I was uneasy that night, as I tried to compose myself for slumber. But the next afternoon brought events so unexpected and momentous as to shock me into feelings of utter horror and panic.

I was preparing to set off for the Chantry farm and was engaged in dressing my hair as neatly as I could and arranging a clean collar to the front of my faded print gown, when there was a knock on the door which then burst open suddenly to reveal, of all people, Marcel Trabut!

My arms were suspended in mid air as I added another comb to keep in check the back curls which were now rather over long, and my startled gaze met the slightly mocking eyes of my tormentor. In that instant, I realized who it was and my heart gave a sudden lurch which sickened me and made me feel faint and weak. I stared at him speechlessly, but there was no way that he was lost for words of course.

He entered confidently, smoothing back the dark hair at his temples and giving me the benefit of his oily smile. As he confronted me, I had a mad desire to run away, as far from the cottage as possible, but somehow, I will never know how, he had managed to extract the big old iron key from its hook and had locked the door behind him. For the first time since I had met Marcel Trabut, I felt in real danger, a danger which I was unable to avoid and that I felt might even cost me my life.

I recognized in him a lack of any moral restraint, particularly where women were concerned, and remembering Edmund's warnings about him, I felt terribly afraid. In the comparative security of Melbury House where Miss Hallburgh was very firmly in control, the worst that this odious toad could do was to try and steal the odd sly kiss, but in the isolated depths of the country, I was far more vulnerable. Apart from the Widow Chantry, no one knew I was here and from the way he was looking at me, Dr Trabut's intentions were certainly less than honourable. I strove to remain calm, but my pulse was racing and my breathing ragged. I felt my face burning. We were so close that I could see his faintly yellowed eyeballs and distended nostrils. His mouth was twisted into a cynical smile and he immediately began to torment me, in his well-remembered way.

'Ah, Miss Grey,' he murmured with mock politeness. 'Well met, my dear. What can have brought you to the delicious seclusion of Dibden Cottage, I wonder?'

I tried to suppress my fear and remain

calm, looking about me for any possible means of escape, but there was none. He read my mind and gave another cruel smile.

'No, my dear Lucy, there is no escape. We are quite alone and will not be disturbed.'

'What do you want from me?' I panted, my eyes staring with the force of my indignation. 'Open the door at once. I do not wish you to trespass in this way.'

'In what way?' he laughed mockingly. 'What is trespass? There is no one who will believe that you did not willingly invite me into your home. In the eyes of polite society, I am merely a welcome visitor at the house of my beloved. We are fond lovers and must come to some arrangement about our situation, Lucy. I think that tomorrow, we should be wed by special licence.'

Overcome by revulsion and panic, I made a rush towards the window, but he was too quick for me. Grasping my wrists, he pulled me towards him and began trying to kiss me.

'Yes, we will be married, at last, my dear. You will be so pleased if I make an honest woman of you. Your little airs and graces will have completely disappeared after a night of love and romance with Dr Trabut.'

'Get away from me,' I screamed, struggling desperately against his loathsome embrace. 'You disgust me, you hateful charlatan. I would never marry you if you were the last man on earth.'

'Oh, yes, you would,' he said triumphantly. 'And you must count yourself lucky that I am offering you the respectability of a wedding ring. No less a person than Miss Hallburgh is prepared to pay for our nuptials and make a financial settlement on you, in order to keep her precious brother from your side, of course. She is sure there will be no hesitation on your part, for you must know, my dear, that there will be no possibility of another post as governess for a young woman who has run away with the French doctor. It will be all over London in a few days. I have taken care to leave a note on your pillow, *cherie*, to say that you love me passionately and cannot live without me. Come. What do you say? To be Madame Trabut is no bad thing, *n'est ce pas?*'

He began to press heavy kisses to the inside of my arm and then my neck, while he repeated his disgusting suggestions. My reply was to twist sideways and bend my head to bite one of the hands which was clamped around my wrist.

This drew blood and with a muffled oath he removed the other hand to clasp the one that was injured. I was thus able to make a dash for the stairs and ran up as though I had wings. Although he chased after me, I had the advantage and drew the big black bolts across the old pine door and then puffed and panted until I had dragged the wash stand in front. Finally, I piled the bedroom chair and my trunk on top of the washstand. Then I stood back trembling, as he hurled himself against my door, again and again, cursing and blaspheming all the while.

Finally, there was silence, but I knew it was only a temporary respite. I would have to come out of the bedroom eventually and unless he grew tired and went back to London, I was a prisoner in Dibden Cottage for as long as he cared to keep me here.

Cautiously, I peered out of the small window. I could see clearly Marcel Trabut's chaise in the lane, with the horses snorting gently as they pawed the ground and I wondered if I could climb out of the window and drive away before he realized it. I looked down doubtfully at the sparse growth of ancient ivies, covering the cottage wall. There seemed no strong foot holds or opportunities for a safe descent from my bedroom window and I withdrew into my room in despair. As the evening shadows lengthened and there was still no sound from Trabut. I first sat on the bed and then rested my head wearily on the pillow. Before I knew it, I was fast asleep.

I awoke in the grey light of dawn. The church clock struck five and I lay for a few more moments on my bed while I recollected my whereabouts and the events of the night before. There was no sound and no sign of the chaise either and very cautiously, I began to remove the furniture from in front of my door. I made frequent pauses, but there was no stirring from downstairs and finally, as silently as I could, I drew back the bolts and crept to the top of the stairs. There was still no sound. Perhaps he had gone. I descended on tiptoe, feeling my way, inch by inch, in the early dawn gloom, and then I heard the sound of snoring. I paused at the bottom of the stairs, holding my breath in an agony of indecision. Perhaps I would still be able to get out of the cottage without waking him. But where was the key? It was too big to go into his pocket. Last night he had placed it on the shelf over the fireplace. Was it still there?

I started cautiously across the floor towards the fireplace. He was wrapped in his greatcoat and lying full out in front of the dead fire. My heart gave a leap as, through the dim light, I discerned the great key, still on the shelf where he had left it. Carefully, I began to make my way towards it.

All of a sudden, he leapt up and dragged me to the ground. The elaborate snores had been a pretence and now I was trapped, pinned to the floor by the weight of his body and utterly helpless. He pinioned my arms above my head and, being the cur he was, he immediately began to gloat, wishing me to beg for mercy. I, meanwhile, refused to do anything so cowardly and instead, looked towards the shelf above the fireplace. The key tormented me. It was still there, but I had no chance of recovering it and effecting an escape. His face was very close to my own and with his breath on my cheek, he began to speak in a low rapid tone of the riches which would be lavished on us by Caroline Hallburgh just as soon as we were married.

'And then, my dear, we shall want for nothing. We will be able to live in La Belle Paris and enjoy the rest of our lives together.'

He felt my body shudder at this thought and, immediately, his expression turned ugly.

'Do not seek to thwart me, Lucy or it will be the worse for you,' he said curtly. 'Now come, give your betrothed a loving kiss. Tomorrow we will be man and wife, but tonight, I shall show you how a real woman can love. Tonight will be ours, Lucy. Just for the two of us, my dear.'

I turned my head aside, squirming to try and avoid his loathsome moist kisses and at that moment, we both froze at the sound of a loud and thunderous knocking on the door.

'Open up. I am a magistrate and will produce a warrant for your arrest if you do not open the door immediately!'

The demand was made with the full force and authority of the Law. It was Edmund Hallburgh.

Trabut let go of me immediately and sprang to his feet at once, standing trembling and indecisive. Then suddenly, he snatched the key from the shelf and ran to the door. I stood up more slowly and, as I turned towards my deliverer, Trabut unlocked the door and made a rush past Edmund, racing away before anyone could stop him.

Edmund seemed hardly to notice. Tossing aside his gloves and greatcoat, he strode into the room and grasped me roughly by the shoulders, almost shaking me with the force of his passionate anger. He was stern-faced as I had never seen him before and I recognized in him the same quality of wild ungovernable passion which drove both his sister and young daughter.

My pulse was pounding as we confronted one another and I could smell the faint lemon balm of his skin as he thrust his face close to mine.

'What do you mean by this, Lucy? What in heaven's name were you about to leave us unannounced, like that? Do you realize how worried I was when that idiot Baxter admitted that he had taken you to the stage-coach?

'I felt I could stay no longer,' I faltered. 'You were first kind and then cold towards me. I . . . had . . . no place in your life. I . . . I . . . left a note for the children. To . . . to . . . explain.'

'Yes,' he said grimly. 'And Yvette brought me the note which she found on your pillow, informing me that the man you had run off with was none other than that scoundrel, Trabut.'

'But this is not true. I would never do such a thing.'

'So you have not agreed to marry Trabut?'

'No. Certainly not,' I cried, with a return to my old spirit. 'I did not run off with him . . . nor would I. How can you think such a thing?'

And I glared at him so fiercely that the ghost of his old smile returned to the grim mouth and he said more gently, 'She also informed me that Trabut is already married — to her! — and has been for the last five years. What a scrape for you to get into.'

'I . . . I . . . did not . . . know this.' I protested miserably. 'I did not write that letter. Doctor Trabut must have written it himself. He . . . he said that Miss Hallburgh had offered him a handsome dowry if he could . . . would . . . marry me, but I refused.'

'Yes,' he said grimly. 'But have no fear, the would-be bigamist will be intercepted by the Watch when he returns to London and will be committed to prison.'

He relaxed his grip and his voice softened somewhat as he said in a more conciliatory tone, 'The two children are crying and inconsolable since you left and there is nothing to be done with them. You must return to London forthwith and marry me. I will brook no refusal.'

I wanted to protest at his high-handed attitude and drew a deep breath, but found it strangely difficult to speak.

Edmund continued in the same soft tone, 'I have loved you since the first moment I saw you. You are all that I want and long for. Now that the misery of the past is behind me I want the future to be ours.'

'But you seemed so changeable,' I said wonderingly. 'First so affectionate and then so distant, as though you wished to escape from everything by your constant travelling abroad. I never dreamt that you could care for me.'

'I know,' he said gently. 'But I felt it very dishonourable of me to offer love to one so young and unspoilt as yourself, whilst I was still dogged by my unhappy memories. Of course, Caroline fed my guilt and doubts about Catherine's death all the time and you are right, I did need to keep escaping from the misery which haunted me. In spite of your obvious warmth, I . . . I . . . began to think that you could never look on me in that way and that I would be doomed to loneliness.'

With the utmost tenderness, he drew me closer to him and whispered, 'Then, when I found you were gone and it seemed I was about to lose you for ever . . . Oh, Lucy, my darling girl, I realized that if I had you, I would never be lonely again. Do you not see that I love only you? Can you not love me in return? Just a little?'

I was quite disarmed by this vulnerability and tried to reply, but could not. Instead, I stood within the safety and warmth of his arms, trying to control my rapid breathing and the frantic pounding of my heart, my eyes returning his passion.

'Yes,' I finally managed. 'Yes. I love you desperately, my darling Edmund.'

My half-dressed hair was hanging in limp, untidy strands against my cheeks; my eyes were full of tears, but I did not care. I raised my eager lips to his and we exchanged a kiss more full of love and desire than I could ever have dreamed of.

'I want you to be with me always, Lucy. Please say that you will marry me and make us all happy.'

Then, with a return to his old teasing manner, he added, 'After all, your reputation as a respectable schoolroom dragon will be utterly ruined, when we finally return to London alone, in my private carriage.'

I began to feel strangely unreal and light-headed. Even now, I doubted the happiness being offered to me. I kept my eyes on his as I asked, wonderingly, 'Can you truly wish to marry me, Edmund? I believed you were about to be engaged to Mrs Marland. I thought you would be seeking someone such as she, who is much more your equal. I never imagined that you could care for someone such as myself.'

'Marry Harriet? No, Lucy. Caroline made it her life's work to try and draw us together, but she was wasting her time. Now that the demon of my unhappiness with Catherine has been defeated and my sister has returned to her own home, I want nothing more in life than marriage to my dear Miss Grey. Come, what do you say?'

'Yes. Oh yes.' I replied, firmly, and sank back happily into his arms.

We do hope that you have enjoyed reading this large print book.

Did you know that all of our titles are available for purchase?

We publish a wide range of high quality large print books including:
Romances, Mysteries, Classics
General Fiction
Non Fiction and Westerns

Special interest titles available in large print are:
The Little Oxford Dictionary
Music Book
Song Book
Hymn Book
Service Book

Also available from us courtesy of Oxford University Press:
Young Readers' Dictionary
(large print edition)
Young Readers' Thesaurus
(large print edition)

For further information or a free brochure, please contact us at:
Ulverscroft Large Print Books Ltd.,
The Green, Bradgate Road, Anstey,
Leicester, LE7 7FU, England.
Tel: (00 44) 0116 236 4325
Fax: (00 44) 0116 234 0205

PROUD HEART, FAIR LADY

Elayn Duffy

Viscount Philip Devlin is not a happy man. From his grave, his father has decreed that the Viscount shall marry a girl he has never met if he is to inherit his beloved Meadowsdene and Kingsgrey Court. For a girl with no dowry to speak of, marrying into one of the oldest, richest houses in England is good fortune indeed. But the Viscount's bride, Kathryn Hastings, faces a grim future for she will be his wife in name only, leaving him to pursue his life as before. Kathryn decides to enact her revenge and turns the tables on Devlin.

DUMMY HAND

Susan Moody

When Cassie Swann is knocked off her bike on a quiet country road, the driver leaves her unconscious and bleeding at the roadside. A man later walks into a police station and confesses, and they gratefully close the case. But something about this guilt-induced confession doesn't smell right, and Cassie's relentless suitor Charlie Quartermain cannot resist doing a little detective work. When a young student at Oxford is found brutally murdered, Charlie begins to suspect that the two incidents are somehow connected. Can he save Cassie from another 'accident' — this time a fatal one?

SHOT IN THE DARK

Annie Ross

When an elderly nun is raped and murdered at a drop-in centre for drug addicts, the police decide it's a burglary gone wrong. Television director Bel Carson sees pictures of the body, and is convinced that this was a ritualistic murder, carried out by a sadistic and calculating killer. Then he strikes closer to home, and Bel determines to track him down. As she closes in on the monster, she senses that someone is spying on her home. And, in a final, terrifying twist, she finds herself caught in the killer's trap . . .

A Tale of Two Cities

A TALE
OF TWO CITIES

Charles Dickens
Edited and abridged by Doris Dickens

Armada
An Imprint of HarperCollins*Publishers*

A Tale of Two Cities was first published in 1859.

This abridged edition was first published in the
UK in Armada in 1991

Armada is an imprint of HarperCollins Children's Books,
part of HarperCollins Publishers Ltd, 77–85 Fulham Palace
Road, Hammersmith, London W6 8JB

Printed and bound in Great Britain by
HarperCollins Book Manufacturing Ltd, Glasgow

Contents

CHAPTER 1

It was the best of times, it was the worst of times, it was the age of wisdom, it was the age of foolishness, it was the spring of hope, it was the winter of despair. We had everything before us, we had nothing before us, we were all going direct to Heaven, we were all going direct the other way – in short, the times were much like the present ones.

There were a king with a large jaw and a queen with a plain face, on the throne of England; there were a king with a large jaw and a queen with a fair face, on the throne of France. It was the year one thousand seven hundred and seventy-five, and while Woodman and Farmer worked unheeded, their Majesties caused stir enough and carried their divine rights with a high hand. Thus did the year one thousand seven hundred and seventy-five conduct their Greatnesses, and myriads of small creatures – the creatures of this story among the rest – along the roads that lay before them.

CHAPTER 2

The Dover road lay before the first of the persons with whom this story is concerned one misty, cold Friday night late in November. The Dover mail coach was lumbering up Shooter's Hill, and this person walked uphill in the mire by the side of the mail as the rest of the passengers did, not because they wanted to, but because the hill, and the harness, and the mud, and the mail, were all so heavy that the horses had three times come to a stop until they had been encouraged by reins and whip to return to their duty.

With drooping heads and tremulous tails, they mashed their way through the thick mud, floundering and stumbling as if they were falling apart at the knees. As often as the coachman rested them and brought them to a stand, with a wary "Wo-ho! so-ho then!" the near leader violently shook his head and everything upon it — like an unusually emphatic horse, denying that the coach could be got up the hill. Whenever the leading horse made this rattle, the passenger started, as a nervous passenger might, and was disturbed in mind.

Two other passengers were plodding up the hill as well. All three men were wrapped to the cheekbones and over the ears, and wore jackboots. Not one of the three could see what the others were like and they were cautious of each other, for anybody on the road might be a robber or in league with robbers. The guard stood on his perch at the back of the coach and kept his head on the arms chest before him. It contained a cutlass, six or eight loaded pistols on top of that and a loaded blunderbuss just under the lid.

The Dover mail struggled on, with the jackboots of its passengers squashing along by its side. They had stopped when the horses rested and they kept close to the coach, for if any one of them had gone ahead into the mist and darkness, he might have been mistaken for a highwayman and instantly shot.

A final burst carried the mail to the summit of the hill. The horses stopped to breathe again, and the guard got down to skid the wheel for the descent, and to open the coach door to let the passengers in.

"Tst! Joe!" cried the coachman in a warning voice, looking down from his box.

"What do you say, Tom?"

They both listened.

"I say a horse at a canter coming up, Joe."

"*I* say a horse at a gallop, Tom," returned the guard, leaving his hold of the door, and mounting nimbly to his place. "Gentlemen! In the king's name, all of you!"

With this charge to his passengers, he cocked his blunderbuss, and stood on the offensive.

The passenger who is concerned in our story was on

9

the coach step, getting in; the other two passengers were close behind him, and about to follow. He remained on the step, half in the coach and half out of it; the others remained in the road below him. They all looked from the coachman to the guard, and from the guard to the coachman, and listened. The coachman looked back, and the guard looked back, and even the lead horse pricked up his ears and looked back as well. The hearts of the passengers beat loud enough almost to be heard, and their breathing was faint.

The sound of a horse at a gallop came fast and furiously up the hill.

"So-ho!" the guard sang out, as loud as he could roar. "Yo there! Stand! I shall fire!"

The pace was suddenly checked, and with much splashing and floundering, a man's voice called from the mist, "Is that the Dover Mail?"

"Never you mind what it is," the guard retorted. "What are you?"

"*Is* that the Dover Mail?"

"Why do you want to know?"

"I want a passenger, if it is."

"What passenger?"

"Mr Jarvis Lorry."

Our passenger showed in a moment that it was his name. The guard, the coachman, and the two other passengers eyed him distrustfully.

"Keep where you are," the guard called to the voice in the mist, "because, if I should make a mistake, it could never be set right in your lifetime. Gentleman of the name of Lorry, answer straight."

"What is the matter?" asked the passenger, then, with mildly quavering speech, "who wants me? Is it Jerry?"

"Yes, Mr Lorry," answered a hoarse voice.

"What is the matter?"

"A despatch sent after you from over yonder. T & Co."

"I know this messenger, guard," said Mr Lorry, getting down into the road. "He may come close; there's nothing wrong."

The guard gave a shout and the figures of a horse and rider came slowly through the eddying mist, and came to the side of the mail coach, where the passenger stood. The rider stooped, and casting up his eyes at the guard, handed the passenger a small folded paper. The rider's horse was blown, and both horse and rider were covered with mud, from the hoofs of the horse to the hat of the man.

"Guard!" said the passenger, in a tone of quiet business confidence.

The watchful guard, with his right hand at the stock of his raised blunderbuss, his left at the barrel, and his eye on the horseman, answered curtly, "Sir."

"There is nothing to fear. I belong to Tellson's Bank. You must know Tellson's Bank in London. I am going to Paris on business. I may read this?"

"If so be you're quick, sir."

He opened it in the light of the coach lamp on that

side, and read – first to himself and then aloud: "Wait at Dover for Mam'selle."

"It's not long, you see, guard. Jerry, say that my answer was, 'Recalled To Life'."

Jerry started in his saddle. "That's a blazing strange answer, too," said he at his hoarsest.

"Take that message back, and they will know that I received this, as well as if I wrote. Make the best of your way. Goodnight."

With those words, the passenger got back in the coach which lumbered on again, with heavier wreaths of mist closing round it as it began the descent. The guard soon replaced his blunderbuss in his arms chest, and, having checked the rest of its contents, and the pistols that he wore in his belt, looked into a smaller chest beneath his seat, in which there were a few smith's tools, a couple of torches and a tinder box. After that, he called softly over the coach roof:

"Tom!"

"Hallo, Joe."

"Did you hear the message?"

"I did, Joe."

"What did you make of it, Tom?"

"Nothing at all, Joe."

"That's a coincidence, too," the guard mused, "for I made the same of it myself."

Jerry, left alone in the mist and darkness, dismounted meanwhile, not only to ease his exhausted horse, but to wipe the mud from his face, and to shake the wet out of his hat brim, which might be capable of holding about half a gallon.

After standing with the bridle over his heavily-splashed arm, until the wheels of the mail were no longer within hearing, and the night was quite still again, he turned to walk down the hill.

"After that there gallop from Temple Bar, I won't trust your forelegs till I get you on the level," said this hoarse messenger, glancing at his mare. "'Recalled to Life'. That's a blazing strange message. Much of that wouldn't do for you, Jerry! I say, Jerry! You'd be in a blazing bad way, if recalling to life was to come into fashion, Jerry!"

CHAPTER 3

Whe n the mail got successfully to Dover, in the course of the forenoon, the porter at the Royal George Hotel opened the coach door as his custom was. He did it with some flourish of ceremony, for a mail journey from London in winter was an achievement to congratulate an adventurous traveller upon.

By that time, there was only one adventurous traveller left to be congratulated: for the two others had been set down at their respective roadside destinations.

The mildewy inside of the coach, with its damp and dirty straw, its disagreeable smell, and its obscurity, was rather like a larger dog kennel. Mr Lorry, the passenger, shaking himself out of it in chains of straw, a tangle of shaggy wrapper, flapping hat, and muddy legs, was rather like a larger sort of dog.

"There will be a packet-boat to Calais, tomorrow, will there, porter?"

"Yes, sir, if the weather holds and the wind sets tolerable fair. The tide will serve pretty nicely at about two in the afternoon, sir. Bed, sir?"

"I shall not go to bed until tonight; but I want a bedroom and a barber."

14

"And then breakfast, sir? Yes, sir. I'll show you to your room. You will find a fine sea-coal fire, sir. This your luggage, sir?"

Presently a gentleman of sixty, formally dressed in a brown suit of clothes, pretty well worn, but very well kept, with large square cuffs and large flaps to the pockets, passed along on his way to his breakfast.

The coffee room had no other occupant that morning than the gentleman in brown. His breakfast table was drawn before the fire, and, as he sat with its light shining on him, waiting for the meal, he sat so still that he might have been sitting for his portrait and presently he dropped off to sleep. The arrival of his breakfast roused him, and he said to the waiter as he moved his chair to it:

"I wish accommodation prepared for a young lady who may come here at any time today. She may ask for Mr Jarvis Lorry, or she may only ask for a gentleman from Tellson's Bank. Please to let me know."

"Yes, sir. Tellson's Bank in London, sir?"

"Yes."

"Yes, sir. We have oftentimes the honour to entertain your gentlemen in their travelling backwards and forwards between London and Paris, sir. A vast deal of travelling, at Tellson and Company's Bank."

"Yes, we are quite a French establishment, as well as an English one."

"Yes, sir. Not much in the habit of such travelling yourself, I think, sir?"

"Not of late years. It is fifteen years since we – since I – came last from France."

"Indeed, sir? That was before my time here, sir. Before our people's time here, sir. The George was in other hands at that time, sir."

"I believe so."

"But I would hold a pretty wager, sir, that Tellson and Company was flourishing a matter of fifty, not to speak of fifteen years ago?"

"You might treble that, and say a hundred and fifty, yet not be far from the truth."

"Indeed, sir!"

Rounding his mouth and both his eyes as he stepped backward from the table, the waiter shifted his napkin from his right arm to his left, dropped into a comfortable attitude, and stood surveying the guest while he ate and drank, as from an observatory or watch-tower, as waiters have always done down the ages.

When Mr Lorry had finished his breakfast, he went out for a stroll on the beach. The little narrow, crooked town of Dover hid itself away from the beach, and ran its head into the chalk cliffs, like a marine ostrich. The beach was a desert of heaps of sea and stones tumbling wildly about, and the sea did what it liked, and what it liked was destruction. It thundered at the town, and thundered at the cliffs, and brought the coast down madly. A little fishing was done in the port and the air between the houses smelt fishy, but many of the inhabitants made a living from smuggling.

As the day declined into the afternoon, and the air, which had been at intervals clear enough to allow the French coast to be seen, became again charged with mist and vapour, Mr Lorry's thoughts seemed to cloud too. When it was dark, and he sat before the coffee room fire, awaiting his dinner as he had awaited his breakfast, his mind was busily digging, digging, digging, in the live red coals.

Mr Lorry had a good bottle of claret with his dinner. He was drinking his last glassful when a rattling of wheels came up the narrow street, and rumbled into the inn yard.

He set down his glass unfinished. "This must be Mam'selle!" said he.

In a very few minutes the waiter came in to announce that Miss Manette had arrived from London and would be happy to see the gentleman from Tellson's.

Mr Lorry emptied his glass and followed the waiter to Miss Manette's appartment. It was a large, dark room lit by two tall candles on a heavy, dark table and it was not until he had got past these candles that Mr Lorry saw, standing to receive him by the table between them and the fire, a young lady of not more than seventeen, in a riding cloak, and still holding her straw travelling hat by its ribbon in her hand.

As his eyes rested on a short, slight, pretty figure, a quantity of golden hair and a pair of blue eyes that met his own with an inquiring look, a sudden vivid likeness passed before him, of a child whom he had held in his

17

arms on the passage across that very Channel, one cold time, when the hail drifted heavily and the sea ran high. The likeness passed away, and he made his formal bow to Miss Manette.

"Pray take a seat, sir." It was a very clear and pleasant young voice, with a slight trace of a French accent.

"I kiss your hand, miss," said Mr Lorry, with old-fashioned manners, as he made his formal bow again, and took his seat.

"I received a letter from the Bank, sir, yesterday, informing me that it was necessary for me to go to Paris concerning the affairs of my poor father, whom I never saw, – so long dead – "

Mr Lorry moved in his chair and looked uncomfortable.

"In Paris, I would meet a gentleman of Tellson's Bank who would assist me, but I now understand that, although that gentleman had left London to undertake the journey, a messenger had been sent after him asking him to await me here, so that I could travel under his protection."

"Myself, miss. I am happy to escort you."

"Thank you, sir. I replied to the Bank that I would do as they suggested, and, as I am an orphan, I would be glad of your help in making the crossing to France and later. I understand that the gentleman will explain to me the details of the business, and that I must prepare myself to find them of a surprising nature and I naturally have a strong and eager interest to know what they are."

"Naturally," said Mr Lorry, "but – but I find it very difficult to begin."

The inquiring look returned. "Are you really quite a stranger to me, sir?"

"Am I not?" Mr Lorry opened his hands, and held them out with a smile.

The young lady took her seat thoughtfully in the chair by which she had been standing.

He watched her as she sat with her eyes cast down, thinking, and the moment she raised her eyes again, went on, "Miss Manette, I want to tell you a story. It is the story of one of our customers. He was a French gentleman; a scientific gentleman; a highly-qualified gentleman – a doctor."

"Not of Beauvais?"

"Why, yes, of Beauvais. Like Monsieur Manette, your father, the gentleman was of Beauvais. I had been working in Tellson's French Branch for the last twenty years and I had the honour of knowing him there."

"Twenty years ago, sir?"

"Yes, miss. This was twenty years ago. The gentleman married an English lady and I was one of the trustees.

"But this is my father's story, sir, and I begin to think that when I was left an orphan through my mother dying only two years after my father, it was you who brought me to England. I am almost sure it was you."

Mr Lorry took the hesitating little hand that she held out to him, and put it to his lips. He then led her to her

19

chair again and stood with his hand on the back, looking down into her face while she sat looking up into his.

"Miss Manette, it *was* I. So far, as you have remarked, this is the story of your father. Now comes the difference. If your father had not died when he did – don't be frightened. You are trembling. As I was saying, if your father had *not* died, if he had disappeared, been spirited away by an enemy to some dreadful place, and had not been heard of since, in spite of his wife having implored the king, the queen, the court, the clergy, for any tidings of him, and all quite in vain – then the history of your father would have been the history of this unfortunate gentleman, the doctor of Beauvais."

"I entreat you to tell me more, sir."

"I will. I am going to. You can bear it?"

"I can bear anything but not knowing."

"I will continue. Now if this lady, who was very brave, had suffered so much before her little child was born from this dreadful happening – "

"The little child was a daughter, sir."

"The child was a daughter. If her mother decided to tell her that her father was dead, in order to spare her suffering – "

"Oh dear, good, kind sir, let me have the truth!"

"You shall have the truth. That is what your mother did. And when she died – I believe broken-hearted – never having ceased to search for your father, she left you, at two years old, to grow to be blooming, beautiful and happy, without the dark cloud upon you of not

20

knowing if your father had died in prison or if he was still there wasting away through the years."

She clasped his wrist and her grip tightened as he continued, "but your father has been found. He is alive. Greatly changed, but he *is* alive. He has been taken to the house of an old servant in Paris, and we are going there. I, to identify him if I can; you, to restore him to life, love, rest, comfort."

She shivered and said, in a low, distinct, awe-stricken voice, as if she were saying it in a dream,

"I am going to see his Ghost! It will be his Ghost – not him!"

Mr Lorry quietly stroked the hands that held his arm.

"There, there, there! See now, see now! The best and the worst are known to you, now. You are well on your way to the poor wronged gentleman, and, with a fair sea voyage, and a fair land journey, you will soon be at his dear side."

She repeated in the same tone, sunk to a whisper, "I have been free, I have been happy, yet his Ghost has never haunted me!"

"Only one thing more," said Mr Lorry, "he has been found under another name; his own name, long forgotten or long concealed. It is best not to talk of the matter, but to remove him – for a while at all events – out of France.

"This is completely secret and I carry about me not a scrap of paper referring to him or to our plan. Our enterprise is code-named 'Recalled to Life' which could mean anything. But what is the matter? She hasn't heard a word! Poor young lady; she has fainted."

Mr Lorry called out loudly for assistance and a wild-looking woman came running into the room in advance of the inn servants. She had red hair and a bonnet like a guardsman's bearskin and, seeing Mr Lorry still holding Miss Manette's hand, she gave him a push which sent him flying back against the nearest wall.

"Why, look at you all!" bawled this figure, addressing the inn servants. "Why don't you go and fetch things, instead of standing there staring at me?

"Go and fetch smelling salts, cold water, and vinegar, quick! Do you hear!"

The servants hurried away and she softly laid the patient on a sofa, and tended her with great skill and gentleness, calling her "my precious!" and "my bird!" and spreading her golden hair aside over her shoulders with great pride and care.

"And you in brown!" she said, indignantly turning to Mr Lorry, "couldn't you tell her what you had to tell her, without frightening her to death? Look at her, with her pale face and her cold hands. Do you call *that* being a banker?"

Mr Lorry was lost for words, and looked on with all humility while the strong woman revived her charge and coaxed her to lay her drooping head upon her shoulder.

"I hope she will do well now," said Mr Lorry.

"No thanks to you in brown, if she does. My darling pretty!"

"I hope," said Mr Lorry, "that you accompany Miss Manette to France."

"A likely thing, too!" replied the strong woman. "If it was ever intended that I should go across salt water, do you suppose Providence would have cast my lot in an island?"

This being another question hard to answer, Mr Jarvis Lorry withdrew to consider it.

CHAPTER 4

A large cask of wine had been dropped and broken in the street. The accident had happened in getting it out of a cart; the cask had tumbled out with a run, the hoops had burst, and it lay on the stones just outside the door of the wine shop, shattered like a walnut-shell.

All the people within reach stopped what they were doing or not doing to run to the spot and drink the wine. The rough stones of the street had caused it to collect in little pools; these were surrounded, each by its own jostling group. Some men kneeled down, made scoops of their two hands joined, and sipped, or tried to help women, who bent over their shoulders, to sip, before the wine had all run out between their fingers.

There was a shrill sound of laughter among the men, women, and children while the wine game lasted, but when the wine was gone it ceased as suddenly as it had broken out.

The man who had left his saw sticking in the firewood he was cutting, began sawing again; the woman who had left on a doorstep the little pot of hot ashes over which she had been trying to warm her fingers and toes

24

and those of her child, returned to it; men with bare arms, uncombed hair and starving faces, who had emerged into the winter light from cellars, moved away, to descend again; and a gloom gathered on the scene that appeared more natural to it than sunshine.

The wine was red wine, and had stained the ground of the narrow street in the suburb of St Antoine, in Paris, where it was spilled. It had stained many hands, too, and many faces, and many naked feet, and many wooden shoes. Those who had been greedy had acquired a tigerish smear about the mouth, and one tall joker in a long night cap, scrawled upon a wall with his fingers dipped in muddy dregs of wine the word – Blood.

The time was to come, when that wine too would be spilled on the street stones, and when the stain of it would be red upon many of the people there.

There was little food, only the leanest scrags of meat, the coarsest bread and not enough of it. Nothing worked except tools and weapons; but the cutler's knives and axes were sharp and bright, the smith's hammers were heavy, and the gunmaker's stock of weapons was murderous. The people were desperate, but the time had not yet come.

The wine shop was a corner shop, better than most others in appearance and the quality of its goods. Its master had stood outside it, in a yellow waistcoat and green breeches, looking on at the struggle for the lost wine. "It's not my affair," said he, with a final shrug of the shoulders. "The people from the market did it. Let them bring another cask." Then, his eyes happening to catch the tall joker writing up his joke, he called to him across the way, "What are you doing, Gaspard?"

The fellow pointed meaningly to his joke, but the wine shop keeper, crossing the road, picked up a handful of mud and smeared it over the word. Then he wiped his hand on the other man's jacket, saying, "This is not the place. Call wine, wine. Is there no other place where such a word as the one you have chosen, can be written?" Then he re-crossed the road and entered the wine shop.

The wine shop keeper was a bull-necked, martial-looking man of thirty, and he should have been of a hot temperament, for, although it was a bitter day, he wore no coat, but carried one slung over his shoulder. His shirt-sleeves were rolled up, too, and his brown arms were bare to the elbows. Neither did he wear anything more on his head than his own crisply-curling short dark hair. He was a dark man altogether, with good eyes set wide apart. Good-humoured looking on the whole, but a man of strong will and a set purpose who would not give way.

Madame Defarge, his wife, sat in the shop behind the counter as he came in. Madame Defarge was a stout woman of about his own age, with a watchful eye that seldom seemed to look at anything, a large hand, a steady face, strong features, and a composed manner. She looked like a woman who did not often make mistakes against herself.

Madame Defarge, being sensitive to cold, was wrapped in fur, and had a large, bright shawl twined about her head which did not hide her large earrings. Her knitting was in front of her, but she had laid it down to pick her teeth with a toothpick. When her husband came in, she gave a slight cough and raised her eyebrows a little which indicated to him that strangers had come into the shop.

The wine shop keeper looked around and saw that an elderly gentleman and a young lady were seated quietly in a corner. Other people were there: two playing cards, two playing dominoes, three standing by the counter lengthening out a short supply of wine. As he passed behind the counter, he noticed that the elderly gentleman said in a look to the young lady, "This is our man."

"What are you doing here?" said Monsieur Defarge to himself, "I don't know you."

But he pretended not to notice the two strangers and began to talk to the three customers who were drinking at the bar.

"How goes it, Jacques?" said one of these to Monsieur Defarge. "Is all the spilt wine swallowed?"

'Every drop, Jacques," answered Monsieur Defarge.

When they exchanged Christian names together, Madame Defarge, picking her teeth with her toothpick, gave another little cough, and raised her eyebrows a little more.

"It is not often," said the second of the three,

addressing Monsieur Defarge, "that many of these miserable creatures know the taste of wine, or of anything but black bread and death. Is it not so, Jacques?"

"It is so, Jacques," Monsieur Defarge returned.

At this second exchange of Christian names, Madame Defarge, still calmly using her toothpick, coughed another little cough, and raised her eyebrows a little higher.

The last of the three now said his say, as he put down his empty drinking vessel and smacked his lips.

"Ah! So much the worse! A bitter taste they have always in their mouths, and hard lives they live. Am I right, Jacques?"

"You are right, Jacques," said Monsieur Defarge.

As the third exchange of Christian names took place again, Madame Defarge put her toothpick away, kept her eyebrows up, and slightly rustled in her seat.

"Gentlemen," said her husband, "my wife."

The three customers pulled off their hats to Madame Defarge, with three flourishes. Madame Defarge bent her head in return, and gave them a quick look. Then she glanced in a casual manner round the wine shop, took up her knitting and became absorbed in it.

"Gentlemen," said her husband, who had kept his bright eye upon her, "good day. The room that you wished to see, and were asking about when I stepped outside, is on the fifth floor. The doorway of the staircase is in the little court yard close to the left here." He pointed with his hand, "near to the window of my establishment. But, now that I remember, one of you has already been there, and can show the way. Gentlemen, adieu!"

They paid for their wine, and left the place. Monsieur Defarge was watching his wife at her knitting when the elderly gentleman advanced from his corner, and begged the favour of a word.

"Willingly, sir," said Monsieur Defarge and quietly stepped with him to the door.

Their conference was very short, but very decided. Almost at the first word, Monsieur Defarge started and became deeply attentive. It had not lasted a minute, when he nodded and went out. The gentleman then beckoned to the young lady, and they, too, went out. Madame Defarge knitted with nimble fingers and appeared to see nothing.

Mr Jarvis Lorry and Miss Manette joined Monsieur Defarge at the doorway off the courtyard which led to the stairs which would take them to the fifth floor. In the gloomy entrance, Monsieur Defarge bent down on one knee to the child of his old master, and put her hand to his lips. His face had changed; the good humour had left his face and he looked a secret, angry, dangerous man. The staircase was steep and they stopped to rest once or twice. At last they reached the top, but there was another staircase above them. This led to a garret room, a sort of attic.

Monsieur Defarge felt in the pocket of the coat he carried over his shoulder and took out a key.

"His door is locked then, my friend?" said Mr Lorry, surprised.

"Yes, he has lived so long locked up that he would be frightened, perhaps come to harm, if his door was left open."

They went up slowly and softly. The staircase was short, and they were soon at the top. Miss Manette was shaking a little.

The staircase had a bend in it, and they came all at once in sight of three men, whose heads were bent down close together at the side of a door, and who were peering into the room to which the room belonged, through some chinks or holes in the wall. On hearing footsteps close at hand, these three turned, and rose, and showed themselves to be the three of one name who had been drinking in the wine shop.

"I forgot them in the surprise of your visit," explained Monsieur Defarge. "Leave us, good boys; we have to be alone here."

The three glided by, and went silently down.

Mr Lorry turned to Monsieur Defarge and asked him in an angry whisper if he made a show of Monsieur Manette.

"I show him, in the way you have seen, to a chosen few."

"Is that right?"

"*I* think it is right."

"Who are the few? How do you choose them?"

"I choose them as men of my name whom I can trust.

I want them to see what has been done. But you are English; it is hard for you to understand what is happening over here. Stay there, for a little moment if you please."

Monsieur Defarge bent down and looked in through the crevice in the wall. Soon raising his head again, he knocked loudly on the door, and turned the key in the lock as heavily as he could.

The door opened inward, and he looked into the room and said something. A faint voice answered. He looked back over his shoulder, and beckoned them to enter. Mr Lorry got his arm securely round the daughter's waist, and held her, for he feared she might faint.

"I am afraid," she said, shuddering.

"Afraid?" he said. "Afraid of what?"

"Afraid of *him*. My father."

"He needs you. Come in, come in."

He led her gently into the room and kept his supporting arm round her.

Defarge drew out the key, closed the door, locked it on the inside, took out the key again, making as much noise as he could, and put it in his pocket. Then he walked slowly across the room to where the window was, stopped there, and faced round.

The garret was dim and dark and it was difficult to see anything, yet some kind of work was going on. With his back towards the door, and his face towards the window where the keeper of the wine shop stood looking at him, a white-haired man sat on a low bench, stooping forward and very busy, making shoes.

CHAPTER 5

"Good day!" said Monsieur Defarge, looking down at the white head that bent low over the shoemaking.

It was raised for a moment, and a faint voice answered as if it were at a distance:

"Good day!"

"You are still hard at work, I see?"

After a long silence, the head was lifted for another moment, and a feeble voice replied, "Yes – I am working," and a sad, dull pair of eyes looked for a moment at the questioner.

"I want," said Defarge, who had not removed his gaze from the shoemaker, "to let in a little more light here. You can bear a little more?"

"What did you say?"

"You can bear a little more light?"

"I *must* bear it if you let it in."

The opened door was opened a little further, and a broad ray of light fell into the garret. It showed the workman with an unfinished shoe upon his lap, pausing in his labour. His few tools and various scraps of leather were at his feet and on his bench. He had a white beard, not very long, a hollow face and exceedingly bright eyes. His hair was white.

His yellow rags of shirt lay open at the throat, and showed his body to be withered and worn. He and his tattered clothes were so worn and faded that it would have been hard to say which was which.

"Are you going to finish that pair of shoes today?" asked Defarge, motioning to Mr Lorry to come forward.

"What did you say?"

"Do you mean to finish that pair of shoes today?"

"I can't say that I mean to. I suppose so. I don't know."

But the question reminded him of his work, and he bent over it again.

Mr Lorry came silently forward, leaving the daughter by the door. After a minute or two, the old man looked up. He showed no surprise at seeing a stranger, but bent down over his shoe again.

"You have a visitor, you see," said Monsieur Defarge.

"What did you say?"

"Here is a visitor."

The shoemaker looked up as before, but without removing a hand from his work.

"Come!" said Defarge. "Here is a gentleman who knows a well-made shoe when he sees one. Show him that shoe you are working at. Take it, monsieur."

Mr Lorry took the shoe in his hand.

"Tell Monsieur what kind of shoe it is, and the maker's name."

"It is a young lady's walking shoe."

"And the maker's name?" said Defarge.

"Did you ask me for my name?"

"Yes."

"One Hundred and Five, North Tower."

"Is that all?"

"One Hundred and Five, North Tower."

With a weary sound which was not a sigh, nor a groan, he bent to work again, until the silence was again broken.

"You are not a shoemaker by trade?" said Mr Lorry, looking steadfastly at him.

"I am not a shoemaker by trade? No, I was not a shoemaker by trade. I learnt it here. I asked leave to teach myself, and I got it with much difficulty after a long while, and I have made shoes ever since."

"Monsieur Manette," said Mr Lorry, handing back the shoe and still looking steadfastly at him, "do you remember nothing of me?"

The shoe dropped to the ground and the old man looked up at his face.

"Monsieur Manette," said Mr Lorry, laying his hand upon Defarge's arm, "do you remember nothing of this man? Look at him. Look at me. Do you not remember your old banker and your old servant?"

He sat looking at them by turns, then dropped his eyes and resumed his work.

"Have you recognized him, Monsieur?" asked Defarge in a whisper.

"Yes. For a moment I saw the face that I once knew so well. Let us draw back; his daughter is coming to him."

She had come forward very near to the bench on which he sat and stood silently beside him as he worked. Presently he had to put down the tool with which he was working and change it for the shoemaker's knife. It lay on that side of him which was not the side on which she stood. He had picked it up, and was stooping to work again, when his eyes caught the skirt of her long dress. He raised them and saw her face. He stared back and said in a faint voice, "What is this?"

With the tears streaming down her face, she put her two hands to her lips, and kissed them to him; then clasped them to her breast as if she laid his poor head there.

"You are not the gaoler's daughter?"

"No."

She sat down upon the bench beside him and laid her hand upon his arm. He sat up at once, put his knife down and sat staring at her.

Her golden hair, which she wore in long curls, had been hurriedly pushed aside, and fell down over her neck. Timidly he took it up and looked at it. Then he put his hand to his neck, and took off a blackened string with a scrap of folded rag attached to it. He opened this, carefully, on his knee; it contained one or two long golden hairs, which he had, many years ago, wound off upon his finger.

He took her hair into his hand again, and looked

closely at it. "It is the same. How can it be? How can it be? When was it? How was it?"

He turned her full to the light and looked at her.

"She laid her head upon my shoulder, that night when they took me away – she had a fear of my going, though I had none – and when I was brought to the North Tower they found these hairs upon my sleeve. They let me keep them. I remember it very well."

He turned to his daughter, "What is your name my gentle angel?"

She fell on her knees before him. "Oh sir, I cannot tell you at this time and I cannot tell you here. I pray you to bless me. Oh my dear, my dear!"

His cold white head mingled with her radiant hair, which warmed and lighted it as though it was the light of freedom shining on him.

She held him close and rocked him like a child. "Your agony is over, dearest, and I am come to take you home to England. We will leave our native France which has been so wicked to you."

He sank down in her arms upon the ground and began to sob. She stayed there beside him with her head upon his arm, and her golden hair drooping over him curtained him from the light.

"If, without disturbing him," she said, raising her eyes to Mr Lorry who was stooping over them, "it could be arranged for our leaving Paris at once, straight from here, it would be best for him."

"But, consider. Is he fit for the journey?" asked Mr Lorry.

"More fit for that, I think, than to remain in this city, so dreadful to him, this city where he has been imprisoned so many years."

"It is true," said Defarge, who was kneeling down beside them. "More than that, Monsieur Manette is, for all reasons, best out of France. Say, shall I hire a carriage and post-horses?"

"I had better do it," said Mr Lorry, "and I will be as speedy as I can."

"Then be so kind," urged Miss Manette, "as to leave my father here with me. I will look after him, and, if you lock us in, we shall be secure from interruption. When you return, we will remove him straight."

Mr Lorry and Monsieur Defarge would have preferred that one of them should stay behind to help her. But, as there were not only carriages and horses to be seen to, but travelling papers as well, and as the day was drawing to a close, they decided to divide the business that was necessary to be done, and hurried away to do it.

Then, as the darkness closed in, the daughter laid her head down on the hard ground close at the father's side, and watched him. The darkness deepened and deepened, and they both lay quiet, until a light gleamed through the chinks in the wall.

Mr Lorry and Monsieur Defarge had made all ready for the journey, and had brought with them, besides travelling cloaks and wrappers, bread and meat, wine, and hot coffee. Monsieur Defarge put these provisions, and the lamp he carried, on the shoemaker's bench (there was nothing else in the garret but a small bed), and he and Mr Lorry roused the old man, and assisted him to his feet.

Whether he knew what was happening, they could not tell. They tried speaking to him but he was so confused, and so very slow to answer, that they took fright at his bewilderment, and agreed for the time being not to worry him.

He had a wild, lost manner of occasionally clasping his head in his hands, that they had not seen in him before, yet he liked to hear his daughter's voice and always turned his face to her when she spoke.

As one who had been accustomed to obey orders for many years, he ate and drank what they gave him to eat and drink, and put on the cloak and other wrappings, that they gave him to wear and was pleased when his daughter drew her arm through his, and took her hand in both his own and kept it there.

They began to descend; Monsieur Defarge, going first with the lamp, and Mr Lorry at the rear. They reached the courtyard; all was quiet and the only person to be seen was Madame Defarge – who leaned against the doorpost, knitting and appeared to see nothing.

The prisoner had got into a coach, and his daughter had followed him, when Mr Lorry was stopped with his foot on the step by his asking, miserably, for his shoemaking tools and the unfinished shoes. Madame

Defarge immediately called to her husband that she would get them, and went, knitting, out of the lamplight, through the courtyard. She quickly brought them down and handed them in; and immediately afterwards leaned against the doorpost, knitting, and appeared to see nothing.

Defarge got up by the driver and gave the command "To the Barrier!" The postilion cracked his whip, and they clattered away under the feeble swinging lamps.

Under the lamps – swinging ever brighter in the better streets, and ever dimmer in the worse – and by lighted shops, cheerful crowds, illuminated coffee houses, and theatre doors, to one of the city gates. Soldiers were there asking to see their papers and Defarge took the officer aside. "These are the papers of the gentleman inside with the white head. They were entrusted to me when I brought him from that place that you know of." A lantern was held up and the officer took a careful look at the white-haired gentleman and his companions. "It is well. Forward!" he said. "Adieu!" said Defarge. And so, under a short grove of feebler and feebler lamps, they went out under the great grove of stars.

All through the night, Mr Lorry, sitting opposite the man who had been as if buried for ages and then dug out, wondered if ever his wits would be restored to him and an old inquiry came to his mind:

"I hope you care to be restored to life?"
And the old answer came back:
"I can't say."

CHAPTER 1

Tellson's Bank by Temple Bar was an old-fashioned place, even in the year one thousand seven hundred and eighty. It was very small, very dark, very ugly and very uncomfortable to work in, but the partners in the Bank were proud of its smallness, proud of its darkness, proud of its ugliness, proud of the discomfort there. A different, more comfortable and more elegant Bank would, they said, be far less respectable and Tellson's was the most respectable Bank in London.

Tellson's had, in the ancient past, been somebody's house. The kitchen and scullery had been made into a strong room and important papers were kept in the family dining-room on a great dining-table which never had a dinner on it.

Cramped in all kinds of dim cupboards and hutches at Tellson's, the oldest of men carried on the business gravely. When they took a young man into the Banking-house, they hid him somewhere till he was old. They kept him in a dark place, like a cheese, until he had the full Tellson flavour and blue mould upon him. Then only was he permitted to be seen, spectacularly poring over large books and adding, in his breeches and gaiters, to the general air of the establishment.

Outside Tellson's – never by any means in it, unless called in – was an odd-job man, an occasional porter and messenger, who served as the live sign for the house. He was a spiky-haired man with a husky voice called Jerry Cruncher and he was never absent during business hours, unless upon an errand, and then he was represented by his son, Young Jerry, a grisly urchin of twelve, who was his express image.

The scene was Mr Cruncher's private lodging in Hanging-sword Alley, Whitefriars: the time half-past seven on a windy March morning in the year seventeen hundred and eighty.

Mr Cruncher's appartments were not in a savoury neighbourhood, and were but two in number, even if a closet with a single pane of glass in it might be counted as one. But they were very decently kept. Early as it was, on the windy March morning, the room in which he lay abed was already scrubbed throughout; and between the cups and saucers arranged for breakfast, and the lumbering deal table, a very clean white cloth was spread.

Mr Cruncher reposed under a patchwork counterpane. At first he slept heavily, but, by degree, began to roll and surge in bed, until he rose above the surface, with his spiky hair looking as if it must tear the sheets to ribbons. At which point, he exclaimed, in a voice of exasperation:

"Bust me, if she ain't at it again!"

A tidy little woman rose hastily from her knees in a corner.

"What!" said Mr Cruncher, looking out of bed for a boot. "You're at it again, are you?" He found a dirty boot and threw it at his wife. He never came back from the Bank with muddy boots, but it was a curious thing that when he got up and looked for them in the morning, they were always covered in muddy clay.

The boot missed its mark.

"What are you up to?" said Mr Cruncher.

"I was only saying my prayers."

"Saying your prayers! What do you mean by flopping down and praying against me?"

"I was not praying against you; I was praying *for* you."

"And what do you suppose, you conceited female," said Mr Cruncher, "your prayers are worth?"

"They come from the heart, Jerry. They are worth no more than that."

"Worth no more than that," repeated Mr Cruncher. "They ain't worth much, then. Anyways, I won't be praised against, I tell you. I can't afford it. I'm out of luck on account of you. If you must do it, do it in favour of your husband and son. Young Jerry, dress yourself my boy, and while I clean my boots, keep an eye upon your mother now and then, and if you see any signs of more flopping, give me a call." With this, Mr Cruncher betook himself to his boot-cleaning, and his general preparation for business. In the meantime, his son, who

43

had spiky hair like his father, but softer, and young eyes close together like his father, kept watch upon his mother. He greatly disturbed that poor woman at intervals, by darting out of his sleeping closet, where he was dressing, with a suppressed cry of, "You are going to flop, mother. Hallo, father!" and then darting back with a mischievous grin.

Exceedingly red-eyed and grim, as if he had been up all night at a party which had not turned out well, Jerry Cruncher worried his breakfast rather than ate it, growling over it like any four-footed animal in a menagerie. Towards nine o'clock he smoothed himself down, and, looking as respectable as he could manage, went off to work.

It could scarcely be called a trade, in spite of his favourite description of himself as "a honest tradesman." His stock consisted of a wooden stool, made out of a broken-backed chair cut down, which Young Jerry, walking at his father's side, carried every morning to beneath the banking-house window that was nearest Temple Bar, where it marked their work place.

On this post of his, Mr Cruncher was as well known to Fleet Street and the Temple, as Temple Bar itself.

Encamped at a quarter before nine, in good time to touch his three-cornered hat to the oldest of the men as they passed in to Tellson's Bank, Jerry took up his position on this windy March morning, with young Jerry standing by him, from time to time darting out to attack boys who might be passing by and were smaller than he was. Jerry stood silently watching the morning traffic in Fleet Street, while the twinkling eyes of Young Jerry restlessly watched his father.

The head of one of the regular indoor messengers attached to Tellson's establishment was put through the door, and the word was given:

"Porter wanted!"

"Hooray, father! Here's an early job to begin with!"

Jerry entered Tellson's; young Jerry took possession of the stool and sat there, thinking.

"Always rusty! His fingers is always rusty!" muttered young Jerry. "Where does my father get all that iron rust from? He don't get no iron rust here!"

CHAPTER 2

"You know the Old Bailey well, no doubt?" said one of the oldest of clerks to Jerry the messenger.

"Yes, sir," answered Jerry, somewhat reluctantly. "I *do* know the Bailey."

"Just so. And you know Mr Lorry."

"I know Mr Lorry, sir, much better than I know the Bailey. Much better," said Jerry, "than I as an honest tradesman, wish to know the Bailey."

"Very well. Find the door where the witnesses go in, and show the doorkeeper this note for Mr Lorry. He will then let you in."

"Into the court, sir?"

"Into the court. The doorkeeper will pass the note to Mr Lorry, and you can make some gesture that will attract Mr Lorry's attention, and show him where you are standing. Then all you have to do is remain there until he wants you."

"Is that all, sir?"

"That is all. He wishes to have a messenger at hand. This is to tell him that you are there."

As the ancient clerk folded and signed the note, Mr Cruncher remarked:

"I suppose they'll be trying forgeries this morning?"

"Treason!"

"That's Death," said Jerry. "Barbarous!"

"It is the law," remarked the ancient clerk, turning his surprised spectacles upon him. "It is the law."

"It's a werry hard law," said Jerry.

"Not at all," replied the ancient clerk. "Speak well of the law. Take care of your chest and voice, my good friend, and leave the law to take care of itself. I give you that advice."

"It's the damp, sir, what settles on my chest and voice," said Jerry. "I leave you to judge what a damp way of earning a living mine is."

"Well, well," said the old clerk, "we all have our various ways of gaining a livelihood. Some of us have damp ways, and some of us have dry ways. Here is the letter. Go along."

Jerry made his bow, told his son where he was going and made his way to the Old Bailey where the Court was sitting. Pushing his way through the crowd, for people paid in those days to see the proceedings as if they were visiting a play, Jerry handed in his letter and squeezed his way into court through a closely guarded door.

"What's on?" he asked in a whisper, of the man he found himself next to.

"Nothing yet."

"What's coming on?"

"The Treason case."

"That's a matter of Death, eh?"

"Ah!" said the man, with relish; "hung, drawn, and quartered, he'll be."

"If he's found Guilty," said Jerry.

"Oh! They'll find him guilty all right. Don't you worry."

At this moment, Jerry saw the doorkeeper making his way to Mr Lorry, with a note in his hand. Mr Lorry sat at a table, among the gentlemen in wigs, not far from a wigged gentleman, the prisoner's counsel, who had a great bundle of papers before him, and nearly opposite another wigged gentleman with his hands in his pockets who was staring at the ceiling. After some gruff coughing and rubbing of his chin and signing with his hand, Jerry attracted the notice of Mr Lorry, who had stood up to look for him, and who quietly nodded and sat down again.

"What's *he* got to do with the case?" asked the man he had spoken with.

"Blest if I know," said Jerry.

"What have *you* got to do with it, then, if a person may inquire?"

"Blest if I know that, either," said Jerry.

The entrance of the Judge stopped their conversation. Everyone stood as he sat down and presently the prisoner was brought in and put to the bar. Everyone present, except the one wigged gentleman who looked at the ceiling, stared at him, and the people at the back stood on tip-toe, the better to see him.

The prisoner was a young gentleman of about five-and-twenty, well-grown and good-looking, with sunburnt cheeks and dark eyes. He was plainly dressed in black, or very dark grey, and his hair, which was long and dark, was gathered in a ribbon at the back of his neck. Although he was sunburnt, his paleness showed through as he bowed to the Judge and stood quietly waiting.

Silence in the court! Charles Darnay had yesterday pleaded Not Guilty to the charge that he was a traitor to the King of England in that he had assisted his enemy Louis, King of France, by coming and going between the two countries and informing the French what forces the English were preparing to send to Canada and North America. This was the charge, and Mr Attorney-General was making ready to speak. It was a hanging matter and everyone, including the prisoner, knew it.

He stood quietly attentive, but before his case was renewed, he gave one glance at two figures who sat in a corner of the Judge's bench. They were a young lady of little more than twenty and a gentleman who was evidently her father. The man was old and white-haired and his face was handsome. At times he seemed to be listening to what passed and then his expression changed and he looked absent-minded and withdrawn. His daughter had one of her hands drawn through his arm, as she sat by him, and the other pressed upon it. Her expression was one of terror and pity for the accused, as she gazed at him.

The Judge leaned back in his seat and looked steadily at the man whose life was in his hands as Mr Attorney-General rose to put his case against the prisoner.

CHAPTER 3

Mr Attorney-General informed the jury that the prisoner had been going between England and France on secret business for several years and was quite unable to give an honest explanation. Nothing of this would have been known had he not aroused the suspicions of an honourable and virtuous patriot who was at the time a friend of the prisoner's. This patriot informed upon him and informed the prisoner's servant of his suspicions and told him what action he had taken. Thereupon, the servant, when his master was out, examined the drawers of his writing-table and took from them a sheaf of papers listing His Majesty's forces on sea and land, exactly where they were and in what state of readiness they were. That the servant had no business looking into his master's drawers was neither here nor there. He was to be commended.

Mr Attorney-General continued that the prisoner would not have had these lists, had he not intended them to be used to convey information to a hostile power – that is to say – France. That the lists were not in the prisoner's handwriting was neither here nor there: it only showed how cunning the prisoner was and how artful to take the precaution of disguising it. His treachery had gone on for a good five years and he should pay for it with his life. He felt sure the jury, being honourable and responsible men, would find the prisoner guilty.

When the Attorney-General ceased, a buzz arose in the court as if a cloud of great blue-flies were swarming about the prisoner as if he was as good as dead.

Mr Solicitor-General then, following his leader's lead, examined the first witness, John Barsad by name. This was the so-called patriot who claimed to have been a friend of the prisoner. He told his story rather too well and rather too exactly and the wigged gentleman sitting next to Mr Lorry rose to cross-examine him.

Had he ever been a spy himself?

Certainly not

How did he make a living?

He had private means.

Had he ever been in prison?

Certainly not.

Never in a debtors' prison?

Didn't see what that had to do with it.

Never in a debtors' prison?

Yes.

How many times?

Two or three times.

Not five or six?

Perhaps.

Ever cheated at dice or cards?

Was accused of that, but it was not true.

Ever borrow money from the prisoner?

Yes.

Ever pay him?

No.

Was not this so-called friendship with the prisoner something that was forced on him in coaches, inns and packet-boats? Only a slight acquaintance?

No.

Sure he saw the prisoner with these lists?

Certain.

Knew no more about the lists?

No.

Had not procured them himself by any chance?

Certainly not.

Expect to get anything for giving this evidence?

No.

Not being paid regularly by the government to spy on people and lay traps?

Oh dear no.

Or do anything?

Oh dear no.

Can you swear that?

Over and over again. All done for love of country.

Take my oath.

John Barsad stood down and the second witness entered the witness-box. He was Roger Cly who was claimed to be the prisoner's trustworthy servant. Roger Cly swore his way through the case at a great rate. He had taken service with the prisoner, in good faith and simplicity, four years ago. He had met the prisoner aboard the Dover to Calais packet-boat, asked him if he wanted a handy fellow, and the prisoner had engaged him. He had not asked the prisoner to enploy him as an act of charity – never thought of such a thing. He began to have suspicions of the prisoner, and began to keep an eye upon him, soon afterwards. In arranging his clothes, while travelling, he had seen similar lists to those found in the prisoner's pockets, over and over again. He had taken these lists from the drawer of the prisoner's desk. He had not put them there first. He had seen the prisoner show these lists to French gentlemen at Calais, and similar lists to French gentlemen, both at Calais and Boulogne. He loved his country, and couldn't bear it, and had given information. He had never been suspected of stealing a silver teapot; he had been falsely accused about a mustard-pot, but it turned out to be only silver-plated, not real silver. He had known John Barsad seven or eight years; that was merely a coincidence. No, he didn't agree that it was a peculiarly curious coincidence; most coincidences were curious. Neither did he disagree that true patriotism was *his* only motive too. He was a true Briton, and hoped there were many like him.

The buzz arose in court again, and Mr Attorney-General called Mr Jarvis Lorry.

"Mr Jarvis Lorry, are you a clerk in Tellson's Bank?"

"I am."

"On a certain Friday night in November one thousand

seven hundred and seventy-five did you travel on business between London and Dover by the mail coach?"

"I did."

"Were there any other passengers in the mail coach?"

"Two."

"Did they alight on the road in the course of the night?"

"They did."

"Mr Lorry, look upon the prisoner. Was he one of those two passengers?"

"I cannot say that he was. We were all so wrapped up and keeping our own counsel."

"You will not swear, Mr Lorry, that he was not one of them?"

"No."

"Mr Lorry, look once more upon the prisoner. Have you seen him before?"

"I have."

"When?"

"I was returning from France a few days afterwards, and, at Calais, the prisoner came on board the packet-boat in which I returned, and made the voyage with me."

"At what hour did he come on board?"

"At a little after midnight."

"In the dead of the night. Was he the only passenger who came on board at that untimely hour?"

"He happened to be the only one."

"Never mind about 'happening', Mr Lorry. He was

the only passenger who came on board in the dead of the night?"

"He was."

"Were you travelling alone, Mr Lorry, or with any companion?"

"With two companions. A gentleman and lady. They are here."

"They are here. Had you any conversation with the prisoner?"

"Hardly any. The weather was stormy, and the passage long and rough, and I lay on a sofa, almost from shore to shore."

"Miss Manette!"

The young lady sitting near the Judge stood up. Her father rose with her, and kept his hand drawn through her arm.

"Miss Manette, look upon the prisoner."

She gazed upon him with a look of intense pity. His hands moved restlessly and it was only with an effort that he controlled his breathing.

The crowd buzzed again.

"Miss Manette, have you seen the prisoner before?"

"Yes, sir."

"Where?"

"On board the packet-boat just referred to, sir, and on the same occasion."

"You are the young lady just now referred to?"

"Yes, sir."

"Did you have any conversation with the prisoner?"

"Yes sir, he helped me make my father comfortable on deck. My father was very weak and needed as much air as possible."

"Did you notice if anybody came on board with the prisoner?"

"Yes sir, two French gentlemen."

"Did they speak together?"

"Yes sir, the three gentlemen spoke together until the boat was due to leave; they then went back in their own boat to the shore."

"Had any papers been handed about among them, similar to these lists which I am holding up?"

"They had some papers, but I was not near enough to see them closely, nor did I listen to their conversation."

"Now, what about the prisoner's conversation, Miss Manette?"

"The prisoner was quite open with me. He was kind and good, and helped my father. I hope," said Miss Manette, bursting into tears, "that I may not repay him by doing him harm today."

"Miss Manette, you know you are obliged to give evidence. Please continue."

"He told me he was travelling on business of a delicate and difficult nature, which might get people into trouble, and that, therefore, he was not travelling under his own name. He said that this business had, within a few days, taken him to France, and might from time to time, take him backwards and forwards between France and England for a long time to come."

"Did he say anything about America, Miss Manette?"

"He tried to explain to me how the quarrel between Britain and America had arisen and said he thought Britain was in the wrong. He added that perhaps George Washington might gain almost as great a name in history as King George the Third, but it was only a joke; he said it laughingly and to pass the time."

The Judge looked up angrily from his notes and the crowd buzzed again.

"Miss Manette, that will be all. Please assist your father to rise."

"Doctor Manette, look upon the prisoner. Have you ever seen him before?"

"Once. When he called at my lodgings in London. Some three years, or three years and a half ago."

"Can you identify him as your fellow passenger on board the packet-boat? Can you confirm that he and your daughter spoke together then?"

"Sir, I can do neither of those things."

"Is there any particular and special reason for this?"

He answered, in a low voice, "There is."

"Has it been your misfortune to undergo a long imprisonment? Without trial, or even accusation, in your own country, Doctor Manette?"

He answered, in a tone that went to every heart, "A long imprisonment."

"Had you just been released when you came on board the boat with your daughter?"

"They tell me so."

"You cannot remember?"

"I cannot remember any of that time except that I knew my dear daughter again, and that under her care my memory of present events is improving."

Mr Attorney-General sat down, and the father and daughter sat down together.

A witness was then produced to say that he had seen the prisoner acting suspiciously those five years ago and leaving the Dover Mail to collect information from a certain person in the coffee room of a hotel along the way.

The prisoner's counsel was cross-examining the witness with no result, except to get from him the fact that this was the only time he had ever seen the prisoner. At this point, the wigged gentleman who had all the time been gazing at the ceiling, wrote a word or two on a little piece of paper, screwed it up, and tossed it over. Opening this piece of paper, the counsel looked with great attention and curiosity at the man he was defending and looked again at the witness.

"You say again you are quite sure that it *was* the prisoner that you saw?"

"Quite sure, sir."

"Did you ever see anybody very like the prisoner?"

"Not so like that I could be mistaken, sir."

"Look well upon that gentleman, my learned friend there," pointing to the man who had tossed the paper over and then look again at the prisoner. "Do you think they are very like each other?"

They were sufficiently like each other to surprise all those present and even more so when the learned gentleman took off his wig.

The Judge inquired whether they were now to try Mr Carton, the learned gentleman, and Mr Stryver, the prisoner's counsel, asked the witness if, having seen that such a likeness was possible, he was probably not mistaken in thinking that he had seen the prisoner.

The witness gave way and his evidence was discarded as of no value.

Mr Stryver continued the case in favour of his client, Charles Darnay. He told the jury that Barsad was nothing but a hired spy and a scoundrel and his friend, the servant Cly, was no better. The prisoner who was French had perfectly good reasons for going to and from France on family business and his conversation with Miss Manette was light-hearted and harmless. Mr Stryver called a few witnesses and urged the jury to acquit his client.

Mr Attorney-General spoke up for Barsad and Cly and said they were patriotic and honest citizens. He urged the Jury to find the prisoner guilty.

The Judge then summed up and, generally speaking, after going through all the evidence, came down against the prisoner and in favour of the witnesses for the prosecution.

And now the Jury turned to consider their verdict.

Meanwhile Mr Carton, hands in his pockets, continued to lean back and gaze at the ceiling. His torn gown was half off him and his untidy wig put on just anyhow. He really did not look like a respectable man of the law and, in spite of his resemblance to the prisoner, the lookers-on said to one another that they would hardly have thought the two were so alike, and Jerry Cruncher said to his neighbour, "I'll lay *he* don't get no law-work to do. Don't look like the sort of one to get any, do he?"

Yet Mr Carton took in more of the details of the scene than he appeared to take in; for now, when Miss Manette's head drooped and she leaned for support on her father, he was the first to see it, and called out, "Officer! Look to that young lady. Help the gentleman to take her out before she faints."

There was much sympathy for Miss Manette and her father as they were helped out of the court. The father had evidently been greatly distressed when his days of imprisonment were recalled and the brooding, withdrawn look which made him seem so much older had been upon him like a heavy cloud ever since.

As he went out, the jury, who had turned back and paused a moment, spoke, through their foreman.

They were not agreed, and wished to retire. The Judge looked surprised but gave them permission and retired himself. The trial had lasted all day, and the lamps in the court were now being lighted. It began to be rumoured that the jury would be out for a long while. Spectators went out to get refreshment, and the prisoner withdrew to the back of the dock and sat down.

Mr Lorry, who had gone out when the young lady and her father went out, now reappeared, and beckoned to Jerry, who, with fewer people in the court, could now easily get near him.

"Jerry, if you want to have something to eat, you can. But keep nearby. You wil be sure to hear when the jury come in. Don't be a moment behind them, for I want you to take the verdict back to the Bank. You are the quickest messenger I know, and will get to Temple Bar long before I can." Mr Lorry gave him a shilling and Jerry touched his forehead. Mr Carton came up at that moment, and touched Mr Lorry on the arm.

"How is the young lady?"

"She is greatly distressed; but her father is comforting her, and she feels better now she has left the court."

"I'll tell the prisoner so." Mr Carton made his way towards the dock.

"Mr Darnay!"

The prisoner came forward at once.

"You will naturally be anxious to hear of the witness, Miss Manette. She is much recovered. You have seen the worst of her distress."

"I am deeply sorry to have been the cause of it. Could you tell her so from me with my fervent acknowledgments?"

"Yes, I could. I will, if you ask it."

Mr Carton's manner was so careless as to be almost insolent. He stood, half turned from the prisoner, lounging with his elbow against the bar.

"I do ask it. Accept my cordial thanks."

"What," said Carton, still only half turned towards him, "do you expect, Mr Darnay?"

"The worst."

"It's the wisest thing to expect, and the likeliest. But I think their withdrawing is in your favour."

Jerry, on his way out of court, heard what passed between them, but loitering not being allowed, he heard no more, but left them – so like each other in feature, so unlike each other in manner – standing side by side, both reflected in the glass above them.

An hour and a half passed in the thief and rascal crowded passages below, as mutton pie and ale were consumed. The hoarse messenger, uncomfortably seated on a form after refreshing himself, had dropped into a doze, when a loud murmur and a rapid tide of people setting up the stairs that led to the court, carried him along with them.

"Jerry! Jerry!" Mr Lorry was already calling at the door when he got there.

"Here, sir! It's a fight to get back again. Here I am, sir!"

Mr Lorry handed him a piece of paper through the throng.

"Quick!" Have you got it?"

"Yes, sir!"

Hastily written on the paper was the word "Acquitted."

"If you had sent the message, 'Recalled to Life,'

again," muttered Jerry as he turned, "I should have known what you meant, this time."

The crowd, still buzzing like baffled blue-flies, swept past him nearly knocking him off his feet, and dispersed in search of other grisly entertainment.

CHAPTER 4

Doctor Manette, Lucie Manette, his daughter, Mr Lorry, solicitor for the defence, and Mr Stryver, counsel for the defence stood gathered round Mr Charles Darnay – just released – congratulating him on his escape from death.

Mr Darnay kissed Lucie's hand fervently and gratefully, and turned to Mr Stryver, thanking him warmly. Mr Stryver was a man of little more than thirty, but looked twenty years older than he was, stout, loud and red in the face. He still had his wig and gown on and he said to the former prisoner: "I am glad to have brought you off with honour, Mr Darnay. It was an infamous prosecution, grossly infamous; but, even so, it might have succeeded."

"I shall remember what you have done for me all my life,' said Charles Darnay, taking his hand.

"I have done my best for you, Mr Darnay, and my best is as good as another man's, I believe," said Mr Stryver, shaking his hand.

"Now, I will appeal to Doctor Manette, to break up this conference and order us all to our homes," said Mr Lorry. "Miss Lucie looks ill; Mr Darnay has had a terrible day; we are all worn out."

"Shall we go home, father?" said Lucie, laying her hand on his.

With a long breath, he answered "Yes." His thoughts had been far away in the past.

Walking between her father and Mr Darnay, Lucie passed into the open air. A hackney-coach was called, and the father and daughter departed in it.

Mr Stryver departed to the robing-room and Mr Lorry returned to Tellson's.

Another person who had not joined the group, but who had stood leaning against the wall where its shadow was darkest now stepped up to where Mr Darnay stood alone upon the pavement. He smelt of port wine and did not appear to be quite sober. Nobody had made any acknowledgment of the part he had played in Charles Darnay's acquittal; nobody had known of it. He had removed his wig and gown and was none the better for it in appearance.

"This is a strange chance that throws you and me together. It must be strange for you standing here with your counterpart, to see another man whose face is identical to yours."

"I hardly seem yet," returned Charles Darnay, "to belong to this world again."

"You speak faintly."

"I begin to think I *am* faint."

"Then why the devil don't you dine? I dined, myself, while those numbskulls were deciding which world you should belong to, this one or the next. Let me show you the nearest tavern to dine well at."

Drawing Darnay's arm through his own, he took him down Ludgate Hill to Fleet Street, and so, up a covered way, into a tavern. Here, they were shown into a little room, where Charles Darnay was soon regaining his strength with a good plain dinner and good wine, while Carton sat opposite to him at the same table, with his separate bottle of port before him, and showing his careless, half-insolent manner.

"Do you feel, yet, that you belong to this world again, Mr Darnay?"

"I am frightfully confused, but I know I am back in the world of the living."

"It must be an immense satisfaction!"

Carton said it bitterly, and filled up his glass again which was a large one. "The greatest desire I have is to forget that I belong to this world. It has no good in it for me – except for wine like this – and I have nothing to give to the world. Indeed, I begin to think that we are not much alike, you and I."

Confused and feeling as if he was dreaming this encounter with his double, so different to himself in manners and outlook, Darnay did not reply.

"Now your dinner is done," Carton presently said, "why don't you call a health, Mr Darnay? Why don't you give your toast?"

"What health? What toast?"

"You know very well. I swear it's on the tip of your tongue."

"Miss Manette, then!"

"Miss Manette, then!"

Looking his companion full in the face while he drank the toast, Carton flung his glass over his shoulder against the wall, where it shivered to pieces. Then he rang the bell and ordered in another.

Darnay said nothing.

"She was mightily pleased when I gave her your message," said Carton. "Not that she showed she was pleased, but I suppose she was."

This remark reminded Darnay that this unattractive companion had, of his own free will, come to the aid of his defence in the heat of the day.

He changed the subject and thanked him warmly.

"I neither want any thanks, nor deserve any," was the careless answer. "It was nothing and I don't know why I did it. Let me ask you a question: do you think I particularly like you?"

"Really Mr Carton," said Darnay, rather ill at ease, "I have not asked myself that question."

"Then ask yourself that question now."

"You have acted as if you do, but I don't think you do."

"*I* don't think I do," said Carton. "I begin to have a very good opinion of your understanding."

"Well, even so," said Darnay, rising to ring the bell, "there is nothing to stop my calling the reckoning and paying for what we have had and for our parting in a friendly manner."

"Nothing in life," said Carton.

Darnay rang the bell and the waiter appeared.

"Do you pay for all?" asked Carton.

"Yes, that is my wish," answered Darnay.

"Then bring me another pint of this same wine, waiter, and come and wake me at ten."

The bill being paid, Charles Darnay rose, and wished him goodnight. Without returning the wish, Carton rose too, with something of a threat of defiance in his manner, and said, "A last word, Mr Darnay: do you think I am drunk?"

'I think you have been drinking, Mr Carton."

"Think? You know I have been drinking."

"Since I must say so, yes I know it."

"Then you shall likewise know why. I am a disappointed drudge, sir. I prepare cases for men like your friend Stryver, but mine are the brains, and withal I care for no man on earth, and no man on earth cares for me."

"Much to be regretted. You might have used your talents better."

"Maybe so, Mr Darnay; maybe not. Don't congratulate yourself on your sober face, however; you don't know what it may come to. Goodnight!"

When he was left alone, this strange being took up a candle, went to a glass that hung against the wall, and studied his face in it. Made wretched by what he saw and contrasting himself with Charles Darnay, he took refuge in his pint of wine for consolation, drank it all in a few minutes, and fell asleep on his arms dreaming of the blue eyes of Lucie Manette.

CHAPTER 5

The quiet lodgings of Doctor Manette were in a street corner not far from Soho Square. On the afternoon of a certain fine Sunday when the Old Bailey trial of Charles Darnay had become a four-month old memory, Mr Jarvis Lorry walked along the sunny streets from Clerkenwell where he lived, on his way to dine with the doctor. Mr Lorry had become the doctor's friend, and the quiet street corner was the sunny part of his life.

A quainter corner than the corner where the doctor lived, was not to be found in London. There was no way through it, and the front windows of the doctor's lodgings looked over a pleasant little vista of street that had a comfortable air of retirement on it.

There were few buildings then, north of the Oxford Road, and forest trees flourished, and wild flowers grew, and the hawthorn blossomed, in the now vanished fields. Country air circulated, and there was many a good south wall, not far off, on which the peaches ripened in their season.

The summer light struck into the corner brilliantly in the earlier part of the day, but when the streets grew hot, the corner was in shadow, but you could still see beyond it into a glare of brightness. It was a cool spot, quiet but cheerful, a wonderful place for echoes, and a very harbour from the raging streets.

The doctor occupied two floors of a large still house, where others pursued their various trades but were seldom seen or heard.

He himself received enough patients to make a modest living and his scientific knowledge and reputation brought him a fair number of requests.

Mr Lorry rang the bell.

'Doctor Manette at home?"

Expected home.

"Miss Lucie at home?"

Expected home.

"Miss Pross at home?"

Possibly at home, handmaid not sure.

"As I am at home myself," said Mr Lorry, "I'll go upstairs."

There were three rooms on a floor, all simply but delightfully furnished by the good taste of the doctor's daughter. The communicating doors between the rooms were open to allow the air to pass through freely, so Mr Lorry smilingly walked from one to another. The first was the best room, and in it were Lucie's birds, and flowers, and books, and desk, and worktable, and box of watercolours; the second was the doctor's consulting-room, used also as the dining-room; the third was the doctor's bedroom, and there, in a corner, stood the disused shoemaker's bench and tray of tools, much as it had stood on the fifth floor of the dismal house by the wine shop, in the suburb of Saint Antoine in Paris.

"I wonder," said Mr Lorry, pausing in his looking about, "that he keeps that reminder of his sufferings about him!"

"And why wonder at that?" was the abrupt inquiry that made him start.

It proceeded from Miss Pross, the wild red woman, strong of hand, whom he had first met at the Royal George Hotel at Dover, and had since grown to know better.

"I should have thought – " Mr Lorry began.

"Pooh! You'd have thought!" said Miss Pross, and Mr Lorry left off.

"How do you do?" inquired that lady then – sharply, and yet as if to express that she bore him no malice.

"I am pretty well, I thank you," answered Mr Lorry, with meekness, "how are you?"

"Nothing to boast of," said Miss Pross.

"Indeed!"

"Ah! indeed!" said Miss Pross. "I am very much put out about my Ladybird."

"Indeed?"

"For gracious sake say something else besides 'indeed', or you'll fidget me to death," said Miss Pross, whose character was shortness.

"Really, then?" said Mr Lorry.

"Really is bad enough," returned Miss Pross, "but better. Yes, I am very much put out."

"May I ask the cause?"

"I don't want dozens of people who are not at all worthy of Ladybird, to come here looking for her."

"Do *dozens* come for that purpose?"

"Hundreds," said Miss Pross, improving on her complaint as she went along.

"Dear me!" said Mr Lorry, as the safest remark he could think of.

"I have lived with the darling – or the darling has lived with me, and paid me for it, which she should certainly never have done, if I could have afforded to keep either myself or her for nothing – since she was ten years old. And it's really very hard," said Miss Pross.

Not seeing exactly what was hard, Mr Lorry shook his head and tried to look sympathetic.

"All sorts of people who are not in the least degree worthy of the pet, are always turning up," said Miss Pross. "When you began it – "

"I began it, Miss Pross?"

"When you brought her father to life, when you brought him back from France. It is not his fault, but it really is doubly and trebly hard to have crowds and multitudes turning up to see him to take Ladybird's affections away from me."

Mr Lorry knew Miss Pross to be very jealous, but her love for Lucie and the service she gave her were unselfish and came from the heart.

74

"There never was, nor will be, but one man worthy of Ladybird," said Miss Pross, "and that was my brother Solomon, if he hadn't made a mistake in life."

Mr Lorry knew that her brother was a heartless scoundrel, who had stripped her of everything she possessed and had abandoned her in her poverty for evermore, with no touch of regret or pity. She kept her faith in him and never spoke against him and this increased the high opinion which Mr Lorry, who understood her well, had of her.

"As we happen to be alone for the moment," he said, as they sat down in a friendly way in the drawing-room, "let me ask you – does the doctor, in talking with Lucie, ever refer to the shoemaking time?"

"Never."

"And yet he keeps that bench and those tools beside him."

"Ah!" returned Miss Pross, shaking her head. "But I don't say he don't refer to it within himself."

"Do you believe that he thinks of it much?"

"I do," said Miss Pross.

"Do you imagine – " Mr Lorry had begun, when Miss Pross took him up short with:

"Never imagine anything. Have no imagination at all."

"Very well; do you *suppose* – you go so far – you go so far as to suppose, sometimes?"

"Now and then," said Miss Pross.

"Do you suppose," Mr Lorry went on, with a laughing

twinkle in his bright eye, as it looked kindly at her, "that Doctor Manette has any idea who sent him to prison without even a trial?"

"I don't suppose anything about it but what Ladybird tells me."

"And that is – ?"

"That she thinks he has."

"He was an innocent man. Why does he never refer to it?"

"To the best of my understanding," said Miss Pross, "he is afraid of the whole subject."

'Afraid?"

"It's plain enough, I should think, why he may be. It's a dreadful remembrance. Besides that, his loss of himself grew out of it. Not knowing how he lost himself, or how he recovered himself, he may never feel certain of not losing himself again. That alone wouldn't make the subject pleasant, I should think."

"It worries me that he shuts it up within himself, Miss Pross. That is why I am talking to you now."

"Can't be helped," said Miss Pross. "If he is reminded of it in any way, he instantly changes for the worse. It is better to leave it alone. Sometimes he gets up in the dead of the night, and we can hear him walking up and down, walking up and down in his room. Ladybird has learnt to know then that his mind is walking up and down, walking up and down in his old prison. Then Lucie goes to him and walks up and down with him until he is peaceful again. But he never says a word of the true reason of his restlessness to her and she thinks it best not to ask. In silence they go walking up and down together, till her love and company have brought him to himself."

The corner where they lived has been mentioned as a wonderful corner for echoes. Now it had begun to echo to the tread of coming feet as though the very mention of that weary pacing to and fro had set it going.

"Here they are," said Miss Pross, rising to break up the conference, "and now we shall have hundreds of people pretty soon!"

As Mr Lorry stood at the open window, looking for the father and daughter whose steps he heard, he fancied they would never approach. It was curious how the echoes died away, as though the steps had gone, but echoes of other steps that never came could be heard instead and then died away when they seemed close at hand. However, father and daughter did at last appear, and Miss Pross was ready at the street door to receive them.

On Sundays, Miss Pross dined at the doctor's table, but on other days persisted in taking her meals at unknown periods, either in the lower regions, or in her own room on the second floor. The day being Sunday, they all sat down together and had a very pleasant dinner.

It was a hot, heavy kind of day, and after dinner, Lucie proposed that the wine should be carried out under the plane-tree, and that they should sit there in the air. As everything turned upon her, and revolved around her, they went out under the plane-tree, and she carried the wine down for the special benefit of Mr Lorry. She had installed herself, some time before, as Mr Lorry's cup-bearer; and while they sat under the plane-tree, talking, she kept his glass filled. Mysterious backs and ends of houses peeped at them as they talked, and the plane-tree whispered to them in its own way above their heads.

The hundreds of people expected by Miss Pross did not present themselves. Mr Darnay presented himself while they were sitting under the plane-tree, but he was only One.

Doctor Manette received him kindly, and so did Lucie. But, Miss Pross suddenly became afflicted with a twitching in the head and body, and retired into the house. She was not unfrequently the victim of this disorder, and she called it in familiar conversation, "a fit of the jerks."

Tea-time came and Miss Pross made tea indoors, with another fit of the jerks upon her, and yet no hundreds of people. Mr Carton had lounged in, but he made only Two.

The night was so very sultry, that, although they sat with doors and windows open, they were overpowered by heat. After tea, they all moved to one of the windows, and looked out into the heavy twilight. Lucie sat by her father; Darnay sat beside her; Carton leaned against a window. The curtains were long and white, and some of the thundergusts that whirled into the corner, caught them up to the ceiling, and waved them like ghostly wings.

"The raindrops are still falling, large, heavy, and few," said Doctor Manette. "It comes slowly."

"It comes surely," said Carton.

They spoke low, as people watching and waiting mostly do; as people in a dark room, watching and waiting for lightning, always do.

There was a great hurry in the streets, of people speeding away to get shelter before the storm broke; the wonderful corner for echoes resounded with the echoes of footsteps coming and going, yet not a footstep was there.

"A multitude of people, and yet a solitude!" said Darnay, when they had listened for a while.

"I sometimes have a fancy," said Lucie, "when I am sitting alone here of an evening listening, that the echoes I can hear are the echoes of all the footsteps that are coming by-and-by into our lives."

"There is a great crowd coming one day into our lives, if that be so," Sydney Carton struck in, in his moody way, "and I see them – by the lightning." He added the last words, after there had been a vivid flash which had shown him lounging in the window.

"And I hear them!" he added again, after a peal of thunder. "Here they come fast, fierce, and furious!"

He spoke of the rush and roar of rain, and it stopped him, for no voice could be heard in it. A memorable storm of thunder and lightning broke with that sweep of water, and there was not a moment's interval in crash, and fire, and rain, until after the moon rose at midnight.

The great bell of St Paul's was striking One in the cleared air, when Mr Lorry, escorted by Jerry, high-booted and bearing a lantern, set forth on his return journey to Clerkenwell. There were solitary patches of road on the way between Soho and Clerkenwell, and Mr Lorry, mindful of footpads, always retained Jerry for this service, though it was usually performed a good two hours earlier.

"What a night it has been! Almost a night, Jerry," said Mr Lorry, "to bring the dead out of their graves."

"I never see the night myself, master – nor yet I don't expect to – what would do that!" answered Jerry.

"Good night, Mr Carton," said Mr Lorry. "Good night Mr Darnay. Shall we ever see such a night again, together!"

Perhaps. Perhaps, see the great crowd of people with its rush and roar, bearing down upon them, too.

CHAPTER 6

Monseigneur, one of the great lords in power at the Court, held his fortnightly reception in his grand house in Paris. He was in his inner room and the crowd of people who wished to see him were in the suite of rooms outside.

Monsigneur was about to drink his morning chocolate and there were four attendants dressed in gorgeous uniforms to help him do it.

The people who wished to see him had one thing in common: they were all dressed as if for a Fancy Dress Ball, and that was how it was among the people who counted, in the Paris of seventeen hundred and eighty.

Monseigneur having finished his chocolate, caused the doors of his inner room to be thrown open and then what bowing and what servility from the elegant people with their humble requests!

Bestowing a word of promise here and a smile there, a whisper to one and a wave of the hand to another, Monseigneur affably walked through his rooms and back again, and so in due course of time got himself shut up in his sanctuary by his attendants, and was seen no more.

The show being over, there was soon but one person left of all the crowd, and he, with his hat under his arm and his snuff-box in his hand, slowly passed among the mirrors on his way out.

"I devote you," said this person, stopping at the last door on his way, and turning in the direction of the sanctuary, "to the Devil!"

With that, he shook the snuff from his fingers as if he had shaken the dust from his feet, and quietly walked downstairs.

He was a man of about sixty, handsomely dressed, haughty in manner, and with a face like a fine mask. The nose, beautifully formed otherwise, was very slightly pinched at the top of each nostril and across his pale face passed, from time to time, a look of treachery. But it was a handsome face and a remarkable one.

Its owner went downstairs into the courtyard, got into his carriage, and drove away. Not many people had talked with him at the reception; he had stood in a little space apart, and Monseigneur might have been warmer in his manner.

Under the circumstances, it appeared rather agreeable to him to see the common people dispersed before his horses, and often barely escaping being run down. His man drove as if he were charging an enemy and his master made no attempt to stop him.

With a wild rattle and clatter, the carriage dashed through streets and swept round corners, with women screaming before it, and men clutching each other and pulling children out of its way. At last, swooping at a street corner by a fountain, one of its wheels came to a sickening little jolt, and there was a loud cry from a number of voices, and the horses reared and plunged as twenty hands held their bridles and the frightened valet got down in a hurry.

"What has gone wrong?" said Monsieur, calmly looking out.

A tall man in a nightcap had caught up a bundle from among the feet of the horses, and had laid it on the base of the fountain, and was down in the mud and wet, howling over it like a wild animal.

"Pardon, Monsieur the Marquis!" said a ragged man, "it is a child."

"Why does he make that abominable noise? Is it his child?"

"Excuse me, Monsieur the Marquis – it is a pity – yes."

The fountain was a little further off, for the street opened into a space some ten or twelve yards square. As the tall man suddenly got up from the ground, and came running at the carriage, Monsieur the Marquis clapped his hand for an instant on his sword hilt.

"Killed!" shrieked the man, in wild desperation, extending both arms at their length above his head, and staring at him. "Dead!"

The people closed round, and looked at Monsieur the Marquis. No one spoke.

Monsieur the Marquis ran his eyes over them all, as if they had been mere rats come out of their holes.

He took out his purse.

"It is extraordinary to me," said he, "that you people cannot take care of yourselves and your children. One or the other of you is for ever in the way. How do I know what injury you have done my horses? See! Give him that."

He threw out a gold coin for the valet to pick up, and all the heads craned forward to see it as it fell. The tall man called out again with a most unearthly cry, "Dead!"

He was stopped by the quick arrival of another man, for whom the rest made way. On seeing him, the miserable creature fell upon his shoulder, sobbing and crying, and pointing to the fountain, where some women were stooping over the motionless bundle, and moving gently about it. They were as silent as the men.

"I know all, I know all," said the latecomer. "Be a brave man, my Gaspard! It is better for the poor little thing to die so, than to live. It has died in a moment without pain. Could it have lived an hour as happily?"

"You are a philosopher, you there," said the Marquis, smiling. "How do they call you?"

"They call me Defarge."

"Of what trade?"

"Monsieur the Marquis, vendor of wine."

"Pick up that, philosopher and vendor of wine," said the Marquis, throwing him another gold coin, "and spend it as you will. The horses there; are they right?"

Without another glance, Monsieur the Marquis leaned back in his seat, and was just being driven away with the air of a gentleman who had accidentally broken some common thing, and had paid for it, and could afford to pay for it, when his comfort was suddenly disturbed by a coin flying into his carriage, and ringing on its floor.

"Hold the horses!" said Monsieur the Marquis. 'Who threw that?"

He looked to the spot where Defarge, the vendor of wine, had stood a moment before but the wretched father was grovelling on his face on the pavement in that spot, and the figure that stood beside him was the figure of a dark stout woman, knitting.

"You dogs," said the Marquis, "if I knew which rascal threw that at the carriage, and if that brigand were sufficiently near it, he should be crushed under the wheels." Among the men not an eye was raised for they knew what such a man could do to them, but the woman who stood knitting looked up steadily, and looked the Marquis in the face. It was not for his dignity to notice it; his contemptuous eyes passed over her, and over all the rest, and he leaned back in his seat again, and gave the word, "Go on!"

He was driven on, other carriages came whirling by, the poor people went inside, but still the woman knitted on with the steadfastness of Fate. The water of the fountain ran, the swift river ran, the day ran into evening, the people slept in their miserable holes and all things ran their course.

CHAPTER 7

Monsieur the Marquis in his travelling carriage (which might have been lighter), conducted by four post-horses and two postilions, fagged up a steep hill. The setting sun struck so brilliantly into the travelling carriage when it gained the hill top, that its occupant was steeped in crimson. "It will die out," said Monsieur the Marquis, glancing at his hands, "directly."

In effect, the sun was so low that it dipped at that moment. When the heavy drag had been adjusted to the wheel, and the carriage slid downhill, in a cloud of dust, the red glow departed quickly and there was none left when the drag was taken off.

But there remained a broken country, bold and open, a little village at the bottom of the hill, a broad sweep and rise beyond it, a church tower, a windmill, a forest for the chase, and a crag with a fortress on it used as a prison. Round upon all these darkening objects as the night drew on, the Marquis looked, with the air of one who was coming near home.

The village had its one poor street, with its poor brewery, poor tannery, poor tavern, poor stable-yard for relays of post-horses, poor fountain, everything poor. It had its poor people too. All its people were poor, and many of them were sitting at their doors, shredding spare onions, and the like for supper, while many were at the fountain, washing leaves and grasses, and anything else that grew and could be eaten.

Heralded by a courier in advance, and by the cracking of his postilions' whips, which twined snake-like about their heads in the evening air, Monsieur the Marquis drew up in his travelling carriage at the posting-house gate. It was right by the fountain and the peasants stopped what they were doing to look at him.

Monsieur the Marquis cast his eyes over them and said to the courier, "Bring me hither that fellow."

The fellow was brought, cap in hand, and the other fellows closed round to look and listen, in the manner of the people at the Paris fountain.

"Did not I pass you on the road?"

"Monseigneur, that is true. I am the road mender."

"Coming up the hill, and at the top of the hill, both?"

"Yes, Monseigneur."

"What were you staring at?"

"Monseigneur, I looked at the man."

He stooped a little, and with his tattered blue cap pointed under the carriage. All his fellows stooped to look under the carriage.

"What man? And why look there?"

"He was under there swinging by the chain that holds the drag."

"Who was he? You must know all the men in this part of the country. Who was he?"

"Monseigneur, I have never seen him before."

"What was he like?"

"Whiter than the miller, all covered with dust, white as a ghost, a very tall ghost."

"You see a thief under my carriage and do not open that great mouth of yours," said the Marquis. "Bah! Put him aside, Monsieur Gabelle!"

Monsieur Gabelle was the postmaster and local tax collector. He had come out of the posting-house and was holding the man in an official manner.

"Bah! Go aside!" said Monsieur Gabelle.

"One moment. Did the man run away when we stopped at the top of the hill and removed the drag?

"He vanished. One moment he was there; the next he was gone."

"Lay hands on this stranger if he seeks to lodge in your village tonight, Gabelle. Drive on!"

The carriage started off again and the horses broke into a quick trot. The sweet scents of the summer night rose all around him, the stars came out and soon Monsieur the Marquis was approaching his home, a large high-roofed house surrounded by over-hanging trees. A man came out with a light and he passed through the great door of his chateau.

"Monsieur Charles, whom I expect, is he arrived from England?"

"Monseigneur, not yet."

CHAPTER 8

It was a heavy mass of building, that château of Monsieur the Marquis, with a large stone courtyard before it, and two stone sweeps of staircase meeting in a stone terrace before the principal door. A stony business altogether, with heavy stone balustrades, and stone urns, and stone flowers, and stone faces of men, and stone heads of lions, in all directions.

Up the broad flight of shallow steps went Monsieur the Marquis. An owl in the great roof of the stable building hooted, but all else was quiet. The great door clanged behind him, and Monsieur the Marquis crossed a hall grim with certain old boar-spears, swords and hunting knives; grimmer with certain heavy riding-whips, of which many a peasant had felt the weight when his lord was angry.

Avoiding the larger rooms, which were dark and made fast for the night, Monsieur the Marquis, with his light-bearer going on before, went up the staircase to a door in a corridor. This thrown open, admitted him to his own private apartment of three rooms: his bed-chamber and two others. They were all fitted in luxurious fashion with exquisite old furniture.

A supper table was laid for two, in the third of the rooms. It was a round room in one of the château's four towers. It was a small lofty room, with its window wide open, and the wooden slatted blinds closed, so that the dark night only showed in slight horizontal lines of black, alternating with their broad lines of stone colour.

"My nephew," said the Marquis, glancing at the supper preparation, "they said he was not arrived."

Nor was he, but he had been expected with Monseigneur.

"Ah! It is probable he may not arrive tonight; nevertheless, leave the table as it is. I shall be ready in a quarter of an hour."

In a quarter of an hour Monseigneur was ready, and sat down alone to his sumptuous and choice supper. His chair was opposite to the window, and he had taken his soup, and was raising a glass of wine to his lips, when he put it down.

"What is that?" he calmly asked, looking with attention at the horizontal lines of black and stone colour.

"Monseigneur! What?"

"Outside the blinds. Open the blinds."

It was done.

"Well?"

"Monseigneur, it is nothing. The trees and the night are all that are there."

The servant who spoke had thrown the blinds wide, had looked out into the empty darkness, and stood, looking round for instructions.

"Good," said his master. "Close them again."

That was done too, and the Marquis went on with his supper. He was half way through it, when he again stopped with his glass in his hand, hearing the sound of wheels. It came on briskly, and came up to the front of the château.

"Ask who is arrived."

It was the nephew of Monseigneur who had been some distance behind his uncle on the road, but had known he was ahead through enquiring at the posting-houses.

He was to be told (said Monseigneur) that supper awaited him then and there, and that he was requested to come to it. In a little while he came. He was known in England as Charles Darnay.

Monseigneur received him in a courtly manner, but they did not shake hands.

"You left Paris yesterday, sir?" he said to Monseigneur, as he took his seat at table.

"Yesterday. And you?"

"I have come direct from London."

"You have been a long time coming to see me," said the Marquis.

"I have been on a special mission and through it, I have been in danger of my life."

"Not in danger of your life, surely?" said his uncle, but the smile on his face was cruel.

"I doubt, sir, if you would have minded. Indeed I think you may have worked for suspicion to fall on me."

"No, no, no," said Monseigneur pleasantly.

"Yes sir. Indeed, if you had not been out of favour at Court at the moment, I think I should have been in a French prison by now."

"Prisons are necessary," said the uncle, "they are the means by which we keep our power over the common people. Unfortunately, things are changing in France."

"We do not agree," said Charles, gloomily. "The way our family has behaved has caused its name to be more detested than any in France."

"Let us hope so, if fear compels these people to know their place."

"Sir," said the nephew, "we have done wrong, and are reaping the fruits of wrong. Even in my father's time, we did a world of wrong, injuring every human creature who came between us and our pleasure whatever it was. My mother, as she lay dying, implored me to do all I could to show mercy and make compensation to those we have wronged, but I receive no understanding or assistance from you, sir."

"You may seek those in vain, my nephew," said the Marquis, touching him on the breast with his forefinger. "It will always be so. I will die, keeping the system under which I have lived."

When he had said this, he took a pinch of snuff and put the box in his pocket.

"Better be a sensible man," he added, after ringing a small bell on the table, "and accept your natural destiny. But you are lost, Monsieur Charles, I see."

"This property and France are lost to me," said the nephew, sadly. "I renounce them."

"Are they both yours to renounce? France may be, but is the property? It is still mine. Your father and I, as twins, inherited it together, you remember."

"If it were mine, tomorrow I would abandon it and live elsewhere and in a different fashion. There is a curse on it, and on all this land."

"And if you renounce your inheritance, how will you live?"

"I will do what others have to do. I will work."

"In England, for example?"

"Yes. The family honour, sir, is safe from me in this country, and in England I am just Charles Darnay."

The ringing of a bell had caused the adjoining bed-chamber to be lighted. It now shone brightly through the communicating door. The Marquis looked that way, and listened for the retreating step of his valet.

"England is very attractive to you considering what a bad time you have had there."

"It is my refuge, sir."

"They say, those boastful English, that it is the refuge of many people. I believe you know another Frenchman who has found a refuge there. A doctor, is it not?"

"Yes."

"With a daughter?"

"Yes."

"Yes," said the Marquis. "You are fatigued. Good night."

"Good night, sir."

"I look forward to seeing you again in the morning. Light Monsieur, my nephew, to his chamber there! And burn Monsieur my nephew in his bed, if you will," he added to himself, before he rang his little bell again, and summoned his valet to his own bedroom.

The valet having come and gone, Monsieur the Marquis prowled up and down the room to prepare himself gently for sleep that hot still night. His softly-slippered feet made him resemble a silent tiger. The events of the day passed unbidden through his mind, ending with the little bundle on the step of the fountain, the women bending over it, and the tall man with his arms up, crying "Dead!"

"I am cool now," said Monsieur the Marquis, "and may go to bed."

So, leaving only one light burning on the large hearth, he let his thin gauze curtains fall around him, and heard the night break its silence with a long sigh as he composed himself to sleep.

For three heavy hours, the stone faces of the château stared blindly at the night. In the village, people and animals slept. The fountain in the village flowed unseen and unheard and the fountain at the château flowed unseen and unheard. Then, the grey water of both began to be ghostly in the light, and the eyes of the stone faces of the château were opened.

Lighter and lighter, until at last the sun touched the tops of the still trees, and poured its radiance over the hill. In the glow, the water of the château fountain seemed to turn to blood, and the stone faces crimsoned. The carol of the birds was loud and high, and on the weatherbeaten sill of the great window of the bed-chamber of Monsieur the Marquis, one little bird sang its sweetest song with all its might. At this, the nearest stone face seemed to stare amazed, and with open mouth and dropped jaw, looked awe-stricken.

Now the sun was up, and movement began in the village. The château awoke later. Doors and windows were thrown open and suddenly the great bell started ringing, people ran up and down the stairs and across the terrace, horses were saddled and ridden away.

The villagers were at the fountain, standing about in their depressed manner, and whispering low, but show-ing no other emotions than grim curiosity and surprise. What did all this mean and why was Monsieur Gabelle, the postmaster, being hoisted up behind a servant on horseback, and why did the horse gallop away with them? It meant that there was one stone face too many up at the château. It lay back on the pillow of Monsieur the Marquis. It was like a fine mask, suddenly startled, made angry and then turned into stone. Driven home into the heart of the stone figure attached to the face, was a knife. Round its hilt was a frill of paper, on which was scrawled: *"Drive him fast to his tomb. This, from* Jacques."

CHAPTER 9

Twelve months had come and gone, and Mr Charles Darnay was established in England as a tutor in French language and literature. He was also a translator, being as fluent in English as he was in French and soon became well-known.

There was only one thing missing: he had loved Lucie Manette since the time of his danger, but he had not yet spoken to her and the assassination of his uncle at the old château in France still preyed on his mind. There was another reason for not telling Lucie the state of his heart and this concerned the strong ties between her and her father. He must speak to Doctor Manette.

It was a warm summer day when Charles turned into the quiet corner in Soho. It was towards the close of day, and he knew that Lucie was out with Miss Pross.

He found the Doctor reading in his armchair by the window. He was much recovered and was now a very energetic man indeed. At the sight of Charles Darnay, he laid aside his book and held out his hand. "We have been counting on your return these three or four days past."

"How is Miss Manette?"

"She is well and your return will delight us all. She has gone out on some household matters, but will soon be home."

"Doctor Manette, I knew she was from home. I took the opportunity of her being from home, to beg to speak to you."

There was a silence.

"Bring your chair here," said the doctor, "and speak on."

"Doctor Manette, I am so happy coming here and feel so close to your family – "

The doctor held up his hand. "Is it about Lucie?"

"Yes, indeed it is."

The doctor withdrew his hand. "It is hard for me to speak of her at any time. It is very hard for me to hear her spoken of in that tone of yours, Charles Darnay."

"It is a tone of deep love and respect."

"I believe it. I believe it."

The doctor turned in his chair, but did not look at Charles or raise his eyes. His chin dropped upon his hand, and his white hair overshadowed his face:

"Have you spoken to Lucie?"

"No."

"Nor written?"

"Never."

"This is out of consideration for me, and I thank you for it." He held out his hand, but his expression was sad.

"Doctor Manette, if ever Lucie consented to become my wife, I can assure you that it would not affect her love for you in any way. I would never come between you."

"I do not know what is the state of her heart, but if she should ever tell me that you are essential to her perfect happiness, I will give her to you. I know that her love for me will never disappear."

"Rather will it grow," said Charles, taking the doctor's hand. "Your confidence in me ought to be returned with full confidence on my part. My present name is not, as you will remember, my own. I wish to tell you what that is, and why I am in England."

"Stop!" said the Doctor of Beauvais.

"I wish to tell you, that I may better deserve your confidence and have no secret from you."

"Tell me when I ask you, not now. If Lucie loves you and agrees to become your wife, you shall tell me on your marriage morning. Do you promise?"

"I promise."

"Give me your hand again. She will be home directly, and it is better she should not see us together tonight. Go! God bless you!"

When Lucie came back, she found him in his reading-chair. His head was bowed and it was only her kiss that brought him back from the memories of his past.

CHAPTER 10

If Sydney Carton ever shone anywhere, he certainly never shone in the house of Doctor Manette. He had been there often, during a whole year, and had always been the same moody and morose lounger there. When he cared to talk, he talked well, but the cloud of caring for nothing which overshadowed him, was very rarely pierced by the light within him.

Yet he did care something for the streets around that house and for the stones that made their pavements. Many a night he wandered there when wine had brought him no feeling of well-being and he could not sleep. Many a dreary daybreak found him still there, but this quiet time brought him some relief and a sense of better things into his mind.

One day in August, his feet, instead of aimlessly wandering, took him with a sense of purpose to Doctor Manette's door.

He was shown upstairs, and found Lucie at her art-work, alone. She had never been quite at her ease with him, and received him rather shyly as he seated himself near her table, but, looking up at his face as they spoke their first words, she noticed a change in it.

"I fear you are not well, Mr Carton!"

"No. But the life I lead, Miss Manette, does not improve my health."

"Is it not – forgive me – a pity to live no better life?"

"God knows it is a shame!"

"Then why not change it?"

Looking gently at him again, she was surprised and saddened to see that there were tears in his eyes. There were tears in his voice too, as he answered:

"It is too late for that. I shall never be better than I am. I shall sink lower, and be worse."

He leaned an elbow on her table, and covered his eyes with his hand. The table trembled in the silence that followed.

She had never seen him like this, and was much distressed. He knew her to be so, without looking at her, and said:

"Pray forgive me, Miss Manette. I break down when I think of what I want to say to you. Will you hear me?"

"If it will do you any good, Mr Carton, if it would make you happier, it would make me very glad!"

"God bless you for your sweet compassion!"

He unshaded his face after a little while, and spoke steadily.

"Don't be afraid to hear me. Don't shrink from anything I say. I am like one who died young. All my life is a might have been."

"No, I am sure the best part of it may still be if you will only help yourself."

"If I knew that I would have you always at my side, it might be possible, but you can never return my love, and indeed, I would not wish it because I should drag you down with me."

Pale and trembling, she replied, "Then how can I help you as a friend? I am afraid I have made you more unhappy than before you knew me."

"That is not true. If anyone could have helped me, you could. You will never be the cause of my becoming worse."

"Have I no power, then for good with you, at all?"

"I have your sweet pity and you have my confidence which I know will be shared by no one."

"You have my promise."

"You will not tell even the dearest one ever to be known to you?"

"Mr Carton," she answered, after an agitated pause, "the secret is yours, not mine, and I promise to respect it."

"Thank you. And again, God bless you."

He put her hands to his lips, and moved towards the door.

"I shall never refer to this again, but I shall like to think, at my death, that you have carried my name and faults, and miseries gently in your heart. May it otherwise be light and happy!"

Lucie wept for him as he stood looking back at her.

"Be comforted. I am not worthy of your tears. But

remember: I would give my life for you. I would give my life to keep a life you love beside you!"

He said, "Farewell!" said a last, "God bless you!" and left her.

CHAPTER 11

Mr Jeremiah Cruncher was sitting on his stool outside Tellson's in Fleet Street with his grisly son beside him, thinking about nothing in particular, when he saw a funeral approaching accompanied by a noisy crowd.

"Young Jerry," said Mr Cruncher, turning to his son, "it's a buryin'"

"Hurrah, father!" cried young Jerry, nodding and winking in a mysterious way.

The crowd approached. They were bawling and hissing round a dingy hearse and dingy mourning coach which had only one uneasy-looking mourner in it. The crowd were making faces at him, groaning and calling out, "Yah! Spies! Yah! Spies!"

Funerals had at all times a remarkable attraction for Mr Cruncher; he always pricked up his senses, and became excited, when a funeral passed Tellson's. One of the crowd bumped against him, and so he asked him: "What is it brother? What's it about?"

"I don't know," said the man. "Spies! Yah! Spies!"

Jerry asked another man. "Who is it?"

"I don't know," returned the man, clapping his hands

to his mouth nevertheless and shouting with the others, "Spies! Yah! Spies!"

Eventually someone better informed tumbled against him, and from this person he learned that the funeral was the funeral of one Roger Cly.

"Was he a spy?" asked Mr Cruncher.

"Old Bailey spy," returned his informant. "Yah! Old Bailey Spies!"

"Why to be sure!" exclaimed Jerry, recalling the Trial of Charles Darnay. "I've seen him. Dead is he?"

"Dead as mutton," returned the other, and can't be too dead. Pull the other one out. Spies! Spies!"

The crowd caught up this idea with great eagerness and pulled open the doors of the mourning coach. The mourner was too quick for them, however, and in a moment he jumped out and ran away up a by-street, after shedding his cloak, hat, long hatband and white pocket handkerchief. These the crowd tore up and then made for the hearse as if to take the coffin out. At that moment, someone had a better idea – they would escort the hearse with the coffin inside to its destination. The mourning coach was immediately filled with eight people inside and a dozen out, while as many people got on the roof of the hearse as could manage to stick on it. Among the first of these volunteers was Jerry Cruncher himself, who modestly concealed his spiky head from the observation of Tellson's, in the further corner of the mourning coach. Young Jerry stayed behind to keep their pitch.

The undertakers protested against these arrangements, but remembering that the crowd was wild and might put them in the nearby river, they soon gave up and the procession restarted with a chimneysweep driving the hearse and a pieman driving the mourning coach. And so the procession went its disorderly way.

Its destination was the old church of St Pancras, far off in the fields. It got there in course of time, insisted on pouring into the burial ground and assisted at the internment of the late Roger Cly in its own way and highly to its own satisfaction.

The dead man disposed of, the crowd gradually dispersed and went off to do further mischief elsewhere.

Jerry Cruncher stayed behind to confer with the undertakers and stood for some little time looking at the railings. "Jerry," he said to himself, "you see that there Cly at the Trial and you see with your own eyes that he was a young 'un and a straight made 'un." Then he turned around and hurried back to Tellson's so that he would be at his post before the Bank closed.

Young Jerry reported No Jobs, the Bank closed, the ancient clerks came out and father and son went home to tea.

"Now I tell you where it is," said Mr Cruncher to his wife, on entering. "If, as a honest tradesman, my affairs goes wrong tonight, I shall make sure that you've been praying against me, and I shall work you for it just the same as if I seen you do it."

The dejected Mrs Cruncher shook her head.

"Why, you're at it afore my face!" said her husband angrily.

"I am saying nothing."

"Well then, don't think nothing either. It's against me just the same. Drop it altogether."

"Yes, Jerry."

"Yes, Jerry," repeated Mr Cruncher sitting down to tea. "You may well say, yes, Jerry. He took a bite out of his bread-and-butter and drank some tea out of his saucer.

"Are you going out tonight?" asked his decent wife, as he took another bite.

"Yes, I am."

"May I go with you, father?" asked his son, briskly.

"No, you mayn't. I'm a going – as your mother knows – a fishing. That's where I'm going to. Going a fishing."

"Your fishing-rod gets rather rusty, don't it, father?"

"Never you mind."

"Shall you bring any fish home, father?"

"Of a kind maybe. We have to live. That's enough questions. I ain't a going out, till you've been long a-bed."

The evening wore away until young Jerry was ordered to bed, and later Mrs Cruncher as well. Mr Cruncher was left alone. He passed the time smoking his pipes and did not start on his excursion until one o'clock.

Towards that small and ghostly hour, he rose up from his chair, took a key out of his pocket, opened a locked cupboard, and brought forth a sack, a crowbar of convenient size, a rope and chain, and other tackle of that nature. Disposing all these things about him in a skilful manner, he extinguished the light, and went out.

Young Jerry, who had only pretended to undress when he went to bed, was not long after his father. Under cover of the darkness he followed out of the room, followed down the stairs, followed down the courtyard, followed out into the streets. He was not worried about getting into the house again, for it was full of lodgers, and the door stood ajar all night.

Young Jerry, keeping as close to house fronts, walls and doorways, as his eyes were close to one another, held his honoured parent in view. The honoured parent had not gone far, when he was joined by another man, and the two trudged on together. Within half an hour, they were out upon a lonely road and here another man came silently up.

The three went on, and young Jerry went on, until the three stopped under a bank overhanging the road. Upon the top of the bank was a low brick wall with an iron railing along its top. In the shadow of bank and wall the three turned out of the road, and up a blind lane of which the wall there, risen to some eight or ten feet high – formed one side.

Crouched down in a corner, peeping up the lane, the next object that Young Jerry saw, was the form of his honoured parent, just showing in the light of a watery and clouded moon, nimbly scaling an iron gate. He was soon over, and then the second man got over, and then the third. They all dropped softly on the ground within the gate, and lay there a little – listening perhaps. Then they moved away on their hands and knees.

It was now Young Jerry's turn to approach the gate, which he did, holding his breath. Crouching down again in a corner there, and looking in, he could see the three men creeping through some coarse grass, and all the gravestones in the churchyard looking like ghosts in white, while the church tower itself looked on like the ghost of a monstrous giant. They did not creep far, before they stopped and stood upright. And then they began to dig.

They dug with a spade at first. Presently the honoured parent appeared to be adjusting some instrument like a great corkscrew. Whatever tools they worked with, they worked hard, until the awful striking of the church clock so terrified Young Jerry, that he made off, with his hair stiff as his father's.

But he wanted so much to know what his father was doing that he crept back, and peered through the gate again.

They were still digging, but now they seemed to have hit something. There was a screwing and a wrenching sound down below, and their bent figures were strained as if by a weight. By slow degrees the weight broke away the earth upon it, and came to the surface. Young Jerry very well knew what it would be, but when he saw the coffin, and saw his honoured parent about to wrench it open, he was so frightened, that he made off again, and never stopped until he had run a mile or more. He thought the coffin must be following him, hopping behind him bolt upright, always on the point of overtaking him or coming up at his side, gaining on him all the time.

When he got to his own door, he was half-dead with fear and thought the coffin was following him upstairs, with a bump on every stair and that it scrambled into bed with him and bumped down, dead and heavy, on his chest when he fell asleep.

From his heavy slumber, Young Jerry in his closet was awakened after daybreak and before sunrise, by the presence of his father in the family room. It seemed that something had gone wrong with him for he had Mrs Cruncher by the ears, and was knocking the back of her head against the headboard of the bed.

"I told you I would," said Mr Cruncher, "and I did."

"Jerry, Jerry, Jerry!" his wife implored.

"You go against my business and me and my partners suffer. You was to honour and obey; why the devil don't you?"

"I try to be a good wife, Jerry," the poor woman protested, with tears.

"Is it being a good wife to go against your husband's business? Is it honouring your husband to dishonour his business? Is it obeying your husband to disobey him on the important subject of his business?"

"You hadn't taken to the dreadful business then, Jerry."

"It's not for you to say when I took to my business. A wife should let her husband's trade alone. If you can't understand that, you'll have to have it knocked into you."

The argument was conducted in a low tone of voice and finished in Mr Cruncher kicking off his clay-soiled boots, and lying down full-length on the floor. After taking a timid peep at him lying on his back, with his rusty hands under his head for a pillow, his son lay down too, and fell asleep again.

There was not much for breakfast and Mr Cruncher was out of spirits and out of temper, but he was brushed and washed at the usual hour, and set off with his son to pursue his daytime calling.

Young Jerry, walking with the stool under his arm at his father's side along sunny and crowded Fleet Street, was a very different Young Jerry from him of the previous night, running home through darkness and solitude from his grim pursuer. His cunning was fresh with the day and his fears had gone with the night.

"Father," said Young Jerry, as they walked along, taking care to keep at arm's length and to have the stool well between them, "what's a Resurrection-Man?"

Mr Cruncher came to a stop on the pavement before he answered, "How should I know?"

"I thought you knowed everything, father," said the artful boy.

"Hem! Well," returned Mr Cruncher, moving on

again, and lifting off his hat to give his spiky hair free play, "he's a tradesman."

"What's his goods, father?" asked the brisk young Jerry.

"His goods," said Mr Cruncher, after turning it over in his mind, "is a branch of Scientific goods."

"Persons' bodies, ain't it, father?" asked the lively boy.

"I believe it is something of that sort," said Mr Cruncher.

"Oh, father, I should so like to be a Resurrection-Man when I'm quite growed up!"

Mr Cruncher was soothed, but shook his head in a dubious and moral way. "It depends upon how you dewelop your talents. Be careful to dewelop your talents, and never say no more than you can help to nobody, and there's no telling at the present time what you may not come to be fit for." As Young Jerry, thus encouraged, went on a few yards in advance, to plant the stool outside Tellson's, Mr Cruncher added to himself: "Jerry, you honest tradesman, there's hopes what that boy will yet be a blessing to you, and will make up for his mother."

CHAPTER 12

There had been earlier drinking than usual in the wine shop of Monsieur Defarge. At six o'clock faces could be seen through the barred windows, drinking and whispering. The wine was thin, the faces gloomy and secretive. This early drinking and whispering had started on Monday; it was now Wednesday and as they glided from seat to seat, corner to corner, the customers seemed more interested in swallowing talk than drink. The talk they consumed with greedy looks.

In spite of the numbers in the wine shop, its master was not present. He was not missed; for nobody who crossed the threshold looked for him, nobody asked for him, nobody wondered to see only Madame Defarge in her seat, presiding over the distribution of wine, with a bowl of battered small coins before her, as much beaten down as the poor people from whose ragged pockets they had come.

It was high noontide when two dusty men passed through the streets of St Antoine and under its swinging lamps. One was Monsieur Defarge, the other a mender of roads in a blue cap. Dusty and thirsty, they entered the wine shop. Their arrival had kindled a flame of excitement in the town, yet, no one had followed them, and no man spoke when they entered the wine shop, though the eyes of every man there were turned upon them.

"Good day, gentlemen!" said Monsieur Defarge.

There was an answering chorus of "Good day!"

"It is bad weather, gentlemen," said Defarge, shaking his head.

Upon which every man looked at his neighbour, and then all cast down their eyes and sat silent. Except one man, who got up and went out.

"My wife," said Defarge to Madame Defarge, "I have travelled a distance with this good mender of roads. He is called Jacques. I met him – by accident – a day and a half's journey out of Paris. He is a good fellow. Give him a drink, my wife!"

A second man got up and went out. Madame Defarge set wine before the mender of roads called Jacques, who doffed his blue cap to the company, and drank. In the pocket of his blouse he carried some coarse dark bread; he ate this between whiles, and sat munching and drinking near Madame Defarge's counter. A third man got up and went out. Defarge refreshed himself with a small draught of wine and stood waiting until the countryman had made his breakfast. He looked at no one present, and no one now looked at him; not even Madame Defarge, who had taken up her knitting, and was at work.

"Have you finished your repast, friend?" he asked presently.

"Yes, thank you."

"Come then! You shall see the appartment that I told you you could occupy. It will suit you very well."

Out of the wine shop into the street, out of the street, into a courtyard, out of the courtyard up a steep staircase, out of the staircase into a garret where once a white-haired man had sat on a low bench making shoes.

No white-haired man was there now; but the three men were there who had gone out of the wine shop singly. Defarge closed the door carefully, and spoke in a subdued voice:

"Jacques One, Jacques Two, Jacques Three! This is the man who has made an arrangement with me, Jacques Four, to tell you his story. Speak Jacques Five!"

The mender of roads, blue cap in hand, wiped his forehead with it, and said, "Where shall I commence, Monsieur?"

"Begin" was Monsieur Defarge's not unreasonable reply, "at the beginning."

"I saw him then," began the mender of roads, "a year ago this summer, underneath the carriage of the Marquis, hanging by the chain. The carriage was slowly climbing the hill, so I saw him easily."

Jacques One interrupted and asked if he had ever seen the man before.

"Never," answered the mender of roads.

"How did you recognize him afterwards, then?" demanded Jacques Three.

"By his tall figure. When Monsieur the Marquis asked me to describe him, I told him 'Tall as a spectre.' He vanished for nine, ten, eleven months."

"No matter the number," said Defarge, "unfortunately, they found him at last. What happened then?"

"I was again at work upon the hillside, and the sun had started going down. I was collecting my tools to descend to my cottage down in the village below, when I raised my eyes, and saw, coming over the hill, six soldiers. In the midst of them was a tall man with his arms bound to his sides – like this!"

With the aid of his cap, he represented a man with his elbows bound fast at his hips, with chords that were knotted behind him.

"When they got nearer, I recognized the tall man, and I could tell by his eyes that he recognized me, but we did not show it to the soldiers. They brought him into the village; all the village ran to look; they took him past the mill, and up to the prison on the hill; all the village saw the prison gate open in the darkness of the night and swallow him up – like this!" He opened his mouth as wide as he could, and shut it with a sounding snap of his teeth. Defarge told him to continue.

"In the morning, with my tools upon my shoulder, I went round by the prison on my way to my work. There I saw him, high up, behind the bars of a lofty iron cage, looking through. He had no hand free, to wave to me. I dared not call to him; he looked at me as if he were a dead man already."

Defarge and the other three glanced darkly at one another. They exchanged dark revengeful looks and had an air of judgement about them as if they were a kind of rough tribunal.

"Go on, Jacques," said Defarge.

"He remained up there in his iron cage for some days and the village watched. When the people assembled to gossip at the fountain, all faces were turned towards the prison. They whispered at the fountain that, although condemned to death, he would not be executed; they said that petitions had been presented in Paris, showing that he was enraged and made mad by the death of his child; they said that a petition had been presented to the King himself. What do I know? It is possible. Perhaps yes, perhaps no."

"Listen then, Jacques," said Jacques Number One, "a petition *was* presented to the King and Queen. We all saw the King take it in his carriage, in the street, sitting beside the Queen. It was Defarge, whom you see here, who, at the hazard of his life, darted out in front of the horses with the petition in his hand."

"And the guards surrounded him and struck him blows," said Jacques Number Three.

"Well, go on Jacques," said Defarge.

"Well, in the end they built a gallows forty feet high above the fountain and there they hung him and left him hanging, poisoning the water. It is frightful. How

CHAPTER 13

Monsieur and Madame Defarge had been away from their suburb of St Antoine on a short visit and going and returning they had to pass through one of the gates of Paris. There was the usual stoppage at the barrier guard-house, and the usual lanterns were brought out for the usual examination and enquiry. Monsieur Defarge alighted from the public vehicle in which they had been travelling. He knew one or two of the soldiers there and was a close friend of one of the police. They passed through the barrier in their covered cart and soon afterwards alighted near the boundary of St Antoine.

As they were picking their way on foot through the muddy streets, Madame Defarge spoke to her husband:

"What did you hear from Jacques of the police?"

"Very little tonight, but all he knows. There is another spy coming to our quarter. There may be many more, for all that he can say, but he knows of one, anyhow."

"Very well," said Madame Defarge, raising her eyebrows with a cool business air. "It is necessary to register him. How do they call that man?"

'He is English."

"So much the better. His name?"

"Barsad," said Defarge and spelt it out for her.

"Barsad," repeated Madame. "Good. Christian name?"

"John."

"John Barsad," repeated Madame, after murmuring it once to herself. "Good. His appearance; is it known?"

"Age, about forty years; height, about five feet nine; black hair; complexion dark; rather handsome face; eyes dark; face thin, long and sallow; nose sharp, but not straight, leans over towards the left cheek; expression, therefore, sinister."

"My faith! It *is* a portrait!" said Madame, laughing. "He shall be registered in my knitting tomorrow."

Next noontide saw Madame Defarge in her usual place in the wine shop, knitting away. A rose lay beside her, and she glanced at it from time to time.

There were a few customers, drinking or not drinking, and it was very hot.

A figure entering at the door threw a shadow on Madame Defarge which she felt to be a new one. She laid down her knitting, and began to pin her rose in her headdress, before she looked at the figure.

It was curious. The moment Madame Defarge took up the rose, the customers ceased talking, and began gradually to go out of the wine shop.

"Good day, Madame," said the newcomer.

"Good day, Monsieur."

"She said it aloud, but added to herself: "Hah! This is the man. Good day one and all!"

"Have the goodness to give me a little glass of old cognac, and a mouthful of cool fresh water, Madame."

Madame gave him his cognac with a polite air.

"Marvellous cognac this, Madame!"

Madame Defarge knew that it was not, but she smiled and took up her knitting.

The visitor watched her fingers for a few moments, then said, "You knit with great skill, Madame."

"I am accustomed to it."

"A pretty pattern too!"

"You think so?" said Madame, looking at him with a smile.

"Decidedly. May one ask what it is for?"

"Just a hobby," said Madame, still looking at him with a smile, while her fingers moved nimbly.

"Not for use?"

"That depends. I may find a use for it one day. If I do – well," said Madame, "I'll use it!"

"John," thought Madame, checking off her work as her fingers knitted, and her eyes looked at the stranger. "Stay long enough, and I shall knit 'Barsad' before you go."

"You have a husband, Madame?"

'I have."

"Children?"

"No children."

"Business seems bad."

"Business is very bad; the people are so poor."

"Ah, the unfortunate, miserable people! So oppressed, too – as you say."

"As *you* say," Madame retorted, correcting him. and deftly knitting an extra something into his name that boded him no good.

"Pardon me. Certainly it was I who said so, but you naturally think so. Of course."

"*I* think?" returned Madame, in a high voice. "I and my husband have enough to do to keep this wine shop open, without thinking. All we think, here, is how to live. We don't think for others. No, no."

The spy, who was there to find out what was going on, and to detect or invent plots, was not getting very far, but he did not allow this to show in his sinister face. He leant his elbow on Madame Defarge's little counter, sipped his cognac and continued:

"A bad business this madame, of Gaspard's execution. Ah! the poor Gaspard. There is much sorrow and anger in Saint Antoine."

"My faith!" returned Madame, coolly and lightly, "if people use knives and kill other people, they have to pay for it. Ah! Here is my husband."

As the keeper of the wine shop entered at the door, the spy saluted him, by touching his hat, and saying, with an engaging smile, "Good day, Jacques!" Defarge stopped short and stared at him.

"Good day, Jacques," the spy repeated, with not quite so much confidence or quite such an easy smile.

"You deceive yourself, monsieur," returned the keeper of the wine shop. "You mistake me for another. That is not my name. I am Ernest Defarge."

"It is all the same," said the spy airily, but discomfited too: "Good day."

"Good day!" answered Defarge, drily.

"I was saying to madame, with whom I had the pleasure of chatting before you entered, that there is much sympathy and anger in Sainte Antoine about the unhappy fate of poor Gaspard."

"No one has told me so," said Defarge, shaking his head. "I know nothing of it."

Having said this, he passed behind the little counter, and stood with his hand on the back of his wife's chair looking at their enemy whom either of them would have shot with the greatest satisfaction.

John Barsad tried another subject:

"I believe that when Dr Manette was released, you, his former servant took him into your care. Is that not so?"

"Yes, that is so."

"It was to you," said the spy, "that his daughter came; and it was from your care that his daughter took him, accompanied by a monsieur called Lorry from the bank of Tellson, over to England."

"That is correct."

"Very interesting memories." said the spy. "I have known Dr Manette and his daughter in England."

"Yes?" said Defarge.

"You don't hear much about them now, do you?" said the spy.

"No," said Defarge.

"We never hear about them," said his wife. "We received the news of their safe arrival, and one or two letters after that and then, nothing more."

"Miss Manette is going to be married."

"Going?" echoed Madame. "She was pretty enough to have been married long ago. You English are cold, it seems to me."

"Oh! You know I am English."

"Of course, by the way you speak."

He did not take this as a compliment, but made the best of it, laughed and finished his cognac.

"Yes, Miss Manette is going to be married, but not to an Englishman. She is going to marry the nephew of Monsieur the Marquis for whose death poor Gaspard was hung. Her future husband lives in England. He is no Marquis there. He is Mr Charles Darnay, a name which comes from his mother's family."

Madame Defarge knitted steadily, but the news had an obvious effect on her husband. Do what he could he could not hide his concern and his hand shook as he tried to light his pipe. The spy would have been no spy if had not noticed it and stored it away in his mind. He paid for his drink and left, saying that he hoped to see Monsieur and Madame Defarge again. For some minutes after he had gone out, the husband and wife remained exactly as he had left them, in case he should come back.

"Can it be true?" said Defarge, in a low voice, looking down at his wife as he stood smoking with his hand on the back of her chair.

"As he has said it," returned Madame, lifting her eyebrows a little, "it is probably false. But it may be true."

"If it is true, and revolution comes, I hope for her sake her husband never comes to France."

"What is to be, will be," said Madame Defarge, knitting on.

"But is it not very strange that after all our sympathy for her father and herself, her husband's name should be knitted into your death list by the side of that infernal dog who has just left us?"

"Stranger things than that will happen when the time comes," said his wife. "I have them both here, of a certainty, and they are both here for good reasons; that is enough."

She rolled up her knitting, and presently took the rose out of the handkerchief that was wound about her head. Her action must have been seen through the window, for people started coming in again and soon the little wine shop looked much as usual.

In the evening, people sat about on doorsteps and window ledges. Most of the men were smoking their pipes and the women were knitting. Madame Defarge passed among them like a missionary and as she went from group to group, the knitting became quicker, the eyes and the thoughts behind them, more fierce. There were many women like her there such as the world will do well never to breed again.

The time was to come when they were to sit knitting, knitting, counting dropping heads.

CHAPTER 14

Never did the sun go down with a brighter glory on the quiet corner in Soho, than one memorable evening when the doctor and his daughter sat under the plane-tree together. Never did the moon rise with a milder radiance over great London, than on that night when it found them still seated under the tree, and shone upon their faces through its leaves.

Lucie was to be married tomorrow. She had kept this last evening for her father, and they sat alone under the plane-tree.

"Are you happy, dear father?"

"Yes, my child."

"And I am very happy tonight, dear father for I love Charles and he loves me, but it will not change my love for you or ever come between us. Are you sure of that in your heart?"

"Quite sure, my darling. In the darkness of my prison, I never could have believed that I would find you and see you happy with such a fine man."

She kissed him and prayed that she might never betray her promise.

There was no one bidden to the marriage but Mr

Lorry; there was even to be no bridesmaid but faithful Miss Pross.

They would still be in the same peaceful house, using some extra rooms which had been empty at the top of the house, and all seemed well.

Presently father and daughter rose under the moonlight and went hand-in-hand indoors towards their new life.

The marriage day was shining brightly, and they were ready outside the closed door of the doctor's room, where he was speaking with Charles Darnay. They were ready to go to church: the beautiful bride, the old friend Mr Lorry, and Miss Pross who was rather sorry that the bridegroom was not to be her brother Solomon.

The door of the doctor's room opened, and he came out with Charles Darnay. He gave his arm to his daughter, and took her downstairs to the carriage which Mr Lorry had hired in honour of the day. The rest followed in another carriage, and soon, in a neighbouring church, where no strange eyes looked on, Charles Darnay and Lucie Manette were happily married.

CHAPTER 15

When the newly-married pair came home, the first person who appeared to offer his congratulations, was Sydney Carton. They had not been at home many hours, when he presented himself. He was not improved in habits, or in looks, or in manner; but there was a certain rugged air of faithfulness about him which had not been noticed before by Charles Darnay.

He watched his opportunity of taking Darnay aside into a window, and of speaking to him when no one overheard.

"Mr Darnay," said Carton, "I wish we might be friends."

"We are already friends, I hope."

"But on the last occasion we met, I was extremely drunk and rude to you. I cannot forget that. Could you forget it?"

"I forgot it long ago. I prefer to remember the service you rendered me when I was on trial for my life."

"Could I come here from time to time as a friend, not a visitor. Could you endure a worthless fellow such as I am coming and going at odd times and being tolerated as one might a piece of furniture for its service? It would not be often, but it would satisfy me to know that I had your permission."

"You have it. Will you try?"

"I thank you, Darnay. I may use that freedom with your name?"

"I think so, Carton, by this time."

They shook hands upon it, and Sydney turned away. Within a minute afterwards, he was, apparently, his usual casual, lounging self.

When he was gone, and in the course of an evening passed with Miss Pross, the doctor, and Mr Lorry, Charles Darnay made some mention of his conversation with Sydney Carton and spoke of him as a problem of carelessness and recklessness which he knew very well himself. He was not hard on him but saw Sydney as he saw himself.

When later on, he and Lucie retired to their rooms, he found her rather quiet.

"We are thoughtful tonight!" said Darnay, drawing his arms about his young wife.

"Yes, dearest Charles, we are rather thoughtful tonight, for we have something on our mind tonight."

"What is it, my Lucie?"

"Will you promise not to press one question on me, if I beg you not to ask it?"

"Will I promise? What will I *not* promise to my Love? Tell me what is troubling you."

"I think, Charles, poor Mr Carton deserves more

consideration and respect than you expressed for him tonight."

"Indeed, my own? Why is that?"

"That is what you are not to ask me. But I know he does deserve it."

"If you know it, that is enough for me. What would you have me do, my Life?"

"I would ask you, dearest, to be very generous with him always, and very understanding about his faults when he is not here. I would ask you to believe that he does not show what is in his heart. There are deep wounds in it. He has shown it to me."

"I am deeply sorry if I have done him any wrong," said Charles, quite astounded. "I did not realize."

"It is so and I fear he cannot change his ways, but he is capable of good things, gentle things, kind things. This I know. And my dearest Love, remember how strong we are in our happiness, and how weak he is in his misery!"

He was touched to the heart and folded her in his arms: "I will always remember it! I will always remember it as long as I live."

If one forlorn wanderer then pacing the dark streets could have heard her innocent request, he might have cried to the night — and not for the first time — "God bless her for her sweet compassion!"

CHAPTER 16

It was a wonderful corner for echoes, that corner where the doctor lived. Lucie sat quietly at her work, listening to the echoing footsteps of years and awaiting the birth of her first child.

Time passed, and her little Lucie came to share their happiness. Later, came a golden-haired boy who died smiling at his papa and mama and went to join his Father in heaven.

Little Lucie played at her mother's side and chattered in English and French, the tongues of the Two Cities that were blended in her life.

The echoes rarely answered to the actual tread of Sydney Carton. Some half a dozen times a year, at most, he claimed his privilege of coming in uninvited, and would sit among them through the evening, as he had once done often. He never came there heated with wine. He was the first stranger to whom little Lucie held out her chubby arms, and he kept his place with her as she grew. The little boy had spoken of him, almost at the last. "Poor Carton! Kiss him for me."

But there were other echoes, from a distance, that rumbled menacingly in the corner all through this space of time. And it was now, about little Lucie's sixth birthday, that they began to have an awful sound, as of a great storm in France with a dreadful sea rising.

On a night in mid-July, one thousand seven hundred and eighty-nine, Mr Lorry came in late, from Tellson's, and sat himself down by Lucie and her husband in the dark window. It was a hot, wild night, and they were all three reminded of the old Sunday night when they had looked at the lightning from the same place.

"I began to think," said Mr Lorry, "that I should have to pass the night at Tellson's. We have been so full of business all day, that we have not known what to do first, or which way to turn. There is such an uneasiness in Paris that our customers over there are sending their property to us for safe-keeping. They cannot do it fast enough."

"That has a bad look," said Darnay.

"A bad look, you say, my dear Darnay? Yes, but we don't know what reason there is in it. People are sometimes quite unreasonable. Where is Manette?"

"Here he is," said the doctor, entering the dark room at that moment.

"I am quite glad you are at home; for these hurries and forebodings by which I have been surrounded all day long, have made me nervous without reason. You are not going out, I hope?"

"No. I am going to play backgammon with you, if you like," said the doctor.

"I don't think I do like, if I may speak my mind. I am

133

not fitted to be pitted against you tonight. Is the teaboard still there, Lucie? I can't see from here."

"Of course, it has been kept for you."

"Thank you, my dear. Is the precious child safe in bed?"

"She is sleeping soundly."

"That's right; all safe and well! I don't know why anything should be otherwise than safe and well here, thank God; but I have been so put out all day, and I am not as young as I was! My tea, my dear. Thank you. Now, come and take your place in the circle and let us listen to those echoing footsteps outside. Only hear them!"

There were footsteps too in the Paris suburb of St Antoine, headlong, mad and dangerous footsteps, footsteps not easily made clean again if once stained red.

Saint Antoine had been that morning a vast mass of half-starved people heaving to and fro. Every man was armed in some way. No one knew where they had come from but muskets were being distributed – so were cartridges, powder and ball, bars of iron and wood, knives, axes, pikes, every kind of weapon which existed or could be devised. People who could lay hold of nothing else, set themselves with bleeding hands to force stones and bricks out of their places in walls. Every man was at fever-pitch and ready to sacrifice his life.

The centre point was the wine shop where Defarge himself issued orders, issued arms, thrust this man back, dragged this man forward, disarmed one to arm another, laboured and strove in the thickest of the uproar.

"Keep near to me, Jacques Three," cried Defarge; "and you, Jacques One and Two, separate and put yourselves at the head of as many of these patriots as you can. Where is my wife?"

"Eh, well! Here you see me!" said Madame, composed as ever, but not knitting today. Madame's resolute right hand was occupied with an axe, and in her girdle were a pistol and a cruel knife.

"Where do you go, my wife?"

"I go," said Madame, "with you at present. You shall see me at the head of women, by and by.'

"Come then!" cried Defarge, in a resounding voice. "Patriots and friends, we are ready! To the Bastille!"

With a roar that sounded as if all the breath in France had been shaped into that detested name, the living sea of people rose, wave on wave, depth on depth, and overflowed the city until they reached the mighty prison. Alarm bells ringing, drums beating, the attack began.

Deep ditches, double drawbridge, massive stone walls, eight great towers, cannon, muskets, fire and smoke. Through the fire and through the smoke – in the fire and in the smoke, Defarge of the wine shop worked like a manful soldier.

Deep ditch, single drawbridge, massive stone walls, eight great towers, cannon, muskets, fire and smoke. One drawbridge down! "Work, comrades all, work!" cried Defarge.

"To me, the women!" cried Madame his wife. "Once the place is taken, we can kill as well as the men!" And to her, with a shrill thirsty cry, trooped the women, variously armed, but all armed alike in hunger and revenge. But still there was the deep ditch, and the single drawbridge, and the massive stone walls, and the eight great towers and still they fought on with Defarge at their head, firing a captured cannon.

A white flag was flown from within the fortress and the drawbridge was lowered. The crowds swept Defarge over it, past the massive stone outer walls and in among the eight great towers which were surrendered to them. He was swept on until he landed in the outer courtyard of the Bastille. There, against an angle of the wall, he made a struggle to look about him. Jacques Three was nearly at his side; Madame Defarge, still heading some of her women, was visible in the inner distance, and her knife was in her hand.

"The Prisoners!"

"The Records!"

"The secret cells!"

"The instruments of torture!" and again:

"The Prisoners!"

When the front ranks of attackers rolled past, bearing the prison officers with them, and threatening them all with instant death if any secret nook remained undisclosed, Defarge laid his strong hand on the shoulder of one of these men – a man with a grey head, who had a lighted torch in his hand – separated him from the rest, and got him between himself and a wall.

"Show me the North Tower!" said Defarge. "Quick!"

"I will faithfully," replied the man, "if you will come with me. But there is no one there."

"What is the meaning of One Hundred and Five, North Tower?" asked Defarge. "Quick!"

"Monsieur, it is a cell."

"Show it to me."

"Come this way."

Through gloomy vaults where the light of day had never shone, past the hideous doors of dark dens and cages, down cavernous flights of steps, and again up steep rugged flights of stone and brick, more like dry waterfalls than staircases, Defarge, the turnkey and Jacques Three who had been by Defarge most of the time, linked hand and arm and went with all the speed they could make. Presently they found themselves winding and climbing up a tower. They were alone.

The turnkey stopped at a low door, put a key in a clashing lock, swung the door slowly open, and said, as they all bent their heads and passed in –

"One Hundred and Five, North Tower!"

There was a small, heavily-grated, unglazed window high in the wall, with a stone screen before it, so that the sky could only be seen by stooping low and looking up. There was a small chimney, heavily barred across, a few feet within. There was a heap of old feathery wood-ashes on the hearth. There was a stool, and table, and a straw bed. There were the four blackened walls, and a rusted iron ring in one of them.

"Pass that torch slowly along these walls, so that I may see them," said Defarge to the turnkey.

The man obeyed, and Defarge followed the light closely with his eyes.

"Stop! Look here, Jacques!"

"A.M." read Jacques Three.

"Alexandre Manette," said Defarge in his ear, following the letters with his forefinger which was deeply engrained with gunpowder. "And here he wrote 'a poor physician' and it was he without doubt who scratched a calendar on this stone. What is that in your hand? Give it to me and hold my gun for a moment."

Defarge turned on the wormeaten stool and table, and beat them to pieces in a few blows.

"Hold the light higher," he said to the turnkey. "Look among those wooden fragments with care, Jacques. Then take this knife; rip open that bed, and search the straw. Hold the light higher, you."

With a threatening look at the turnkey, he crawled upon the hearth, and peering up the chimney, struck and prised at its sides with the crowbar, and worked at the iron grating across it. In a few minutes, some mortar and dust came dropping down, just missing his face, and in this rubble, and in the old wood-ashes, and in a crevice in the chimney into which his weapon had slipped, he groped with a cautious touch.

"Nothing in the wood, and nothing in the straw, Jacques?"

"Nothing."

"Let us collect them together, in the middle of the cell. Light them, you."

The turnkey fired the little pile, which blazed high and hot. Stooping again to come out, they left it burning, and retraced their way to the courtyard, where the mob was surging about looking for Defarge to take charge of the Governor who had defended the Bastille and shot the people. Otherwise he might escape judgement and the people's blood would be unavenged.

In all the crowd which surrounded this grim old officer conspicuous in his grey coat and red decoration, there was but one quite steady figure, and that was a woman's. "See, there is my husband!" she cried, pointing him out. "See, there is Defarge!" She stood immovable, close to the grim old officer, and remained close to him through the streets, as Defarge and the rest bore him along; remained close to him when he was got near his destination, and began to be struck at from behind; remained close to him when the long-gathering rain of stabs and blows fell heavy; was so close to him when he dropped dead under it, that, suddenly, she put a foot upon his neck, and with her cruel knife – long ready – hewed off his head.

Seven prisoners were released. They were carried high on men's shoulders. Seven prisoners released, seven gory heads on pikes, a guard hung from a lamp-post, the keys of the accursed fortress, the footsteps of the people of Saint Antoine echoing through the Paris streets in mid-July, one thousand seven hundred and eighty-nine. Now, pray Heaven those feet stay far from the life of Lucie Manette! For they are headlong, mad, and dangerous, and in the years so long after the breaking of the cask at Defarge's wine shop door, they are not easily purified when once stained red.

CHAPTER 18

Three years had passed, and the terror in France increased.

Little Lucie was three years older and lived her peaceful life at home, but although the quiet home did not change, the inmates listened many a night and day to the echoes in the corner, with hearts that failed them when they heard the thronging feet. For the footsteps had become to their minds as the footsteps of a people, tumultuous under a red flag and with their country declared in danger, their people changed into wild beasts, by terrible enchantment long persisted in.

The court had gone and with it Monseigneur and the rich corrupt people who came there, the Royal family was besieged in its palace and many noble families had sought refuge in London. Tellson's Bank became their meeting place and Tellson's Bank looked after such money as they had managed to bring to England.

On a steaming, misty afternoon, Mr Lorry sat at his desk and Charles Darnay stood leaning on it, talking with him in a low voice. It was within half an hour or so of closing time.

"Although you are the youngest man that ever lived,"

said Charles Darnay, hesitating a little, "I wish you were not going."

"You think I am too old?" said Mr Lorry.

"Unsettled weather, a long and difficult journey, a city that may not even be safe for you."

"My dear Charles," said Mr Lorry, with cheerful confidence, "it is safe enough for me; nobody will care to interfere with an old fellow, when there are so many other people to interfere with. I am needed in Paris to offer assistance from Tellson's and I am proud to go as its representative of many years now."

"I wish I were going myself," said Darnay. "They have burnt down my uncle's château. I do not know what has happened to those people who worked for him. If it were not for my family, I would go and chance it."

"You have no idea what it would be like for you," said Mr Lorry. "Papers and other matters were brought to Tellson's today by the strangest bearers you can imagine, every one of whom had his head hanging on by a single hair as he passed through the barriers. At another time, our parcels would come and go, as easily as in business-like old England; but now, everything is stopped."

"And are you really going tonight?"

"I must; for the case has become too pressing for me to delay."

"Who will you take with you?"

"All sorts of people have been proposed to me, but I will have nothing to say to any of them. I intend to take Jerry Cruncher. Nobody will suspect Jerry of being anything but an English bull-dog, or of having any idea in his head but to fly at anybody who touches his master."

"I heartily admire your gallantry and youthfulness."

"Nonsense, nonsense! When I have finished this little mission, I shall, perhaps, accept Tellson's proposal to retire and live at my ease. Time enough, then, to think about growing old."

In spite of saying he thought he should not go to France because of the danger and how it could affect his family, Charles Darnay felt restless and uneasy. Refugees continued to come to Tellson's from France and he heard them talking about the dreadful events there. Yet, he could not go and see for himself. He was still worrying as to where his duty lay, when something happened which made up his mind for him.

Before the two friends parted, Mr Lorry was handed a soiled and unopened letter which had been brought to Tellson's, and the messenger asked him if had any idea how the person to whom it was addressed might be traced. The letter was laid down so close to Darnay that he could see it was addressed to *him* under his true name: To Monsieur the former Marquis St Evrémonde, of France. Care of Tellson's Bank, London. England. It was marked VERY URGENT.

On the marriage morning, Doctor Manette had made it his one request that Charles Darney should not reveal his true name unless he gave his permission. Nobody, except the doctor knew that he was the Marquis St

Evrémonde; his own wife did not know and nor did Mr Lorry. Mr Lorry was at a loss what to do with the letter.

"I know the fellow," said Darnay.

"You do?" said Mr Lorry, "then will you take charge of the letter? You know where to deliver it?"

"I do."

"Would you please explain that Tellson's had no address for this gentleman and that the letter has been here some time."

"I will do so. Do you start for Paris from here?"

"From here, at eight."

"I will come back, to see you off."

Very ill at ease with himself, Darnay made his way into the quiet of the Temple, opened the letter and read it. These were its contents:

Prison of the Abbaye, Paris.

Monsieur, Formerly The Marquis

After having been long in danger of my life at the hands of the village people, I have been seized, with great violence and indignity, and brought a long journey on foot to Paris. On the road I have suffered a great deal. Nor is that all; my house has been destroyed – razed to the ground.

The crime for which I am imprisoned is that I have acted against the people by remaining true to your commands. Those nobles and others who have left

France are deemed to be emigrants and enemies of the people. It is in vain that I explain to them that I have acted *for* and not against them, according to your commands. It is in vain that I explain to them that I have released them from their taxes and have charged them no rent. The response is that I have acted for an emigrant and that emigrants are traitors and where is that emigrant?

Ah monsieur, I send my desolate cry across the sea, hoping it may perhaps reach your ears through the great Bank of Tellson known at Paris!

For the love of Heaven, I implore you Monsieur to come and help me. My only fault is that I have been true to you. I pray that you may be true to me. From this prison of horror, I send you my faithful duty.

Your unhappy Gabelle.

But he had oppressed no man, he had imprisoned no man, he had given up his right to tax his peasants, he had come to England and made his way without any advantages or favours. He had earned his own bread. Monsieur Gabelle had been given instructions to help the people with fuel and produce and to let them off any money they owed the late Marquis. Surely all this would tell in his favour if he were arrested!

By such reasoning, Charles Darnay came to his desperate resolution to return to Paris and, in spite of the known danger to try and help his old servant Gabelle.

As he walked to and fro with his resolution made, he considered that neither Lucie nor her father must know of it until he was gone. Lucie should be spared the pain of separation, must be spared the anxiety of knowing that he was considering such a step. The step must come first.

He walked to and fro, with thoughts very busy, until it was time to return to Tellson's and take leave of Mr Lorry. As soon as he arrived in Paris, he would present himself to this old friend, but he would say nothing of his intention now.

A carriage with post-horses was ready at the Bank door, and Jerry was booted and equipped.

"I have delivered that letter," said Charles to Mr Lorry, "I do not think it would be wise to give you a written answer, but perhaps you could arrange for a message to be sent."

"That I will, and readily," said Mr Lorry, "if it is not dangerous."

"Not at all. Though it is to a prisoner in the Abbaye."

"What is his name?" said Mr Lorry, with his open pocket-book in his hand.

"Gabelle. And what is the message to the unfortunate Gabelle in prison?"

"Simply, that he has received the letter, and will come."

"Any time mentioned?"

"He will start upon his journey tomorrow night."

"Any person mentioned?"

"No."

He helped Mr Lorry to wrap himself in a number of coats and cloaks, and went out with him from the warm atmosphere of the old Bank, into the misty air of Fleet Street.

"My love to Lucie, and to little Lucie," said Mr Lorry at parting, "and take precious care of them till I come back."

Charles Darnay shook his head and doubtfully smiled, as the carriage rolled away.

That night – it was the fourteenth of August – he sat up late, and wrote two letters; one was to Lucie, explaining why he had to go to Paris and reassuring her as to his safety; the other was to the doctor, confiding Lucie and their dear child to his care and explaining why he thought he would be safe in France. To both he promised letters, in proof of his safety, immediately after his arrival.

It was a hard day, being with them, and not telling them of his plans. It was especially hard not to tell Lucie, as she had always aided him in everything he did, and she trusted him completely. That night he embraced her and, making some excuse that he had to go out, but would be back later, he left the house, and, picking up a small case which he had hidden outside, emerged into the heavy mist of the heavy streets, with a heavier heart. He left his two letters with a trusty porter, to be delivered half an hour before midnight, and no sooner; took horse for Dover and began his mission of rescue with a sinking heart, as he left all that was dear on earth behind him.

Book the Third

CHAPTER 1

Travelling from England to Paris was difficult and slow in the autumn of the year one thousand seven hundred and ninety two. The roads, carriages and horses to be had were all bad.

Every town-gate and village taxing house had its band of citizen patriots, with their national muskets in a most explosive state of readiness, who stopped all comers and goers, cross-questioned them, inspected their papers, looked for their names in lists of their own, turned them back, or sent them on, or arrested them, as seemed best for the new Republic they were building of Liberty, Equality, Fraternity, or Death.

Charles Darnay had not travelled far in France when he realized that he would not be able to return home unless he was declared a good citizen in Paris. He must now go on to his journey's end. Every time a barrier closed behind him, he felt that his freedom had completely gone.

This universal watchfulness hindered him at every stage. He had been days upon his journey in France, when he went to bed tired out, in a little town on the high road, still a long way from Paris. He would not have got as far as this place if he had not had Gabelle's letter from the Abbaye prison with him. As it was, his difficulties in this small place had been such that he felt his journey to have come to a crisis point. And he was, therefore, as little surprised as a man could be, to find himself awakened at the small inn where they had placed him until morning, in the middle of the night.

He was awakened by a timid local official and three armed patriots in rough red caps and with pipes in their mouths, who sat down on the bed.

"Emigrant," said the official, "I am going to send you on to Paris, under escort."

"Citizen, I desire nothing more than to get to Paris, though I could do without the escort."

"Silence!" growled a red-cap, striking at the coverlet with the butt end of his musket. "Be quiet, aristocrat."

"It is as the good patriot says," observed the timid official. "You are an aristocrat, and must have an escort – and must pay for it."

"I have no choice," said Charles Darnay.

"Choice? Listen to him!" cried the same scowling red-cap. "You are lucky to be protected from the people. You could be hung from a lamp-post like many others."

"It is as the good patriot says," observed the official. "Rise and dress yourself, emigrant."

Darnay obeyed, and was taken back to the guard-house, where other patriots in rough red caps were smoking, drinking, and sleeping by a watch-fire. Here he paid a heavy price for his escort and started out with them on the wet, wet roads at three o'clock in the morning.

The escort were two mounted patriots in red caps and tricoloured cockades, armed with national muskets and sabres, who rode one on either side of him. Darnay controlled his own horse, but a loose line was attached to his bridle, the end of which one of the guards kept tied round his wrist.

In this state they set forth with the sharp rain driving in their faces, clattering at a heavy trot over the uneven town pavement, and out upon the muddy roads. They travelled like this, changing horses and resting from time to time, until they reached Beauvais the following eventide, and here the aspect of affairs was very alarming.

An ominous crowd gathered to see him dismount at the posting-yard, and many voices called out loudly, "Down with the emigrant!"

He stopped in the act of swinging himself out of his saddle, stayed mounted for safety, and said, "Emigrant, my friends! Do you not see me here, in France, of my own will?"

"You are a cursed emigrant," cried a farrier, rushing at him in a furious manner, with a hammer in his hand, "and you are a cursed aristocrat!"

The postmaster put himself between this man and the rider's bridle (which he was making for), and soothingly said, "Let him be, let him be. He will be judged in Paris."

"Judged!" repeated the farrier, swinging his hammer.

"Ay! and condemned as a traitor." At this the crowd roared approval. Checking the postmaster, who was for turning his horse's head towards the yard, Darnay said, as soon as he could make his voice heard:

"Friends, you deceive yourselves, or you are deceived. I am not a traitor."

"He lies!" cried the smith. "He is a traitor since the new decree. His cursed life is not his own."

At the instant when Darnay saw a rush in the eyes of the crowd, which another instant would have brought upon him, the postmaster, who still had his hand on the bridle, turned his horse quickly into the yard, the escort rode in close upon his horse's flanks, and the postmaster shut and barred the rickety double gates. The farrier struck a blow upon them with his hammer, and the crowd groaned, but no more was done.

"What is this decree that the smith spoke of?" Darnay asked the postmaster, when he had thanked him, and stood beside him in the yard.

"It is a new law for selling the property of emigrants."

"When was it passed?"

"On the fourteenth."

"That was the day I left England!"

"Everyone says the decree is but one of several, and that there will be others – if there are not already – banishing all emigrants from France, and condemning all who return. That is what he meant when he said your life was not your own."

"But have these laws been passed yet?"

"How do I know?" said the postmaster, shrugging his shoulders. "If they are not passed already, they will be soon."

They rested on some straw in a loft until the middle of the night, and then rode forward again when all the town was asleep.

Daylight at last found them before the wall of Paris. The barrier was closed and strongly guarded when they rode up to it.

"Where are the papers of this prisoner?" demanded a resolute-looking man in authority, who was summoned out by the guard.

Darnay said at once that he was no prisoner but a French citizen, travelling with an escort for which he had paid.

The man paid no attention to him at all and repeated, "Where are the papers of this prisoner?"

One of the patriots had them in his cap and handed them over. Casting his eyes over Gabelle's letter, the man in authority looked a little shaken and surprised, and looked at Darnay with close attention. Then he turned round without a word, leaving the others waiting on their horses and went into the guard room.

Charles Darnay watched the barrier and noticed that, while it was quite easy to get into Paris, it was very difficult to get out. The people passing through were mostly peasants bringing in country produce or taking out their empty carts. Those going home seemed to wait a long time. Both men and women wore the red cap and tricolour cockade.

When he had sat in his saddle some half-hour, taking note of these things, Darnay found himself confronted by the same man in authority, who directed the guard to open the barrier. Then he delivered to the escort a receipt for the prisoner, and requested him to dismount. Darnay did so, and the two patriots, leading his tired horse, turned and rode away without entering the city.

Darnay accompanied his conductor into a guard room, smelling of common wine and tobacco, where soldiers were standing and lying about. Some lists were lying on a desk and a coarse-looking officer was seated in front of these.

"Citizen Defarge," said he to Darnay's conductor, as he took a slip of paper to write on. "Is this the emigrant Evrémonde?"

"This is the man."

"Your age, Evrémonde?"

"Thirty-seven."

"Married, Evrémonde?"

"Yes."

"Where married?"

"In England."

"Of course. Where is your wife, Evrémonde?"

"In England."

"Of course. You are consigned, Evrémonde, to the prison of La Force."

"Just Heaven!" exclaimed Darnay. "Under what law, and for what offence?"

The officer looked up from his slip of paper for a moment.

"We have new laws, Evrémonde, and new offences, since you were here." He said it with a hard smile and went on writing.

"Please note that I have come here of my own free will to help a fellow-countryman who is in trouble. I am only asking that I should be allowed to do this. Isn't that my right?"

"Emigrants have no rights, Evrémonde," was the calm reply. The officer wrote until he had finished, read over to himself what he had written, and handed it to Defarge, with the words "In secret."

Defarge motioned with the paper to the prisoner that he must accompany him. The prisoner obeyed, and a guard of two armed patriots attended them.

"Is it you," said Defarge, in a low voice, as they went down the guard house steps and turned into Paris, "who married the daughter of Doctor Manette, once a prisoner of the Bastille, now destroyed?"

"Yes," replied Darnay, looking at him with surprise.

"My name is Defarge, and I keep a wine shop in Saint Antoine. Possibly you have heard of me."

"My wife came to your house to reclaim her father whom you were sheltering. Yes, I have heard of you."

The word "wife" seemed to bring a gloomy look to the

155

face of Defarge, and he said impatiently, "why did you come to France?"

"You heard me say why, a minute ago. Do you not believe that is the truth?"

"A bad truth for you," said Defarge, with a worried frown, and looking straight before him.

"I am quite at a loss here. Everything is so unusual, so changed, so sudden and unfair, that I am totally confused. Will you render me a little help?"

"None." Defarge spoke, always looking straight before him.

"Will you answer me a single question?"

"Perhaps. Say what it is."

"In this prison that I am going to so unjustly, shall I have some free communication with the world outside?"

"You will see."

"Am I to be kept there as if I were buried without any means of presenting my case?"

"You will see. But what if that is so? Other people have been buried like that in worse prisons, before now."

"But never by me, Citizen Defarge."

Defarge glanced darkly at him for answer, and walked on in a steady and set silence.

Darnay tried again: "It is of the utmost importance to me that Mr Lorry of Tellson's Bank in London who is at present in Paris should know that I have been thrown into the prison of La Force. Could you arrange for this to be done?"

"I will do nothing for you," Defarge replied. "My duty is to my country and the people. I am the sworn servant of both against you. I will do nothing for you."

Charles Darnay felt it was hopeless to ask anything of Defarge and, indeed, he was too proud to do so. As they walked on in silence, he could see that the people were quite used to seeing prisoners passing along the streets and even the children scarcely noticed him. Nobody seemed to think it was any more strange that a man in good clothes was going to prison than that a man in working clothes should be going to work.

In one narrow, dark and dirty street through which they passed, an excited man, mounted on a stool, was addressing an excited audience on the crimes against the people of the king and royal family. It was from the few words he managed to catch that Darnay gathered that the king was in prison and that the foreign ambassadors had one and all left Paris. He knew now that he was in the greatest possible danger, but he still hoped. He could not know of the guillotine and the frightful deeds that were soon to be done. No ordinary good-living person could imagine such things. He expected prison and separation from his wife and child, but beyond this he dreaded nothing distinctly.

At last they arrived at a dreary prison courtyard. They were at the prison of La Force.

A man with a bloated face opened the strong wicket gate. He gave Defarge a receipt for the prisoner and

Defarge and the two patriots went away, still keeping their silence.

The prison of La Force was a gloomy prison, dark and filthy with a horrible smell about it.

"In secret, I see," said the gaoler, "come with me, emigrant Evrémonde."

Through the dismal prison twilight, the gaoler accompanied him by corridor and staircase, many doors clanging and locking behind them, until they came into a large, low, vaulted chamber, crowded with prisoners of both sexes. The women were seated at a long table, reading and writing, knitting, sewing and embroidering; the men were for the most part standing behind their chairs, or lingering up and down the room.

They all rose to receive him with every courtesy and aristocratic grace. Ghosts all: they awaited a second death. They had suffered the first in coming there.

"In the name of the assembled companions in misfortune," said a gentleman of courtly appearance, coming forward, "I have the honour of giving you welcome to La Force, and of condoling with you on the calamity that has brought you among us. May I ask who you are?"

Darnay told him and the courtly gentleman greeted him again and added, following the gaoler with his eyes as he moved across the room, "But I hope that you are not 'in secret'."

There was a murmur of pity as Charles Darnay crossed the room to a grated door where the gaoler awaited him, and many voices gave him good wishes and encouragement. He turned at the grated door, to render the thanks of his heart; it closed under the gaoler's hand and the apparitions vanished from his sight for ever.

The wicket-gate opened on a stone staircase, leading upward. When they ascended them, the prisoner counted forty steps, the gaoler opened a low black door, and they passed into a solitary cell. It struck cold and damp, but was not dark.

"Yours," said the gaoler.

"Why am I imprisoned alone?"

"How do I know?"

"Will I be able to buy pen, ink and paper?"

"Such are not my orders. You will be visited, and can ask then. At present, you may buy your food, and nothing more."

There were in the cell a chair, a table, and a straw mattress. When the gaoler went out, Darnay said to himself, "Now am I left, as if I were dead."

"Five paces by four and a half, five paces by four and a half, five paces by four and a half. The prisoner walked to and fro in his cell, counting its measurements, and the roar of the city rolled like muffled drums with a wild swell of voices added to them. And he thought they were saying, "He made shoes, he made shoes, he made shoes."

Tellson's Bank, established in the Saint Germain Quarter of Paris, was in the wing of a large house, approached by a courtyard and shut off from the street by a high wall and a strong gate. The house belonged to Monseigneur, the great nobleman, but he had fled the troubles and it had been confiscated and given over to the patriots. The wing was separate from the house.

On the night of the third of September, Mr Lorry, who occupied rooms in the bank sat by a newly-lighted wood fire, and on his honest and courageous face there was a deeper shade than the hanging lamp could throw – a shade of horror.

From the streets behind the high wall and the strong gate, there came the usual night hum of the city, with now and then a strange ring in it, weird and unearthly, as if unusual sounds of a terrible nature were going up to Heaven.

"Thank God," said Mr Lorry, clasping his hands and shivering, "that no one near and dear to me is in this dreadful town tonight. May He have mercy on all who are in danger!"

Soon afterwards, the bell at the great gate sounded, and he sat listening, but there was no noisy invasion of people, as had happened before, and he heard the gate clash again, and all was quiet.

Suddenly his door opened and two figures rushed in, at the sight of which he fell back in amazement.

Lucie and her father! Lucie with her arms stretched out to him. Lucie in distress and deadly pale.

"What is this?" cried Mr Lorry, breathless and confused. "What is the matter? What has happened? What has brought you here?"

Still clinging to him, Lucie cried out, "Oh my dear friend! It is my husband!"

"Your husband, Lucie?"

"Charles."

"What of Charles?"

"Here."

"Here, in Paris?"

"He has been here some days – three or four – I don't know how many – I can't collect my thoughts. Unknown to us, he came here to try and help somebody; he was stopped at the barrier, and sent to prison."

The old man could not repress a cry. Almost at the same moment, the bell of the great gate rang again, and a loud noise of feet and voices came pouring into the courtyard.

"What is that noise?" said the doctor, turning towards the window.

"Don't look!" cried Mr Lorry. "Don't touch that blind!"

The doctor turned with his hand upon the fastening of the window, and said, with a cool, bold, smile:

"My dear friend, I have a charmed life in this city. I have been a Bastille prisoner. There is no patriot in Paris or in all France who, knowing this, would touch me, except to overwhelm me with embraces, or carry me in triumph. Through my misfortune, I have a power that has brought us through the barrier, and gained us news of Charles there, and brought us here. I knew it would be so. I knew I could help Charles out of all danger. I told Lucie so. What is that noise?" His hand was again upon the window.

"Don't look!" cried Mr Lorry, absolutely desperate. "No, Lucie, my dear, nor you!" He got his arm around her, and held her. "Now tell me which prison Charles is in. I had no idea, even, that he was over here."

"He is in La Force."

"La Force! Lucie, you can do nothing tonight and you must not go out. Yu must do as I say for Charles's sake. You must let me put you in a room at the back here. You must leave your father and me alone for two minutes, and as there are Life and Death in the world, you must not delay."

"I can see in your face that I must do as you say. I know I can trust you."

Mr Lorry kissed her and hurried her into his own room. Then he came hurrying back to the doctor, and opened the window and partly opened the blind and put his hand upon the doctor's arm, and looked out with him into the courtyard.

They looked out upon a throng of men and women, forty to fifty of them in all. The people in possession of the house had let them in at the gate, and they had rushed into work at a large grindstone; it had evidently been set up there especially for them because it was a quiet and convenient place.

But such awful workers, and such awful work!

The grindstone had a double handle, and, turning it

madly were two men, whose faces were more horrible and cruel than those of the most barbarous of savages.

As these ruffians turned and turned, their matted hair now flung forward over their eyes, now flung backward over their necks, some women held wine to their mouths that they might drink. Most of the men were stained with blood and it was hard to see where the blood ended and the wine began.

Their hatchets, knives, bayonets, swords were all red with blood and as the frantic wielders of these weapons snatched them from the stream of sparks which came from the grindstone and tore away into the streets, the same blood red was in their frenzied eyes.

Mr Lorry and the doctor drew back from the window, and the doctor looked for explanation in his friend's ashen face.

"They are murdering the prisoners," said Mr Lorry. "If you really have the power you think you have – as I believe you have – tell these devils who you are and get taken to La Force. It may be too late, I don't know, but you could try."

Doctor Manette pressed his hand, hastened bare-headed out of the room, and was in the courtyard when Mr Lorry pulled up the blind. His streaming white hair, his remarkable face and his confidence carried him in an instant among the men who were sharpening their weapons at the grindstone. Mr Lorry saw that he was talking to them and then he saw him in the midst of a line of twenty men, all linked shoulder to shoulder, and hand to shoulder, being hurried out with cries of "Long live the Bastille prisoner! Help for his son-in-law in La Force. Save the prisoner Evrémonde in La Force" and a thousand answering shouts.

Mr Lorry closed the window, pulled down the blind and hastened to Lucie, and told her that her father was assisted by the people and had gone in search of her husband. He found her little girl and Miss Pross with her, but it never occurred to him to be surprised that they were there until a long time afterwards when he sat watching them in the night, holding Lucie's hand.

Miss Pross had laid little Lucie down on his own bed, and her head had gradually fallen on the pillow beside her pretty charge. The mother was half fainting and moaning and this continued through the long, long night, with no return of her father and no news.

CHAPTER 3

Mr Lorry knew that he could not keep the wife of an emigrant prisoner on premises belonging to Tellson's Bank, so he consulted Lucie. She said that her father had spoken of hiring a lodging for a short term, in that Quarter, near the Banking-House; so Mr Lorry went out to look for such a lodging, and found a suitable one, high up in a side street where most of the houses were deserted and had their blinds down.

To this lodging he at once removed Lucie and her child, and Miss Pross, giving them what comfort he could, and much more than he had himself. He left Jerry to guard them, and returned to his work with a heavy heart.

The day wore itself out, and wore him out with it, until the Bank closed. He was again alone in his room of the previous night, considering what to do next, when he heard a foot upon the stair. In a few moments, a man stood in his presence, who, with a keenly observant look at him, addressed him by his name.

"Your servant," said Mr Lorry. "Do you know me?"

He was a strongly made man with dark curling hair, from forty-five to fifty years of age. For answer, he replied, "Do you know *me*?"

"I have seen you somewhere."

"Perhaps at my wine shop?"

Much interested and agitated, Mr Lorry said, "Do you come from Doctor Manette?"

"Yes, I come from Doctor Manette."

"What does he say? Have you a message for me?"

Defarge gave into his anxious hand an open scrap of paper. It bore the words in the doctor's writing: "Charles is safe, but I cannot safely leave this place yet. The bearer of this note has kindly brought a letter from Charles to his wife. Let the bearer see his wife."

The note from Doctor Manette had been written from La Force about an hour ago.

"Will you come with me to his wife's lodgings?" asked Mr Lorry, very much relieved.

"Yes," answered Defarge.

Scarcely noticing as yet that Defarge was speaking in a curiously reserved and mechanical way, Mr Lorry put on his hat and they went down into the court yard. There, they found two women; one of whom was knitting.

"Madame Defarge, surely!" said Mr Lorry, who had left her in exactly the same attitude some seventeen years ago.

"It is she," observed her husband.

"Is Madame coming with us?" inquired Mr Lorry, seeing that she moved as they moved.

"Yes. So that she may be able to recognize the faces and know the persons. It is for their safety."

Beginning to be struck by Defarge's manner, Mr Lorry

looked doubtfully at him, and led the way. Both the women followed; the second woman being her friend, the Vengeance.

They passed through the intervening streets as quickly as they might, ascended the staircase of the new lodging, were admitted by Jerry, and found Lucie weeping alone. Her tears vanished when she heard Mr Lorry's news and clasped the hand that delivered her husband's note, little thinking what that hand had been doing during the night, and, but for a chance, what it might have done to Charles.

This was the note Charles had sent her: "Dearest, take courage. I am well, and your father has influence around me. You cannot answer this. Kiss our child for me."

That was all the writing. It was so much, however, to Lucie, that she turned from Defarge to his wife, and kissed one of the hands that knitted. But the hand made no response – dropped cold and heavy, and took to its knitting again.

There was something in its touch that gave Lucie a check. She stopped in the act of putting the note near her heart and looked, terrified, at Madame Defarge.

"My dear," said Mr Lorry, trying to explain, "there are frequent risings in the streets and Madame Defarge wishes to see those whom she has the power to protect, so that she can identify them in case of need. Am I right Citizen Defarge?" His voice became more and more uneasy as he looked at the three stony faces.

Defarge looked gloomily at his wife and gave a grunt of agreement.

"Lucie," said Mr Lorry, doing all he could to improve the atmosphere, "you had better have the dear child here, and our good Pross. Our good Pross, Defarge, is an English lady, and knows no French."

Miss Pross, who was quite sure she was a match for any foreigner and was not to be shaken by distress and danger, appeared with folded arms, and observed in English to the Vengeance whom her eyes first encountered, "Well, I am sure Boldface! I hope *you* are pretty well!" She also bestowed a British cough on Madame Defarge; but neither of the two took much heed of her.

"Is that his child?" said Madame Defarge, stopping in her work for the first time, and pointing her knitting needle at little Lucie as if it were the finger of fate.

"Yes, Madame," answered Mr Lorry, "this is our poor prisoner's darling daughter, and only child."

The shadow attendant on Madame Defarge and her party seemed to fall so threatening and dark on the child, that her mother instinctively kneeled on the ground beside her, and put her arms round her. The shadow attendant on Madame Defarge and her party seemed then to fall, threatening and dark, on both the mother and the child.

"It is enough, husband," said Madame Defarge, "I have seen them. We may go."

"As a wife and mother," cried Lucie most earnestly, "I implore you to have pity on me and not to use any power which you possess against my innocent husband, but to use it to help him."

Madame Defarge looked coldly at Lucie and said, turning to her friend the Vengeance:

"The wives and mothers we have been used to see, since we were as little as this child, and much less, have not been greatly considered. We have known *their* husbands and fathers laid in prison and kept from them, often enough. All our lives we have seen our fellow-women suffer, in themselves and in their children, poverty, hunger, thirst, sickness, misery, oppression, and neglect of all kinds."

"We have seen nothing else," returned the Vengeance.

"We have borne this a long time," said Madame Defarge, turning her eyes again upon Lucie. "Think! Is it likely that the trouble of one wife and mother would be much to us now?"

She resumed her knitting and went out. The Vengeance followed. Defarge went last and closed the door.

"Courage, my dear Lucie," said Mr Lorry, as he raised her from the floor. "So far all goes well with us. Cheer up, and have a thankful heart."

"I am not thankless, I hope, but that dreadful woman seems to throw a shadow on me and all my hopes."

"It *is* only a shadow, Lucie," said Mr Lorry, "only a shadow, dear."

But the shadow of the manner of these Defarges was upon himself, for all that and in his secret mind it troubled him greatly.

CHAPTER 4

Doctor Manette returned in the morning four days later. He told them that there had been an attack upon the prisons, that all political prisoners had been in danger, and that some had been dragged out by the crowd and murdered. The crowd had taken him to the prison of La Force. There he had found a self-appointed Tribunal sitting, before which the prisoners were brought one by one. They were ordered to be sent out to be massacred, or to be released or to be sent back to their cells.

The men who had conducted him to La Force had presented him to this Tribunal and he had identified himself by name and profession and told them that he had been a secret and unaccused prisoner in the Bastille for eighteen years. Defarge who was one of the people sitting in judgement had identified him and confirmed what he had said.

Doctor Manette had then pleaded for the life and liberty of his son-in-law. The Tribunal had seemed on the point of releasing him, when there was an unexplained check – not clear to the doctor – and a secret conference among the men sitting in judgement. Presently the President informed him that Darnay must still be held in prison, but that he would be held in safe custody. The doctor had remained at the prison to make sure that this was done and that Charles, by some error, should not be delivered to the butchers outside.

All this he told them but to Mr Lorry only did he give an account of the horrors he had seen which, at one point, had caused him to faint. But Doctor Manette remained calm and resolute and determined to save the husband of his beloved daughter. He soon managed to get himself appointed as visiting physician at La Force and two other prisons. This meant that he could bring regular news of Charles to Lucie.

He was no longer confined alone, but was mixed with the general body of prisoners and was able to send loving messages to Lucie whenever he saw his father-in-law. No letters were allowed, however, from one to the other.

But, though the doctor tried hard, and never ceased trying to get Charles Darnay set at liberty, or at least to get him brought to trial, the tide of events was too strong and fast for him. The new era began; the king was tried, doomed and beheaded and the Republic of Liberty, Equality, Fraternity or Death declared against the world for victory or death.

There was no pause, no pity, no peace, no rest. The executioner had shown the people the head of the king and eight months later the head of his fair wife with hair gone grey during the weary months of imprisoned widowhood and misery.

There was a revolutionary tribunal in the capital, and

forty or fifty thousand revolutionary committees all over the land; there was too, a law of the Suspected, which struck away all security for liberty or life, and delivered over any good and innocent person to any bad and guilty one. The prisons were full of people who had committed no offence, and could obtain no hearing. These things became the established order and soon became quite normal.

Above all one hideous machine grew as familiar as if it had always been there. It was the Guillotine, often referred to as a female – Madame Guillotine. In one morning it lopped off the heads of twenty-two people in as many minutes.

Among all these terrors the doctor walked with a steady head, treating good and bad alike and trusted by all. He was confident that he would, in the end, obtain the release of Lucie's husband, but things got worse and worse, more and more prisoners were murdered, and Charles Darnay remained in La Force.

CHAPTER 5

One year and three months had passed. During all that time Lucie was never sure, from hour to hour, that the Guillotine would not strike off her husband's head the next day. Every day, through the stony streets, the carts, known as tumbrils, now jolted heavily, filled with the condemned. Lovely girls; bright women, brown-haired, black-haired, and grey; youths; stalwart men and old; gentle born and peasant born; all on their way to the Guillotine.

Lucie tried to keep her little household as if her husband was there and little Lucie she taught, as regularly as if they had all been united in their English home, but sometimes, on kissing her father goodnight, she would burst into tears and tell him that, under God, all her hopes were on him. He always resolutely answered. "Nothing can happen to him without my knowledge, and I know that I can save him, Lucie."

They had not been in their lodging many weeks, when her father said to her, on coming home one evening:

"My dear, there is an upper window in the prison, to which Charles is sometimes able to come at three in the afternoon. When he is able to get to it, he thinks he might see you in the street, if you stood in a certain place that I can show you. But you will not be able to see him, my poor child, and, even if you could, it would be unsafe for you to make any sign."

"Father! Show me the place, and I will go there every day."

From that time, in all weathers, she waited there two hours. As the clock struck two, she was there, and at four she turned sadly away. When it was not too wet or windy, she took little Lucie with her; at other times she was alone but she never missed a single day.

It was the dark and dirty corner of a small winding street. A hut belonging to a cutter of wood into lengths for burning, was the only house at that end; all else was wall. On the third day of her being there, he noticed her.

"Good day, citizeness."

"Good day, citizen."

This way of addressing people was now the law.

"Walking here again, citizeness?"

"Yes, as you can see, citizen."

The wood-sawyer, (he had once been a mender of roads) cast a glance at the prison, and remarked, "But it's not my business." And he went on sawing his wood.

Next day he was looking out for her and approached her the moment she appeared.

"What? Walking here again, citizeness?"

"Yes, citizen."

"Ah! A child too! Your mother, is it not, my little citizeness?"

"Do I say yes, mama?" whispered little Lucie, drawing close to her.

"Yes, dearest."

"Yes, citizen."

"Ah! But it's not my business. My work is my business. See my saw! I call it my Little Guillotine. La, la, la; La, la, la! And off his head comes!" The piece of wood fell as he spoke.

"See here again! Loo, loo, loo; Loo, loo, loo! And off *her* head comes. Now, a child. Tickle, tickle; Pickle, pickle! And off *its* head comes. All the family!"

Lucie shuddered as he threw two more pieces of wood into his basket, but it was impossible to be there while the wood-sawyer was at work, and not be in his sight. After this, to secure his good will, she always spoke to him first, and often gave him drink money, which he readily received. He was an inquisitive fellow, and sometimes when she had quite forgotten him in gazing at the prison roofs, and in lifting her heart up to her husband, she would come to herself to find him looking at her, with his knee on his bench and his saw stopped in its work. "But it's not my business!" he would generally say at those times, and would briskly start sawing again.

In all weathers, in the snow and frost of winter, in the bitter winds of spring, in the hot sunshine of summer, in the rains of autumn, and again in the snow and frost of winter, Lucie passed two hours of every day at this place, and every day on leaving it, she kissed the prison wall. Her husband saw her (so she learned from her father) it might be once in five or six times: it might be twice or three times running: it might be, not for a week or a fortnight together. It was enough that he could and did see her from time to time, and on that possibility she would have waited all day if necessary, seven days a week.

December came and snow was falling lightly when Lucie took up her usual post in the afternoon. After a few moments, she was joined by her father.

"Lucie, I came to tell you that I have just left Charles climbing to the window. There is no one here to see at the moment. You may kiss your hand towards that highest shelving roof."

"I do so, father, and I send him my soul with it!"

"You cannot see him, my poor dear."

"No, father," said Lucie, weeping as she kissed her hand, "no."

A footstep in the snow. Madame Defarge, "I salute you, citizeness," from the doctor. "I salute you, citizen." This in passing. Nothing more. Madame Defarge gone, like a shadow over the white road.

"Give me your arm, my love. Pass from here with an air of cheerfulness and courage for his sake. That is good. Now, I have to tell you that Charles is summoned to go before the Tribunal tomorrow."

"For tomorrow!"

"Yes. He has not received the notice yet, but I have been given the information. You are not afraid?"

She answered faintly, "I trust in you."

"Do so. Your suspense is nearly ended, my darling; he shall be restored to you within a few hours. I have surrounded him with all the protection I can. I must see Lorry." He stopped. There was a heavy lumbering of wheels within hearing. They both knew too well what it meant. One. Two. Three. Three tumbrils rattling away with their dread loads over the snow.

"I must see Lorry," the doctor repeated, turning her another way.

It was almost dark when they arrived at the Bank. The former residence of Monseigneur was altogether blighted and deserted. Above a heap of dust and ashes in the court, ran the letters: National Property. One United Republic. Liberty, Equality, Fraternity, or Death!

Who could that be with Mr Lorry – in the back room – who must not be seen? From whom, newly arrived, did he come out, agitated and surprised? To whom did he appear to repeat her faltering words, when, raising his voice and turning his head towards the door of the room from which he had just issued, he said: "Summoned to appear before the Tribunal tomorrow."

CHAPTER 6

The dread Tribunal of five Judges, Public Prosecutor, and determined Jury, sat every day. Their lists went forth every evening, and were read out by the gaolers of the various prisons to their prisoners. The standard gaoler-joke was, "Come out and listen to the Evening Paper, you inside there!"

"Charles Evrémonde, called Darnay!"

So at last began the Evening Paper at La Force.

When a name was called, its owner stepped apart into a spot reserved for those who were thus fatally recorded. Charles Evrémonde, called Darnay, had reason to know the usage; he had seen hundreds pass away so.

His gaoler, who wore spectacles to read with, glanced over them to assure himself that he had taken his place, and went through the list, making a similar short pause at each name.

There were twenty-three names, but only twenty people responded. One of the prisoners had died in gaol and been forgotten, and two had already been guillotined and forgotten. The list was read in the vaulted chamber where Darnay had seen the associated prisoners on the night of his arrival. Every one of those had perished in the massacre; every human creature he had since cared for and parted with, had died on the scaffold.

There were hurried words of farewell and kindness, but the parting was soon over. The prisoners spent the night in cold cells which were infested with rats and other vermin. Next day, fifteen prisoners were put to the bar before Charles Darnay's name was called. All the fifteen were condemned, and the trials of the whole occupied an hour and a half.

"Charles Evrémonde, called Darnay," was at length called.

His judges sat upon the bench in feathered hats; but everyone else except the prisoners wore the rough red cap and tricoloured cockade. The Jury and the audience were the worst types in the city, low, cruel, and bad. They were noisy, sometimes applauding, sometimes disapproving; some ate and drank as they looked on.

Of the men, the greater part were armed in various ways; of the women, some wore knives, some daggers; many knitted. Among these last was one, with a spare piece of knitting under her arm as she worked. She was in a front row, by the side of a man whom he had not seen since he was detained at the barrier, but whom he at once recognized as Defarge. He noticed that she once or twice whispered in his ear, and that she seemed to be his wife; but, what he noticed most was that although they were very close, they never looked towards him. They seemed to be waiting for something, and they looked at the Jury, but at nothing else. Below the

President sat Doctor Manette. As far as the prisoner could see, he and Mr Lorry were the only men there, apart from the Tribunal, who wore respectable clothes.

Charles Evrémonde, called Darnay, was accused by the public prosecutor as an emigrant, whose life was demanded by the Republic of France, under the law which banished all emigrants on pain of Death. It did not matter that the decree was dated after he returned to France. There he was, and there was the decree; he had been arrested in France, and his head was demanded.

"Take off his head!" cried the audience. "He is an enemy of the Republic!"

The President rang his bell to silence those cries, and asked the prisoner if it was not true that he had lived many years in England.

Yes, it was true.

He was an emigrant then. What else could he call himself?

Not an emigrant, he hoped, within the sense and spirit of the law.

Why not? the President desired to know.

Because he had given up his title and position which he disliked and had left his country, before the word emigrant, in the present sense, was in use to live by his own hard work in England, rather than by the work of the overladen people of France.

What proof had he of this?

He handed in the names of two witnesses: Théophile Gabelle, and Alexandre Manette.

But he had married in England, the President reminded him.

True, but not an English woman.

A citizeness of France?

Yes, by birth.

Her name and family?

"Lucie Manette, only daughter of Doctor Manette, the good physician who sits there."

This had a good effect on the audience, some of whom applauded.

The questions continued and Charles Darnay answered them according to the instructions given him previously by Doctor Manette, who had prepared the way for him.

The President wanted to know why he had not returned earlier. Charles Darnay told him he had no means of earning a living in France. He had only returned to save a citizen's life and to tell the truth. Was that criminal in the eyes of the Republic? Cries of "No!" from the audience.

The President required the name of the citizen. The accused replied that the citizen was his first witness. His letter, asking for help, had been taken from him at the barrier, but doubtless was among the papers in front of the President.

The doctor had taken care that it should be there, and it was produced and read. Citizen Gabelle was called to confirm it and did so. Citizen Gabelle hinted, with the greatest politeness, that he was now free because the accusation against him was answered, as to himself, by the surrender of the citizen Evrémonde, called Darnay.

Doctor Manette was next questioned. He told the Tribunal that the accused was his first friend on his release from his long imprisonment. He had remained in England, always faithful to his daughter and himself in their exile. He was not working for the aristrocratic government in England, but had actually been tried for his life by it, as the foe of England and friend of the United States. Monsieur Lorry, an English gentleman who was present, had been at that trial and would confirm what he had said. At this point, the Jury declared that they had heard enough, and that they were ready with their votes if the President would like to receive them.

The Jurymen voted aloud and individually. At every vote, the crowd set up a shout of applause. All the voices were in the prisoner's favour, and the President declared him free.

The crowd carried him home on their shoulders into the courtyard of the building where he lived. Lucie's father had gone ahead to prepare her and when her husband stood upon his feet, his wife fell, fainting, into his arms.

As he held her to his heart, the crowd started dancing and finally danced themselves away into the nearby streets, along the bank of the river and over the bridge.

After grasping the doctor's hand, as he stood victorious and proud before him; after grasping the hand of Mr Lorry, who came panting in after his struggle through the dancers; after kissing little Lucie, who was lifted up to clasp her hands round his neck; and after embracing the ever faithful Miss Pross, he took his wife in his arms, and carried her up to their rooms.

When they came back, Lucie went straight to her father. He was happy and proud and they all thanked God together.

"Don't tremble so, my darling," said the doctor. I have saved him."

CHAPTER 7

"**I** have saved him." It was not another of the dreams in which he had come back to her. He was really there, and yet his wife trembled, and a vague but heavy fear was upon her. Her father though, was happy. He had accomplished the task he had set himself, his promise was redeemed, he had saved Charles. Let them all lean upon him.

They lived very simply, not only because that was the safest way of life, giving the least offence to the people, but because they were not rich, and Charles, throughout his imprisonment, had had to pay heavily for his bad food, and for his guard, and towards the living of the poorer prisoners. Partly on this account, and partly to avoid a domestic spy, they kept no servant and Jerry, almost wholly transferred to them by Mr Lorry, had become their daily servant and had his bed there every night. His name and that of Charles Darnay were added to the list of inmates of the house which had, by law to be painted on the door or doorpost of every house.

In the universal fear and distress that darkened the time, all the usual harmless ways of life were changed. In the doctor's little household, as in many others, the daily food was purchased every evening, in small quantities and at various small shops. To avoid attracting notice, and to prevent envious people talking, was the general idea.

For some months past, Miss Pross and Mr Cruncher had done the shopping. Every afternoon, at about the time the public lamps were lighted, they went out together and brought back what was needed for the next day or so.

They neither of them spoke French, so Miss Pross pointed to what she needed, the shopkeeper held up a number of fingers to indicate the price of the goods, and Miss Pross held up one less.

"Now, Mr Cruncher," said Miss Pross, one afternoon, "if you are ready, I am."

Jerry hoarsely professed himself at Miss Pross's service. He had worn all the rust off his fingers long ago, but nothing would file his spiky head down.

"There's all kinds of things wanted," said Miss Pross. "We want wine, among the rest, and, speaking of wine, I hope we may not run into any of these redheads drunk with it or there'll be Murder and Mischief which is all these creatures understand."

"Pray, pray be cautious, dear!" cried Lucie.

"Yes, yes, yes, I'll be cautious, but I may say among ourselves that I do hope there'll be none of that crazy dancing going on in the streets. It only leads to trouble. Now, Ladybird, never you stir from that fire till I come back! Take care of that dear husband you have recovered, and don't move your pretty head from his shoulder as you have it now, till you see me again! May I ask a question, Doctor Manette, before I go?"

"I think you may take that liberty," the doctor answered, smiling.

"For gracious sake, don't talk about Liberty; we have quite enough of that," said Miss Pross.

"Hush, dear," said Lucie.

"Well, my sweet," said Miss Pross, nodding her head emphatically "the short and the long of it is, that I am a subject of His Most Gracious Majesty King George the Third," Miss Pross curtseyed at the name, "and as such, my maxim is, Confound their politics, Frustrate their knavish tricks, On him our hopes we fix, God save the King!"

Mr Cruncher, inspired with loyalty, growlingly repeated the words after Miss Pross, like somebody at church.

"I am glad you have so much of the Englishman in you, though I wish you had never caught that cold in your voice," said Miss Pross approvingly. "But the question is, Doctor Manette, is there any prospect yet, of our getting out of this place?" The good creature was as anxious as they all were, but, as was her way, she approached the subject in a light, somewhat casual way.

"I fear not yet. It would be too dangerous for Charles."

"Heigh-ho-hum!" said Miss Pross, cheerfully keeping back a sigh as she glanced at her darling's golden hair in the light of the fire, "then we must have patience and wait; that's all. We must hold up our heads and fight low, as my brother Solomon used to say. Now, Mr Cruncher! Don't you move, Ladybird!"

They went out, leaving Lucie and her husband, her father, and the child, by a bright fire. Mr Lorry was expected back presently from the Banking House. Miss Pross had lighted the lamp, but had put it aside in a corner so that they might enjoy the firelight undisturbed.

Little Lucie sat by her grandfather with her hands clasped through his arm, and he began to whisper a story to her about a great and powerful Fairy who had opened a prison wall and let out a captive who had once done the Fairy a service.

All at once, footsteps were heard upon the stairs and a blow was struck at the door. Lucie cried out and clutched her husband. The doctor took the lamp in his hand, crossed the two intervening outer rooms, and opened it. There was a clattering of feet over the floor, and four rough men in red caps, armed with sabres and pistols, entered the room.

"The Citizen Evrémonde, called Darnay," said the first man.

"Who seeks him?" answered Darnay.

"I seek him. We seek him. I know you Evrémonde; I saw you before the Tribunal today. You are again the prisoner of the Republic."

The four men surrounded him where he stood with his wife and child clinging to him.

"Tell me how and why I am again a prisoner."

"It is enough that you return to the prison, and will know tomorrow. You are summoned to appear before the Tribunal tomorrow."

Doctor Manette put the lamp down, went over to the speaker, and taking him by the loose front of his red woollen shirt, said:

"You know him, you have said. Do you know me?"

"Yes, I know you, Citizen Doctor."

"We all know you, Citizen Doctor," said the other three.

"Then, will you tell me, how does this happen?"

"Citizen Doctor," said the first man, reluctantly, "he has been denounced by the Section of Saint Antoine. This citizen," pointing out the second who had entered, "is from Saint Antoine."

The man he had indicated nodded his head and added:

"He is accused by Saint Antoine."

"Of what?" asked the doctor.

"Citizen Doctor, ask no more. You will know tomorrow. Now, Evrémonde, we have no time to spare."

"One word," the doctor entreated, "will you tell me who denounced him?"

"It is against the rules," answered the first man, "but you can ask the Citizen from Saint Antoine, if you wish."

The doctor turned his eyes upon that man, who moved uneasily on his feet, rubbed his beard a little, and at length said, "he is denounced by the Citizen and Citizeness Defarge. And by one other."

"What other?"

"Do *you* ask, Citizen Doctor?"

"Yes."

"Then," said the man from Saint Antoine, with a strange look, "you will be answered tomorrow. Meanwhile, I am dumb."

CHAPTER 8

Happily unconscious of the new calamity at home, Miss Pross threaded her way along the narrow streets and crossed the river by the bridge of the Pont-neuf, making a list in her mind of the purchases she had to make. Mr Cruncher, with the basket, walked at her side. They both looked to the right and to the left and avoided groups of people.

Having purchased a few small articles of grocery, and some oil for the lamp, she remembered the wine. After peeping into several wine shops, she stopped at the sign of the Good Republican which had a quieter look than any other place they had passed, and, though red with patriotic caps, was not so red as the rest. Sounding Mr Cruncher, and finding him of her opinion, she ventured in to the Good Republican escorted by her cavalier. They approached the counter, and showed what they wanted.

As their wine was being measured out, a man parted from another man in the corner, and rose to depart. In going, he had to face Miss Pross. No sooner did he face her, than Miss Pross uttered a scream, and clapped her hands.

"What is the matter?" said the man who looked French but spoke in a low voice in English.

"Oh, Solomon, dear Solomon!" cried Miss Pross, clapping her hands again, "after all this time, I find you here!"

"Don't call me Solomon. Do you want to be the death of me?" asked the man, in a furtive, frightened way.

"Brother," cried Miss Pross, bursting into tears. "How can you be so hard to me?"

"Come outside if you want to talk to me," said her brother. "Pay for your wine and come out. Who's this man?"

Miss Pross, shaking her head at her far from affectionate brother, said through her tears, "Mr Cruncher."

"Let him come out too," said Solomon. "Does he think I'm a ghost?"

To judge from his looks, Mr Cruncher did think that, but he said nothing. Miss Pross paid for the wine, and they all went outside.

"Now," said Solomon, stopping at the dark street corner, "What do you want?"

"How dreadfully unkind of a brother," cried Miss Pross, "to give me such a greeting, and show me no affection."

"There. Confound it! There," said Solomon, giving her a peck on the cheek. "*Now* are you satisfied?"

Miss Pross only shook her head and wept in silence.

"If you expect me to be surprised," said her brother, "I am not surprised; I knew you were here; I know of most people who are here. If you really want to protect me, you will go your ways as soon as possible, and let me go mine. I am busy. I am an official."

"But now that I have found you, I don't want to leave you, Solomon!"

"I knew you would say that," said Solomon. "You want to be the death of me. I shall be rendered Suspected by my own sister. Is that what you want?"

"Heavens forbid!" cried Miss Pross. "I have ever loved you truly, and ever shall. Say but one affectionate word to me, and tell me there is nothing wrong between us, and I will detain you no longer."

Poor, good Miss Pross! If anything was wrong between them, it would be no fault of hers, but his for spending her money and leaving her. Mr Lorry knew all about it.

At this moment, Mr Cruncher, who had been looking rather confused throughout their conversation, touched him on the shoulder and said, "I say! Might I ask the favour? As to whether your name is John Solomon, or Solomon John?"

The official turned towards him with a sudden mistrust. He had not previously uttered a word.

"Come on," said Mr Cruncher. "Speak out, you know. John Solomon or Solomon John? She calls you Solomon, and she must know being your sister. And I know you're John, you know. Which of the two goes first? And regarding that name of Pross, likewise. That weren't your name over the water."

"What do you mean?"

"Well, I don't know all I mean, for I can't call to mind what your name was, over the water."

"No?"

"No. But I'll swear it was a name of two syllables."

"Indeed?"

"Yes. I know you. You was a spy-witness at the Old Bailey. What, in the name of the Father of Lies, own father to yourself, was you called at that time?"

"Barsad," said another voice, striking in.

"That's the name for a thousand pound!" cried Jerry.

The speaker who struck in was Sydney Carton. He had his hands behind him under the skirts of his riding-coat, and he stood at Mr Cruncher's elbow as carelessly as he might have stood at the Old Bailey itself.

"Don't be alarmed, my dear Miss Pross. I arrived at Mr Lorry's, to his surprise, yesterday evening; we agreed that I would not present myself elsewhere until all was well, or unless I could be useful; I present myself here, to beg a little talk with your brother. I wish you had a better employed brother. I wish for your sake Mr Barsad was not a Spy of the Prisons."

The spy turned pale and started to bluster but Carton interrupted him:

"There is no point in denying it, Mr Barsad. I saw you coming out of the prison of the Conciergerie an hour or more ago and I followed you here. You have a face to be remembered, and I remember faces well. Wondering what you were mixed up in now and remembering Mr Darnay's trial at the Old Bailey, I followed you. I walked into the wine shop here, close after you and sat near you. I heard your conversation with others in here, and I had no difficulty in working out what your occupation was. You are most certainly a Prison Spy and I think you might be useful to me."

"In what way?" asked the spy uncomfortably.

"Come to the office of Tellson's Bank, and I will tell you."

"And what if I refuse?"

"That would be unwise, Mr Barsad. I know who you are and what you do. But I have a little proposal to make to you that might interest you. Will you come to the Bank?"

"I'll hear what you have got to say. Yes, I'll go with you."

"I propose that we first conduct your sister safely to the corner of her own street. Let me take your arm, Miss Pross. This is not a good city, at this time, for you to be out in, unprotected; and as I know Mr Barsad, I will invite him to Mr Lorry's with us. Are we ready? Come then."

They left her at the corner of the street, and Carton led the way to Mr Lorry's, which was within a few minutes' walk. John Barsad – otherwise Solomon Pross – walked at his side.

Mr Lorry had just finished his dinner, and was sitting before a cheery log or two of fire. He turned his head as they entered, and showed the surprise with which he saw a stranger.

"Miss Pross's brother, sir," said Sydney. "Mr Barsad."

"Barsad?" repeated Mr Lorry, "Barsad? I seem to know the name and the face."

"I told you you had a remarkable face, Mr Barsad," observed Carton, coolly. "Pray sit down."

As he took a chair himself, he reminded Mr Lorry of the connection with Barsad, by saying to him with a frown, "Witness at that trial." Mr Lorry immediately remembered, and regarded his new visitor with a look of dislike.

"Mr Barsad has been recognized by Miss Pross as the brother she is so devoted to, but has not seen lately and he has acknowledged that she is his sister. I pass to worse news. Darnay has been arrested again. I have the news from Mr Barsad."

"But I left him safe and free within these two hours," exclaimed Mr Lorry in horror, and am about to return to him."

"When was it done, Mr Barsad?"

"A short time ago, I believe. I heard it at the wine shop where we spoke together."

"I own to you I am shaken, Mr Lorry, by Doctor Manette's not having had the power to prevent the arrest."

"He may not have known of it beforehand," said Mr Lorry, confused and very shaken himself.

"But that, in itself, is a very bad sign."

"That's true," Mr Lorry acknowledged, with his

troubled hand at his chin, and his troubled eyes on Carton.

"In short," said Sydney, "this is a desperate time, and desperate times need desperate measures. Mr Lorry, you know my weakness. I should be glad if you would give me a glass of brandy."

He drank off a glassful and then another and sat thinking for a few minutes. Then he said, "We need a man at the Conciergerie. Mr Barsad, you have been in the service of the English Government, an enemy of France, you have been in the service of the French Government, which has now been overthrown, and you are now in the service of the French Republican Government as prison official at the Conciergerie. Do you not think you are, with that kind of past, in grave danger of denunciation to the Revolutionary Tribunal followed by a short journey to the Guillotine? For all they know, you might still be spying for your former employers. Perhaps you are. *I* could denounce you, could I not?"

John Barsad thought rapidly. His position was worse than even Sydney Carton suspected. He had spied on the Defarges in their wine shop for the former French Government. He remembered with fear and trembling, that Madame Defarge had knitted when he talked with her, and how she had looked at him. He had since seen her, in the Section of Saint Antoine, over and over again produce her knitted registers, and denounce people whose lives the guillotine then surely swallowed up.

He appealed to Mr Lorry: "I think, sir that I may appeal to a gentleman of your years and good nature, to put it to this other gentleman, so much your junior that he *is* a gentleman and should not lower himself by betraying me to my employers. I admit that *I* am a spy – a spy is despised, though some persons do that kind of work; but this gentleman is no spy. Why should he behave like one?"

"Mr Barsad," said Sydney Carton, "unless you accept the proposal which I propose to make to you, I shall denounce you. I have thoroughly made up my mind about it."

The smooth manner of the spy received such a check from Carton's words, that it faltered, and he was at a loss to know how to reply.

While Barsad sat there, with his confidence quite gone and fear on his face, Carton said in a thoughtful way:

"And indeed, now I think again, there is something else. Who was that friend and fellow spy I saw you with in the wine shop, the Good Republican?"

"French. You don't know him," said the spy, quickly.

"French, eh?" replied Carton, thoughtfully, "well, he may be."

"He is, I assure you," said the spy; "though it's not important."

"Not important," said Carton. "No. Yet I know the face."

"I think not. I am sure not. It can't be," said the spy.

"It can't be", muttered Sydney Carton. "He spoke good French, yet like an Englishman, I thought."

"From the country," said the spy.

"No. English!" cried Carton, striking his open hand on the table, as a light broke clearly on his mind. "Roger Cly! Disguised, but the same man. We had that man before us at the Old Bailey."

"Now, there you are hasty, sir," said Barsad, with a smile. "Cly, who, I will admit was a partner of mine, has been dead several years. I attended him in his last illness. He was buried in London, at the church of St Pancras-in-the-Fields. I helped to lay him in his coffin."

Here, Mr Lorry became aware, from where he sat, of a most remarkable goblin shadow on the wall. Tracing it to its source, he discovered it to be caused by a sudden extraordinary rising and stiffening of all the risen and stiff hair on Mr Cruncher's head.

"Let us be reasonable," said the spy, "and let us be fair. To show you how mistaken you are, I will lay before you a certificate of Cly's burial, which I happened to have carried in my pocket-book. There it is. Look at it. It's no forgery."

Here Mr Lorry perceived the reflection on the wall to lengthen, and Mr Cruncher rose and stepped forward, his hair still violently on end.

Unseen by the spy, Mr Cruncher stood at his side, and touched him on the shoulder like a ghostly bailiff.

"That there Roger Cly, master," said Mr Cruncher, with an accusing face. "So *you* put him in his coffin?"

"I did."

"Who took him out of it?"

Barsad leaned back in his chair, and stammered, "What do you mean?"

"I mean," said Mr Cruncher, "that he weren't never in it. No! Not he! I'll have my head took off, if he was ever in it."

The spy looked round at the two gentlemen: the both looked in astonishment at Jerry.

"I tell you," said Jerry, "that you buried paving-stones and earth in that there coffin. Don't go and tell *me* that you buried Cly. It was a take in. Me and two more knows it."

"How do you know it?"

"What's that to you? It's you I've got a grudge against, it is, doing a tradesman out of a job! I'd catch hold of your throat and choke you for half a guinea."

Sydney Carton who, with Mr Lorry, had been lost in amazement at this turn of the business, here requested Mr Cruncher to quieten down and explain himself.

"At another time, sir," answered Jerry hastily. "What I say is the truth and he knows well what that there Cly was never in that there coffin, and if he says he was, I'll choke him."

"Well, I see one thing," said Carton. I hold another

advantage over you, Mr Barsad. Associate of an English spy, pretending to be French who faked his own death and came to life again. In the present atmosphere of suspicion, that is quite enough to get you denouced, tried and sent to the Guillotine."

"I give up," said the spy. "I must confess we fled from England to get away from the mob who were after us. I only just escaped and Cly never would have got away at all, if he hadn't faked his death. Though how this man knows it was a sham, is a wonder of wonders to me."

"Never you mind about that," said Jerry. "I just wish I could choke you, that's all."

The Spy of the prisons turned away from him and spoke to Sydney Carton:

"It has come to a point. I go on duty at the prison soon, and can't overstay my time. You told me you had a proposal. What is it? What do you want with me?"

"Not very much. You are a turnkey at the Conciergerie?"

"I am sometimes."

"Can you choose the time?"

"I tell you once and for all, there is no such thing as an escape possible," said the spy firmly.

"Why need you tell me what I have not asked? You are a turnkey at the Conciergerie. Can you choose the time when you are on duty?"

"I can pass in and out when I choose."

Sydney Carton filled another glass with brandy,

poured it slowly out upon the hearth, and watched it as it dropped. When it was all gone, he said rising:

"So far we have spoken before two others. Now, come into the next room, and let us have one final word alone."

CHAPTER 9

While Sydney Carton and Barsad, the Spy, were in the adjoining room, speaking so low that not a sound was heard, Mr Lorry looked at Jerry in considerable doubt and mistrust. Jerry, for his part, was looking extremely uncomfortable, and whenever Mr Lorry's eyes caught his, he was taken with a peculiar kind of short cough requiring the hollow of a hand before it, which made him look more shifty than ever.

"Jerry," said Mr Lorry. "Come here."

Mr Cruncher came forward sideways, with one shoulder in front of the other.

"What have you been, besides a messenger?"

After some thought, Mr Cruncher replied, "Something in the agricultural way, sir."

"I suspect," said Mr Lorry, that you have used the respectable and great house of Tellson's as a cover for an unlawful occupation of an evil description. I suspect you Jerry of digging up bodies buried in hallowed ground and selling them to doctors who then use them to teach their students. If you have been doing this, don't expect me to befriend you when you get back to England. Don't expect me to keep your secret. You cannot use the fact that you are a messenger for the Bank to make you seem respectable. Tellson's shall not be imposed upon."

"I hope sir," said Jerry pleadingly, "that a gentleman like you what I have had the honour of taking messages for for many years would think twice about harming me, even if I was doing it – I don't say I *was* doing it, but even if I was, there's two sides. There's the doctors too, going around in their carriages. Nobody asks them about my visits!"

"Ugh!" cried Mr Lorry, seeing his argument nevertheless. "I am shocked at the sight of you."

"I don't say I *was* doing it."

"Don't tell me lies," said Mr Lorry.

"I'm not sir," said Jerry, as if nothing were further from his thoughts.

"No, I will not sir. What I would humbly offer you, sir is this. Upon my stool outside Tellson's sits that their boy of mine, brought up and growed up to be a man, what will do your errands for you, take your messages, do any light jobs what need doing. Let that there boy take my place and take care of his mother, and let me go and dig graves and put the bodies in, instead of taking 'em out. That is what I respectfully offer you, sir. Don't blow upon me, sir. I have told you about that there Roger Cly, and I could have held it back."

"That at least is true," said Mr Lorry. "Say no more now. It may be that I shall yet stand your friend, if you deserve it, and repent in deeds not words. I want no more words."

Mr Cruncher touched his forehead, as Sydney Carton and the spy returned from the adjoining room. "Good-bye, Mr Barsad," said Carton, "we have made our arrangements. You have nothing to fear from me."

He sat down in a chair on the hearth beside Mr Lorry. When they were alone, Mr Lorry asked him what he had done.

"Not much. If it should go badly with the prisoner, I have made sure I shall at least be able to see him once."

Mr Lorry's face fell.

"It was all I could do," said Carton. "If I asked too much, Barsad might be charged and go to the guillotine. That's the weakness of the position. There is no help for it."

"But going to see him, if it should go badly with him before the Tribunal, will not save him," said Mr Lorry.

Mr Lorry's eyes sought the fire; the anxiety of the last few days was too much for him and his tears fell.

"You are a good man and a true friend," said Carton in a gentler voice. "I could not respect your sorrow more if you were my father. Fortunately for you, however, you are not my father."

Though he said the last words with a slip into his usual manner, there was a true feeling and respect both in his tone and in his touch, that Mr Lorry, who had never seen the better side of him, was wholly unprepared for. He gave him his hand, and Carton gently pressed it.

"To return to poor Darnay," said Carton. "Don't tell

Lucie about my plan. It would not make it possible for her to see him. Better not to speak of me. I had better not see her. I can give her any little help that I can without that. You are going to her, I hope. She must be very desolate tonight."

"I am going at once."

"I am glad of that. She is so fond of you and relies so much on you. How does she look?"

"Anxious and unhappy, but very beautiful."

"Ah!"

It was a long grieving sound, like a sigh – almost like a sob.

For a while, Carton sat gazing into the fire, then he turned to Mr Lorry and said, "Have your duties drawn to an end now, sir?"

"Yes. I have done all I can do here. I hoped to have left them in perfect safety, and then to have left Paris. I have my permit to go through. I was ready to go."

They were both silent.

"Yours is a long life to look back upon, sir," said Carton, wistfully.

"I am in my seventy-eighth year."

"You have been useful all your life; trusted, respected, and looked up to."

"I have been a man of business, ever since I have been a man. Indeed, I may say that I was a man of business when a boy."

"See what a place you fill at seventy-eight. How many people will miss you when you leave it empty!"

"A solitary old bachelor," answered Mr Lorry, shaking his head. "There is nobody to weep for me."

"How can you say that! Wouldn't Lucie weep for you? Wouldn't little Lucie?"

"Yes, yes, thank God. I did not quite mean what I said."

"It *is* a thing to thank God for; is it not?"

"Surely, surely."

"Perhaps, it is not too late for me."

"No, not too late; you are young."

"I am not old, but my young way was never the way to age. Enough of me. Let me help you on with your coat, sir."

"And enough of me, I am sure," said Mr Lorry. "Are you going out?"

"I will walk with you to her gate. You know my vagabond and restless habits. If I should prowl about the streets a long time, don't be uneasy; I shall reappear in the morning."

"Are you going to the Court tomorrow?"

"Yes, unhappily."

"I shall be there, but only as one of the crowd. My Spy will find a place for me. Take my arm, sir."

Mr Lorry did so, and they went downstairs and out into the streets. Sydney Carton left the old gentleman at Lucie's gate and made his way through several dark and dirty streets to a chemist's shop, which the owner was closing with his own hands. It was a small, dim, crooked shop, kept by a small, dim, crooked man.

Greeting this citizen, Sydney went quickly up to his shop counter, wrote something down on a scrap of paper and laid it before him.

"Whew!" the chemist whistled softly as he read it. "Hi! hi! hi!"

Sydney Carton took no heed, and the chemist said, "For you, citizen?"

"For me."

"You will be careful to keep them separate, citizen. You know what will happen if you mix them?"

"Perfectly."

Certain small packets were made and given to him. He put them, one by one, into the breast pocket of his inner coat, counted out the money for them, and left the shop.

"There is nothing more to do," said he, glancing upward at the moon, "until tomorrow. I can't sleep." They were the words of a tired man, who had wandered and struggled and got lost, but who at length stuck into his road and saw its end.

Long ago, when he had been famous among his earliest competitors as a youth of great promise, he had followed his father to the grave. His mother had died, years before.

These solemn words, which had been read at his father's grave, arose in his mind as he went down the dark streets, among the heavy shadows, with the moon and the clouds sailing on high above him. "I am the resurrection and the life, saith the Lord: he that believeth in me, though he were dead, yet shall he live: and whosoever liveth and believeth in me, shall never die."

Now that the streets were quiet and the night wore on, the words were in the echoes of his feet, and were in the air. Perfectly calm and steady, he sometimes repeated them to himself as he walked; but he heard them always.

He crossed the Seine, the night wore on, and after a few hours wandering, he saw that it was coming to an end.

He stood upon the bridge listening to the water as it splashed the river walls of the Island of Paris, where the picturesque confusion of houses and cathedral shone bright in the light of the moon; the day came coldly, looking like a dead face out of the sky. Then the night, with the moon and the stars, turned pale and died, and for a little while it seemed as if creation was dying.

But the glorious sun, rising, seemed to strike those words, that burden of the night, straight and warm to his heart in its long bright rays. And looking along them, with reverently shaded eyes, a bridge of light appeared to span the air between him and the sun, while the river sparkled under it.

The strong tide, so swift, so deep, and certain, was like a friend in the morning stillness. He walked by the stream, far from the houses, and in the light and warmth of the sun fell asleep on the bank. When he awoke and was afoot again, he lingered there yet a little longer, watching a small whirlpool that turned and turned without purpose, until the main stream absorbed it, and carried it on to the sea – "like me!"

Mr Lorry was already out when he got back, and it was easy to guess where the good old man had gone. Sydney Carton drank nothing but a little coffee, ate some bread, and having washed and changed to refresh himself, went out to the place of trial.

He found an obscure corner among the crowd. Mr Lorry was there, and Doctor Manette was there. Lucie was there, sitting beside her father.

Every eye was turned to the jury. They were the same people as yesterday and the day before, and the days before that. They looked eager and like nothing so much as dogs awaiting their time to hunt the deer.

Every eye then turned to the five judges and the Public Prosecutor. No hope at all there. Silence was called and everyone leaned forward with a strained attention.

The Public Prosecutor introduced the prisoner:

Charles Evrémonde, called Darnay. Released yesterday. Accused again and arrested again. Suspected and Denounced as an enemy of the Republic. An Aristocrat, one of a family of tyrants who had oppressed the people.

The President asked if the Accused was denounced openly or secretly.

"Openly, President."

"By whom?"

"Three voices. Ernest Defarge, winekeeper of Saint Antoine."

"Good."

"Thérèse Defarge, his wife."

"Good."

"Alexandre Manette, physician."

A great uproar took place in the court, and in the midst of it, Doctor Manette was seen, pale and trembling, standing where he had been seated.

"President, I indignantly protest to you that this is a forgery and a fraud. You know the accused to be the husband of my daughter. My daughter, and those dear to her, are far dearer to me than my life. Who and where is the false conspirator who says that I denounce the husband of my child?"

"Calm yourself, Citizen Manette. To disobey the authority of the Tribunal would be to put yourself out of Law. As to what is dearer to you than life, nothing can be so dear to a good Citizen as the Republic."

Loud acclamations hailed this rebuke. The President rang his bell, and with warmth resumed:

"If the Republic should demand of you the sacrifice of your child herself, it would be your duty to sacrifice her. Listen to what is to follow. In the meanwhile, be silent!"

Frantic acclamations were again raised. Doctor Manette sat down, with his eyes looking around, and his lips trembling; and his daughter drew closer to him.

Defarge was produced, when the court was quiet enough for him to be heard, and rapidly told the story of the imprisonment, and of his having been a mere boy in the Doctor's service, and of the Doctor's release, and of the state he was in when he was released and delivered to him. This short examination followed, for the court was quick with its work.

"You did good service at the taking of the Bastille citizen, I am told."

"I believe so."

Here an excited woman screeched from the crowd, "You were one of the best patriots there. You were among the first to enter the accursed fortress when it fell. Why not say so?"

It was the Vengeance who shouted out. The audience cheered.

The President rang his bell, but the Vengeance, encouraged by the applause, shrieked, "I defy that bell!" More cheers.

"Inform the Tribunal of what you did that day within the Bastille, citizen."

"I knew," said Defarge, looking down at his wife, who stood at the bottom of the steps on which he was standing, looking steadily up at him; "I knew that this prisoner, of whom I speak, had been confined in a cell known as One Hundred and Five, North Tower. I knew it from himself. He knew himself by no other name than One Hundred and Five, North Tower when he made shoes under my care at my home. I decided that as soon as the Bastille fell, I would examine the cell where he had been.

The Bastille fell and I climbed many steps up to the cell with a fellow citizen who is a member of the Jury today. We were taken up by one of the gaolers. I examined the cell very closely. In a hole in the chimney, where a stone had been removed and replaced, I found a written paper. This is that written paper. I know the handwriting of Doctor Manette and this is his writing. I give this paper now into the hands of the President."

"Let it be read."

All eyes were intent upon the doctor and the paper was read as follows.

CHAPTER 10

"I, Alexandre Manette, unfortunate physician, born in Beauvais, and afterwards resident in Paris, write this paper secretly in my miserable cell in the Bastille, during the last month of the year, 1767. I am going to hide it in the wall of the chimney where some pitying hand may find it, when I and my sorrows are dust.

I am writing with a rusty nail, dipped into scrapings of soot and charcoal from the chimney mixed with my blood.

I have no hope at all of release and I fear that, in time my reason will go, but as I write this, I am of sound mind, my memory is perfect and I write the truth.

This is my story:

"One cloudy moonlight night in the third week of December in the year 1757, I was walking by the River Seine in the refreshing frosty air, at an hour's distance from my place of residence in the Street of the School of Medicine, when a carriage came along behind me, driven very fast. As I stood aside to let it pass, a head was put out of the window, and a voice called on the driver to stop.

The carriage stopped as soon as the driver could rein

in his horses, and the same voice called to me by my name. I answered. The carriage was then so far in advance of me that two gentlemen had time to open the door and alight before I came up with it. I observed that they were both wrapped in cloaks, and appeared to conceal themselves. As they stood side by side near the carriage door, I also observed that they both looked of about my own age, or a little younger and they were greatly alike, in height, manner, voice, and (as far as I could see) face too.

"Are you Doctor Manette?" said one.

"I am."

"Doctor Manette, formerly of Beauvais," said the other, "the young physician and expert surgeon, who within the last year or two has made a rising reputation in Paris?"

"Gentlemen," I answered, "I am that Doctor Manette of whom you speak so graciously."

"We have been to your residence," said the first, "and not being so fortunate as to find you there, and being informed that you were probably walking in this direction, we followed, in the hope of overtaking you. Will you please enter the carriage?"

This seemed more like an order than a request, and they both moved, as these words were spoken, so as to place me between themselves and the carriage door. They were armed. I was not.

"Gentlemen," said I, "pardon me, but I usually inquire

who is asking my assistance and what is the nature of the case to which I am summoned."

The second man spoke again: "Doctor, your clients are important people and, as to the nature of the case, we are confident that you will be able to see for yourself when we get there. Enough. Will you please enter the carriage?"

I had to obey, and I entered the carriage in silence. The carriage was turned round, and drove on at its former speed.

We soon left the streets behind, passed the North Barrier, and emerged upon the country road. Some time later, we left this road and presently stopped at a solitary house.

We all three alighted, and walked, by a damp soft footpath in a garden where a neglected fountain had overflowed, to the door of the house where we were admitted by a servant. I now perceived that the two brothers were twins.

From the time of alighting at the outer gate, which had been unlocked by one of the brothers and relocked after us, I had heard cries proceeding from an upper chamber. I was taken straight there, the cries growing louder as we ascended the stairs, and I found a patient in a high fever, lying on a bed.

The patient was a woman of great beauty, and young; she was not much past twenty. Her hair was torn and ragged, and her arms were bound to her sides with sashes and handkerchiefs. I noticed that these bonds were all pieces of a gentleman's clothes. On one of them, a fringed scarf, I saw the armorial bearings of a nobleman, and the letter E. She was lying on her face.

I turned her gently over, placed my hands on her to keep her down and looked into her face.

Her eyes were dilated and wild, and she constantly uttered piercing shrieks, and repeated the words, "My husband, my father, and my brother!" and then counted up to twelve, and said "Hush!" For an instant, and no more, she would pause to listen and the piercing shrieks would begin again, and she would repeat the cry, "My husband, my father, and my brother!" and would count up to twelve, and say "Hush!" There would be a pause after this, and then she started the same thing all over again.

"How long," I asked, "has this lasted?"

I will call the brothers the elder and the younger. The elder brother seemed to have the most authority, and it was he who answered, "Since about this hour last night."

"She has a husband, a father, and a brother?"

"A brother."

"I am not speaking to the brother?"

He answered with great contempt, "No."

"She has some recent association with the number twelve?"

"With twelve o'clock," replied the younger brother impatiently.

Because the brothers had not cared to tell me the nature of my patient's illness, I had no medicine with me, but, in any case, I did not carry my bag with me when I was out walking. I pointed this out and one of the brothers produced an old medicine chest. I found something in this that I could give my patient to quieten her and made her swallow, with some difficulty, the dose that I desired to give. Then, I sat down by the bed, holding her hand and a timid woman, who was the wife of the servant who had admitted us, waited in attendance in a corner.

I had sat by the side of the bed for half an hour, with the two brothers looking on, before the elder said:

"There is another patient."

I was startled, and asked, "Is it an urgent case?"

"You had better see," he carelessly answered, and took up a light.

The other patient lay in a back room across a second staircase, which was a kind of loft over a stable.

On some hay on the ground, with a cushion under his head, lay a handsome peasant boy – a boy of not more than seventeen at the most. He lay on his back, with his teeth set, his right hand clenched on his chest, and his eyes staring straight upward. I could not see where his wound was, as I kneeled on one knee over him; but I could see that he was dying of a wound from a sharp point.

"I am a doctor, my poor fellow," said I. "Let me examine it."

"I do not want it examined," he answered; "let it be."

It was under his hand, and I persuaded him to let me move his hand away.

The wound was a sword thrust, received from twenty to twenty-four hours earlier, but no skill could have saved him if he had had immediate attention. He was dying fast. As I turned my eyes to the elder brother, I saw him looking down at this handsome boy whose life was ebbing out, as if he were a wounded bird, or hare, or rabbit; not at all as if he were a fellow creature.

"A crazed young common dog! A serf! Forced my brother to draw upon him, and has fallen by my brother's sword – like a gentleman."

There was no touch of pity or sorrow in what he said. He had no feeling about the boy or his fate. It was just inconvenient to the brothers that this had happened.

The boy turned his eyes to me and spoke:

"They are very proud, these nobles, but we have our pride too. They think they can have their shameful way with our daughters and sisters, but we have had good girls among us. My sister is a good girl and was betrothed to a good young man, a tenant of this man. We were all tenants of his – this man who stands here. The other is his brother, the worst of a bad race."

"My sister married her lover. He was not strong, poor fellow. She had not been married many weeks, when that man's brother saw her, and asked that man to lend her to him. He was willing, but she was not, so to make her husband persuade her, they put him in the shafts of a cart and drove him until he collapsed. They took him out of his harness – it was striking twelve noon – he sobbed twelve times, once for every stroke of the bell and died in his wife's arms."

"Then, with that man's permission and even help, his brother took the poor widow away to have his pleasure with her. I saw her pass me on the road. When I told my father, his heart failed and he could not speak. I took my younger sister to a place of safety. Then I tracked the brother to this old place, and last night I climbed in with an old soldier's sword in my hand. He offered me money and then struck at me with a whip. I attacked him with my sword and forced him to draw his own sword. He thrust at me with all his skill and wounded me to death as you can see.

Lift me up, doctor. Where is that man? Proud as these nobles are, he is afraid to see me." I raised the boy's head against my knee, but, filled with an extraordinary power, he raised himself completely, obliging me to rise too.

"Marquis," said the boy, turning to him with his eyes opened wide, and his right hand raised, "in the days when all these things are to be answered for, I summon you and yours, to the last of your bad race, to answer for them. I mark this cross of blood upon you, as a sign that I do it. In the days when all these things are to be answered for, I summon your brother, the worse of the bad race, to answer for them separately. I mark this cross of blood upon him, as a sign that I do it."

Twice, he put his hand to his wound, and with his

forefinger drew a cross in the air. He stood for a moment with the finger still raised, and, as it dropped, he dropped with it, and I laid him down dead.

When I returned to the bedside of the young woman, I found her still raving. I knew that this might last for many hours, and that it would probably end in the silence of the grave.

"Is she dead?" asked the Marquis, whom I will still describe as the elder brother, coming booted into the room from his horse.

"Not dead," said I, "but like to die."

I was sitting by the bed; he ordered the woman in attendance away, and said in a subdued voice, "Doctor, when my brother got himself in this difficulty, I recommended that your aid should be invited. Your reputation is high, and, as a young man with your fortune to make, you are probably mindful of your own interest. The things that you see here, are things to be seen, and not spoken of."

I listened to the patient's breathing, and avoided answering.

"Are you listening to me, doctor?"

"Monsieur," said I, "in my profession, the communications of patients are always treated in confidence." I was careful what I said to him, for I was troubled in my mind with all that I had heard and seen. After this, I felt that I was watched by the brothers. They were waiting for the young woman to go and went out on their horses to pass the time.

Two or three days passed. She spoke faintly to me and asked me who I was and where she was. I told her and I asked her family name. She shook her head upon the pillow, and kept her secret as her brother had done.

My patient died, two hours before midnight that night. I was alone with her, when her forlorn young head dropped gently on one side, and all her earthly wrongs and sorrows ended.

The brothers were waiting in a room downstairs, impatient to ride away. "Is she dead?" said the elder, when I went in.

"She is dead," said I.

"I congratulate you, my brother," were his words as he turned round. He had before offered me money, which I had postponed taking. He now gave me a packet of gold coins. I took it from his hand, but laid it on the table. I had considered the question, and had resolved to accept nothing.

"Pray excuse me," said I. "Under the circumstances, no."

They exchanged looks, but bowed to me as I bowed to them; we parted without another word on either side.

Early in the morning, I found the packet of gold in a box with my name on it outside my door. I had decided to report the whole matter to whichever Government Minister would deal with such an affair, but court influence was strong and the nobles were powerful, so I had not much hope that anything would be done. But I felt I must do it to relieve my own mind.

I was very busy that day, and was not able to complete my letter that night. I rose long before my usual time next morning to finish it. It was the last day of the year. The letter was lying in front of me just completed, when I was told that a lady waited, who wished to see me.

The lady was young, charming, and handsome, but looked frail. She seemed very agitated. She told me she was the wife of the Marquis St Evrémonde, and I realized at once that her husband was one of the noblemen I had been with very lately.

She knew part of the story, of her husband's share in it and of my being brought there. She did not know the girl was dead and had been hoping to show her, in secret, a woman's sympathy to atone for the hateful deeds of the family she had married into.

She had heard that there was a young sister living, and her greatest desire was to help that sister. She had hoped that I might be able to tell her where she could find her, but beyond confirming that there was a younger sister, I was unable to help her. I only knew that her brother had taken her to a place of safety.

She was a good, kind lady who was not happy in her marriage. How could she be! Her brother-in-law disliked her and distrusted her, and all his influence was against her. She was frightened of him and of her husband too. When I escorted her to the door, I saw that there was a child, a handsome boy from two to three years old in her carriage.

"For his sake, doctor," she said, pointing to him in

tears, "I must make amends for what his family has done. Otherwise, one day it will be required of him. I will do all I can to help her if she can only be found."

I kissed her hand, said a word to the little boy, and never saw her more.

As she had mentioned her husband's title to me in the belief that I already knew it, I made no mention of it in my letter, but sealed it, and, not trusting it out of my own hands, delivered it myself that day.

That night, the last night of the year, towards nine o'clock, a man in black clothes rang at my gate, demanded to see me, and softly followed my servant, Ernest Defarge, a youth, upstairs. When my servant came into the room where I sat with my wife – oh my wife, beloved of my heart! My fair young English wife! – we saw the man, who should have been waiting at the gate, standing silent behind him.

"An urgent case in the Rue St Honoré", he said. "It should not take long" He had a coach in waiting.

It brought me here, to the Bastille. It brought me to my living grave.

When we were clear of the house, a black scarf was drawn tightly over my mouth from behind, and my arms were tied down. The two brothers crossed the road from a dark corner, and identified me with a single gesture. The Marquis took from his pocket the letter I had written, showed it to me, burnt it in the flame of a lantern that was held, and extinguished the ashes with his foot.

Not a word was spoken. I was brought here; I was brought to my living grave.

During all these frightful years, I have had no news of my wife and no mercy. On this last night of the year 1767, I, Alexandre Manette denounce those brothers and all their descendants to the last of their race. I denounce them to Heaven and to earth."

A terrible sound arose when the reading of this document was done. A sound of craving and eagerness that had nothing in it but blood. The Defarges had bided their time and kept the Doctor's document to use when the time was ripe. Charles Evrémonde, known as Darnay, was doomed.

"Much influence around him has that Doctor Manette," murmured Madame Defarge, smiling to her friend the Vengeance. "Save him now, Doctor, save him if you can!"

At every juryman's vote, there was a roar. Another and another. Roar and roar. They were of one mind. An Aristocrat, an enemy of the Republic, a known enemy of the People. Back to the Conciergerie, and Death within four-and-twenty hours!

CHAPTER 11

The judges, having to take part in a demonstration, the Tribunal adjourned. The quick noise and movement of the court's emptying itself by many passages had not ceased when Lucie, who had first fallen stricken when she heard the sentence, but quickly risen again, stood stretching out her arms towards her husband, with nothing in her face but love and consolation.

"Let me touch him! Let me embrace him once! Oh, good citizens, have pity on us."

There was only one gaoler left, along with two of the four men who had arrested him last night, and Barsad. The people had all poured out to the show in the streets. Barsad proposed to the rest, "Let her embrace him then; it is but a moment." There was silent agreement and they passed her over the seats in the hall to a raised place, where he, by leaning over the dock, could fold her in his arms.

"Farewell, dear darling of my soul. My parting blessing on my love. We shall meet again, where the weary are at rest!"

"I can bear it, dear Charles. I am supported from above. Don't suffer for me. A parting blessing for our child."

"I send it to her by you. I kiss her by you."

Her father had followed her, and would have fallen on his knees to both of them, if Darnay had not put out a hand and seized him, crying:

"No, no! You have done nothing wrong that you should kneel to us. We know now what you underwent when you suspected my descent, and when you knew it. We know now how, in spite of the wrong my family had done you, you accepted me for her dear sake. We thank you with all our hearts, and all our love and duty. Heaven be with you!"

As he was drawn away, his wife released him, and stood looking after him with her hands touching one another in the attitude of prayer, and with a radiant look upon her face, in which there was even a comforting smile. As he went out at the prisoner's door, she turned, laid her head on her father's shoulder, tried to speak to him, and fell at his feet.

Then, coming from the obscure corner from which he had never moved, Sydney Carton came and took her up. Only her father and Mr Lorry were with her. His arm trembled as it raised her, and supported her head. Yet, there was an air about him that was not all of pity – that had a flush of pride in it.

"Shall I take her to a coach? I shall never feel her weight."

He carried her lightly to the door, and laid her tenderly down in a coach. Her father and Mr Lorry got into it, and he took his seat beside the driver. When they were home, he lifted her again, and carried her up the staircase to their rooms. There, he laid her down on a couch, where her child and Miss Pross wept over her.

"Oh, Carton, Carton, dear Carton!" cried little Lucie, springing up and throwing her arms round him, in a burst of grief. "Now that you have come, I think you will do something to help mamma, something to save papa!" He bent over the child and laid her blooming cheek against his face. He put her gently from him, and looked at her unconscious mother.

"Before I go," he said, and paused – "May I kiss her?"

It was remembered afterwards that when he bent down and touched her face with his lips, he murmured some words. The child, who was nearest to him, told them afterwards, and told her grandchildren when she was a handsome old lady, that she heard him say, "A life you love."

When he had gone out into the next room, he turned suddenly to Mr Lorry and her father who were following, and said to her father:

"You had great influence, only yesterday, Doctor Manette. Let it at least be tried. These judges, and all the men in power, are very friendly to you, and very appreciative of your services; are they not?"

"Nothing connected with Charles was concealed from me. They promised me that I would be able to save him; and I thought I had."

He returned the answer in great trouble, and very slowly.

"Try them again."

"I intend to try," said Doctor Manette. "I will go direct to the Prosecutor and the President, and I will go to others whom it is better not to name. But, wait a minute, there is a demonstration in the streets, and I shall not be able to see anybody until it is dark."

"It will be dark soon after four. If I go to Mr Lorry's at nine, shall I hear what you have done, either from our friend or from yourself?"

"Yes."

"May you prosper!"

Mr Lorry followed Sydney to the outer door, and touching him on the shoulder as he was going away, caused him to turn.

"I have no hope," said Mr Lorry, in a low and sorrowful whisper.

"Nor have I."

"In any case, I doubt if any one of them would dare to save him after that demonstration in the court."

"I doubt it too. I heard the stroke of the Guillotine in that sound."

Mr Lorry leaned his arm upon the doorpost and bowed his face upon it.

"Don't despond," said Carton, very gently, "don't grieve. I encouraged Doctor Manette in this idea, because I felt it might one day be a consolation to his daughter. Otherwise she might think nothing more had been done to try and save him, and that might trouble her."

"Yes, yes, yes," returned Mr Lorry, drying his eyes, "you are right. But he will perish; there is no real hope."

"Yes. He will perish; there is no real hope," echoed Carton. And he walked with a firm step downstairs.

CHAPTER 12

Sydney Carton paused in the street, not quite decided where to go. "At Tellson's Banking-House at nine," he said thoughtfully, "but perhaps it would be a good plan to show myself somewhere else as well first so that these people should know I am still here."

He turned his face towards Saint Antoine.

Defarge had described himself, that day, as the keeper of a wine shop in the Saint Antoine suburb. It was not difficult for one who knew the city well, to find his house without asking any questions. Having found for himself the place where it was, Carton came out of the smaller streets again, and dined at a place of refreshment and fell sound asleep after dinner. For the first time in many years, he had no strong drink. Since last night he had drunk nothing but a little light thin wine, and last night he had dropped the brandy slowly down on Mr Lorry's hearth like a man who had done with it.

It was as late as seven o'clock when he awoke refreshed, and went out into the streets again. As he passed along towards Saint Antoine, he stopped at a shop window where there was a mirror, and slightly altered the untidy arrangement of his loose cravat, and his coat collar, and his wild hair. This done, he went on direct to Defarge's, and went in.

There happened to be no customer in the shop but Jacques Three. This man whom Carton had seen upon the Jury, stood drinking at the little counter, in conversation with the Defarges, man and wife. The Vengeance assisted in the conversation, like a regular member of the establishment.

As Carton walked in, took his seat and asked (in very poor French), for a small measure of wine, Madame Defarge cast a careless glance at him, and then a keener one, and then a keener one still, and then came forward to him herself, and asked him what it was he had ordered.

He repeated what he had already said.

"English?" asked Madame Defarge, inquisitively raising her dark eyebrows.

Carton answered in his former strong foreign accent. "Yes Madame, yes. I am English!"

Madame Defarge returned to her counter to get the wine and he heard her say to her husband, "I swear to you, just like Evrémonde."

Defarge brought him his wine and took a long look at him. Carton picked up a newspaper, and pretended to be reading it as he sipped his wine.

Those at the counter were speaking in low voices. There was a silence for a minute or two, as they looked at Carton to see if he was listening, but were satisfied when they saw him apparently trying to read the French words in the newspaper and running his finger along the lines, so they resumed their conversation.

"It is true what Madame says," observed Jacques Three. "Why stop? There is great force in that. Why stop?"

"Well, well," reasoned Defarge, "but one must stop somewhere, but at what point does one stop?"

"When they are all accounted for," said Madame.

"Magnificent," said Jacques Three. The Vengeance also approved highly.

"In general, I would say nothing against that," said Defarge, rather troubled, "but Doctor Manette has suffered much; you have seen him today; you have observed his face when his paper was read."

"I have observed his face!" repeated Madame, contemptuously and angrily. "Yes. I have observed his face. I have observed his face to be not the face of a true friend of the Republic. Let him take care of his face!"

"He also has to observe the anguish of his daughter," said Defarge. "That must be a terrible anguish for him!"

"I have observed his daughter," repeated Madame, "yes, I have observed his daughter, more times than one. I have observed her today, and I have observed her on other days. I have observed her in the court, and I have observed her in the street by the prison. Let me but lift my little finger, and that will be the end of her."

"The citizeness is superb," said the Juryman.

"She is an Angel!" said the Vengeance, and embraced her.

"As to you," went on Madame, addressing her husband, "if it depended on you — which happily it does not — you would rescue this man even now."

"No!" protested Defarge. "I would not. But I would leave the matter there. Stop there."

"This family is on my register, doomed to die — all of them and has been so for a long time," cried Madame Defarge. "Is that not true, husband?"

"That is true," assented Defarge.

"You remember well when you found that paper of the doctor's hidden in his cell in the Bastille. We brought it here and read it. We heard it again at the trial. You remember the whole story?"

"I remember the whole story."

"You remember that, of the whole family destroyed by the Evrémondes, there remained a girl, a sister of the boy who died. She had been taken to a place of safety. You remember?"

"I remember," said Defarge.

"Friends! Defarge will tell you, that I was that girl, the only one left. Those dead are my dead, and that summons to answer for those things descends to me. Ask him, is that so?"

"It is so," assented Defarge once more.

"Then tell Wind and Fire where to stop," returned Madame, "but don't tell me."

The wrath of Madame Defarge was terrifying to behold and her husband said no more.

Customers entered the wine shop, and the group was

233

broken up. The English customer paid for what he had had, and left.

At the appointed hour, he presented himself in Mr Lorry's room again, where he found the old gentleman walking to and fro in restless anxiety. He said he had been with Lucie until just now, and had only left her for a few minutes, to come and keep his appointment. Her father had not been seen since he quitted the Banking-House towards four o'clock. Lucie had some faint hopes that he might be able to save Charles, but they were very slight. He had been more than five hours gone: where could he be?

Mr Lorry waited until ten; but, Doctor Manette not returning, and he being unwilling to leave Lucie any longer, it was arranged that he should go back to her, and come to the Banking-House again at midnight. In the meanwhile, Carton would wait alone by the fire for the doctor.

He waited and waited, and the clock struck twelve; but Doctor Manette did not come back. Mr Lorry returned, and found no tidings of him, and brought none. Where could he be?

They were discussing this question and wondering if it was a hopeful sign, when they heard him on the stairs. The instant he entered the room, it was plain that all was lost.

Whether he had really been to anyone, or whether he had been all that time wandering in the streets, was never known. As he stood staring at them, they asked him no question, for his face told them everything.

Doctor Manette collapsed into a chair. He was crying, and they could see in him the poor, hopeless prisoner of the Bastille. They did what they could for him, but time was pressing and Lucie was foremost in their minds. The doctor was sobbing quietly and appeared lost in his thoughts. They spoke quietly: Carton was the first to speak:

"The last chance is gone: it was not much. Perhaps he should be taken to her. But, before you go, will you, for a moment, steadily attend to me? Don't ask me why I am asking certain things of you or why I shall ask you to make a certain promise to me. I have a reason – a good reason."

"I do not doubt it," answered Mr Lorry. "Say on."

Carton stooped to pick up the doctor's coat, which lay where he had dropped it. As he did so, a small case, in which he was accustomed to carry the list of his day's duties, fell lightly on the floor. Carton took it up, and there was a folded paper in it. "We should look at this!" he said. Mr Lorry nodded his consent. He opened it, and exclaimed, "Thank God!"

"What is it?" asked Mr Lorry, eagerly.

"A moment! Let me speak of it in its place. First," he put his hand in his coat, and took another paper from it, "that is the certificate which enables me to pass out of this city. Look at it. You see – Sydney Carton, an Englishman."

Mr Lorry held it open in his hand, gazing in his earnest face.

"Keep it for me until tomorrow. I shall see Charles tomorrow, you remember, and I had better not take it into the prison."

"Why not?"

"I don't know; I prefer not to do so. Now, take this paper that Doctor Manette has carried about him. It is a similar certificate, allowing him and his daughter and her child, at any time, to pass the barrier and the frontier. You see?"

"Yes!"

"Put it carefully with mine and your own. I never doubted until within this hour or two, that he had such a paper. It is good, until recalled, and I have reason to think it will be."

"They are not in danger, are they?"

"They are in great danger. They are in danger of denunciation by Madame Defarge. I know it from her own lips. Since then, I have seen the spy, Barsad, and he says the same. He knows that a wood-sawyer, living by the prison wall, is under the control of the Defarges, and has been rehearsed by Madame Defarge as to his having seen Lucie making signs and signals to prisoners. It is easy – they will accuse her of plotting and perhaps her father and her child too, for both have been seen with her at that place. It could involve their lives. But don't look so horrified. Yu will save them all."

"Heaven grant I may, Carton! But how?"

"I am going to tell you how. It will depend on you, and it could depend on no better man. Any denunciation would not be until after tomorrow, so we have a little time."

"Very well. What do you want me to do?"

"You have money, and can buy the means of travelling to the coast as quickly as the journey can be made. Your preparations have been completed for some days, to return to England. Early tomorrow have your horses ready, so that they may be ready to start at two o'clock in the afternoon."

"It shall be done."

"You have a noble heart. Tell them they *must* go and that it was the last wish of her husband. You think that her father will do what she asks, even in his present sad state?"

"I am sure of it."

"I thought so. Quietly and steadily have all these arrangements made in the courtyard here, even to the taking of your own seat in the carriage. The moment I come to you, take me in, and drive away."

"And I wait for you whatever happens?"

"You have my certificate in your hand with the rest, you know, and will reserve my place. Wait for nothing but to have my place occupied, and then for England!"

"Why then," said Mr Lorry, grasping his eager but so firm and steady hand, "it does not all depend on one old man, but I shall have a young and ardent man at my side."

"By the help of Heaven you shall! Promise me solemnly that nothing will make you change the plan which we have agreed between us."

"Nothing, Carton. I hope to do my part faithfully."

"And I hope to do mine. Now, goodbye!" Though he said this, he did not part from him then, but helped Mr Lorry take the poor doctor home to his unhappy daughter.

He did not enter the house, but stayed in the courtyard and remained there for a few minutes alone, looking up at the light in the window of Lucie's room. Before he went away, he breathed a blessing towards it, and a Farewell.

CHAPTER 13

In the black prison of the Conciergerie, the doomed of the day awaited their fate. They were in number as the weeks of the year. Fifty-two were to die that afternoon.

Charles Darnay, alone in a cell, had no hope of escaping the Guillotine now, but it was not easy, with the face of his beloved wife fresh before him to reconcile himself to his fate, and even if he had done so, he knew that Lucie and little Lucie would have to bear the sorrow for the rest of their lives. Nevertheless, their future peace of mind would depend on his quiet strength and presently, he found that he was able to pray, and he was comforted.

He had been allowed pen and paper and a light, and he sat down to write until such time as the prison lamps should be extinguished.

He wrote a long letter to Lucie, showing her that he had known nothing of her father's imprisonment, until he had heard of it from herself and had been as ignorant as she of his father's and uncle's responsibility for it until Doctor Manette's Bastille paper was read. He entreated her to make him realize that the arrest and denunciation was not his fault, since he had either forgotten the paper existed or thought it had been destroyed with the Bastille, since there was no mention of it among the relics of prisoners which had been discoverd there, and which had been described to all the world.

She knew already that it was her father's wish that he should change his name.

He confided to her the care of their dear child, and prayed her, as they would meet in Heaven, to comfort her father.

He wrote as well to Doctor Manette asking him to look after the family. He put this very strongly, hoping that it would arouse him from the despair into which he had sunk.

To Mr Lorry, he commended them all, and explained his worldly affairs. That done, with many added sentences of grateful friendship and thanks, all was done.

He never thought of Carton. His mind was so full of the others, that he never once thought of him.

He had time to finish these letters before the lights were put out. When he lay down on his straw bed, he thought he had done with this world. But Lucie came to him in his sleep and told him it was all a dream, and he had never gone away. He awoke in the sombre morning, not knowing where he was or what had happened until it flashed upon his mind, "This is the day of my death!"

He walked up and down, counting the hours. He had been told the executions started at three, so he thought they might come for him at two o'clock. He began to pray that he might be strong and be able to strengthen others.

Walking regularly to and fro with his arms folded, a very different man from the prisoner who had walked to and fro at the prison of La Force, he heard one o'clock strike without surprise. Devoutly thankful to Heaven that he was calm and in control of himself, he said, "There is but another hour now," and he turned to walk again.

There were footsteps in the stone passage outside the door. He stopped. The key was put in the lock, and turned. As the door opened, he heard a man say in a low voice, in English, "He has never seen me here. I have kept out of his way. Go in alone. I will wait here. Lose no time!"

The door was quickly opened and closed, and there stood before him face to face, quiet and with a finger on his lips and the light of a smile upon his face, Sydney Carton.

There was something so bright and remarkable in his look, that, for the first moment, the prisoner thought he had imagined him. But he spoke, and it was his voice; he took the prisoner's hand, and it was his real grasp.

"Of all the people upon earth; you least expected to see me," he said.

"I could not believe it to be you. I can scarcely believe it now. You are not" – the fear came suddenly into his mind – "a prisoner?"

"No. I happen to have some power over one of the keepers here, and that is how I come to stand before you. I come from your wife, dear Darnay."

The prisoner clasped his hand.

"I bring you a request from her."

"What is it?"

"It is something she earnestly wishes you to do. We have no time to discuss what it is. But you *must* do what she asks. Take off those boots you are wearing, and draw on these of mine."

"There was a chair against the wall of the cell, behind the prisoner. Carton, pressing forward, had already, with the speed of lightning, got him down into it, and stood over him, barefoot.

"Draw on these boots of mine. Put your hands to them; put your will to them. Quick!"

"Carton, there is no escaping from this place; it never can be done. You will only die with me. It is madness."

"It would be madness if I asked you to escape; but do I? Now, change that cravat for this one of mine, that coat for this of mine. While you do it, let me take this ribbon from your hair, and shake out your hair like this of mine."

With wonderful quickness, Carton forced these changes upon him. The prisoner was like a child in his hands.

"Carton! Dear Carton! It is madness. It cannot be done. It has been attempted before and has always failed. I implore you not to add your death to the bitterness of mine."

"Do I ask you, my dear Darnay, to pass the door? If I ask that, refuse. There are pen and ink and paper on this table. Is your hand steady enough to write?"

"It was when you came in."

"Steady it again, and write what I shall decide. Quick, friend, quick."

Pressing his hand to his bewildered head, Darnay sat down at the table. Carton with his right hand inside his coat, stood close beside him.

"Write exactly as I speak."

"To whom do I address it?"

"To no one." Carton still had his right hand hidden.

"Do I date it?"

"No. If you remember," said Carton, dictating, "the words that passed between us, long ago, you will readily understand this letter when you see it. You do remember them I know. It is not in your nature to forget them."

He was drawing his hand out a little; the prisoner chancing to look up in his hurried wonder as he wrote, the hand stopped, closing upon something.

"Have you written that?" Carton asked.

"I have. Is that a weapon in your hand?"

"No; I am not armed."

"What is that in your hand?"

"You shall know in a minute. Write on; there are but a few words more." He dictated again. "I am thankful that the time has come, when I can prove them. It is no cause for regret or grief." As he said these words with his eyes fixed on the writer, Carton's hand slowly and softly moved down close to the writer's face.

The pen dropped from Darnay's fingers on the table, and he looked about him vacantly.

"What vapour is that?" he asked.

"Vapour?"

"Something that crossed me."

"I don't notice anything. Take up the pen and finish. Hurry, hurry!"

"If it had been otherwise, and I did not use this opportunity, I should have had so much the more to answer for. If it had been otherwise – " Carton looked at the pen and saw that it was wandering off the paper.

Carton's hand moved back inside no more. The prisoner sprang up with a reproachful look, but Carton's hand was firm and close to his nostrils, and Carton's left arm caught him round the waist. For a few seconds he faintly struggled with the man who had come to lay down his life for him; but, within a minute or so, he was stretched insensible on the ground.

Quickly, but with hands as true to the purpose as his heart was, Carton dressed himself in the clothes the prisoner had laid aside, combed his hair, and tied it with the ribbon the prisoner had worn. Then he softly called, "Come in!" and the Spy, Barsad, presented himself.

"You see," said Carton looking up, as he kneeled on one knee beside the insensible figure, putting his letter to Lucie inside the breast pocket of Darnay's coat, "you are not taking any great risk."

"Not if you are true to your bargain," said the Spy nervously.

"Don't fear me. I will be true to the death. Now get assistance and take me to the coach."

"You?" said the Spy, who was shaking a little.

"The man with whom I have exchanged. You go out at the gate by which you brought me in, but he is Carton, now, and I am Darnay."

"Of course."

"Carton was weak and faint when you brought him in, and now he is even fainter as you bring him out. Saying goodbye to Darnay has overpowered him. That is what you tell the guards. Your life is in your own hands. Quick! Call assistance!"

"You swear not to betray me?" said the trembling Spy, as he paused for a last moment.

"Man, man!" returned Carton, stamping his foot; "I have sworn to go through with this. "Don't waste precious moments now. Take him yourself to the court-yard you know of, show him yourself to Mr Lorry, tell him yourself not to try and rouse him, but to let him have plenty of air. Tell him to remember my words of last night, and drive away!"

The Spy withdrew, and Carton seated himself at the table, resting his forehead on his hands. The Spy returned immediately with two men. They raised the unconscious figure, placed it on a litter they had brought to the door, and bent to carry it away.

"The time is short, Evrémonde," said the Spy, in a warning voice.

"I know it well," answered Carton. "Be careful of my friend, I entreat you, and leave me."

"Come then, comrades," said Barsad. "Lift him, and come away!"

The door closed, and Carton was left alone. Straining his powers of listening to the utmost, he listened for any sound which might indicate that the alarm had been raised. There was none. Keys turned, doors clashed, footsteps passed along distant passages. No cry was raised or hurry made, that seemed unusual. Breathing more freely in a little while, he sat down at the table, and listened again until the clock struck two.

He heard several doors opening in succession, and finally his own. A gaoler, with a list in his hand, looked in, merely saying, "Follow me, Evrémonde!" and he followed him into a large dark room, at a distance.

It was a dark winter day, and he could only just see the others who were brought there to have their arms bound. Some were standing; some seated. Most of them were silent and still, looking fixedly at the ground.

As he stood by the wall in a dim corner, while some of the fifty-two who were to die that day were brought in after him, one man stopped in passing to embrace him, as if he knew him. At that moment, he had a great dread of discovery; but the man went on. A very few moments after that, a young woman, with a slight girlish form, a sweet spare face in which there was no vestige of colour and large widely opened patient eyes, rose from the seat where he had observed her sitting, and came to speak to him.

"Citizen Evrémonde," she said, touching him with her cold hand. "I am a poor little seamstress, who was with you in La Force."

He murmured for answer: "True. I forget what you were accused of."

"Plots. Though Heaven knows I am innocent of any. Is it likely? Who would think of plotting with a poor little weak creature like me?"

The forlorn smile with which she said it, so touched him, that tears started from his eyes.

"I am not afraid to die, Citizen Evrémonde, but I have done nothing. I am not unwilling to die, if the Republic which is to do so much good to us poor, will profit by my death; but I do not know how that can be, Citizen Evrémonde. Such a poor weak little creature!"

As the last thing on earth that his heart was to warm and soften to, it warmed and softened to this pitiable girl.

"I heard you were released, Citizen Evrémonde. I hope it was true."

"It was. But I was again taken and condemned."

"If I may ride with you, Citizen Evrémonde, will you let me hold your hand? I am not afraid, but I am little and weak, and it will give me more courage."

As the patient eyes were lifted to his face, he saw a sudden doubt in them, and then astonishment. He pressed the work-worn, hunger-worn young fingers, and touched his lips.

"Are you dying for him?" she whispered.

"And his wife and child. Hush! Yes."

"Will you let me hold your brave hand, stranger?"

"Hush! Yes, my poor sister; to the last."

The same shadows that were falling on the prison were falling, in that same hour of the early afternoon, on the Barrier with the crowd about it, when a coach going out of Paris drove up to be examined.

"Who goes here? Whom have within? Papers!"

The papers were handed out and read.

"Alexandre Manette. Physician. French. Which is he?"

The poor old doctor, now helpless and murmuring to himself, was pointed out.

"Apparently the Citizen Doctor is not in his right mind. The Revolution fever will have been too much for him!"

"Yes, as you can see," said Mr Lorry.

"Ha! Many suffer with it. Lucie. His daughter. French. The wife of Evrémonde. Is this she?"

"Yes," said Mr Lorry.

"Ha! She has an important appointment elsewhere?"

"Yes," said Mr Lorry.

"Lucie, her child. English. This is she?"

"Yes," said Mr Lorry.

"Sydney Carton. Advocate. English. Is that he, in the corner there?"

"Yes," said Mr Lorry. "He is still in a swoon having said goodbye to his friend who dies today."

"Well, what of it? Many enemies of the Republic will die today. Jarvis Lorry. Banker. English. Is that you?"

"Yes, it is I," replied Mr Lorry, who had alighted and was standing with his hand on the coach door, replying to a group of officials.

"Here are your papers then, Jarvis Lorry. The coach may go. A good journey!"

Mr Lorry got back into the coach and the postilions started up the horses. The first danger was passed! But, there was still terror in the carriage, in case they should be pursued and Mr Lorry was constantly looking back.

Out into the country they went, then in again among ruinous buildings, cottages and solitary farms. They changed horses and were stopped once by some soldiers who wanted to know how many were going to the Guillotine that day. They were pleased with the answer given at the staging-post: "Fifty-Two today!"

They travelled on, looking constantly back. The wind was rushing after them, and the clouds were flying after them, and the moon was flying after them, and the whole wild night was in pursuit of them; but, thus far, they were pursued by nothing else.

CHAPTER 14

At the same time as the fifty-two awaited their fate, Madame Defarge was having a conference with the Vengeance and Jacques Three of the Revolutionary Jury, in the shed of the wood-sawyer, formerly a mender of roads. The wood-sawyer was not part of the council, but waited at the side until he was needed.

"Citizens," said Madame Defarge, "we are here to discuss this Doctor Manette. My husband is a good Republican and a bold man, but he has his weaknesses, and one of them is that he is loyal to this doctor, for whom he once worked and whom he cared for after he was released from the Bastille. He would never denounce him."

"It is a great pity," said Jacques Three. "That is not quite like a good citizen; it is a thing to regret."

"Well," said Madame, "I care nothing for this doctor. He may wear his head or lose it, for any interest I have in him; it is all one to me. But, the Evrémonde people are to be put to death, and the wife and child must follow the husband and father; the whole family must be exterminated."

"Jacques Three and the Vengeance gave this their

250

strong approval, and Madame Defarge continued, "We are of one mind as I thought, but I cannot trust my husband in this matter. I am afraid that if I tell him of my plans, he might warn them, and they might escape. He has not my reason for pursuing the Evrémondes to death, and I have not his reason for his feelings towards the doctor. I must therefore act for myself. Come here, citizen."

The wood-sawyer, who held Madame Defarge in respect and fear, advanced, touching his red cap.

"About these signals that the wife made to prisoners from the street where you work, you are ready to bear witness to them this very day, are you?"

"Ay, ay, why not!" cried the wood-sawyer. "Every day, in all weathers, from two to four, always signalling, sometimes with the child, sometimes without. I know what I know. I have seen with my eyes."

"Clearly plots," said Jacques Three. "Transparently!"

"There is no doubt of the Jury? Can we trust them?" asked Madame Defarge, letting her eyes turn to him with a gloomy smile.

"Rely upon the patriotic Jury, dear citizeness. I answer for my fellow Jurymen."

"Now, let me see," said Madame Defarge, pondering again. "Yet once more. Can I spare this doctor to my husband? I have no feeling either way. Can I spare him?"

"He would count as one more head," observed Jacques

Three, in a low voice. "We really have not heads enough; it would be a pity, I think."

"He was signalling with her when I saw her," said Madame Defarge; "I cannot speak of one without the other; and I must not be silent, and trust the case wholly to our citizen here. For I am not a bad witness."

Jacques Three and the Vengeance declared that she was the most admirable and marvellous of witnesses. The citizen wood-sawyer, not to be outdone, declared her to be a heavenly witness.

"He must take his chance," said Madame Defarge. "No, I cannot spare him. We shall all meet, I expect, at three o'clock to see the batch of today executed. After it is over – say at eight tonight, come to me in Saint Antoine, and we will give information against these people at my section." When the wood-sawyer had left, Madame Defarge said to the others, "She will now be at home, awaiting the moment of his death. She will be mourning and grieving. She will be in a state of mind to criticize the justice of the Republic. She will be full of sympathy for its enemies. I will go to her."

"What an admirable woman; what an adorable woman!" exclaimed Jacques Three, rapturously. "Ah, my cherished!" cried the Vengeance and embraced her.

"Take my knitting," said Madame Defarge, placing it in her lieutenant's hands, "and have it ready for me in my usual seat. Go there straight, for there will probably be more people there than usual today."

"I willingly obey the orders of my Chief," said the

Vengeance with alacrity and, kissing her cheek, "you will not be late?"

"I shall be there before the commencement."

"And before the tumbrils arrive. Be sure you are there, my soul," said the Vengeance, calling after her, for she had already turned into the street, "before the tumbrils arrive!"

Madame Defarge slightly waved her hand, to imply that she heard, and might be relied upon to arrive in good time, and so went through the mud, and round the corner of the prison wall.

It was nothing to her, that an innocent man was to die for the sins of his forefathers; she saw, not him, but them. It was nothing to her, that his wife was to be made a widow and his daughter an orphan; that was insufficient punishment, because they were her natural enemies and her prey, and as such had no right to live. To appeal to her, was made hopeless by her having no sense of pity, even for herself. If she had been ordered to the Guillotine tomorrow she would not have pitied herself, but would have gone to her death with no other feeling than a fierce desire to change places with the man who sent her there.

Such a cold heart Madame Defarge carried under her rough robe. Carelessly worn, it was a becoming robe enough, in a certain weird way, her face was beautiful in a savage kind of way, and her dark hair looked rich under her coarse red cap. Lying hidden in her bosom, was a loaded pistol. Lying hidden at her waist, was a sharpened dagger. Thus armed, and walking with the confident tread of such a character, and with the supple freedom of a woman who had habitually walked in her girlhood, barefoot and barelegged, on the brown sea-sand, Madame Defarge took her way along the streets.

Now, when the journey of the travelling coach, at that very moment waiting for the completion of its load, had been planned out last night, Mr Lorry had realized that if Miss Pross and Jerry came with them, they would be overloaded and two more people might delay them at the Barrier, when their escape might depend on the saving of only a few seconds here and there. Finally, he had proposed, after much thought, that Miss Pross and Jerry, who were free to leave the city, should leave it at three o'clock in a light-wheeled carriage. They would have no luggage with them, so should soon overtake the coach, and be able to go ahead and order the change of horses before the coach arrived. This would greatly help the progress of the coach during the precious hours of the night, when delay was the most to be dreaded.

Miss Pross and Jerry were even now concluding their arrangements to follow the coach, which they had seen off, as Madame Defarge drew nearer and nearer to their lodging in which they were holding a consultation.

"What do you think, Mr Cruncher," said Miss Pross who was extremely agitated, "would it be better not to start from this courtyard? Another carriage having already gone from here today, it might awaken suspicion."

"My opinion, miss," returned Mr Cruncher, "is as you're right. Likewise what I'll stand by you, right or wrong."

"I am so worried about the others," said Miss Pross, beginning to cry, "that I am incapable of forming any plan. Are *you* capable of forming any plan, my dear good Mr Cruncher?"

"Respectin' my future, miss, I hope so. Respectin' any present use of this here blessed old head of mine, I think not. Would you do me the favour, miss, to take notice of two promises, and vows what it is my wishes fur to record in this here crisis?"

"Oh, for gracious sake!" still crying, "record them at once, and get them out of the way, like an excellent man."

"First," said Mr Cruncher, who was all in a tremble, and spoke with an ashy and solemn face, "them poor things well out of this world, never no more will I do it, never no more!"

"I am quite sure, Mr Cruncher," returned Miss Pross, "that you will never do it again, whatever it is, and I beg you not to think it necessary to mention what it is."

"No miss," returned Jerry, "it shall not be named to you and never no more will I interfere with Mrs Cruncher's flopping on her knees, never no more!"

"Whatever housekeeping arrangement that may be," said Miss Pross, striving to dry her eyes and compose herself, "I am sure that must be Mrs Cruncher's business and she is well able to take care of it. – Oh my poor darlings!"

While they were talking, Madame Defarge, making her way along the streets, came nearer and nearer.

"If we ever get back to our native land," said Miss Pross, "I shall remember everything you have said, and I shall bear witness to your being thoroughly in earnest at this dreadful time. Now, pray let us think! My esteemed Mr Cruncher, let us think!"

Still Madame Defarge, making her way along the streets, came nearer and nearer.

"If you were to go ahead," said Miss Pross, "and stop the carriage and horses from coming here where we might be observed, and if you were to wait somewhere for me; wouldn't that be best?"

Mr Cruncher thought that might be best.

"Perhaps by the cathedral door," said Miss Pross. "Would it be much out of the way, to take me in near the great cathedral door between the two towers?"

"No, miss," answered Mr Cruncher.

"Then, like the best of men," said Miss Pross, "go to the posting-house straight, and change the arrangement."

"I am doubtful," said Mr Cruncher, hesitating and shaking his head, "about leaving you, you see. We don't know what may happen."

"Heaven knows we don't," returned Miss Pross, "but have no fear for me. Pick me up at the cathedral, at three o'clock, or as near it as you can, and I am sure it will be better than our going from here. I feel certain of it. There! Bless you, Mr Cruncher. Do not worry about me, but think of the lives that may depend on both of us!"

This decided Mr Cruncher. With an encouraging nod or two, he immediately went out to alter the arrangements, and left her by herself to follow as she had proposed.

Miss Pross looked at her watch and it was twenty minutes past two. She had no time to lose, but must get ready at once. She got a basin of water and began bathing her eyes which were swollen and red with crying, for she did not wish to attract attention in the streets. She was very frightened and did not like her eyes being blinded for a minute at a time by the dripping water, and she constantly paused and looked round to see that there was no one watching her. In one of these pauses she fell back and cried out, for she saw a figure standing in the room.

The basin fell to the ground broken, and the water flowed to the feet of Madame Defarge. By strange stern ways, and through much staining blood, those feet had come to meet that water.

Madame Defarge looked coldly at her, and said, "The wife of Evrémonde; where is she?"

It flashed upon Miss Pross's mind that the doors were all open, and would look as if there had been a hurried escape, so she quickly shut them. There were four doors in the room, and she shut them all. She then placed herself before the door of the room which Lucie had occupied. Madame Defarge's dark eyes followed her as she did this, and rested on her when she took her stand, but Miss Pross measured Madame Defarge with *her* eyes, every inch.

"You might, from your appearance, be the wife of the Devil himself," said Miss Pross, breathing hard. "Nevertheless, you shall not get the better of me. I am an Englishwoman."

Madame Defarge looked at her scornfully, but she saw before her a firm, hard, wiry woman. She knew full well that Miss Pross was the family's devoted friend; Miss Pross knew well that Madame Defarge was the family's declared enemy.

"On my way yonder," said Madame Defarge, with a slight movement of her hand in the direction of the place of execution, "where they reserve my chair and my knitting for me, I have come to make my compliments to her in passing. I wish to see her."

"I know that you have come for no good," said Miss Pross, "and you may depend upon it, I'll hold my own against you."

Each spoke in her own language; neither understood the other's words; both were very watchful and trying to guess from their look and manner what the other one was saying.

"It will do her no good to keep herself concealed from me at this moment," said Madame Defarge. "Good patriots will know what that means. Let me see her. Go and tell her that I wish to see her. Do you hear?"

"No, you wicked foreign woman," said Miss Pross. "I am your match."

Madame Defarge could not follow exactly what Miss Pross was saying, but she realized she was being defied.

"Woman imbecile and pig-like," she said, frowning. "I take no answer from you. I demand to see her. Either tell her that I demand to see her, or stand out of the way of the door and let me go to her." She waved angrily at the door before which Miss Pross stood firm.

"I little thought," said Miss Pross, "that I should ever want to understand your nonsensical language; but I would give all I have, except the clothes I wear, to know whether you suspect the truth, or any part of it."

Madame Defarge advanced one step, still keeping her eyes on Miss Pross.

"I am a Briton," said Miss Pross, "I am desperate. I don't care an English Twopence for myself. I know that the longer I keep you here, the greater hope there is for my Ladybird. I'll not leave a handful of that dark hair upon your head, if you lay a finger on me!"

"Wretch!" laughed Madame Defarge. "What are you worth? I address myself to that doctor." Then she raised her voice and called out, "Citizen Doctor! Wife of Evrémonde! Child of Evrémonde! Any person but this miserable fool, answer the Citizeness Defarge!"

Perhaps the following silence and a certain expression on Miss Pross's face, whispered to Madame Defarge that they were gone. Three of the doors she opened swiftly, and looked in.

"Those rooms are all in disorder, there has been hurried packing, there are odds and ends upon the ground. There is no one in that room behind you! Let me look."

"Never!" said Miss Pross, who understood the request as perfectly as Madame Defarge understood the answer.

"If they are not in that room, they are gone, and can be pursued and brought back," said Madame Defarge to herself.

"As long as you don't know whether they are in that room or not, you are not sure what to do," said Miss Pross to herself, "and you shall not know that, if I can prevent your knowing it; and you shall not leave here while I can hold you."

Madame Defarge made for the door. Miss Pross seized her round the waist in both her arms, and held her tight. It was in vain for Madame Defarge to struggle and to strike; Miss Pross clasped her tight, and even lifted her from the floor in the struggle that they had. The two hands of Madame Defarge buffeted and tore her face; but Miss Pross, with her head down, held her round the waist, and clung to her with more than the hold of a drowning woman.

Soon, Madame Defarge's hands ceased to strike, and felt at her waist. "Your knife is under my arm," said Miss Pross, in smothered tones, "you shall not draw it. I am stronger than you, I bless Heaven for it. I'll hold you till one or other of us faints or dies!"

Madame Defarge's hands went to her blouse. Miss Pross looked up, saw what it was, struck at it, struck out a flash and a crash, and stood alone – blinded with smoke.

All this was in a second. As the smoke cleared, leaving an awful stillness, it passed out on the air, like the soul of the furious woman whose body lay lifeless on the ground.

In the first fright and horror of her situation, Miss Pross passed the body as far from it as she could, and ran down the stairs to call for help. Luckily she realized this would not be wise, so she went back up the stairs. It was dreadful to go in at the door again; but she did go in, and even went near it, to get her bonnet and other things that she must wear. These she put on, out on the staircase, first shutting and locking the door and taking away the key. She then sat down on the stairs a few moments to breathe and to cry, and then got up and hurried away.

By good fortune she had a veil on her bonnet, or she could hardly have gone along the streets without being stopped. The marks of Madame Defarge's fingers were deep in her face, and her hair was torn. She had pulled her dress together as best she could.

In crossing the bridge, she dropped the door key in the river. Arriving at the cathedral she found Mr

Cruncher waiting for her with a conveyance. He took her in and took her away.

"Is there any noise in the streets?" she asked him.

"The usual noises," Mr Cruncher replied; and looked surprised by the question and by her appearance.

"I can't hear you," said Miss Pross. "What are you saying?"

It was in vain for Mr Cruncher to repeat what he had said; Miss Pross could not hear him. "So I'll nod my head," thought Mr Cruncher, amazed, "at all events she'll see that." And she did.

"Is there any noise in the streets now?" asked Miss Pross again, presently.

Again Mr Cruncher nodded his head.

"I can't hear it."

"Gone deaf in an hour?" said Mr Cruncher to himself much disturbed; "what's come to her?"

"I feel," said Miss Pross, "as if there had been a flash and a crash, and that crash was the last thing I should ever hear in this life."

"Blest if she ain't in a queer condition!" said Mr Cruncher, more and more disturbed. "What can she have been a takin', to keep her courage up? Hark! There's the roll of them dreadful carts! Can you hear that, miss?"

"I can hear," said Miss Pross, seeing that he spoke to her, "nothing. Oh, my good man, there was first a great crash, and then a great stillness, and that stillness seems to be fixed for ever, never to be broken any more as long as my life lasts."

"If she don't hear the roll of those dreadful carts, now very nigh their journey's end," said Mr Cruncher, glancing over his shoulder, "it's my opinion that indeed she never will hear anything else in this world."

And indeed she never did.

CHAPTER 15

Along the Paris streets the death carts rumble, hollow and harsh. There are six tumbrils today and, as their sombre wheels go round, they seem to plough up a long crooked furrow among the populace in the streets. Ridges of faces seem to be thrown to this way or that as the tumbrils go steadily onward. So used are the regular inhabitants of the houses to the spectacle, that in many windows there are no people at all. The wretched men and women in the carts do not appeal by word or look for any pity from the crowds, but seem lost in their own thoughts and some have their eyes shut.

There is a guard of horsemen riding alongside the tumbrils, and faces are often turned up to some of them, and they are asked some question. It would seem to be always the same question, for, it is always followed by a rush of people towards the third cart. The horsemen riding beside that cart, frequently point out one man in it with their swords. This man stands at the back of the tumbril with his head bent down, so that he can talk to a young girl who sits on the side of the cart, and holds his hand. He has no curiosity or care for the scene about him, and always speaks to the girl. Once in a while he shakes his hair a little more loosely about his face. He cannot easily touch his face, his arms being bound.

On the steps of a church, awaiting the coming-up of the tumbrils, stands Barsad the Spy. He looks into the first of them: not there. He looks into the second: not there. He already asks himself, "Has he betrayed me?" when his face clears, as he looks into the third.

"Which is Evrémonde?" said a man behind him.

"That one. At the back there."

"With his hand in the girl's?"

"Yes."

The man cries, "Down, Evrémonde! To the Guillotine all aristocrats! Down Evrémonde!"

"Hush, hush!" the Spy entreats him, timidly.

"And why not, citizen?"

"He is going to pay the penalty: it will be paid in five minutes more. Let him be at peace."

But the man continues to exclaim. "Down, Evrémonde!"

The face of Sydney Carton is for a moment turned towards him. Carton then sees the Spy, and looks attentively at him, and goes his way.

The clocks are on the stroke of three, and the tumbrils are turning into the place of execution. The people close in behind the last one, for all are following to the Guillotine.

In front, in chairs, as if in a public garden, are a number of women, busily knitting. On one of the chairs in the front row, stands the Vengeance, looking about for her friend.

"Thérèse!" she cries, in her shrill tones. "Who has seen her? Thérèse Defarge!"

"She has never missed before," says a knitting woman of the sisterhood.

"Bad Fortune!" cries the Vengeance, stamping her foot on the chair, "and here are the tumbrils! Evrémonde will be despatched in a wink, and she is not here! See her knitting in my hand, and her empty chair ready for her. I cry with vexation and disappointment!"

As the Vengeance gets down from her chair, the tumbrils begin to discharge their loads. The servants of the Guillotine – the executioners – are robed and ready. Crash! – a head is held up, and the knitting women, who scarcely lifted their eyes a moment ago, count One.

The second tumbril empties and moves on; the third comes up. Crash! – And the knitting women, never faltering or pausing in their work, count Two.

The man, thought to be Evrémonde, descends, and the little seamstress is lifted out after him. He has managed to keep hold of her hand as he promised, and gently places her with her back to the crashing machine that constantly whirrs up and falls, and she looks into his face and thanks him.

"But for you, dear stranger, I should not be so composed, for I am naturally a poor little thing, faint of heart; nor should I have been able to raise my thoughts to Him who was put to death, that we might have hope and comfort here today. I think you were sent to me by Heaven."

"Or you to me," says Sydney Carton. "Keep your eyes upon me, dear child, and look at nothing else."

"I mind nothing while I hold your hand. I shall mind nothing when I let it go, if they are quick."

"They will be quick. Fear not!" They stand in the fast-thinning throng of victims as if they were alone. They have come together on the dark highway, and are going home together.

"You comfort me so much. Am I to kiss you now? Is the moment come?"

"Yes."

She kisses him. He kisses her. They solemnly bless each other. Her hand does not tremble as he releases it. She goes next before him – is gone; the knitting women count Twenty-Two.

"I am the Resurrection and the Life, saith the Lord: he that believeth in me, though he were dead, yet shall he live: and whosoever liveth and believeth in me shall never die!"

The murmuring of many voices, the upturning of many faces, the pressing on of many footsteps in the outskirts of the crowd, so that it swells forward in a mass, like one great heave of water, all flashes away. Twenty-Three.

They said of him, in the city that night, that his was the most peaceful man's face ever beheld there. Many added that he looked noble and prophetic. If he had been able to express his thoughts at that time, they would have been these:

"I see John Barsad and Roger Cly, Ernest Defarge, the Vengeance, the Jurymen, the Judge, long ranks of the new oppressors who have risen on the destruction of the old ones, dying by this same instrument, the Guillotine.

I see a beautiful city and a brilliant people finding peace at last, and I see the evil of this time and the evil which came before and was the cause of it, wearing out and the bad redeemed by the good.

I see the lives for which I lay down my life, peaceful, useful, prosperous and happy, in that England which I shall see no more. I see Lucie with a child clasped to her heart who bears my name. I see her father, aged and bent, but otherwise restored, and faithful to all men in his healing work, and happy. I see Jarvis Lorry, so long their friend and helper, leaving them all he has in ten years time, and passing peacefully to his reward.

I see that I hold a sanctuary in their hearts and in the hearts of those who come after them and I see the child who bears my name winning his way up in the path of the Law which was once my path. I see him winning it so well, that my name is made illustrious by the light of his and I see him bringing his own son one day to this place and telling him my story.

It is a far, far better thing that I do, than I have ever done; it is a far, far better rest that I go to, than I have ever known."

Armada
Gift Classics

An attractive collection of beautifully illustrated stories, including some of the finest and most enjoyable children's stories ever written.

Some of the older, longer titles have been skilfully edited and abridged.

Little Women	*Louisa M. Alcott*	£1.95 ☐
Peter Pan	*J. M. Barrie*	£1.95 ☐
The Wizard of Oz	*L. Frank Baum*	£1.95 ☐
Lorna Doone	*R. D. Blackmore*	£1.95 ☐
What Katy Did	*Susan M. Coolidge*	£1.95 ☐
What Katy Did at School	*Susan M. Coolidge*	£1.95 ☐
What Katy Did Next	*Susan M. Coolidge*	£1.95 ☐
The Wind in the Willows	*Kenneth Grahame*	£1.95 ☐
The Secret Garden	*Frances Hodgson Burnett*	£1.95 ☐
The Phantom of the Opera	*Gaston Leroux*	£1.95 ☐
The Railway Children	*E. Nesbit*	£1.95 ☐
The Scarlet Pimpernel	*Baroness Orczy*	£1.95 ☐
Black Beauty	*Anna Sewell*	£1.95 ☐
Kidnapped	*R. L. Stevenson*	£1.95 ☐
Treasure Island	*R. L. Stevenson*	£1.95 ☐
Dracula	*Bram Stoker*	£1.95 ☐
Gulliver's Travels	*Jonathan Swift*	£1.95 ☐
The Adventures of Tom Sawyer	*Mark Twain*	£1.95 ☐
Around the World in 80 Days	*Jules Verne*	£1.95 ☐

All these books are available at your local bookshop or newsagent, or can be ordered from the publisher. To order direct from the publishers just tick the title you want and fill in the form below:

Name _____

Address _____

_____

Send to: Collins Childrens Cash Sales
          PO Box 11
          Falmouth
          Cornwall
          TR10 9EN

Please enclose a cheque or postal order or debit my Visa/Access –

  Credit card no:

  Expiry date:

  Signature:

– to the value of the cover price plus:

UK: 80p for the first book and 20p per copy for each additional book ordered to a maximum charge of £2.00.

BFPO: 80p for the first book and 20p per copy for each additional book.

Overseas and Eire: £1.50 for the first book, £1.00 for the second book. Thereafter 30p per book.